KINDERGARTEN FRIEND

TRESSA OLDEN

Library of Congress Control Number: 2020914208
ISBN: 979-8-89465-035-7 (sc)
ISBN: 979-8-89465-036-4 (e)

Printed in the United States of America.

Integrity Publishing
39343 Harbor Hills Blvd Lady Lake,
FL 32159

www.integrity-publishing.com

Dedication

Dedicated to Jesus Christ Son of God
who made this all possible.

Written by Tressa Ann Olden

CONTENTS

Foreword

Can you remember the days of yester-year? Do you take the time to recap your life's journey? As you rewind back the tape (DVD) and pull sound bits and snippets from years gone by you recall and ponder the journey with a smile, a tear, a pause to meditate that snapshot so clear and vivid. You attempt to remember the details, the essence that embodied the memory the relationships that etched the memories so vividly in mind. You pause tilt your head slightly upward and slide back to fully capture what is now only a fleeing thought. What made it so special, how did it become and indelible imprint in your journey of life?

Kindergarten Friend unfolds with delightful episodes of how a young man journeys though life with special and significant events that lead to inspiration, delight, disappointment, and intrigue. It will allow you to stop and reminisce about what it was like for you when you encountered your first friend(s) to those who stayed with you through adult hood and those who you wished you knew their life's path. It presses your imagination to recall those very special moments and times that define who and how you are today. Each phase of his development is filled with exciting and mysterious aspects of life.

The author introduces a delightful and compassionate little boy whose story begins with his earliest years of life. Through careful and deliberate inserts of his yester-years his journey is illuminated through snippets of church, elementary, high school and college with the Hand of God guiding and maneuvering this boy into a man. But to enjoy and know this story you must begin in Kindergarten…

Philanders J. Olden
Loving husband

Prologue

Billy (William John Parker finds himself in a relationship that last a lifetime. All along the way there are guiding hands to help in his decision making. His life starts as a very young boy who finds himself alone with his mother whom through unfortunate circumstance has left her marital relationship to be by herself. Billy comes to accept as a child where he is in life and starts to flourish with his own friends and relationships. He is aware of his absent father whom he sees often though starts out not knowing why they're not living under the same roof. He has developed a close bond with his mother but loves both parents equally. Billy finds friends along the way that will make you laugh as you identify with them. Feel the love that Tetra Billy's mother continues to share for each person she meets despite the hand in life she was dealt. As Billy grows he builds relationships with the church community as well as other families in his neighborhood. We watch through the pages of this book how he relates with situations that he encounters as he moves forward in age. We see how a bonded friendship lasts over the years as Billy and Glen his best friend are moved from each other when Glen's Father is called to go to another state to minister. Billy and Dorca his girlfriend, how their relationship is tried and retried as he puts his life on hold awaiting her return. And the intimate love that was shared between Billy and Jillian now his fiancée with stood the test of time. His parents David and Tetra demonstrated how their love for each other was renewed by the spoken word of God and forgiveness from one another. And feel how David's love for his son lead him to see all the ways Gods shows himself everywhere if we're willing to stop and take the time to listen. Tetra's giving spirit of love to the Center and all the lives that were touched by a young boy's love for his mentor Mr. Parsons that continued flowing through his mother. You will find yourself laughing with the characters. Crying with the families and many times rejoicing with them. Ask yourself eliminating money would you still have problems in your life? Imagine how Dorca must have felt in her big home? Or how Doris her older sister who had come to her ropes end in life but with help from Dorca the younger sister she was able to start new. You'll hopefully remember situations in life where you met someone that touched your life that changed your thoughts and caused you to see life new refreshed. Sit at the table with Jillian as she shares her good news about Billy with her mother or exhaust yourself in the waiting room with Cheryl as she finds out the fate of her man. This book many times may keep you on the edge waiting to see what will happen next as the young man's life unfolds right before your eyes. Sit on the edge of your sit as Jillian runs around trying to locate Davie who she is responsible for while his mother is away. It's delightful, mysterious, and I trust uplifting. Go into Tetra's kitchen and cook a meal or dine out with the couples on caviar and wine. Take this journey through life where the thought of money is no object and careers are a budding success. Go on the golf course with the restored David Parker and feel the pain as Ariel talks to her mom regarding her family. There is a bit of all of us in this book. It' intriguing, and imaginative as we try to keep up with Dorca and her many personalities that will keep you wondering what will she do next and is there any hope of a future with her true love Billy Parker? Visit Kansas with Desmond and Mossy Owens when finding a perfect Christmas tree lands Desmond at the tree's top hanging from it. Stand in the pulpit with Dr. Hathaway and one of his inspiring messages. You will find yourself taking a ride on the skateboard with Horace the neighbor's kid. Or maybe sitting in the living room of Pastor and Mrs. Reed as they discuss what has happen to their daughter. Wherever you find yourself in this book whether shopping in New York with Jillian at Neiman's or sitting through a joyous service, be prayerful that God is still in control of whatever is going on in life. Keep your eyes on Jesus as I have taken examples of real-life relationships and situations, and a whole lot of fictional imagination to delight you and brought them to the light in this inspired book. From beginning to end we're left trying to figure out the age-old problem, how long as this been going on? We continue reading to find out about this little girl's life. We all must walk this journey of life where relationship plays a big part often, times stepping out beyond what we can see. We frequently go through life thinking we are controlling it. But God and only He knows the total outcome of every situation.

Sincerely
Tressa Ann Olden

CHAPTER 1

Be quiet dear

Mom and I entered the little building with its tall pointed top. She said it was a church. We had just moved to town and mom felt she needed somewhere to go. There were other mommies there with their children, but only a few men, some daddies' I guess. We walked in and sat on a long hard bench next to others who had gotten there before us. Mommy gave me one of the soft pillows, that laid stretched out on the benches, I remember they were nice and soft. I sat next to my mother listening and watching this man talk a lot. Every now and then mommy and the others present would say "amen". "Mommy, mommy what are they saying?" I kept asking." Who are they talking about?" "Shhh! Mom would scold, "He is talking about Jesus" "Jesus who?" I asked. "Our redeemer" you will understand when you're older" I thought to myself the words are getting harder, Jesus, redeemer" oh well maybe I will because I sure can't make sense of it now" he whispered under my breath.

We must have sat there for hours, so it seemed but I enjoyed the songs they were singing. Mom knew a lot of them she learned them growing up she told me. I continually got in trouble for giggling as I watched some of the ladies dancing around and beating a tingly thing mom called a tambourine.

After a long time, mom caught me by my hand and we walked to the door. The man who mom told me was a preacher stood shaking everyone's hand as they left through the front entrance of the small church. I waved to some of the other children as they left. We were all glad to finally be able to talk and run and do anything but be quiet.

When my mother was tucking me into bed, I asked about Jesus who the man talked about so long. Mom explained as best she could to a five- year old. I really didn't understand I just said I did so she would stop talking about it. Mom had started sounding like the preacher man we heard earlier that day and it was too much. "Okay mommy, I see okay goodnight".

The next day, I would be going to school in my neighborhood where most of the children I played with went I thought. We had not lived there long. Some boxes were still packed with our things from our old house where dad lived. I liked my old house it had tall stairs and lots of space to run around. This house was smaller and not as pretty as my other one but mom said this one, she could pay for by herself. I think she always wanted to go back to our old house someday. Dad had not moved with us and mommy used to cry a lot. I always thought she was lonely. She seemed to feel better when we would go to the little church. She met some new friends who she says were nice I thought so too.

Mom got up early and I could hear her humming one of the songs from that little church as she cooked grits and eggs my favorite breakfast next to pancakes of course. "Lots of butter mom" I would always remind her as I finished getting dressed and rushed to the table to eat.

The school wasn't far from our house. Mom said it was a private school, so while I was at school, she would be looking for work. "Gotta keep busy," she'd say. She said she would meet me "right here" when I ended my school day.

I knew exactly where we were going, we had come earlier in the week and filled out all the papers and found my classroom. It was right in front of a large play area filled with toys, a slide and a merry-go-round. Mom watched as I walked into my classroom. I looked back to wave goodbye and "oops" I bumped into this little girl who changed the way I looked at my life forever. "I'm sorry" I said. She just looked and smiled "no problem". Then she turned and walked in to find a seat. I sat in the desk next to her. "Are you afraid I asked her seeing some of the other children crying from being left there by their parents. "No, are you?" she asked, returning the question. "no not really". "My name is William Parker but everyone calls me Billy". "I'm Dorca Williams and my friends call me Dorca. She said smiling at me. "You have a big smile, are you always this happy? I asked. Then she stopped smiling and sat silently without saying another word. I didn't mean to hurt her feelings.

As other children entered the room became noisy, "Quiet, quiet please children, a voice came from the front of the classroom. My name is Sister Mary Martha, welcome to kindergarten" "You all looked very nice today. Everyone looked the same to me we wore uniforms. There were mommies also wiping tears and assuring them it was going to be fun. I thought about when I was in that situation and mom and dad took me to pre-school it was not pretty.

After a while, things settled down and our day began. We all introduced ourselves those who wanted to. Some refused and Sister Martha didn't insist, being it was the first day she said. Dorca stood up when it came to her turn and sat again in silence. We had lots of fun. Our room had lots of fun stuff to play with also. On our playground outside I played with all the children. Mom said the classes were small so each child could get the attention he or she needed. It didn't take me long to start remembering names. Ryan and I played catch with a football. We rode tricycles and even played on the monkey bars. Kerrie and Arianna played hopscotch on the blacktop when they weren't sliding on the playground slide. And Dorca sat under a tree and watched all the activities going on. She would only talk to me when I would stop playing and run over to where she was sitting. Kerrie asked her to join their game but she refused. Back in class we recited out loud all the letters of the alphabet and played games with colors. Soon our day was over it had gone a lot faster than sitting through church I thought.

I met my mother right outside. She hugged me and asked how was my day? I told her all about it all the way home. I talked so much I forgot to ask her about hers, dad use to do that.

I was up early and ready to go out the door. "You're up early Billy mom replied, "are you excited?" "yes mom, I met some new friends and the teacher can't remember her name yet but she's nice. We are going to paint today!" "That's wonderful dear mom said continuing to cook breakfast. The bacon was sizzling in the pan when the phone rang. "Hello" she said. Her next words were "fine" then I heard "he's fine". "Mom, mom is that dad? I quickly asked. "yes, Billy would you like to say something?" Handing me the phone. "Hi dad, I'm in school and I have some friends, and" "hold on son, you've been busy." "Yes dad, and we're going to paint today!" Remember the pictures I gave you dad?" "do you still have them?

I asked excitedly. "Yes, Billy I have them" "I love you dad bye." I gave the phone back to mom. Very little was said and she hung up.

Soon it was off to school another day. The week went by fast and I tried to tell mom everything that went on each day. I was so excited I liked my new school, my new teacher and my new friends. Dorca and I played together a lot. She would let Arthur and Arianna play with us sometimes. We had loads of fun. I painted lots of beautiful pictures for mom she seemed happy.

Dorca only played with me most of the time. When she was upset with me for any reason then she would play with Kerrie, Arianna and Arthur also. She didn't want to play with me alone she'd say which was fine with me I liked playing with everybody. I told mom about it she would just say "strange behavior". Often Dorca would be withdrawn that's what Sister Mary Martha called it when mom shared my concerns with her. Some days were all right no problems at all. She was seldom quiet around me. So they concluded it was just part of her make-up and that she would grow out of it. She told them she enjoyed playing with me.

I always arrived at school before Dorca and greeted her good morning as she entered the classroom. We often talked about leaving St. Theodore or what it would be like to go to Washington Elementary the public school. Glen and some of the other children from our neighborhood went there. Mom had taken me to Washington's school carnival they had every year. It was a big event in our neighborhood. The children enjoyed throwing the balls to dunk the teacher in the water below. "Mom can I have some money to get more tickets for the dunk booth?" I'd asked with Glen nudging me from the back. And of course, they sold lots of cotton candy. Glen and I both had a stomachache all night. I liked our school but I wanted a chance to ride the big yellow bus with all the children I played with in the neighborhood. Our school did not have a bus we came in cars. The big bus would always pass mom and I in the car waving as they went by. The children seemed to be having so much fun. I knew mom wouldn't let me change schools yet though I begged her every day to please let me go to Hamilton middle school with Glen in the fall. Mom promised she would think about it. Hamilton was the middle school everyone went to after leaving Washington elementary. Winnie was going there too and a few other children from our church. Winnie and I often invited children from our neighborhood to church on bring a friend to Sunday school day and some just kept coming and brought their parents too. After a lot of asking mom finally conceded and said I could go to Hamilton after sixth grade. I was so happy and when I told Glen we jumped around "Yeah! Yeah! We both were overjoyed. Dorca Williams said she'd ask again to attend Hamilton but like always we never got an answer. I was always hoping to see her but we never did. I was her friend too. So, each Sunday in class I would say a prayer for her and hope she would come but I'd have to wait and see. She never attended church with me but I never stopped asking her. She would just ignore me and change the subject. I wanted her to know about Jesus because it made mom happy and I wanted her to be happy too. Sometimes she was. I would sit out under the tree with her at noon and read from my bible. I would share and teach her everything we had learned in our class on Sunday mornings. I even gave her a bible which I had won during one of Mrs. Parson's bible quiz sessions once a month. Mrs. Trina Parsons was a creative teacher. That's the word mom gave me after I told her about Mrs. Parson. I found her class interesting. Everyone said she was a schoolteacher that's why? Later she explained it was a gift from God. She worked at a bank. Boy was she a great teacher! Her husband Mr. Parson's worked with the youth ministry at the church. I signed on the first page of Dorcas bible TO MY KINDERGARTEN FRIEND ALWAYS BILLY.

One day while she had come to play, I asked if she would like to attend church with me and mom. She left to go and ask and never came back to play that day. I wasn't trying to get her in trouble but somehow it always seems to turned out that way.

Sunday was here and Dorca hadn't given me an answer. She somehow had promise she'd surely ask this time. I wanted her to come because this week again we were asked to bring a friend. Glen had come with me before many times. He would come all the time but his dad was the Pastor at another church in the city and he had to attend with his family most of the time. "Mom I said "I asked Dorca if she wanted to attend church with me". She said she would like too. Can we go get her?" Billy asked with a childlike concern for a friend. Tetra didn't know where Dorca lived and thought it best to wait. "I'll ask her mom Billy, when I see her at school." mom stated we must go we're going to be late! I sat again squirming in my seat all the way through service. I enjoyed the singing not much else mostly because I did not understand it. They were going to start children's church and I thought it has to be better than this. But this Sunday I just sat and twiddled my thumbs thinking about Dorca.

When I got home, I hurried and changed my clothes and went out to play, but no Dorca. I didn't see her until school the next day. She said she went to visit her grandparents for the weekend with her family. "Well I'm glad to see you, did you have fun? I said hoping she had. "It was all right! Dorca confided. "I missed you yesterday did you ask your mom about coming to church with me? Billy was very persistent. I though somehow getting Dorca to church would make her happy all the time. "Yes, I asked, I told you I would! She stated, now let's go play on the merry-go-round with Arthur" and off she ran. The day was over before we knew it. That night at the dinner table I told mom what Dorca had said. And then I realized again she never gave me an answer.

The weeks went by fast. Dorca and I became best friends mostly because I was the only one willing to adjust to her changes. The girls would just play games by themselves and Dorca and Arthur would argue all the time about anything. She and I played together every day. Mom told me to be sure and play with the other children including Dorca. I promised I would.

The months and years went even faster Dorca didn't always like playing with the others every day. Some days she would just totally refuse and sit under the tree at recess by herself. I couldn't break my promise to mom but I was the only one who would adjust to her moods. I tried to keep the peace. Despite everything we had fun days and remained best friends. She continued to be the master of avoiding my questions about the church and I knew that! But there was something about her that I was drawn to. And I liked her, I guess. I felt she would not have anybody for a friend if I didn't play with her. I accepted her and was content to have her as my best friend.

The days months and years continued to past quickly it seemed. Dorca and I grew up overnight. I never saw her during the summers but every year until sixth grade we attended the same school "St. Theodore". Arthur's family was in the military and he moved away when we were in the third grade. During some summers when I didn't visit my dad in Maine I played with the other children in the neighborhood. Glen and I formed a baseball team and won the championships each summer. We had lots of fun. Our small upscale neighborhood filled with cape- cod style homes and rolling lawns was a wonderful place for a young man to grow up. I heard mom say that to her friend Christine Guillory as they talked on the phone.

Dorca was learning to share our friendship and was less possessive of my time. Her mom always picked her up after about an hour of play. The park was only a block away we all wondered where she lived. Glen and I made plans to follow her one time. But Mrs. Thompkins, was watching Raymond who was a lot younger than we were playing outside and she was looking and made us go home. Dorca always said she would give us a ride in her Rolls Royce. But never did. Once when her mom came to pick her up Glen jumped in the Rolls' back door entrance. He got to the corner before being discovered and they tossed him out. The next day Dorca brought candy for all of us. She said she still wanted to be our friend. We laughed at the situation and Glen laughed the hardest bragging he was the only one who ever rode in Dorca's Rolls Royce. Glen survived the whipping and our parents decided after hearing the story to always have a parent there to oversee our play every day at the park.

One day mom happened upon Dorca's mom as she dropped her off at school. She explained that our children are good friends and wanted to invite them to visit church any Sunday. Mrs. Williams was very frank mom said. She was pleased Dorca had friends but was not interested in a friendship other than school for her. And no, they would not be attending and please don't ask again. That's exactly what she told mom, I got in trouble for listening in on mom's conversation with Ms. Christine. Mom just told me we would pray about it.

We continued to go to the little church. It was quite a way by freeway from our neighborhood. She said she liked it because it reminded her of when she was a little girl growing up. The little church after years had grown in size under the leadership of Pastor Cornelius Hathaway. We watched as construction began on our small building. Now in its place were beautiful stain glass windows in the entrance that sat over two sets of tall large oak wooden doors facing the street. It could easily seat 2000 people comfortably and had soft benches from end to end. There were no signs of pillows. It had two stories with classrooms on either floor. Most classrooms were on the second floor with the administrative offices. There were four or five entrances in the circular building. The main floor had a large elevated stage where one of our choirs sings every Sunday. It is magnificent! This is what Jesus had done for us mom explained.

I knew a little of what she meant. Mrs. Ann my Sunday school teacher had taught us about Jesus when we were still in our little building with its hard benches and the room so cold that she would allow us to keep our coats, caps and gloves on. She was very nice. Mom and I bought caps and gloves for everyone in my Sunday class.

Mrs. Ann had a way of making learning fun. Our class grew and grew. She soon had other parents and members helping in children's church. We no longer had just one class we had classes starting at daycare, preschool continuing up to high school. Pastor Hathaway often said we were growing past our property line. We owned and had taken up a whole city block. Mom was always helping Mrs. Guillory in the church's administrative office. Mrs. Christine Guillory was Pastor Hathaway's secretary she and mom were good friends.

I enjoyed Sunday mornings seeing friends I hadn't seen all week and learning more about Jesus. Even after I was no longer in Mrs. Ann's class I would still stop by and say hello and just talk to her.

Dad always called to talk to me and mom. Conversations were getting longer between them. He even visited us at least twice a month. Every time he would leave, I would be full of questions that were unanswered and mom didn't want to talk about either. I could hear her praying to Jesus, she'd say some things about dad. I don't know all of what she would pray about the door was usually closed. I fell asleep one night by her door listening she put me to bed…

CHAPTER 2

Decisions, decisions, decisions

I had made up my mind that over the summer I would go and ask Dorca's parents if she could attend Sunday services with mom and I. I would explain we would bring her home immediately when services were over. Mom and I often had friends over after church especially during the holidays. Mom loved to cook and I certainly couldn't eat all that she would prepare even for dinner most of the time.

I settled in my mind that I was going to do this. But I must first find out where she lived. I had asked her many times, but she would say not far from here and change the subject. She would even get mad if I was persistent. She'd say "not far we go to the same school silly" with a quaint smile on her face.

Yes, I knew we went to the same school. But St. Theodore is a private school and she and I went everyday by car as well as many others from all parts of the city. Mom told me it was very expensive and not everyone could afford to go. But public schools in this area were second to none. Besides I told her you come every day in a Rolls, you go everywhere in a Rolls Royce are you rich? "No, she told me "my parents are!" She wasn't the only one that came to school in an expensive car but she was the only one in our class. A lady who we called Ms. Williams would wave and say something to Dorca and quickly get back in the car and drive away. As the school year came to an end, I wondered more about the public middle school and thought how much fun it would be sharing classes together with Glen and Dorca.

Homework was keeping me busy these days and Dorca had the same homework as I in Father Dutart's sixth grade class. We didn't play outside as often Dorca hardly at all. The day before school ended that finally year

I quickly ran from the classroom after the bell rang. Dorca said she looked around for me to say goodbye but I was gone.

I came streaking around the corner across the lawn of the school "oops, and down the streets behind the big car. Wherever Dorca and her mom were going was not around the corner. Soon I was passing the administration building where mom worked. I knew that was far. Mom couldn't walk to work even when she was having her Benz tires rotated. She had Ms. Guillory to take her to work or get another car.

I'd better turn around I thought. I was afraid I was tired and Dorca and her mom were still going around another corner and another. Soon I found myself crossing over a bridge to get to the other side of the freeway. Just as I was about to give up the car pulled in a driveway of a humongous brick house with a beautiful large yard with lots of flowers in it. I stayed back far enough so that no one could see me. Dorca got out and ran to a woman and embraced her. Soon another car pulled in while they were still in the yard. The man got out and hugged Dorca. I thought this must be her parents? But they were Caucasian. Then Edith Williams the one who always brings her to school got out the car with Dorca's books and took them in the house. I was really confused, two mothers? I didn't know what to think or what was going on. All I knew is that I had better get home because it was getting dark soon and I have a long way to go. When I arrived, mom was home waiting for me. She had called Glen and he was sitting there too. I finally told her what happened. With Glen almost rolling on the floor in laughter I concluded my story. That night after I was in bed mom sit in my room and told me what Dorca's mom had said. She thought I should let her decide when she wanted to attend church. After a day like today I thought that would be best also.

I thought about a lot over the summer. How to ask Dorca about what I had seen? But then I would have to tell her how I had followed her home that day. I didn't want to risk losing her friendship after all I had worked hard to bring her out of that shell. I felt I had already lost my dad. "No, it's not worth it!"

That night dad called he needed to talk with mom. He was considering selling the house in Maine and needed to discuss it with her. Mom hung up the phone seemingly disappointed though she never said it. I always knew she never really wanted to leave it, and sure she hoped to return one day. I had been back to visit my dad several times over the years and spent a lot of summers there. Some of the time I spent with my grandparents too. They lived in Maine also. The house in Maine was too big for just him dad would say. It felt empty and lonely. "David Parker was always on the go most of the time. It was business trips. Tetra told Billy. As Tetra stood remembering how she never liked the fact that his secretary always accompanied David even when she would go along with her husband. After Billy was born Tetra and he were always waving goodbye to David". "See you soon" Tetra would always say.

Dorca did not attend the middle school with us. I had asked my mom over and over during the summers to let me go to Hamilton Jr. High with Glen and after continually asking mom conceded. Dorca apparently went to St. Miguel because I never saw her. Despite what my mom had said I went by Dorca's house several times hoping to see her. But I never saw her on either trip by her home. One day Glen and I went to St. Miguel. Glen promised he wouldn't tell my mom so I let him come along. When we entered through the doors of the school, we were met by Sister Elizabeth who kindly escorted us out. Another story for Glen's laugh file. I had given up hope of ever seeing Dorca again after that. But there was still a chance she might show up at the high school. I did spot the Rolls Royce several times heading out of the neighborhood. I kept hoping to see her but I'd have to wait.

Glen and I had good times in middle school after I stopped trying to find Dorca around every corner. He and I were always doing something that brought attention to ourselves. Glen was always getting into scraps and often took me with him. One day we were caught giving our buddies two slices of pizza as we worked in the cafeteria during lunch. Mrs. Sullivan made us wash dishes for both lunch periods for a week. Glen's father was a minister and he got teased a lot about being a p.k. "Preachers kid,". He wasn't the only one but Glen was such a personable guy he could handle it well. Mom liked him too and she would sit and talk with us for hours when he came over. He was always at my house or I was at his. He had a younger sister so he preferred my house most of the time. Once while we were talking Glen told my mom he wanted to live in Florida and work at Disney World. Mom never discouraged any of our dreams big or small. "I know you young men can do anything you put your minds to she'd say. "Mrs. Parker until I get my job at Disney World can I have some of your homemade cookies?" He knew mom always had something sweet and homemade around the house. "Help yourselves boys" she'd replied. Glen was a friend magnet. Everyone liked him and he loved to make people laugh. He could even get Dorca to relax and that was not easy to do. Once Glen and I decided we were going to be different this year and get dates for our eighth grade, dance. I asked Briana Glen's sister to come with me. She went there and had her own set of friends so I knew I would not have to keep her company. Glen asked Winnie Hathaway my Pastor's daughter. She said yes because she would really be with me. We also decided to wear our Sunday suits and ties that we would not be caught in except Easter Sunday. After laughing at each other we asked Mrs. Reed to take us to the school and mom would pick us up. When we walked in everybody looked at us. Everyone else had on jeans and "t "shirt after all it was just an end of semester dance. "Look at you two handsome gentlemen Mr. Rato, the school principal said, "you two are setting a great example". We had all the girls wanting to dance with us. And we tried to dance with them all. Winnie vowed to never talk to us again saying we were immature. I slept well that night I was tired of jumping around to the Hully Gully for each dance.

In spite of our antics we were good students always competing for honor roll status. Winnie stayed on the honor roll all three years we were in Jr. high school. And let us know it! All the teachers liked us well they knew us anyway but answering to Minister Reed, Pastor Hathaway and mom, not necessarily in that order for either of us. We were for the most part well behaved.

One day Glen came to school saying he was moving away. I didn't believe him he was always getting what we referred to as his morning attention. But I found out later from his mom it was true. They had planned a swim party for all the young people of their church. Minister Reed Glen's father had been called to Pastor a church in another state. They would be moving at the end of the summer. I knew I would miss my buddy. I had spent countless hours in that pool and at his house. His mom had purchased me a bean- bag chair like Glen's for their great room while we played video games. We promised always to call or write. Briana invited me to the swim party as if I needed to be invited. But she was always calling for something after that eighth grade, dance. We nicknamed her "pest." She and her friends were constantly bothering us. The swim party was great. Glen and I wet everybody doing cannon balls in the pool. He won the back flip, contest because he wasn't going to let a girl win, he explained. This family was going to be missed. Mom told me God was sending them off to continue his work they were gifted people.

For weeks my heart was heavy the Reeds were like family. Mrs. Reed and mom were always exchanging recipes over the years. They frequented each other's women groups and of course shopped together especially around the holidays for Glen and I. Things would not be the same without them. Mom and Mrs. Guillory put together a surprise dinner party for the Reeds. They invited both churches. Our church supplied the food and Community Central was the invited guest. There was everything imaginable and lots of it. Fried chicken, greens, potato salad, corn on the cob, cakes sweet potato and apple pies. Lots of southern food mom told me. Well I knew it was different from the food we served at dad's dinner parties in Maine. Dad volunteered with the men's group to barbeque ribs and chicken. There was so much food that all the 200 plus well-wishers were fed. This would have been perfect for the home in Maine. But our living room and the great room along with the large dinning, area was occupied by someone. Our backyard was filled also, but we all enjoyed ourselves and laughed and cried all day. Many of the guest left well wishes and blessings for the Reed family.

On the summer before entering high school I went to visit dad. I didn't want to leave Washington. Since my buddy had left, I was getting to know some other friends that went to the gym near the administration building where mom worked. I worked on some of my basketball skills and toned my muscles. I knew I should go to dads' now instead of over the holidays. The holidays were always more fun with mom. There were lots of guest from church over at our home and mom enjoyed being with friends around the holidays. She loved entertaining. Besides Winnie whose name was Erica Winifred Hathaway, the pastor's daughter had not given up hope of ever having me. She had invited me to a social at the church. She was always inviting me somewhere. I knew she liked me, though I never told anyone, my heart belonged to Dorca. I hadn't seen her since sixth grade at St. Theodore but I still thought of her a lot.

Glen called before I left to visit my dad in Maine. He wanted to tell me about the school he would be attending in Texas. He would surely be playing baseball for them, his words were, he was sent there to help the team". I'm glad to know he hasn't changed. I told him I was on my way to Maine again before school starts and was so glad, he had called. "How's the pest? I asked and your mom and dad. "We're all doing fine he said, "mom is letting the pest date now, so she's not in my hair as much". Now I give her little boyfriends a hard time. He continued laughing the whole time. "Have you found Dorca yet? He joked. He was laughing so hard remembering the time mom caught me after staying off to late. He couldn't hear what I was saying anyway. "Glen it's good to hear from you man." "I'm going to miss you this year", but the good thing is I won't get in any trouble" I told him" "oh he said now you're being the funny one! We would go on like that for close to an hour. Finally ended with I get the next call. "take care and give my love to the family". "tell the pest I have to approve him too. I said laughing as I hung up the phone. That's just like Glen he would have to bring up Dorca. I hadn't thought about her for a least a week I chuckled to myself. I was intrigued by that quiet little girl full of secrets yet to learn. I will probably grow out of it. But I had run out of excuses to Winnie so off to my dad's in Maine I went.

Visiting dad wasn't that bad, I just hated leaving mom alone. She was always busy with work at the office and at the church. Mrs. Guillory came by almost every day she was good for mom. Mom would always say as I was leaving "enjoy yourself" that usually put me at ease it made her feel better anyway. At dads I got a chance to see old friends of mom and his. I really didn't remember them they boasted of how I had grown, and ask about mom.

One morning dad left for the office. I became bored to tears by noon. Television no! video games no! no! Where were the children? probably in their rooms, with their nannies or off at boarding school. That's' when I really missed mom. At home I would be out playing with my friends at the park or gym anyway.

Bored stiff I began to explore. I went into mom and dad's old room. The large bedroom seemed even bigger compared to our house now in Spokane Washington. Dad had moved into the smaller bedroom down the hall on the other side of the house. Searching around under the huge poster bed I found a box of papers. Some were letters from mom. Most had our current address on them. I thought should I read these? Am I old enough to handle what I might find? That's what mom and dad would always say "when you're old enough". Time went fast. I read letter after letter. Most of them were not saying much, just that Billy and I are find hope you're happy, Sincerely Tetra. Suddenly there it was this large brown envelope addressed to dad. It looked important so I opened it carefully has not to mess it up. Across the top of the document in bold letters read: Birth Certificate. Thinking it was mine I quickly pulled it out and began to read it: Father: David Parker, Mother: Katherine Heller. Child: Justin Parker. That was my dad's name, but that wasn't mom's name and not mine. I had heard Katherine before but couldn't remember where. What was I looking at? Maybe I should have waited I thought.

I sit looking at the piece of paper lost in thought I heard, "Billy, Billy" it was dad he was coming up the stairs. I quickly gazed at the birth date again. I noticed he was younger than me two years to be exact. I hurried and stuffed it back in the box and shoved the box under the bed, and ran out to meet dad in the hallway at the top of the stairs. "Hey sport" Busy day", he asked. "No dad not really not much to do today around here" "But Mrs. Peeler makes an awesome lunch though, I said as I gathered my thoughts. "She sure does son I agree dad added, reminds me of your mother, she loves to cook that's why I hired her he continued talking. Mrs. Peeler was a lot older than the other housekeeper's dad had over the years. Her blue gray hair and rimmed glasses hinted to her age. Her hair was pulled back in a bun and over all she was easy on the eyes. She said she enjoyed my visit's it gave her something more to do. Occasionally dad would have a dinner party or dinner guest for that matter. "I think he needed her to keep him grounded.

CHAPTER 3

She's back

I HAD GROWN SO MUCH OVER THE SUMMER, and looked forward to my new friends. I had hoped I could talk to mom about my visit to dad's but somehow never found the time. Now I realized Dorca wasn't the only one with secrets.

"Good Morning Billy", came a voice across the large court, the gathering place for everyone starting the morning. It was Winnie. She had spotted me standing there. I was still looking for Dorca. Would I even recognize her? I couldn't be rude. 'hi Winnie I like your outfit", I said hoping to lighten the conversation." Thank You Billy", and quickly asked, "may I see your schedule?" "Do we have classes together?" "When's lunch?" She wasn't allowing me to answer any questions. I kept trying to be polite, after all she was my pastor's daughter. "Let's see taking the schedule from my hand." "We have four classes together guess we will be hanging out" she suggested. Then "hi Billy", I turned to see Dorca, she had changed over the years, her pig tales were gone and well she looked different all over a lot different. Winnie looked at Dorca, hi she said, "I'm Erica Winifred Hathaway". Billy and I have classes together and we attend the same church do you remember? Will you be hanging out with us too?" She questioned. I didn't have a lot to say, I was floored with Dorca's new look. I spent the summer with my dad. Plainly I had missed a lot. Winnie looked different too but I had seen her at church last Sunday. But Dorca was breathtakingly, beautiful, overwhelming. How are you? Finally came out. It's good to see you. You look so different, pleasingly different." I replied. "Mom lets me wear my hair down, now that I'm in high school", I didn't want to go to St Regis I wanted to come here with you". She said smiling at me. "I guess that's it" I said. "Did you get your schedule yet?" Winnie asked quickly taking it from her hand. "Oh sorry, Billy only lunch" Winnie chided. I wasn't disappointed after all we spent all our elementary school together over lunch. She handed the schedule back to Dorca and looked at me. "I'll see you in first period", Winnie remarked and walked away to meet other friends from church.

I knew I didn't have much time so I asked if we could meet here for lunch and talk about our summers. Dorca agreed just as the bell rang. "Okay see you soon" she said walking away. I stood amazed still at her looks. Hmmm. "Billy, Billy", you're going to be late" Winnie yelled as she moved in the direction of our first period class.

It seemed lunch would never come. We were carrying around loads of books waiting for locker assignments that would not take place until sixth period. Besides the books, I had Winnie in four classes. Why? I thought, I always pray when asked.

When the bell rang for lunch, I quickly gathered my books and ran to where I would meet Dorca. She walked slowly carrying an arm full of books and dropping them to the table. We took turns watching each other's belongings and got lunch, which didn't leave us much time to talk. We did agree we would make the most of our time. Dorca said her parents are letting her ride the bus to and from school. They were thinking of getting her a car soon and she would let me know. "that's wonderful" I told her. I was really confused now but I didn't let Dorca know it. I was happy to know she was getting a car maybe we would have more time together. I didn't realize how much I had missed her and looked forward to spending more time with her. Lunch now just wasn't enough.

After school everyone met directly in front near the main office. There were lines and lines of students waiting to get on the buses. It was visible lockers had been assigned for no one was weighed down with books. I stood looking around at the long lines for Dorca. Then I thought which bus would she be on? Which one goes where she lives? "Billy you're going to get left if you don't get on this bus". I turned to see Dorca hanging her head out of the window of the bus I ride to get home. I quickly ran to the door and on the bus to the seat she had saved for me. Winnie sat across on the other side. She dominated the conversation all the way home.

When we got near the St. Theodore School the bus stopped. Dorca quickly said goodbye and got off. I sat wondering should I get off here or wait another five or six blocks to the next stop. I looked over at Winnie and ran off behind Dorca. "see you tomorrow" Winnie yelled as I left the bus. I ran to catch up with Dorca wondering where she was going. She ignored me and kept walking. Soon up pulled her Rolls and off she went.

Mom was waiting for me when I got home. She was glad to see me and wanted to know about my day, my classes and new friends. But I could see something was visibly wrong she was home. "Why are you home so early? I asked surprised she was there at this time of day. She explained she had gotten a call from dad and he had decided to sell the house in Maine and move. His plans aren't final yet he'd be in touch.

She said she didn't feel like dealing with the day. She had taken a sick day and truthfully, she was. Mom had devoted herself only to my needs and me. We didn't want for anything I knew we had money dad always saw to that, but mom had money too. She wanted me to continue in private school to protect me she says. But I wanted to know what it was like to live in the real world besides public school seemed more fun. She worked to keep busy with her degree in business she enjoyed her director's job in the huge Commissioners of state building near midtown. She didn't attend a lot of there after work functions the church held her heart. There were single men there. Some looked to be mom's age. She wasn't interested and would tell them she was married. Which wasn't a lie but she and dad were not together. Not like that. I guess she wasn't ready to give dad up. Divorce wasn't in her vocabulary.

It's time I thought it was clear. I was always told, you're mature for your age Billy. I needed answers. Mom I paused; "when I heard you praying one day, many times I heard the same prayer." I hesitated before going on. "you always ask God to help you forgive dad for his mistake so you could live with it." "Mom' I sighed; "were you talking about me?" "Oh no Billy" she replied. "I'm sorry if I made you think that". "This has nothing to do with you" she continued. I knew it wasn't about me, but I was trying to find out and make her feel better. What was she thinking? I told her my Sunday youth class was studying about the truth setting one free. And I wanted her to be free from guilt of any kind. I wanted her to know I would love her and would be there no matter what. I quoted James 5:19-20 brethren if anyone among you wanders from the truth and someone turns him back. Let him know that he who turns a sinner from the error of his way will save a soul from death and cover a multitude of sins.

Mom looked at me lovingly. Somehow, I sensed she knew I knew what was troubling her. "My little man has grown up before my eyes." She got her bible from the counter. She had just finished reading it before I came in, she confessed. She handed it to me and I turned to the passage and read it again out loud. Mother's eyes filled with tears and she began to pray. I joined her, embraced her, and let her cry on my shoulder as long as she needed.

CHAPTER 4

Depending on God

I assisted my new teacher Mrs. Hathaway the pastor's wife who had taken over for Mrs. Nancy the Sunday youth class teacher. She was out after having a new baby and would return in about 2 or 3 weeks. Winnie made it a point to have me as the other assistant to assure I would always be there since her mom was teaching the class. Our church had grown so fast it was hard to keep up with the ever-changing new faces. Many of us went to the same school, but certainly not all. Mrs. Hathaway was an all right teacher with the class though quite different from Mrs. Nancy. She shared a lot of great conversation points of discussion for our class. We all applauded her when she immediately recognized that Winnie was dominating the class and taking over most of the questions raised for discussion. Mrs. Hathaway put a stop to it quickly being her mother I guess made it easier. She told Winnie maybe you're to advanced, for this class and should consider moving to the young adult class down the hall. We all snickered quietly to ourselves. Or maybe you would like to teach the younger children in children's church or perhaps you're ready to train with the leadership group on Sunday mornings. All of those were good options but she knew Winnie didn't want to leave the class; truly she was a bright young lady, over bearing sometimes. We all knew Winnie was going places we just wanted her to go. Mr. Parson's was over the men ministry and he and I worked closely on a lot of projects. His son Tyler was my age and we talked a lot about his love for music. Mr. Parsons loved working with the youth, and young men especially those whose father was not in the home. He would mentor us. His daughter Chelsea was holding down the choir with her angelic voice. Her looks we guys knew would come later but her voice was beautiful. His children worked with the music department so he took me under his wing to be his counterpart. The young adult men were going on a retreat to Bear Mountain and he wanted me to be in charge of getting things set up and ready to go. He had asked Tyler to do it but he was busy with an upcoming music event and couldn't give it the time it needed. Tyler was in the first chair with his trumpet he was very gifted with it. It was obvious Mr. Parsons had inherited a musical family of which he was very proud. I liked working with him and was always willing to lend him a hand.

The day before leaving on the retreat Dorca had left a message saying she wanted to talk to me after school. She had also left a message on my home phone. I had saw her at school and we had lunch together she had not mentioned wanting to see me about anything after school. That was the message she had left but I never got it until that dreadful day after I returned home with mom. As the day arrived to go to Bear Mountain I was running late after school. I wanted to finish up my science project for the science fair. I told Dorca I wouldn't be riding the bus home and hoped to see her when I came back from Bear Mountain. She could not see how that would be fun. I told her there were lots of activities planned and a great study of God's word. Dorca said I could study with her. I tried again to explain it wasn't the same, besides I have committed to Mr. Parsons and I really want to go. I didn't argue the point with her I closed the conversation letting her think about it.

I needed an hour longer to work on my project to get everything up and ready for Monday morning. We were not returning from the mountain until very late Sunday night the following week. I will get mom to pick me up from school and drive me to the last pickup stop for the bus. Then I would ride on the bus with the others. That would give me plenty of time to finish and get there in time. I had been so busy these past weeks getting things arranged and supplies ordered for our weeks stay at Bear Mountain not to mention the schoolwork, which was assigned my science project had been neglected and a few other things too. But I looked forward to going and wanted it to be a success for everyone especially Mr. Parsons. He worked so hard with all of us old and young men alike. I called Mr. Parsons to let him know I was working on my science project and would meet him at the last stop. He wasn't pleased I had neglected my school project and said to be sure it's completed before you come up that hill young man. "I look forward to seeing up there," he added with a smile. I called mom and left a message for her to please pick me up from the school and I would explain later. I continued working to finish on time and meet mom at 5:30.

The bus was loaded everyone was excited and anxiously awaiting the much talk about retreat. The group had been on many trips before, but this one boasted Timothy Wonters the much talk about Television Evangelist, and Motivator from California would be this year's facilitator. Mr. Parsons certainly wanted me there. He had told us so much about this man, his teaching style and beliefs we felt like we knew him already. He always said to reach high and achieve greatness through Jesus Christ. Mr. Parsons wanted to expose us to God's people. He would always say that to us also.

I looked at my watch it read 5:0 clock, I couldn't believe I still had that much time left. So, I took a few more minutes and called to see if mom was on her way. She picked me up and off we went down the highway. Mom did you remember those big boots dad gave me? Did you put them in my bag? I asked. I was feeling a little nervous because I had waited to finish the project and almost missed out on going to the retreat. Mom said yes, everything I had asked for was in the duffel styled bag. We settled in for the ride up to the last stop. Mom I asked why are you driving so slowly? You're going to miss the bus. "I thought I was taking you up" she said. "We have plenty of time." I'll switch over a highway 32 and probably meet the bus coming in mom explained. I said I wanted to ride up with everyone else, and was just trying to get to the last stop that the bus had to pick up the others going on the retreat. Mom asked, why did you wait so late to call me Billy? "Late! I said, it's only, my heart stopped, and so had my watch, it had the same time when I looked at it at school. What time is it mom? It's 6:00 clock Billy".

Suddenly the traffic stopped! Mom sit up in the seat to see what was going on. We both stopped and sat there impatiently for about 10 minutes. "People are getting out of their cars" mom said. I got out and ran around the curve of the road to see what was going on. All I could see was flashing lights. The sirens could be heard from the highway below. I ran back to the car; turn the radio on "KVEW" the traffic station in our area. Someone shouted loudly "a bus went over the rail of the highway!". Then the news came on over the radio a bus going on a retreat had went over an embankment of the highway at 5:30 pm. Didn't yet know the severity of casualties but there were bodies thrown from the bus. The first two vehicles had pushed the bus off the main road on the embankment it was resting on its side. Ambulances and other law enforcement vehicles covered the highway. OH MY God, Tetra said. I was at the church when Mr. Parsons called to speak with Pastor Hathaway about the final delivery to the camp. He also asked for Trina his wife she had left for home. I hope he got her there. I slumped over in my seat. I felt I had been kicked in the stomach. Tears filled my eyes and began running down my face. Mom and I began to pray, she put her arms around me. I couldn't believe the news! I couldn't believe I was spared from that bus. I searched my heart for answers. Then John 14:1 came to me, LET NOT YOUR HEART BE TROUBLE, you believe in God believe also in me. I go to prepare a place for you and I will come again. I still didn't know how bad it was, but I felt a horse had kicked me in the gut……and already I missed my mentor Mr. Parson.

The days ahead were the saddest ever. I had never encountered this feeling in my life. I've felt saddest when dad would leave, but I always knew he would come back. This sadness felt final. I thought all my friends were gone. There were fifty-six people on that bus. It never made it to the final stop where at least 50 more were to board. Mr. Parson's had been rushed to the hospital but lived only a short while. We had to pray. Mt Nebo had to pray, if we were too recovered from this disaster God's surely present in this place. Eight of the fifty-six men went home to be with the Lord. Some find it hard to understand. Many are still thanking God for a miracle.

Seems we were having funeral after funeral. Pastor Hathaway spoke with the families and asked if we could have the remaining three funerals together. I thanked God the families agreed, for it was hard on everyone. There was Mr. King who had been at Mt. Nebo since the doors opened. He had a wife children and grandchildren and a new grandchild born just last month. Earl Potts was a new member who joined because his wife had been going for months, two of our Sunday school teacher's Carl Mosley, and Lonnie Greedy. Henry Fields a young energetic senior wanting to be an engineer. Thomas Kinncade, and Joseph Sinclair both were newlyweds at Mt. Nebo and of course Henry Parsons the man who had mentored me most of my life. And I was finding it hard for me to bear. I thought what else Lord? The night before one of the funerals I was having a rough day.

I was questioning the Lord. I called Mr. Reed I needed to understand. Mrs. Reed answered and I greeted her and she was surprised I asked for her husband instead of Glen. She knew me well so she asked. "Billy is everything alright with you and your mom?" "Yes ma'am" we're fine, I went on to explain to her about what had happened in our church family. She was wondering how that was affecting us. She had heard about it from some of the old members of Community Central. She knew I was taking it hard and said she'd be praying and gave the phone to Pastor Reed. He talked to me about God's ways and how his understanding does not line up with ours. He talked with me about 1 Thessalonians 5:18 giving thanks in all circumstances. He shared God knows us and will be there for us and he read 1 Peter 5:7 cast all your cares on him because he cares for you. He told me I could call him any time of day if I needed to talk or had questions, or just wanted to pray. He prayed with and for me and said he'd be in touch soon. I thanked him and asked him to please tell Glen I said hello. Though those days are very hard for me I sure felt better knowing I had him to talk to.

There were many sad years at Mt. Nebo Church. Tyler Parsons was taking it hard and rightly so he was devastated. He was on the bus but God had spared his life. Why he thought had he spared me to suffer. After he recovered from his injuries he moved to live with his aunt in another state. I hope wherever he is God is holding his heart.

CHAPTER 5

Surprise, surprise

I was growing up as fast as our congregation and we were growing by leaps and bounds. God had blessed us through those sad years. Hearts were mending everyone was determined to be there for one another. It wasn't an easy task keeping the core of our young adults intact. We had experienced a massive loss to a lot of families. We rested on the fact that God controls all things. I spent a lot of silent hours during lunch with Dorca. She was supportive at times but just couldn't understand why I felt the loss because we were not related. She knew me better than most, but became a little impatient with me sometimes. Many times, opting to have lunch with someone else since some days I just didn't want to talk. But for months after she would bring lunch for the both of us encouraging me to eat, I'd feel better. She was kind enough to read Psalms to me from her new bible which I had given her, and had me to read too. I must admit it made me feel better if only for a short time. Dorca did a lot of the reading, I know now it couldn't have hurt. She was always thinking of ways to ease the hurt for me. She asked her mom to pick her up a little later from her stop. We would sit and talk. I felt comfortable with her and could pour out my heart. Though, I don't think she ever really understood how or why this impacted me, she was willing to listen, and that alone was help for me.

I spent a lot of time at church now. One because I was now in charge of the Youth Ministry and another because it allowed me time alone to be myself in a place that Mr. Parsons loved. I missed a lot of Dorca's phone calls in the evening. She always commented to the fact. I would always find time at school walking with her between classes and bringing us lunch from home. She finally got around to telling me, that her parents didn't think she was quite ready for dating except special occasions. That meant I could look forward to the prom. I could feel the tension sometimes between us when I missed seeing her. She'd say things like 'you don't like me anymore!" So, I decided to get help and lighten my load of the youth ministry. I prayed and asked James Captain to assist me with this ministry he and I had worked alongside Mr. Parsons and I knew he truly loved the Lord.

One day at lunch Dorca presented me with an idea. She knew how much I liked and appreciated Mr. Parsons and never wanted to forget what he'd done or stood for. He had helped not only me but so many others with his generosity and kindness. A man that spared no expense to see that everyone was equal, no one was lacking. He was always giving. He would tell us God blessed him and he always will try and be a blessing to someone else.

Billy, she said, "Why don't your church build a center, multipurpose complex adjoined to the church in honor of Mr. Parsons. You can even give it his name "Henry Parsons Center" and it will serve all especially those youth he was passionate about. What do you think? I looked up, refreshed from sad thoughts, "what a wonderful idea. The idea was wonderful, but at this moment the fact that Dorca thought of it made it marvelous. "Well Billy, what do you think? She asked me again. 'That's a great idea, I like it". It will take a lot of work, time and money I said hesitantly" but if you help me, I'm going to try.

The months ending sophomore proved to be challenging. I would have to present and sell my idea to Pastor Hathaway and his staff and wait to hear if it's a go. Dorca and I worked after school, during lunch, and an occasionally weekend when she was available on the presentation. I talked to my father and other businessmen to acquire the needed information to make this idea a reality. We were two busy young people. I knew Dorca was doing this for me. She was on several committees at school and keeping up a very impressive grade point average. She was a campaign manager for one of her classmates but she always found time to help me with this project.

I excelled academically also but I relaxed by playing basketball. I was all right at it too. Dorca and I sat often brainstorming about a campaign slogan for her candidate. We would sit laughing and enjoying one another's company. We spent a lot of time together mostly at school.

By years end I was meeting one night with Pastor Hathaway and his staff to find out if we could continue pursuing the project we had presented regarding the Center. The next day I met Dorca near the cafeteria door of the school. "Well, well" she said before I could get a word out. "Now the works begins" I said grinning from ear to ear. Dorca was glad too I think she saw the bubbly kindergartener of long ago. My point guard skills showed up again in our victory win that night over the rival school.

After the school bus trip home, I was surprised to see the Rolls Royce already waiting. I always had a little time with her. What was going on I thought? She hurried off the bus and ran right to her car, "SEE YOU LATER" she yelled and off she went. I walked home silently. I wanted to share and idea with her but it will have to wait. Just as I settled into my big cozy leather chair after getting a snack and all the paperwork laid out for the Center my doorbell rang. I wasn't expecting anyone and I felt interrupted but hurried to open the door. This had better be good I thought opening the door. Much to my surprise it was Dorca. I could hardly get the words out. "Hi I'm surprised"! I said. "Sure, you are," she said I planned it that way" are you busy? "not yet I told her I'm just getting started." I dropped my head, I wanted to tell her I knew where she lived. I wanted to tell her about the day I followed her home years ago. How could I? She had come all this way to surprise me by coming over. We had worked on the presentation at lunch after school while she waited to be picked up from the bus stop a few times. But now she was standing in my doorway. "I'm, I'm glad to see you please come in" I finally said. "I have an idea I'd like to run by you.

Now in our junior year we worked on the plans for the Center for an hour before mom came home. I was glad for she had not formerly been introduced to the girl I was taking to the prom and spending time with. Mom had watched Dorca growing up during elementary school and always wondered if she had changed. Her personality I mean she'd say. All she knew about Dorca is what I had shared. Which now I realize wasn't much. Mom this is Dorca Williams" "Dorca this is my mom Tetra Parker" "It's good to finally meet you dear, mom said. "Billy has talked a lot about you over the years". 'All good things I hoped Dorca replied then she added "it's nice to meet you also Mrs. Parker. "O.K. I'll let you two continue if you need something Billy let me know. "Thanks mom, I said. She smiled and walked out of the room.

We finished all the planning and sat and talked for an hour. It was getting late and I was getting concerned about the time. "I'd better get going I have homework in Mr. Bicker's class to finish. I knew Mr. Bicker's class was college prep courses not to be taken lightly. "I understand I told her. Can I walk you home? I asked hesitantly. 'No, and she got up and went out of the door. I was now very concerned should I tell her now? I didn't want her walking home alone. All that way it would surely be dark before she arrived. I turned to go and ask mom to take her home, but by then she was on the lawn in my front yard headed for the street. Dorca! I called out "wait I have something to tell you". "Tell me tomorrow Billy I have to go". "See ya" she hurried down the street. I was not about to let her go that distant by herself. And I didn't have time to explain to mom. Dorca was a true friend coming all that way to help me, besides I really liked her a lot. I ran to my garage and took the bicycle from the bike hooks on the wall. Don't ride much anymore dad was convincing mom I was ready for a car. I raced down the street in the direction Dorca went. Around the corner I went, no Dorca another corner, nothing. I thought she could not have walked that fast, where could she be?

I slowly started back home. As I rode looking hopelessly around up and down the street, I spotted her sitting on a local bus bench 'Dorca". My heart leaped from under my shirt. Relieved she was all right I started to ride toward her. When around the corner came the Rolls! Dorca's Rolls Royce. She smiled and got in. I waited a way off as not to be seen. That's how she does it I thought. The car drove away. I was glad she was in safe hands. But what would I tell her tomorrow?

CHAPTER 6

Prom Time

Dad had sold the house in Maine and promised to let us know where the location of his move would be and other plans he had made. He and mom had been talking more but I didn't know what plans they had laid out. I knew the decision to sell wasn't easy because he was trying to please mom, he told me that. I thought all the long conversations were regarding the house sell. It was now my senior year and I wanted to share with him my plans. I was trying to make the right decisions on what college to attend. Should I stay close in the area with mom? Or take one of the athletic scholarships to an all-black college? Mr. Parsons and I had talked about that a lot. He was a Brown University's man and very proud of the fact. When dad had settled, I plan to sit down with he and mom and discuss options. I wasn't sure of Dorca's plans but I'd hoped they included me somehow. I knew Dorca said her parents wanted her to go to Paris before deciding on a college. She wasn't sold on the idea. I had a feeling she would get her way. She still hadn't shared what college she would attend if any. There were many offers I saw some of the letters they had sent her. She had received back many responses after applying and was trying to decide as well. She was boarding brilliant I'd say.

The next day when I arrived at school there were signs everywhere. Senior prom tickets go on sell at noon. As if I couldn't see all the poster's up around the campus Winnie thought she would point them out. "Billy the prom is coming! Now Winnie had gotten me to accompany her to several functions at the church, but not the prom I was set on taking Dorca. "Yea I see, hear it's going to be great. The guys are all talking about it and looking for dates they all plan to attend". "I know you have a date already

Winnie? I stated hoping the answer was yes. "I do if you're asking" she replied. "No! I mean not really, I've already asked Dorca she has accepted sorry," I said looking down for I had lied and couldn't look her in the face. But I wanted to take Dorca and Winnie had tripped me up before and I wasn't taking any chances. If there was a chance to go with Dorca I wasn't going to blow it. I'm leaving all options open. Dorca walked up while we were still talking. "Hi Dorca, I hear you are Billy's date for the prom" Winnie hissed. "RANG! RANG! The school bell ranged. "I'll see you in first period" Winnie chided and walked off. I looked at Dorca it was an awkward moment. I knew I hadn't asked her. I had just found out about ticket sales. Winnie had spilled the beans she had told her. What was she thinking? "I'll talk to you later Billy. I don't want to be late for class. Lunch o.k." she finally said. "O.k. lunch I said walking to Mr. Bicker's class still wondering about what she was thinking? I had never been on a date with her. She always came to dances alone and left right away after it was over "I knew I'd see you all tomorrow no need to lose my beauty sleep chatting" she'd say. Would she even want to go with me? Well I'd have to wait and see.

I waited anxiously but nervously at our usual lunch spot. She was taking longer than usual. Was she upset because I had lied? Was she even going to show? After about fifteen minutes she came walking by with Nicole Fleming a cheerleader from the school's squad team. Not your stereotypical blonde Nicole had brains to go along with her beauty. Dorca hung out with her most of the time. Probably because she was near the team players and knew what went on. I never knew, didn't ask. Dorca knew from her Winnie wasn't a threat. They seemed to have a genuine friendship, which was very rare for Dorca, she often tolerated Winnie she'd say.

'I'll call you with the color of my dress, when I decide what it's going to be, o.k. she said as she continued to pass me by. Nicole and I are having lunch today. "I'll see you on the bus" Dorca added. Was she having lunch with someone else just to spite me for lying? I thought. She said she'll call. We didn't always have lunch together. But why was she having lunch with someone else today?

I walked over and purchased lunch at the snack bar. Then I found a group of my team buddies who after giving me a hard time about not being with Dorca discussed the homecoming game against Edison High

School. They boasted the number one quarterback of our conference. And they were going to put the lights out on our parade party. We laughed and joked through the entire lunch hour.

After school I waited on the bus for Dorca. The ride home was wonderful. She said she would love to accompany me to the prom and added "thanks for asking." I waited impatiently for mom to come home so that I could share with her about the prom. The phone rang. 'Hello! hello son, how are you? Hi dad I'm good, got a date for the prom. "Sure, wish you could meet her?". When are you coming? Well that's what I need to talk with Tetra about, is she there? Not yet dad soon! "Please let her know I will be there tomorrow, but have her call me when she gets in okay". "Okay dad, look forward to seeing you". I need to talk with you about my college decisions also". "Is it that time already" David said with a smile in his voice" time flies." "Alright son I'll see you soon bye" "bye dad." I said hanging up the phone.

"Ring, ring, "hello" "hi Billy" "hi Dorca" "what are you doing? 'just got off the phone with my dad" What are you doing? "I told you I would call". With Dorca I learned never to expect. She somehow seems to change plans on a whim. Well I'm calling did you get a concert date? "Oh, oh, I was still thinking about the prom, we had planned a concert to raise the money to continue the construction on the new Center. Everything was in place except the date for it. We had to coordinate the speakers, singer's choirs, dancers, into a four or five-hour, show. So many had responded to perform, we soon decided on two days instead of the one previously. So, we were adjusting schedules to find dates that met our needs. We needed a month notification on most groups, which we understood. James and I thought we would get Timothy Wonters the television motivator/evangelist to speak for us. That would be very fitting. "I'm meeting tonight with Pastor Hathaway and his staff to finalize the program and the date and get it out to everyone" 'I' will let you know Dorca, "I'm excited too I shared.

I paused for a minute then asked, "are you coming to the concert? "it's for everyone you know. Bring your mother or your parents for that matter I said. Dorca sat silent for a moment then said "I'm glad you're excited, though I don't know if I'm coming, Nicole and I might show up who knows". I'm glad it's going to happen. It is for a good cause." Billy I'll talk with you tomorrow bye" and Dorca abruptly hung up the phone.

If she and Nicole showed up, that would be great. Nicole does own a car. It would be a first but nothing Dorca did surprised me anymore. I hung up thinking she didn't even mention the prom. I somehow sensed she liked the tease factor of things but one thing at a time first the concert then the prom.

CHAPTER 7

Making life changing decisions

Dad arrived early. I had not left for school when the doorbell rang. I walked over peeked out and opened it. "Good morning," "good morning son" "it's good to see you" you too dad" Then I turned my head and yelled "mom, dad's here!" Mom came out from her room down the hall. 'You said you'd be early" how was your flight?" "flight was good, but little can be said for the best breakfast on the plane" he said looking at the pancakes and bacon mom had prepared for us. "come in sit down there's plenty, "mom told him. I hurried and ate my breakfast and said I would like to talk with dad later if he had plans to be there. He assured me he would, I kissed mom and ran out the door.

I went to talk with coach Geary about some letter offers I had received and share with him on some decisions I had already made with others. I knew that Harvard was first choice if I wasn't playing sports of any kind. Many letters came offering a basketball scholarship. Dad was the expert there. But sports were something I played for fun. I didn't know if I wanted to make a living of it. Since my father was in the business a lawyer for some of the top National Basketball Association player's agents, I most certainly valued my dad's opinion. He was always featured in Fortune magazines and Business Week just to name a few. Most of the guys on the team knew who he was just from his popularity status. So, I knew exactly what it took to be in that arena. I had seen and heard a lot of stories good and bad about players and their lives.

Grambling would be fun I could meet a lot of lifetime friends while getting a great education. Mr. Parsons had brought so much of black colleges to life for us as he told the stories. Most of my exposure with Black's was when mom brought me here to live. Dad's world was glitz and glamour, lots of entertaining people of all races but mostly Caucasians. Mother always said she wanted me grounded. Growing up in two worlds has its advantages neither of which I regret, thanks to mom. If I wasn't going to pursue basketball, and I knew I wasn't as good as some of my teammates whom I would say was gifted. I had lots of decisions to make. Most of the teammates liked me. Some because of who my dad was. The guys envied me saying because of my dad I was a shoe in to the NBA. I sure didn't see it that way. I wanted to sit and talk with my parents before making any decisions. Coach Geary understood. "Son do weight all options, no quick decisions often costly." I'll be here," coach said. 'Thanks coach I said, thanks for the information.

I walked down the long hallway into a group of girls standing near my locker. Dorca was one of them. "Hi Billy" the girls giggled loudly. "Hi Dorca, Nicole, Eykuha what are you all up to I asked. "Dorca I've got the dates for the concert it's June 12th and 13th at Mt. Nebo's in the west end main sanctuary. God had blessed our church it had grown despite the oppositions. God had brought us through. It now covered the large parcel of land it owned. It was a beautiful group of buildings. The sanctuary with it seats that were in a half circle that stopped on either side of a large stage. The seats descended as they went to the top. Perfect setting for what was about to take place. Sound system state of the art. We were ready.

Everyone pulled together and advertised the concert it was a community effort. Ticket sales went through the roof and God was blessings. We had to turn some group's offers down, promising to do it again. Everyone knew and loved Mr. Parsons he had been around a long time. Two glorious nights were planned in which to praise and uplift the Lord and honor a man who meant so much too so many.

"That's wonderful" Dorca said, by the way I'm wearing peach". "Peach" I repeated puzzled, 'for the prom silly". "oh o.k. I'll remember that. I still have some things to get done before school starts. See you at lunch if you're not busy" I said as Dorca and the girls walked away.

Everything was in place for the concert now I could concentrate on the prom. It was right around the corner only months away. I needed to buy tickets and a peach color corsage. How would I get there? Would she let me pick her up? That's what usually happens. I walked over to a long line of students waiting to purchase tickets and stood talking as the line moved slowly upward to the small ticket window, made with a table across the door. "May I help you Billy?" "2 tickets please" I replied. "$45.00 dollars" I handed Michelle the money, as she gave me the change back, she said. "I'm looking forward to the concert Billy you have put together some great groups". "Thank you, Mimi, everyone helped, you know it's for a good cause, see you around". I wasn't trying to be rude, but couldn't be late again for Mrs. Cloretta's class so I cut the conversation short and hurried off.

I put the tickets in my backpack and headed for class meeting Winnie at the door, 'good morning Billy" "good morning Winnie" "Mom said you did a great job organizing the concert" Winnie confessed. "Why thank you, it was a joint effort you know", I continued "but please thank Mrs. Hathaway personally for me". "Whatever" Winnie remarked sharply and walked away. "By the way is Dorca coming? "I don't know," I said "you'll have to ask her" "she's invited of course I added, "everyone's invited". Seeing that she had not succeeded in ruining the start of my day, Winnie replied, "I'll be there Billy rooting you on". "I'll let mom know what you said also." Without another remark I went to my desk, getting the last word with Winnie was impossible. No ones, life is that long.

When I arrived at the church early to get all the last minute, arrangements in order Fred, James and Leeta, were just a part of those who had come in to help make things run smoothly. Everyone was moving about and performers were showing up. Pastor Hathaway had arrived to greet the visiting Evangelist Wonters and to make him welcome and comfortable until he was ready to go out. Pastor's office was equipped for him to rest if he desired or just relax from his flight in. The church had put him up at the Sheraton Inn for his two day stay with us, but he was flying in today coming from a conference and would, just get in hours before he was to speak with us. We wanted him to be well taken care of and comfortable.

People began pouring in from everywhere from every walk of life, just like Mr. Parson's would have wanted. He never turned anyone away. Mr. Parsons often purchased fares for the outings when their families couldn't afford it. He and his wife took children to his home especially around the holidays and shared what God had blessed them with. The Church was full to capacity the music played softly. Prayer was led by Pastor Hathaway, and a solo by Chelsea Parsons. Each act was uplifting and praise worthy. There was shouting, praised tears of joy hand clapping the spirit was high. Evangelist Wonters exhorted, explained and compelled through his encouraging words. Everyone left that place different just for being there.

We raised enough in the two glorious nights to get final construction underway. We also presented a plaque to Mrs. Trina Parsons who continues to weather the storms of life. She is still very active in women ministries with the women's circle. The plaque is a replica of the one to be attached to the front entrance of the Center that reads: Suffer little children to come unto me and forbid them not for such in the kingdom of heaven Matthew 19:14 "Henry Parson's Center".

August twelfth was approaching quickly. Dad had relocated in the city and had purchased a home in Granite Heights. A very posh community miles from the high school and the church. It was about midway point from where mom and I lived by freeway, and the homes reminded me of our home in Maine. Dad talked about how long he took him to find it. He wanted it to be right. It would be a surprise for mom. And boy was she surprised! He and mom were getting together talking more often having an occasional dinner or two. I didn't want her hurt. I could see she liked having him around. I wasn't sure what was happening or how this would work out. So, I prayed about it every night before going to bed. I knew mom better than dad, because I had spent most of my life with her personality. I knew dad was always there for us. One thing was certain my decision about leaving mom alone vanished!

I sat my parents down at one of mom's great dinners. A spicy, almost smoky pork chop encrusted with coarsely ground spices and a fruity rice and barely plum pilaf meal one of dad's favorite dinners. I knew that. I helped mom place the salad mixed with apples on the table and got the blue cheese dressing from the frig. The sautéed vegetables that set in the center of the table steaming slightly smelled so delicious. "My favorite dinner guys you have out done yourselves" dad warmly said with a smile. He knew mom loved to cook she was always helping the chefs prepare dinners in Maine. "Thank you very much' mom said" but leave room for dessert pear upside down cake". Dad got up from the big armed chair and went over to his briefcase and pulled out a bottle of Sauvignon Blanc "perfect "I stopped by Ron and Joanne's vineyard in Norfolk on my way here." "They wanted me to give you their love, hope to see us soon." "Oh, Tetra said how are they doing, "I do miss my dear friends, I'll have to call them." She continued moving over to the dining room table. Let's eat. Dad and I walked over and sat down. Mom handed dad the wine corkscrew that he placed beside the chilled ice bucket that held the wine she had placed on the table to chill.

After a brief prayer from dad we began eating. Conversation was light and cheerful. I was waiting to finish dinner before I began discussing my college options. Dad had told us he had hired a manager to lighten his load at the office. One who would do most of the traveling for him now. He'd only go in extreme cases as needed. That made mom smile, a lot. Dad had poured three goblets with the wine. I continued to eat until I saw mom pick the glass up and drink. I stopped and looked at her. She had not drunk before why now? "Drink dear she told me, there is no alcohol in it. I looked at dad and got the parental nod, and smiled. I soon emptied the glass. "Wow haven't had that before." Only the grape juice they call wine at church mom". "That's good to know Billy, I pray you keep it that way" she smiled. I picked up the bottle of wine for further inspection. Non-alcohol "that's good to know you can have wine with your dinner and not suffer for it" When things settled again, I brought up college. I told them I had been discussing it with coach Geary. And I did some research and also talked with my other teachers. Mom and I had spoken in great details weeks earlier after a recruiting trip. "But dad I need to know what you think?" I laid out some details with papers I had gotten from my bedroom. "I really want your opinion I told him.

My father looked at me. Then he looked at mom. "Tetra you have done a great job raising our son. I know I wasn't always there. I made a mistake that caused me to separate from your lives and I have paid dearly. I need you to forgive me. And I'm asking now that you forgive me." Tears were now forming in dad's eyes. I never stopped loving you and Billy. I so want to be a part of your life. I never knew how to ask for forgiveness or even how to come to you. "How could you ever forgive me?" Mom nor dad had said anything to me but I knew what he was talking about now. Didn't understand why he was bringing it up though things seemed to be going well at this point. Dad didn't stop talking it was as if someone was pouring it into him and it was flowing out uncontrollably. "I now want to be a part of your life Tetra. "I'm tired of traveling without you. Living in hotels heavens knows business meetings are endless and watching Billy grow up from a far. I know I can't change the past, but I'm asking for a future with you. I have always sustained a good life a comfortable life but it means nothing without you. Please let me love you again." The room went silent and all that could be heard was breathing. I took mom by the hand. You could hear a pin dropped on plush carpeting the silence in the room was massive. "Tetra", dad finally said. "I wanted to rush right over after the concert, but talked my way out of it". "Evangelist Wonters talked about a second chance". "God forgives it's never too late". "I hesitated, thought to hard, lost my courage got on a plane and left". "I sat in my hotel room vowing that if I had another opportunity to ask, I was not going to let it pass". 'You are precious to me" "Please give me a chance to get it right."

Mom wasn't making this easy; because she was saying nothing so everything was going through my mind. God only knows what was going through dads. I was all set to discuss my future and college. I didn't even know dad was at the concert, neither did mom. He surprised us both with that revelation. I didn't know what would happen next but I sure wanted God in it.

I walked over and took dad by his hand and began to pray a prayer of forgiveness and deliverance in this situation. The words came flowing out of me. Tears flowed down our faces, forgiveness, found our hearts. Joy was restored to our family. Happiness was imminent. We stood in that dining room crying and embracing one another allowing healing to overshadow doubt. We were a whole family again. We didn't know what tomorrow held for us. We only knew God was holding it.

CHAPTER 8

Move in day

The prom was approaching fast and Dorca had not given me her address. Even though I knew where she lived. I was thinking would she let me pick her up? Or would she pick me up in the Rolls? I needed to finalize my plans for prom night. Mom had agreed to move in with dad in the huge house he had purchased for us. Made sense to me she hadn't been intimate with anyone else over the years that I knew about and I didn't miss much that went on with mom. Why not dad? I would definitely feel better going off to college knowing she wasn't alone.

It wasn't going to be an easy adjustment mom had become accustomed to doing things her way. She and I have lived together so long we knew each other well. But if she was willing to work to make it happen, and willing to forgive him surely, I was.

The movers drove up to the new house. Mom and I were following them in our Benz. We went around the van as we headed down this curved path of the driveway. Pulling in I noticed a brand-new Ford Mustang parked in one of the spaces in front of the garage entrance. I figured this was a car dad hadn't taken back yet. I beckoned to the van driver to pull in so they could begin unloading. I wanted to hurry and get things settled so that I could call Glen and Dorca.

As we approached the front entrance of the Mediterranean style home I looked out on the crescent shaped lawn. There were a variety of flowers and plants all over. Rhododendrons, roses and lots of shrub like plants fenced the beautiful spacious lawn. As I stood admiring the view, a grassy path ran down the side of the house with flowers and foliage on either side. Across the turf was a stone walkway to the front door. The two-story home had three sets of beautiful French double doors across the front entrance. The upper level boasted a balcony off the master bedroom. Unlike our home in Maine this one had a large wrap around porch in elegant taste for this house. Dad talked about how he enjoyed sitting out in the evening and just relaxing. The gorgeous outdoor furniture mom helped dad pick out weeks ago had arrived. I teased her" mom the furniture you picked out for dad's client looks great!" She just slapped me on the shoulder and smiled. That's what dad had told her when they went out to purchase it. Mom handed me the key. I opened the door to this illuminating large entrance. The laid stone flooring caught mom's eye. It was just like our floors in Maine. I looked up at the high cathedral ceiling motif. I turned to mom and smiled "we're home" I said. I ran up the wide spiraling staircase and looked for the space I would call my room. There were three large rooms in addition to the master suite to choose from. I chose the bedroom overlooking the backyard it also had a balcony. Down below I could see a pond, waterfall and a vibrant mix of shrubs and flowers and green lawn as far as the eye could see. There's a wooden deck with chairs for relaxing in the garden setting and a basketball court as well as a large swimming pool.

The house so reminded me of our Maine home but this one was full of color bursting out all over the grounds. Dad had spared no expensive in making this home right for mom and me and it showed. Mom walked around sizing up where everything would go. Realizing with two houses both full of furniture some furnishings would have to go. She found herself sorting and replacing or discarding altogether many of the pieces. She loved her furnishings she and dad had purchased in Maine. So, most of the pieces she and I had accumulated were stored in the storage basement until she decided what to do with them. I was tired I helped the movers with the last furniture pieces so I could get showered and settled and talk with Dorca. The installer had given me the thumbs up several hours ago regarding the phone lines. I had called and left a message with the new number, but still had not heard from Dorca. I had never called Dorca she always called me. Had she gotten my message? I did tell her about the move and that my schedule would change a bit maybe her parents didn't even know I existed. Well I'd just wait until she called, I was tired anyway. "Mom I'm just going to rest in my room O.K." I laid down on my frumpy large bed and closed my eyes.

My schedule was hectic it's any wonder that Dorca could keep up with it. I barely could and mom was always having me write it down. "Where am I picking you up from today Billy" she'd say. Between school after school activities and the Center I was always somewhere. I worked very closely with Pastor Hathaway's committee with the new Center, which by the way was moving along as scheduled.

I lay there on the bed for what seemed minutes when I heard 'Billy, Billy, are you hungry? I have prepared lunch". I gazed at my watch and realized I had laid down two hours earlier." "Mom did anyone call? I asked. No dear, "who has the number?" "Glen and Dorca mom" "I should have known" "no Billy she hasn't called yet," "but I'm sure she will soon". "I hope so I've got basketball practice at 2:30 at the school mom, can you take me? "not a problem, eat your lunch, I'm going to finish putting away this China."

As mom and I were gathering our things heading for the door dad came in. "Well Tetra do you like it? "It's wonderful David, you know me quite well", mom teased. "I'd like to think so anyway" David remarked. "Billy, I have something for you too". He walked over to his briefcase. Dad seemed to keep everything in that briefcase. He beckoned for mom, and whispered in her ear. She smiled and gave that parental nod. "What! what is it"? I asked not knowing but excited just the same. He reached in his pocket and tossed me a set of keys. Oh boy! I leaped. Where is it dad? "out front." Did you drive it here? I asked as we walked out to it. When we got out front dad pointed to the Mustang parked in the driveway. It was fire engine red. "Thanks dad, thanks mom".

I thought it was time, thanks Dave" Tetra said kissing him lightly on his cheek. He was running me raggedy with his schedule. Besides he's a good kid he deserves it. I sat under the wheel; dad got in on the passenger side. Mom waved us on. We went around the block and to the freeway. 'Handles well dad, I'll keep it under the speed limit". "Please do Tetra will have both of us if you don't". I drove dad back home Dorca still hadn't called. She was probably out of town it was the weekend. I'll talk with her tomorrow. Glen I called later that night and we got caught up on each one lives.

Mom had dinner on the table at six o clock. Dad asked mom to be sure and hire someone to help her with the house, if only 3 or 4 days a week. She promised she would if needed. She had gotten accustomed to doing it herself but this house was much larger than our previous one. Tetra had put most of the fine China away and other items for her kitchen, and had cleared the kitchen table for an informal dinner.

David had come in from the den to help get things ready. "Well Tetra, do you really like our new home? "I do Dave" and I'm noticing all the things you had done to make it more enjoyable, special touches, the flooring in the front." "Remember what fun we had picking it out for the house in Maine? "Yes, I was afraid I wouldn't be able to duplicate it. David told her reaching casually over to kiss her on the check. How was your day? Tetra asked. I closed the New York office today. And the one here should be ready or very near ready next week. I'm Looking forward to not having to travel so much" David told her. That's wonderful, we will take it one day at a time." she remarked.

David and Tetra had finished dinner when the phone rang. It was Billy informing them he would be going over to the church to talk with the construction supervisor about the new floor for the Center and would come home after that. David had change clothes and was helping Tetra put away the dinner dishes. They laughed and shared with one another regarding those missing years keeping things purposely light. "Tetra, Dave questioned, 'did you talk with Billy about what happened? I mean what I did?" "What you did! Tetra came back. "The affair with Katherine your secretary" Tetra remarked "no I was waiting for him to get older, then I was waiting for you to tell him, I guess I didn't want it to interfere with your relationship." I do still plan to tell him I think he should know" "or you may want to tell him that's fine too" somehow I think he should know why our lives was interrupted from you." "I wanted to get as far away from you as I possibly could David". But no matter how far I went away I couldn't stop hurting." Billy was always asking "when were you coming home?" I realized I was missing you in between those visit as much as Billy. I couldn't tell you to stop." Believe it or not, "I thank you for what you did" not because it was right" you hurt me badly" but because through the hurt and pain I found Jesus again. Dave I find myself quoting psalms 34: I will praise the Lord at all times his praise will continually be in my mouth. Some days or harder than others, I've finished crying about that. I've placed it in God's hand. I have asked Him to help me to forgive, and daily thank Him for mending my broken heart.

"Hi mom," she turned to wipe her face as I entered the room, I could see she had been crying. Is everything alright? I asked looking now at dad. Everything's fine son your mom is a bit emotional about her new place, dad said embracing her in his arm. 'I'll just warm dinner, "is this the microwave on the oven's top? I said pointing at all the new stainless steel, appliances. Mrs. Peeler would always let me mess around in the kitchen, while she prepared dad's meals. I was always turning the wrong buttons. Mom now composed said, Billy your food is in the conventional oven, it should still be warm." "Thanks mom" I pulled the warming dish from the oven the grilled garlic chicken made my mouth water. I put it in a plate and sat down to eat. "Dad was talking softly with mom, everything at this moment seemed fine. "Dad I got a letter from Brown University, and Grambling I'd like to talk with you and mom after I eat okay, and dad the guys loved my Mustang!" We sat there talking about everything mostly about my college options. Dad had gone the Yale route, but wasn't pushing me to go there. "Your choice" he'd say. He felt Granddad made him go but he'd have to admit he really enjoy those years. Granddad was always so serious. I spent time with them when my summer visits conflicted with dads travel schedule. Grandma was sweet. He tried to make dad and aunt Sarah dad's sister the same way very serious. Dad was always saying he is never going to be like granddad. Perhaps mom understood that because he was totally opposite from granddad in personality.

I had made up my mind about Harvard. My parents had already set it up that way anyway. But they were still letting me go on two more recruiting trips. Seymore wanted me to go and I was accompanying him it was fun. He was a McDonald All American and everyone was after him. I didn't really want to play basketball my heart was not always in it. They say I could for the most part put together a good game. So, consistency is what I needed if I was going to make a living of it. I had watched over the years many dishearten wives and players who came to know it as a fast life and for the players a business. You have to be mentally ready dad always said. I wanted to do something I was good at. And talking through a problem to find a solution, negotiating, and arguing a point I was there. So, I thanked mom and dad and headed for my room. Mom had been in while I was gone. All the clothes were put away and my bed wasn't frumpy anymore.

I took a shower and sat on my bed looking over a homework assignment when the phone rang. It was Dorca "hi Billy" got your message. I was at my grandparents did you get moved in? She asked "I sure did" I replied "We decided to stay the whole weekend my grandfather is sick. So, we are spending more time with him she added. "Oh, I see well I was calling about the prom" am-I-picking-you-up? I said slowly breaking each word up individually. I got a new car today it's a Ford Mustang convertible, you'll see it tomorrow" "Great Billy, gotta go" hurrying me off the phone. "I'll be at school early" I said hurriedly now before she hung up. "You'll have to see my car. I can pick you up for school if you give me your address" I said insistently. "Tomorrow Billy O.K. goodnight and the phone buzzed loudly in my ear.

CHAPTER 9

Pastor Cornelius Hathaway

The Center was beautifully constructed. The ribbon cutting ceremony drew crowds from several neighborhoods and communities. We called and invited the groups that did not get a chance to share a performance at the concert. They sang and danced for hours on an open stage we had brought in for the day. We arranged an outdoor affair with lots of activities for children and adults alike. There was barbeque on the grill, hot dogs and hamburgers with all the trimmings. It was a wonderful event. Mayor Calvin Reeves was our Honoree and presided over the ribbon cutting ceremony. After the ceremony everyone toured the facilities. There were plenty of activity rooms for the children, a large computer room, a large open space with a pool table and other group games as well as a large library that allowed us to incorporate the smaller one in Pastor Hathaway's office. It was a huge multiplex, multipurpose complex. My dad and other business owners had made large donations to the Center. We even received a very large donation from an anonymous donor. I have my thoughts on where that came from. The day the doors opened was a proud day for Mt. Nebo the community and a proud day for the now Dr. Cornelius Hathaway.

Dad was now a member and attending services regularly. He travels once maybe twice a month. He still had not committed to one particular ministry but loved being with the men at their monthly meetings of fellowship. On Sundays when he walked in with mom and me all heads turned around. There were those who talked but most of them were happy for us especially Christine Guillory mom's best friend.

I parked my Mustang convertible in the student lot with all the other student's cars and stood around talking before school. Some guys from the team came over and gathered looking in and around it. 'This is sharp man! Check out the wheels! Chrome, right? Man, this is just in time for the prom" Walter interjected. "Thanks guys, just trying to keep up, I said "speaking of the prom though I'd better go and find Dorca". Bill is she picking you up in the Rolls? Won't you let us join you all! Everybody was trying to talk at once. "Not my call guys, besides I prefer driving my own car". "See you all later I finally said and off I went. At the student square I found Dorca standing near the cafeteria door with Blaine and Nicole "Hey guys" I said walking toward them. "Are you two ready for the prom?" Blaine says, "I'm ready, are you driving those fancy wheels? "or will you be stuck in that cold steel Rolls Royce? He continued to ask, despite Nicole elbowing him in his side. "Haven't decided yet I replied pulling Dorca away to speak with her alone. "Dorca can we talk?" continuing to pull her away I replied see you guys later." Dorca and I walked over to an empty bench away from the crowd. "Would you like to see my car?" I asked her before sitting next to her on the bench. 'Not yet Billy there is plenty of time" "I hear it's nice". Well are you going to give me your address so I can come and get ya? I joked to lighten the moment. Dorca looked at me. Her look was puzzling and I wasn't sure what she was thinking; even what she was about to say. "Billy, I want to go to the prom with you, but you will have to meet my parents" she told me. I got passed that whew*@!* that's it, that's wonderful. How hard could that be? "I've already met your mom, right?" looking now with this silly smile forming on my face. "That lady is Edith my housekeeper kinda" "you've heard the joke about the weird little rich girl?" She was asking as if I would answer. That was a joke the guys used when teasing me, I had never told her that but then there was Nicole. "Edith escorts me around everywhere, but it doesn't take a genius to figure that out" she continued. "Well I said, honestly I have thought about it, you have to admit it's different. She lets me go and do things without having my parents looking over my shoulder" Dorca shared. Edith has lived with me all my life, and allows me to do things, that does not necessarily need approval from them. My parents are older and somewhat protective to put it mildly Dorca continued. I like Edith a lot she's always been there as long as I can remember. Every time we go to Oregon to my grandparents, she takes me over to this lady's house. There's a girl there named Doris and she and I talk and share stories. We talk about everything. Besides her Edith is the only one who understands me. "I really didn't know why Dorca was sharing all this or even where she was going with this conversation so I just listened. "Edith would bring me to play at the park after school if I would ask her, she said. "I would ask her to pick me up around the corner. 'That was my idea she said I didn't want you and the children laughing at me and added I hate that car! I enjoy coming to school, and being out of that house Dorca stated. Things are very different Billy and so are my parents she said putting her head down. "What do you mean Dorca?" I asked seeing her sadden face. My mom is Black and my dad is Caucasian, is that what you're calling different?" I asked. "Oh, you probably wouldn't understand" she acknowledged and changed the subject. "I live quite a distant from here Billy she said smiling and moving to the other side of the bench from where I was sitting. I knew where she lived but couldn't let her know, so I just sat in silence. And Dorca rambled on. "Edith helped talk my parents into letting me come to this school after I refused to eat if they made me to go St. Regis High" Dorca confessed to Billy. "They agreed as long as I maintain good grades and stay out of trouble I could come here". "That's why I work so hard in my classes; I don't want to go back with the Nuns!" she affirmed. "I have plans of being a psychiatrist so I can help people like me". "Edith says they were helping her cope with things in her life" Dorca chided. Edith also said we all need someone to talk to "do you agree?" Dorca asked me. I was trying all I knew how to leave for class. The smile she gave me when she stated that sent chills up my spine. "Edith had a way with people even my parents when it came to me" Dorca said as she continued talking. "When Edith is around, she takes care of me. She protects me from" then she stopped again and looked off as if swatting a fly. "You know Billy Edith brings me to all the dances when my parents go out of town or to one of their many charity events" And as long as I came right out when it was over, she would allow me to come to every dance if I wanted to". Then Dorca sat down next to me. "I'm sure going to miss her." MISS HER! I said very loud after sitting silent for so long. 'Where is she going?' I asked. "They are sending her to live in Oregon with their parents" my dad's parents I mean" His dad is sick and they don't just trust anyone living with them out there Dorca confided and they can't live alone." They will just hire someone else to drive me around for a while. Until I get my car anyway. Edith didn't want to go I remembered they argued a lot about it in their room. Billy you're not responding! Do you even understand what I'm saying?" Dorca sat waiting for me to say something but what I thought?" 'So, my life will probably be different! She paused again waiting for a response. Well I said, "I'm surprised you're telling me this now! Are you saying you're not going to the prom?" I questioned which to me right now was sounding pretty good. I didn't wait for and answer I felt as if she was practicing on me already. Dorca, "I'm glad to know this now it really helps me to understand you and your moods a lot better" I think?" I said lifting my eyebrows high into my forehead. "My moods, what do you mean Billy?" Dorca asked as if she hadn't noticed her mood changes. I was talking but at this point even I wasn't sure of what I was saying or just what to say. I chose my next question very carefully. "Why are you telling me all this now?" I asked again confused at this point. "Is there a problem?" we don't have to go!" Honestly, she was making me nervous. "Is there something I really need to know?" I continued to question. Dorca Williams was a beautiful mocha browned skinned girl with hair to her shoulders and curves placed to fit a Greek goddess no doubt about it! Very intelligent and for the most part had a good sense of humor with me. So, all this talking she felt she had to do now was a little unsettling. Mrs. Edith is all I knew her as. She looked a lot like her but she was much darker and of course older and she wore her hair up off her shoulders in a French roll style. "Billy, Dorca finally confided I am adopted since birth is what I understand from Edith". "She made me promise not to tell the Demato's I knew". They would be devastated" "And I admit for a long time I didn't know until children started treating me different and saying mean things to me" teasing me about my wavy hair that frizzies and my dark skin. "When I got older a lot of things changed Dorca said looking directly at Billy. "Edith told me she was hired as my live-in sitter for the Demato's as you know they are Caucasian too. I'm often mistaken for someone else's child most of the time" Dorca admitted". "I look a lot like you don't you think but only lighter" she smiled rubbing my face. "I remember the other women wouldn't bring their children around to play when I was little because they thought my color would rub off on them. So, by making Edith my mother they accepted me and it made life a lot easier" Dorca told me. "One day a little girl told me how lucky I was that my mom gave me chocolate milk when I was a baby that's what her mom had said regarding my color." When I asked my parents why my skin was darker, they said it was in my genes somewhere. They'd research it. but never got around to telling me despite my constant asking." This girl as gone through a lot I though as I sat there, "I knew what it was like being mixed and somehow my problems didn't impact me. I noticed the difference more with my dad's friends than my mom's. But most of dad's friends knew mom so there were few questions. I think because they were trying to keep the adoption a secret was the problem. "Dorca do you still read your bible?" I asked her, surely there was something in there to help her I reasoned. "I do, but there is so much I don't understand about it" she replied. "Well I'll be glad to help you with it anytime, just let me know! "Billy, you're the only one who knows all this about me please don't tell anyone! She requested I'm confiding in you because I feel I can trust you and I'm tired of hiding the real me from you", Dorca explained. I'd be so ashamed! Okay I said you can count on me." So, seeming to feel better she held on to my hand. "If you don't want to take me to the prom I will understand." getting up and standing directly in front of me as I sat on the lower bench of the table. I didn't say anything. Dorca turned and started to walk away. Something inside of me said let her go! Ignoring it I caught Dorca's hand. Again, I heard my buddy Glen's voice saying, "are you sure man?" Again, I ignored it. I had been in love with this girl since kindergarten. How bad could she be? I thought. "I'll be there at 6:30 p.m. dinner reservations are at 7:30 p.m. at Perago's we should arrive at the prom at 8:30 or 9:00 pm. Depending how you eat! I teased feeling better I had got passed that moment. "Now! What is your address?" I asked confidently standing up facing Dorca. Without another word she said, 5408 Richvale Meadows. "Think you can find it?" she smiled. I was feeling pretty good, no great! "Sure, I said I know my way around" playfully holding Dorca's hand. "Billy please don't be nervous" she told me my parents are really not bad and thanks again for being a good friend". I really needed to talk with someone I have not seen my friend in Oregon in a long-time thanks for listening" she said and kissed me on the side of my cheek. I smiled. I had all the information I needed and was ready to move on but I soon realized it wasn't over. Dorca started talking again. I sat back on the bench hoping the bell would ring, but a quick glance at my watch say's it wasn't. "I remember Edith and I played games. She would make me tell her all that went on in the house when she was away". And then she would lie down and let me practice on her by asking questions that pertained to what I just told her". Sometimes I would cry, but she said it's okay to cry every now and then." Edith also taught me how to read from her medical books she worked at a hospital you know!" Dorca explained. I sat as long as I could "Dorca! I don't want to hear any more of this okay!" I started getting up from the bench. And as if that's all I had to say she stopped and changed the subject. "Billy do you think peach is a nice color for the prom?" I would just be devastated if you didn't take me to the prom! She said laughing and hitting me lightly as if the conversation we were having never existed. She had been confessing about slumber parties and family secrets and color issues. God, I thought could surely help this girl! If only I could get her to church. She questioned her color and her difference, her kinky hair and I thought I had it bad! She said one day while in Edith's room she came across some interesting papers. She was going to ask Richard and Victoria Demato about them but Edith came home. Edith said she would tell her all about them if she promised not to let the Demato's know what she had found. I stood looking at the hall that led to my class thinking if what she is telling me is half right "Prom and I'm out of here! I thought to myself. She said according to Edith her real mother died in childbirth. She had and older sister but wasn't sure where she was. And Mrs. Demato suspected Mr. Demato was the father. Edith went on to tell Dorca that Mrs. Demato chose her. "So little Dorca you should feel special." I finally shared with Dorca that I looked forward to seeing her parents but I really wished this whole thing was over. I left with more information about Dorca Williams those few minutes than all the years I had known her. Did I really want to go further in this world of hers that seemed so mysterious that's what Glen called it? Surely God knows Dorca I thought to myself. I wasn't sure what the future held for me with Dorca. I would have to think about it as she smiled at me departing to go our separate ways.

CHAPTER 10

Prom night

The day of the prom arrived and I was glad the wait was finally over. The school day seemed to be two days long I just wanted it to end. Dorca and some of the other girls had left earlier for hair appointments and other last-minute girly things that needed their attention. After that long day of school, I stopped by the florist and picked up my boutonnière and a peach colored flower corsage wristlet for Dorca. Winnie's date Wyston came in too. The florist told us a lot of students had come in from the high school to make purchases. She had been very busy all day. She said there were only a few orders left and she was so looking forward to closing shop and going home for the evening. She gave Wyston his change and explained the flowers requested must go directly to the frig until they were ready to be worn. "leave it up to Winnie to want something that needs special attention" he said as he walked out the door "I'll see you tonight" he told me.

I dressed early and went down stairs where my mom had the camera ready. "stand still dear" she said fixing my shirt collar. "you look so handsome I could cry". Dad sat near with the camcorder mom had given him to operate. "Are you bringing Dorca by so we can see her?" "Sure mom, I said "if you stop fussing over me and let me finish getting ready". I took my jacket out of the closet and put it on for more pictures. I kissed mom and dad and hurried out the front door with dad standing pointing the camcorder at me and mom clicking the camera. "I'll be back before we go to dinner" I yelled back to them. And got into my car and drove away.

I pulled out the map Dorca had given me that morning before school, so I wouldn't get lost or be late picking her up. She still wasn't aware I knew where she lived and I had driven by several times after getting my new car. I got to Dorca's house at about 6:15 pm. That would give me time to meet her parents and quickly stop by and let my mom and dad see us all decked out for the evening. I surely wasn't going to break a promise to mom. I walked slowly to the door. 'Hello young man, came a voice up the sidewalk. "visiting the Dematos? Haven't seen them all day, he usually walks with me to the park I guess he was too busy", strange though never missed in two years. "No sir 'I'm here to get their daughter for the prom" I replied seeing he was a friend of the family. "oh you're taking Dorca out" she was here earlier, but left a good while ago, didn't see her come back, but I could have missed her", the old gentleman said walking back to his home with the large picture window that looked out toward the Demato's home.

I glanced again at my watch and walked closer and rang the bell. The sound of ding, dong echoed has if it was down in a cave slowly again ding, dong. I stood there expecting some fancy maid or butler to come to the door. But no one came. Did I get it wrong? Was this the right house? I took the paper from my pocket and checked the address. It matched the gold numbers that was etched on the mailbox slot near the door. Address was correct. Now I was puzzled, maybe the old gentleman was right. I stood there, should I ring again? I didn't want them to be angry when they came to the door. Did she even tell them I was coming? I thought I'll go back home and call her. As I walked back to my car the Rolls pulled up. Dorca got out. She was dressed and ready to go. "Running quite late" she said. "I'm sorry, do you like my hair?" She was stunting. "Yes, I said you are lovely" handing her the peach corsage wristlet. "Is your parent'-s home?" "no-one answered the door" I questioned. "They had to go out we'll see them when we return". She quickly put the wristlet on and said "ready let's go"

I was a little confused but since Dorca was who I had come for and she was ready to go so was I. I walked over and opened the car door for her to get in. "I met your neighbor", he wondered why your dad hadn't come out for his walk." "Mr. Grover, he's a lonely busy-body, dad listens to his stories about how his children is taking everything from him, and won't let him remarry" What did he have to say to you?" Dorca asked. "He seemed to enjoy the walks he takes with your dad. He found it surprising that he hadn't seen him today." "Is that all he said?" "Pretty much, I concluded. I could sense Dorca did not want to talk about her nosy neighbor.

Do you mind if I stop by and let my parents see how lovely you are Dorca? I chose my words very carefully sensing how quiet she was after I told her about Mr. Grover. 'That's fine" she said perking up "I'd love to meet your parents". Mom and dad were very understanding and Dorca and I made our 7:00 reservations for dinner. Dorca said she was pleased that my parents had gotten back together after all those years and had worked out their differences.

Dinner was fun. We talked about our college expectations and leaving Spokane. I didn't dare change the mood of the moment by asking questions about her parents, but they were surely questions floating around in my head. After a lovely dinner we were off to the prom. The prom was wonderful too. The committee went all out on this one and it showed. The table centerpieces came right out of a magazine. The decorations looked priceless and the huge floral arrangements that sat at either end of the stage were the talked of all the girls wedding plans. Everyone was having a good time dancing, laughing to the latest tunes being played. I won tickets to the skating rink from the raffle. We were given numbers when we entered the prom and my number was chosen. Dorca promised to be my date when I used them. Jacqueline Dobbs and Mykal Carrington were voted king and queen. Dorca and I were also part of this year's royal court.

And Winnie joined us also. She is a very pretty girl. She almost looked regal until she started ordering Wyston around. Then the true Winnie came out. The prom committee headed by Nicole Fleming had done a great job planning this event. The evening could not have gone better. "Where's everyone going after this? yelled Dorca loud enough for Nicole and Blaine to hear. "Don't know" Nicole said are you and Billy going to join in tonight?" "Thinking about it" Dorca replied. I didn't say anything I was in shock, or amazed not sure which. Everyone went to his car. "We're going to Asleigh's her parents are out of town" who's game?" "Let's go" someone said and off we went. I was glad we were getting out with friends but in the back of my mind questions lingered. "Shouldn't we clear this with your parents first Dorca?' I just had to ask. I knew my curfew would cover time after the prom so I wasn't to worry about me. "They're probably gone by now" she confessed. Ms. Ruth is probably there now and she won't mind. "Are you sure?" I insisted with the questions. "Stop worrying, relax and let's have some fun", Dorca told me. She caught my hand and led me across the street and up the walk to Asleigh's house with the five others couples not including Winnie and Wyston close in front. It was a side of Dorca I had not seen before, she was wild and we all had fun. We finally concluded at 3:30 in the morning. And now I felt guilty and my parents! For it was after my curfew now! Mom I know will be wanting to speak with me. But first I would have to face the Demato's. What are they going to think?

I drove slowly around the corner to Dorca's house and saw flashing lights, lots of flashing lights and police cars all over the place leading to Dorca's home. The streets were cordoned off with tape. We stopped a few blocks down and walked up to the house. Mr. Grover met us coming up the walkway. "What's going on? Dorca asked. Mr. Grover just shook his head and walked back toward his house. "it was you!" could be heard from Mr. Grover as he was escorted by a policeman back to his home to answer questions. What's going on!' Dorca yelled running up to her house. Dorca and I pushed our way very close to the front door before being stopped abruptly by an officer in uniform. "You are not allowed to go any further" he told us holding out his large hand to our faces. "But this is my house" Dorca explained. "Where are my parents?' I thought that was odd to ask, she had said they were not home. Shouldn't she ask about Ms. Ruth? Maybe it's just the moment. Apparently, the maid had come home and found the couple dead in their home that's all he would say. Dorca was now crying unreasonably at times, she wanted and needed answers. 'Who would want to hurt her parents? What had Grover seen? He was always looking.

It was now early morning the sun had peeked over the darkness and several hours had passed before we got any answers to what was going on. I had called my parents and informed them as best I could to what was told to us and gave them the directions to Dorca's home. The officer had questioned Dorca and I separately and said he'd be in touch with us in a few days. Dorca and I sat in my car waiting for my parents to get there. She wasn't ready to move yet. She needed me and I wasn't going anywhere without her I was in love.

My parents showed up about half hour after I had called them. "What's going on son? Dad asked puzzled, walking to my little car. He could see clearly all the chaos still going on. Dorca and I got out of the car she was still crying. "I don't' know! I explained. "I came to bring

Dorca, home after the prom and this is what we found" I told him. "What time was that", he continued asking questions. I was sure you were upstairs in your bed when the phone rang and woke us up." 'Well dad, I said hesitating knowing there would be lots of questions to follow. "We went out with friends after the prom. Well not out exactly we went to one of the other student's home and sat around talking and having fun until about 3:00 am." "William Parker!" Tetra joined in. "What were you thinking? She admonished. "Well I guess it would have been worst if you and Dorca were here or encounter the ones who did this" Tetra said. "You're right mom, but we have no idea what has happened we're waiting for answers too.

Dorca turned to David "can you help Mr. Parker? "Can you get some answers? "Are my parents' home, are they alright? Tetra put her coat around Dorca's bear shoulders. "I will see what I can find out, he said. "Stay here I'll be right back.

Dad walked over to who he thought was the officer in charge. He stood talking with him for about fifteen or twenty minutes. The officer handed him a card like the one he had given Dorca and I. Dad shook his hand and made his way back to us. He looked at me; giving me the sense that it was not good news. I stood next to Dorca with my arms around her for support if needed. They are not releasing any names at this time but apparently a couple was murdered here tonight. There does not at this time seem to be forceful entry, they suspect the couple knew the intruder. Dorca, backed up and sat slumped over on the car seat crying. "Was it my parents?" came out through her tears. "I don't know he wouldn't give me names. They are investigating the crime scene, gathering all the evidence details right now or sketchy and it's going to be a long day. Let's go home and try to rest".

CHAPTER 11

Who picked her up?

The weeks ahead were very confusing for me. I knew my life could not stop, but I wanted to be there every moment for Dorca. Graduation was only months away and I still had to appoint someone to take the job at the Center. I had decided with everything that had happened I surely needed to get away and I thought it would be good for Dorca also. College was going to be my escape and I knew Dorca losing both parents wasn't going to be easy. I would be there for her, inviting her to come to Harvard with me until she decided what's best. She said she'd think about it since Radcliff was one place she had been accepted.

The newspaper and the media regarding the Demato's were everywhere I went around town. Every local news channel carried the story throughout the town. Most did not paint a pretty picture, probably because there wasn't one. For weeks Dorca stayed in our home she was so sad. I felt for her. I could only imagine how she was feeling, her mom and dad. Often, she'd sat outback looking into the blue sky silently. I would have been devastated. I remembered my dear friend Mr. Parsons. Dorca kept to herself and just cried. Mom understood and we all just left her alone to grieve. I spent a lot of time with her and tried to be there for her. Mom would comfort her as best she could and always told me to pray. Mom said no child should have to go through this ordeal. With everything else I needed to get done before leaving home it was wearing on me. Dorca wasn't attending school not that anyone expected her to so I kept her informed about graduation and upcoming events. Just to keep her mind on something else. It probably helped a little. She didn't seem interested at all. "Billy" she said to me one day I arrived home to find her sitting in the living room looking out of the window. "Ms. Edith is coming to get me. Strange she would never talk to Edith before. Edith tried several times calling continually. Dad finally told Edith to give Dorca some time she would come around." I'm going to my grandparent's home for a while at least until this case is settled. "I want you to know that I will always remember prom night and the wonderful time we had." I just need time alone. I need to be by myself. "Please thank your parents for everything". "You're saying that as if I will never see you again" I spoke sadly to her. "I'll see you Billy" she returned with a smile in her voice. Dorca walked to the open door and went outside to a car with Edith behind the wheel driving up. She got out and waved at me. Dorca greeted her with a hug on the sidewalk and got in the car. Then Dorca put her head out of the window and yelled "take care Billy, I'll be in touch". "How will I know where you are? If you are all right? I kept asking. 'I'll call I promise I'll call as soon as I get there Dorca insisted. As I stood watching the car suddenly stopped from its backing down the driveway. Dorca's door opened. She ran over to me and hugged me so tight. "You are a true friend Billy I love you. I felt a tear run down my cheek as I stood still watching the car pull away.

It had been weeks and I had not heard from Dorca. I tried calling the number to the house in Richvale. But it had been vacated a few weeks after the police had finished the investigation. I had ridden by time and time again noticing the yellow tape was gone but it still seemed eerie. Mr. Grover could still be spotted looking out of the large window. It would be interesting to hear his story I thought. The media reports had said although they couldn't find forced entry into the house, there were items missing that pointed to burglary. It looked as though about 2:00 pm in the afternoon they were surprised by someone while sitting at their table having lunch. This person or persons shot them both at close range. Victoria and Richard Demato never suspected anything. It appears they knew the persons who had committed this crime. Mr. Grover the neighbor spotted their daughter home earlier that day, but that wasn't unusual she had come home during the day a few times he says. He knew they were all right after she left, he said Richard had given her permission to drive the car. That was one thing Victoria and Dorca disagreed on. He felt things had been solved Richard came out and watered is prize garden filled with blue Aconitum and yellow Thalictrum flowers what a beautiful rose garden. He waved and went back into the house. Soon his car left so he figured they had left for the farm to visit his elderly parents. "Nothing unusual, he saw, Mr. Grover had told them. Investigation was still ongoing.

I couldn't get excited about what I had considered a big day for me. I still had not heard from Dorca. She left so suddenly and seemed to disappear off the map. Where was she? Why hadn't she called? Surely the police knew where she was, they weren't saying if they did. I needed answers they had questioned all of the friends who was with us that prom night. Nicole was constantly asking me about Dorca. I did not have answers and was about to find some, but where? I went to the school office to get and additional address or phone number for Dorca that was requested on the enrollment form. Mrs. Perkins greeted, "good morning Billy may I help you". "yes, good morning Mrs. Perkins, I'd like to get a forwarding address for Dorca Williams or a contact number if you have it?" "Why Billy Parker, I can't give you that information" she insisted, you'd better get to your class before the bell rings." "Is that the girl the police are always in here asking about?" "Yes, yes, it is, she's my friend and I'm concerned about her". I told her. "Well according to police no information goes out on this one" "now go to class". Mrs. Perkins turned away to other activity-taking place along the extended counter in the office.

As I walked toward the door Winnie was coming to talk to Mrs. Perkins. "Hi Billy," "hi Winnie" what's up?" I asked. Winnie told me she had to let Mrs. Perkins know she would be late for her office assistant class, still trying to finalize graduation plans. Graduation plans I had been totally out of the loop of activities going on. "How's Dorca" she asked. Everyone's talking about what happened, it would be hard to come back to school is she all right? 'I hope so Winnie but I really don't know. Winnie continued to question me. Not surprised though she wasn't the only one. "Who knows Billy if you don't?" you two were always together at school anyway!" "Winnie! I interrupted, "are you headed to class? I'll walk with you." Winnie and I walked slowly to our first period class talking, I was mostly listening. "Why are you going to be late for Perkins class? I asked her after she took a breath between sentences. "We're putting together a skit for the senior assembly shouldn't be too late why?" "Oh, just asking trying to keep up with things you know". "When is that taking place?" "Fifth period silly, during your lunch period, would you like to join us

Billy?" "No, the team is planning something too. "I was just asking. As the day went on, I needed answers information anyway. I hoped my good friend Winnie would be the one to get it for me.

My mom had not bothered me regarding Dorca, but I'm sure she had lots of questions too. Mom knew I was having a hard time with her leaving now it seems she had disappeared. Not knowing anything other than through the media she and dad both gave me reasonable space regarding Dorca. "I saw the invitations dear, what are you wearing?" mom asked me. "Nothing special, for you slacks and a shirt okay." "Have you heard from Dorca? Will she be there?" "No mom I haven't heard, I've had lots of sleepless nights wondering what has happened to her since she left that day. I don't have a number or anyway of finding her, I confided. "Mom can you help?" "Billy, I don't know what I can do, regarding her whereabouts. God knows, I know that's not what you wanted to hear, but it's true. Seems right now he's the only one who does. Have you tried asking him? I was always good about praying for someone else's need. It had not accrued to me to go to him for answers for myself. I really missed Dorca and was concerned about her wellbeing. That night I poured my heart out before the Lord for answers.

Lord you said that I could call on you in the day of trouble and you would hear my call. I have always prayed to you many times not understanding why, and you've always brought answers. Dear God I come now asking about my friend Dorca. Please God bring me to and understanding in you to accept that wherever she is it's where you want her to be. Lord I struggle not knowing please help me with your decision. I would love to hear from her to know that's she's all right. Please let your will for me be done. Amen.

The next day I returned to school determined to get information about Dorca. Revived from a much-needed good night's rest I went to see Nicole. Dorca and Nicole left at noon the day of the prom for hair appointments. But to his surprise Nicole didn't have the answers he was looking for, or did she? She told him that was the plans the two had made to leave together at noon. However, Dorca's mother picked her up in the student lot as they were leaving Nicole said. Dorca informed her she'd see them later and when she came to the prom with you everything seemed fine. Where was she that day? Who picked her up? Was it, Mrs. Demato or Edith? What really happened in the Richvale home that day? Is she involved in this? Questions? questions? Lord help me I pleaded because I don't know and not even sure if I want to know. But I love her.

Fifth period came around. "Hi Winnie" "hello Billy not having lunch today? "I came to see you" "me" Winnie said astonished. Shhh! I looked over Mrs. Perkins was sitting at the desk sorting papers. Why? Are you shhhing me? Winnie hissed. "I have this information you asked for". Winnie finally got the hint that I wanted something and I needed it from her. She walked down to the far end of the tall counter from where Mrs. Perkins sat. I followed her asking for a piece of paper to write on. She quickly handed me a piece of paper and a pen. "Please write it down Billy I wouldn't want to forget it". I gave her back the paper and thanked her for the use of her pen, while now being watched by Mrs. Perkins for being in the office to long. 'See you later" I said loud enough so Mrs. Perkins could hear me as I left out the office.

I knew I'd see Winnie at seventh period and it took all I had in me to wait. I hurried and showered got dressed after P.E. class and went and stood at the entrance of out next class. I knew that if I was going to get answers to this it would have to be today, we were graduating and school would soon be closed to students. As Winnie walked up, she proclaimed, "you owe me Billy, you owe me big time!"

I had rushed home to get ready for graduation night. Excited about the information Winnie had got for me an address and a phone number. I hurried up to my room and dialed the number. 'Ring, ring, ring hello, came a voice at the other end it was Dorca. "Dorca" I said relieved. How are you? There was only silence at the other end. "hello! Hello! Hello! She had hung up the phone. So, I hung up and dial again this time I got a recording. I did leave a message that said I miss you hope to see you soon, please call me". That was her voice but why did she hang up? At least I know she's all right Thank you God.

I felt better knowing she was with her grandparents even if she didn't want to talk yet. I looked at my watch and hurried to the civic auditorium downtown where they were having the ceremony for our senior class. I looked anxiously at the crowd of parent's family and friends gathering to be a part of the night's activity. I peeked from behind the large draped curtain to see my parents walking down the aisle to their seats. Pastor Hathaway and his wife were seated up front near the stage. He needed quick access to the stage to give the opening prayer. The program went off as planned. I thought a lot about my dear friend, how we had planned and waited for this day to come. Jane Brown gave her closing remarks as class valedictorian the applause started. It could still be heard as Principal Ridgeway stood up and with one motion of his arm the class of 1984 began another life journey across the stage. "William John Parker" rang out loud and I could hear my mom through all the cheering that was going on. Each student made his or her way on stage to shake hands and receive their diplomas. Parents and friends alike were proud as each greeted their graduates in the main hallway of the civic center. Mt Nebo had prepared a "be safe all night" celebration for graduating seniors and friends. Our church family was proud of each one of our accomplishments. I sure missed not having Dorca there.

Glen had enjoyed his big day too. We had talked about it during the years and though we didn't graduate at the same school. We were both graduating and very proud we were. San Antonio is where his family had settled. I told him I would come and visit him when I got settled in Harvard and asked of his plans. He told me he had been accepted at the University of Texas in Austin and was moving there to live. He was concentrating his studies in engineering and still hoped to live in Florida one day. He told me he and his parents had driven down and looked around the campus so his commuting home was not that long. 'Only a few miles he smiled". He confided that the pest had gotten herself in trouble and had not yet told their mom or dad. Seems she after seating under the same teaching as he had, had gotten herself pregnant. Now Brianna was getting by in school, but she just had other interest that prevented her success. Meldon Jenkins a young boy who attended church with his grandmother had stolen her heart, but as he put it that wasn't all. He seemed to be a nice young man and wanted to do the right thing but either he or Brianna was really ready for marriage. She was afraid and came to him Glen said, but he didn't know what to tell her so he went to their mom on her behave. Their mom and dad sat down with them and with disappointment written on both her parent's faces they talked to them civilly. They explained to them with bible passages and from a marriage prospect what they had just entered. They asked Meldon what his life expectations were and what he planned to do to get ready for the life he was bringing in this world. He was as honest as one frightened young man could be. Glen says he doesn't think he realized what this situation really meant. Meldon explained that he was raised by his grandmother and never knew his father. He asked dad to help him be the best dad for his child. And Glen thinks he honestly meant it. He has changed. He was always a good kid but he's matured. I really think this is going to work out for them Glen told me. Their dad said after Brianna graduates from high school, he would do the honors of their wedding. Brianna apologized to her parents and asked their forgiveness and thanked them for being so understanding. Mrs. Reed called mom and talk with her and ask her to pray for her. She said it's not easy trying to tell other young ladies how they should live when your own goes against the grain. "But I'm trusting in the Lord that he knows all about it and will make me stronger through it" Mr. Reed cried a lot after each sermon several Sundays. He told us God was dealing with him and he was going through in spite of the opposition.

I had informed Glen about the events that had taken place since Dorca came back in my life. 'Billy are you sure this girl is for you? He asked me. "She's gone again, buddy maybe just maybe God is trying to tell you something. "Are you listening to him? "Glen I don't know what it is about this girl that fascinates me. Except for the night after the prom she really never gave me much play, I confided. She seems to be gone for good, so it's out of my control. "Well Glen said, for you I hope so". But the girls at U.T. aren't bad I checked them out on my visit. He ended "I'll set you up" 'Thanks man I'll be in touch".

CHAPTER 12

College bound

Detective Diamicci had come by our home again for the second time this week. He was still investigating the case but came by to give me and my parents the good news that I had been cleared to go out of state to college. He was now calling the murders senseless but stated everyone was being cooperative in the matter. I went over again everything I knew about prom night and the day Dorca left. He avoided questions I asked about Dorca. I sensed he knew where she was but couldn't or wouldn't say. Detective Diamicci stood up to leave saying "I'll let you know if some things change in this case" good luck young man", shaking my hand and then leaving. That night mom prepared a great dinner. It is my favorite pasta dish. Penne pasta prepared with fresh salmon steak. The mushrooms wine sauce olive oil and other ingredients aromas filled the room. I wrote it out so I could make it to impress my Harvard friends. Mom just smiled at me. 'Billy set the table please your dad will be home soon." she said. She slapped my hand as I reached for a phyllo log appetizer she was arraigning on a tray. "Hello honey, came a voice from the front of the house, surprised to see you here this time of day son said dad walking into his study to put down his briefcase. "It came finally." David said looking at the world globe in his study. Yes, dear I just unpacked it and with Billy's help I placed it on its stand, it's gorgeous. Its rich cherry finished mimicked the large grandfather clock that stood in the home's entry. The colors are impeccable. Solid wooden legs added the perfect accent to mom's room décor. David's very large-scale model of the world globe for his study arrived and he was very pleased with it. After admiring his new piece for his study, he came into the kitchen where Tetra and Billy had just finished setting the table. "Hello again honey, he walked over and kissed her gently on the lips "got a little distracted dear sorry about that". "Dave, we got good news from Detective Diamicci, not that it was a concern but they have cleared Billy to go out of state." "I thought for a moment with all this uncertainty he would have to put his future on hold". Tetra informed him. "That's wonderful, David replied, is the case closed?" "as far as we're concerned" she told him "though I do think about that sweet little girl" what's going to happen to her? With the table all set to mom's delight we all sat down. Dad led us as always at dinner-time in prayer. He not only thanked God for the delicious meal mom had prepared but also for the good news we had received. And he asked a special blessing for Dorca.

The days went by too fast for mom. She wasn't ready for me to leave. Knowing mom, she would never be ready. She hurried around the house making sure I had everything packed and something to carry on the plane to eat. "Mother's" I said under my breath so she wouldn't hear me. The plan was to stop by dad's office on the way to the airport. Mom grabbed a box of Kleenex from the counter as we went to the door. "You're not going to cry are you mom?" I asked knowing the answer. "It's not the first time you've put me on a plane." "I know, I know, but you're all grown up now and you'll be gone longer" she added. "Be sure to call as soon as you arrive". "Mom I will we've went over this several times now I will call". Can we go now I do want to talk too dad.

Mom and I talked all the way to dad's office, getting further instruction for being away. I knew she was going to cry when we got to the airport no doubt in my mind. When I entered the building where dad worked, we were greeted with banners and well-wishers. I guess dad had let them know what was going on. One large banner that hung across the ground level of the high rise read: Our C.E.O. is the proud father of a Harvard student. Talking about pressure to succeed.

"Well son this is it! dad said walking over to put his arms around me. "I'm not worried about you doing well, I know you will, just have fun and keep safe. You know your mom and I are just a phone call away". "I know dad, I know". They were starting to make me cry. I thanked everyone that was standing around the office and corridor and entered the elevator going up to dad's office suite.

I wanted to talk to dad alone and asked mom to get some of the hors d'oeuvre they had put out on the ground floor office. "a guy as, got to eat"

I joked. Mom sensed I wanted to be alone for a moment. "all right you two." I'll be right back.

I had asked dad to help me locate Dorca's whereabouts and I didn't want mom to worry. I had given him the address Winnie had supplied for me and phone number though it was giving a disconnect recording the next week after I had called. "Why was I so obsessed with this girl? With the exception of prom night she had always been self-centered in a way. Then David said "I'm going to Oregon this week and I'll check on this address. There's a prospect there at the college I'm going to talk with for one of my agents." "I'll call you when I return." "Thanks dad". I was swirling around in dad's executive chair as mom walked in "I'm ready I said. She had her arms full of goodies. "Here's a plate for you Dave" no one could possibly eat all that buffet in a day." 'Let's go'. Mom kissed dad on the cheek and headed for the door. "Wait Tetra he said let's have a word of prayer for our son's safe flight. We all stood near dad's big desk and thanked God for everything in our lives. We thanked him for what he has done and thanked him for a safe flight. We all needed one of mom's Kleenex tissues when prayer was over.

"Thanks dad I love you" we embraced. Dad had walked with us out to the car for the final goodbye. I wanted it this way. It was my way of letting mom have me all to herself one more time. Mom tried very hard not to continue crying as I waited to board my flight. She even had another woman convinced who understood crying with her. "Mom it's college not war" I just wanted her to smile.

The plane ride wasn't bad after all I had spent a lot of time on planes. I had frequent flyer miles to use. I spent my growing up between Washington State and Maine on a plane food hadn't got any better though. Soon I was walking down the narrow halls of Harvard University. I had done some research and had talked to former lawyers who were students there. I was not coming here to fail. I was going to succeed. Someday someone very important to me may need my help. You just never know. I went up one flight of stairs then two flights of stairs before finally going to the door of my dorm room. It was on the third floor of Stoughton Hall. Other freshmen wondered why I wasn't living in residential housing being I was a sophomore. My status as an honor student coming here brought this about. I settle into my dorm and went exploring the campus. I had left mom and dad a message so mom wouldn't worry and walked past the museum of Archaeology. All the museums were in the same area, some distant between them though. I was very interested in the college observatory that maintains radio facilities in Massachusetts and Texas. I knew I would be assigned to Cambridge Campus. And had information on the tutorial plans because of my sophomore status. Being younger than most sophomores there I knew all eyes were on me.

Winnie had decided on Yale she was our school politician. She had a great gift of gab and a leadership style second to none for a girl we all thought. Her persuasiveness during a debate was definitely a plus she would succeed or surely be noticed for trying.

The university had paired me with another young sophomore named Desmond Owens, from California. This guy was groomed for law with his sharp fast tongue and charming good looks. Desmond's parents were both lawyers and he was carrying on the tradition. He had talked me into dating one of the girls from Radcliff. Which at this time in my life didn't take much persuasion? I knew dad's trip to Oregon did not result in a lot of information but he was planning a return trip. He didn't get a response from anyone at the address but the place was well kept so he promised to try again. Desmond and I had wondered out and met some of the Radcliff girls that he and I started seeing regularly. I was not looking to get into a serious relationship with anyone yet I was still thinking about Dorca. I flew back to Washington a lot my first year it kept mom from calling so much. She's getting better I must admit, she usually will go a week or two between calls. On major holidays Desmond and I would trade off visiting each other's parents. I always thought California would be an interesting place to live. We spent one summer caddying for his dad at the Pebble Beach golf course in Monterey. One weekend on a whim we flew down to Connecticut to visit Winnie at Yale University. She had secured a job working on the "Yale Daily News" paper and was well respected and known around campus, but wasn't into the partying scene. We still enjoyed our stay with her meeting and a few choice friends. She said she'd return the favor someday. She and Desmond got into a lot of debates during our stay regarding how much better Yale is since allowing women to attend. He didn't have a problem with equal rights but wasn't going to pass up and opportunity to argue a point. I said society was not ready for those two together not on the same planet anyway. There were plenty of guest rooms at our home since dad and mom took over the master suite together. I couldn't miss the opportunity to tease dad about that. But I was very glad to know life for them was still progressing. They liked Desmond and thought he was good for me. 'Very positive" dad would say. Desmond loved the home cooked meals mom prepared every day we were there.

Dad had some property in Maine that needed to be sold and Mom was flying into Maine next week and wanted me to meet her and help make a decision on it. I hadn't seen mom in a few months so I got things scheduled so that I would be available to go. Mom was so excited it had been a while since she flew to Maine. She would take a trip now and then with dad when he insisted. Saying you need to get away for a little while Tet. She flew in early grabbed a snack from Hilton's snack locker and waited to have lunch when she picked me up from the airport. I had time to finish an exam and catch a flight out to meet mom by noon. Mom had got the car and surprised me at the airport. "Didn't expect you here already mom, how was your flight? Have you been waiting long? "About two hours; and I'm starving let's find something to eat" Mom insisted. We drove along catching up on happenings since we last talked. Mom decided we would go to Burham Tavern. It was one of the places she and dad would come with me. Great seafood! The view was right off a post card. It overlooked a fleet of fishing boats where the tides went in and out.

What cha having? I asked teasing mom. "Lobster dear and what's your favor? Mom joked back. 'I'll try the Perch; dad would always order it for him and let me have it against the waiter's suggestion. "too many small bones for such a young lad don't you think?"

After lunch we walked along the harbor talking about how classes were going, how was Desmond? And was there a girl in my life yet? She wanted to know had I given up on finding Dorca and moved on with my life. I shared with her I did date occasionally, but Dorca still crossed my mind every now and then. "God only knows what's best" she said. "She always had a way about her that was different. "Mom how's things with you and dad?" I questioned changing the subject matter. "They're in order" Tetra replied. "In order what does that mean?' I inquired "we're doing well, she paused we have a lot of lost time to make up for. "There are years and years of mending, but we're moving forward". Some days are harder than others". We both want it to work". Your dad has changed a lot and that was needed. We are committed to this relationship but more than that. I stopped her in mid-sentence "what could be more than that? I asked. Well Billy she said relieved, we're both committed to God and that's the difference". We continued walking along the sandy harbor. I tossed out some small stones in the water as we walked slowly down by the water's edge. Suddenly mom bent over in pain, "Billy!" mom said looking up "something's wrong!". She was noticeably in pain. "please get me to a hospital Billy!".

CHAPTER 13

A unforgettable gentleman

David had gotten the directions to a rural route on the out skirts of town. After driving for about an hour he came upon a large farm style home. As he drove down the long trail path that led to the front entrance, the house still appeared to be empty. Looking around the grounds he could see that the grounds were maintained regularly and the home was in great shape. Getting closer David could see a for sale sign hanging from a post standing in the front yard. The property was fenced in with a white picket fence that seemed to be the space for the family yard area only. Portland Realty: Realtor Darby Smith (748-3269) David wrote down the information and continued looking around the property. The property extended out much further than the picket fence which set out about 100 ft from the main house. There was another smaller house seemly to be occupied. David turned to head back to his car and heard" hello, hello young man can I help you?" It was an elderly gentleman who explained he was the grounds keeper. "just waiting for the property to sell so I can get on with my life" he told him. David smiled but he guessed it's all how you look at things. He told David he had worked for the Demato family for some thirty years and was looking forward to going back to Kansas where his children lived. He and Richard's father were good friends. He had known Richard since he was a young boy and his wife Clara taught school. She had gone on to be with the lord he told him. "Tragic just tragic but we were always warning him about that headstrong maid." "So rude to Mrs. Vickie "never understood why they kept her around." "She was very possessive too." Are you planning to buy this place? "No sir" I was looking for a young lady. Dorca Williams" "Oh Dorca' the old timer said smiling, she was a handful. Kept us all busy around here for years.

"After the police picked up Edith Wright for questioning, she left. They took Mr. Jessie and Miss Olivia to a rest home in town". "Not quite sure where she went son." She seemed to have grown up to be a nice young lady. Hope she's not with that Wright woman". "It's pretty quiet around here these days don't get much company", he continued to talk. "Thank you, sir," David told him and proceeded to leave. 'You take care". "I'm ready to eat son want to join me?" "Thanks, but no thanks, you enjoy it o.k." "few more places I need to go before it gets late".

David got into his car and drove to the Portland Realty Co. and located the realtor in charge of the Demato's farm account. David learned that Dorca was set to inherit the property after the death of the grandparents who for now resides in Chateau /convalescent Hospital in Portland. She had become next in line after the death of Victoria and Richard her adoptive parents. David wondered if his son knew Dorca was adopted he had never spoke about it. On to see Detective Mansony he was the one assigned to the case and could give him more details about it. When he arrived at the precinct the next day detective Mansony was filing the case away. 'Good morning; David said cheerfully rested after riding around all day yesterday he had gotten a good night's rest. 'I'm looking for Detective Mansony. 'Well you're looking at him" what can I help you with sir? "I'm wondering what you can tell me about the Demato case or Dorca Williams. "Yes, that case, the one out of Washington." Yes, I'm filing it away right now. I remember a few months ago this young lady walked in and turn in the former maid who confessed to the murders". She had paper work from where the maid had falsified papers from a hospital and evidence, we needed to convict the maid Edith Wright for the murders." Strange though" something still didn't seem quite right though she did confess. Apparently, all these years she was blackmailing the Demato's under their own roof. They all worked together at the hospital where Dorca was born. Mrs. Vickie Demato was the hospital Administrator. She couldn't have children so when the mother of this baby died Vickie and Edith plodded to keep her. Edith became the live-in maid for the Demato's. Mr. Demato had watched his wife suffer for years trying to have children. She somehow knew he was involved with Faye, Edith's daughter so he went along with the scheme also. Everything went as planned until Dorca got older and started asking questions. Edith who we found later to be her real grandmother became threaten and felt she was being closed out of the young lady's life. The Demato's insisted that Edith come to Oregon to live and take care of their parents. She felt they were trying to get rid of her. She was trying to make up for lost years she said. The Demato's had everything she needed and could take care of Dorca so she went along with the maid story. She didn't explain why there were years to make up. She did explain when she drove back to Spokane to see Dorca for the prom the Demato's became enraged is what she told me. They called her possessive and said Dorca was a grown young lady now. Then they scolded her regarding their parents "by the way who's caring for our parents while you're away?" Edith alleged she pleaded with them to hire someone else for their parents she did not want to live in Oregon she wanted to be near Dorca. After they had given her an affirmed no! to all of her suggestions and telling her they would pay her for her time and services she snapped. Edith says she then pulled out a gun and shot them both. We never found the murder weapon. That was her story. And she told me with a blank look on her face. She made sure everything was ready for Dorca that evening. And made sure Grover was satisfied she just knew he was watching; he always did! She stated. Making sure Grover saw somebody leave in Dorca's clothes. She then left for Oregon with the Demato's lying dead on the kitchen floor. Edith says she waved to Grover as the Rolls Royce pulled out of the driveway. "Good evening" Mr. Grover, Mr. Demato and the Mrs. are heading to Oregon is what she said and pulled away down the street.

Then Dorca Williams called me from the farm said Detective Masony. She said she was afraid Edith would hurt her friend Billy Parker, in Washington for what he had done with her prom night. So when Billy was safe far away from Spokane she turned her in. We actually surprised her at the farm after Dorca called. Edith just looked forlorn and didn't even put up a fight she just smiled a puzzled smile and walk out of the door and got in our patrol car Masony told David. She wanted the death sentence she said what she had done was unforgivable and showed no remorse for the Demato's deaths. Edith Wright is in custody and the death penalty has been set. She didn't won't a trial she blatantly refused to even discuss it with a prosecutor Masony said closing up the files once again. "Where is Dorca?" David asked he still had questions. He was hoping she was not heading to Billy things were still stretchy in his mind right now. "When she was here in my office, she was sick to her stomach I suppose she threw up a couple of times right in my wastebasket, apologized though, seems to be a nice girl" Masony added. Dorca said she would be available when the farm sold and soon left my office. David was relieved on one hand it was over but still not knowing where she was still left a lot of questions. They would just keep wondering. She is out there somewhere, but where? Why was she still hiding now? Maybe just maybe that was a good thing!

CHAPTER 14

Don't panic

I helped my mom walk to the car and headed for Maine General hospital a few blocks away I was told. As I proceeded out on the highway I was forced in the far lane and could not get over to make the assigned ramp off to the Maine General exit. Mom now moaning in pain I began to panic. I was not familiar with this town. I needed to head back to find the hospital now. I had gone about 3 or 4 miles in the opposite direction and could not find a sign or anything that resembled the hospital. Mom was telling me not to worry we'll find it. I did the unthinkable. I pulled into a gas station and asked for directions. I came out with the directions but it sure didn't seem we had traveled 10 miles out of the way. I got back up on the same freeway I thought and headed to Maine General. After driving a few minutes, I spotted the hospital sign next right. Relieved I turned off and headed to the emergency entrance of it. By now mom was changing colors and the pain she said was excruciating. I parked across the doorway and hopped out to help mom get out of the passenger side. "Move please move" I shouted, trying to get mom passed the activity going on near the nurse's station. "My mom is in a lot of pain!" I told the nurse at the counter. "What happened? The nurse asked. We were walking down the shore after eating and she bent over in pain!" "what did she eat?" "Lobster I said lobster and crab from Burham Tavern.

They put her on a gurney and wheeled her into one of the emergency rooms. Please wait here. A doctor pushed back the curtain and began to work on mom. After a time, they told me to go to the waiting room, she was going down for x-rays. It seemed like hours and I sat waiting to hear something about mom. I phoned dad and let him know what was going on and that I was waiting to get information from the doctors. Dad didn't mix words. "I'll be on the next flight out son. What hospital are you at? Without hesitation I answered, "Maine General" what's the address location son?" I got up to ask the address of the hospital. "Wait dad hold on" "excuse me what is the address of this hospital?' 345 Vernon Street she told me and continued writing on her charts. I gave the information to dad and continued to wait. "Maine General o.k. got it dad said keep me informed I'm on my way.

I sat there an hour or so nodding and pacing back and forth in the waiting room. I remembered the 88 psalms "oh lord of my salvation, I have cried day and night before thee. Let my prayer come before thee. Incline thy ear unto my cry for my troubles and my" I looked up and stopped to see a young man dress in hospital greens standing waiting for me, he introduced himself "hello I'm Justin Parker your mom's x-ray technician how are you doing? He asked. "I'm okay returning the greeting, how's my mom? I asked anxiously. "She's resting now, has Dr. Acker spoke with you yet? "No not yet, I confided. He sensed my concern and added. "she resting now, appeared to be food poisoning he told me. Doc will talk to you soon and walked off as Dr. Acker came near me. "Hello' son I'm Dr. Acker extending his hand. Your mom is fine, seems it was food poisoning" "food poisoning from lobster?" I asked surprised "well bottom-line son, crab is shell fish and that does happen". "Two days rest and she should be as good as new". He said now smiling sensing my relief. "Doctor when can I see her?" "She's sleeping now after having us working on her for so long she's exhausted though you're welcome to see her" he told me. Thanks doctor. Dad had told me he was flying out and should be there in a few hours at best. I had spent the entire night sitting in the chair that felt like cement cold and hard. I tossed and stood trying to find comfort for just a few minutes. The nurses were coming in every 2- or 3-hours checking vital signs and charting her progress.

I woke up to dad standing over me the next day. "Been here long dad? I asked rubbing my eyes to focus. "No just got here he replied. "long layover out of Washington? I questioned. "No, Billy you gave me the wrong hospital so I have been waiting on a cab to get here." I thought it would be easier than driving it myself" he confided. "what do you mean the wrong hospital dad?" "Well, when I got to the airport, I just asked the cabbie to drive to Maine General Hospital." When I got there, I was in a hurry, I didn't look at the address I just got out and went in to find you and your mom" he shared. After being persistent about you being there, I found out the address and name didn't match. "This is Seaside Memorial Hospital several miles away from General". "I understand son you were worried about your mother "how is she?" She's resting dad, "food poisoning from shellfish the doctor says. She should be fine in two or three days. Tetra woke up for breakfast drank some orange juice and went back to sleep. Dr Acker came in to check on her at 10 0 clock everything was fine. "You look like warmed over hash" dad remarked looking at me, "why don't you go to your room and get some rest." "I'll stay with your mom". I was exhausted I hadn't rested since my feet hit Maine yesterday. I was more than willing to take dad up on his offer, after all the doctor said mom was progressing. David sat in Tetra's room thinking of his horrible night. How he was in total panic when he couldn't find Tetra or Billy. He sat in Maine General about an hour having someone find his wife and son who had called him from there. David had forgotten to charge is battery on his cell phone so he had to rely on finding a phone to use. Next to him was a young lady who had been waiting for hours to have her son seen by the doctor. Apparently, he had woken up in the middle of the night with an extremely high fever. He watched the restless child move around in her arms. Up and down from her lap he went she appeared weary. But she was friendly and very polite continuing to smile through it all. David could hear her praying quietly to herself. Her smile seemed so familiar to him. He thought about Tetra and Billy the more. "God bless you, young lady and give you strength, I know that can't be easy raising a child by yourself he added. "It's all right sir we're fine" she said. "Well alright David remarked "If you can have that smile in adversity, I think you will be all right. The young child two maybe three years of age hard to tell drew a picture on a piece of paper and handed it to him.

"Mr. Parker" you're at the wrong hospital. You want Seaside Memorial. David thanked the attendant for the information and walked outside to wait for a cab putting the child's drawing in is pocket.

Billy walked out to get some much-needed rest and went past the nurse's station. He needed to sign insurance papers for his mom. "Justin are you going tonight?' the receptionist asked. Billy looked to see the x-ray technician behind him getting some of the patient's charts. "I'll have to let you know, big exam tomorrow he replied walking off. Something about is name struck him but whatever it was wasn't overshadowing the sleep he needed now. By evening mom was feeling better and was sitting up drinking some fruit juice and a light liquid diet for nutrition. I had returned after spending most of the day at the room in the Hilton. "How are you feeling mom? I asked upon entering she was sitting up in bed. I walked over and hugged her and kissed her on her forehead. "Where is dad? I asked relieved that she was better. "He went down to the chapel for a while when Dr. Acker came in to exam me." Should be right back she added. "Mom you're not giving them a hard time about the food in this place are you! I said teasing her to get a much-needed smile from her. She and I talked a bit longer. She felt bad about how our visit had turned out. "I'm just glad you are alright mom you scared me!" "Thank you, Billy for your prayers. "I'll go down to the chapel and let dad know I'm back he had a pretty rough night getting here he needs to rest". "You both are going out of here tonight so I can rest, you both worry too much", she said very lovingly.

I passed the nurses station to inquire when mom would be released to go home. I had called Desmond and informed him I wouldn't need his services and I should be home soon. "Hello, I turned to see the x-ray tech standing by the charts. "hello I said, "how's my favorite girl?" I asked sounding relieved. "I understand from Doctor Acker sir she will be released tomorrow" he informed. "This will be a visit to remember" I said quietly. "Are you from this area?" he asked me. I told him I was born here but haven't been here for a while, I was just here looking at property". "This is a beautiful place he confided been here all my life. I am a student at Bowdoin College and I work here as an x-ray technician until I can get into medical school, I want to be a doctor" he went on to tell me. "Maybe then I will get a chance to see other parts of this great country we live in." I stood looking at this intelligent younger man. "I apologize I said we have not been formally introduced "I'm William Parker" I was in such a panic when I brought my mother in. "Parker" the young man came back with. "We could be related you know" jokingly. "I'm Justin Parker just teasing about that common name, I'm an only child" he added. Then it hit me like a ton of bricks. The name of the birth certificate he found long ago. This young man could possibly be his brother! 'Nice talking with you Justin and I turned and headed to the chapel to find dad. Has dad figured it out? does he know, or even suspect? Dad was sitting in the small little chapel with his head down. I moved in close to him on the bench.

"He acknowledged my presence and kept praying. "Amen" "How's Tetra doing?" dad asked me. "She's fine ready to go home" I told him. "She's fine then, I was just thanking God for the outcome of things. "Things happen so quickly you know" dad acknowledged.

I paused and looked at dad, I talked to Justin dad. "did he say something I should know regarding your mother Billy? "No dad mom is fine by the way she says we worry too much," I told him smiling. Have you spoken with him dad? "Spoken with who Billy? David questioned. I sensed he wasn't getting what I was trying to say. "Why all the questions" Billy? "Well dad, remember the birth certificate? I found it under your bed one summer when I visited you." dad I'm not sure but I think that's Justin, your other son!" David looked at his son Billy "you knew all this time about that?" "Yes dad, but mom doesn't know I do, and that's how I want to keep it" alright. "I wanted to tell you Billy, you forgave me, Tetra forgave me I told myself I wouldn't take it to my grave, "I'm sorry you had to find out like this" "I'm not sure that's him and honestly Billy if I could have gotten out of here not knowing it would be alright with me." GOD PLEASE FORGIVE ME" I really don't want to upset your mother" 'now what?"

There were a few days left on their planned time in Maine. They decided to put business on hold and drive Billy back to Harvard and fly out of Massachusetts to Washington. On the drive back David nor Billy mentioned any of the personnel who help make Tetra's stay comfortable, even when she mentioned the nice young man who x-rayed her when she came in. And she said he had come by every day she was there to say hello. David filled Billy in on the trip to Oregon. He said the case was closed and every detail he could remember about it he shared. Tetra was pleased Dorca Williams was all right and she hoped she had moved on. 'Now Billy you can find a nice girl to marry after you finish college." "Mother you're rushing things" I said. David told them about the young lady he saw a Maine General with the young child and her wonderful smile. Something about her struck me, but my mind was on finding you and Tetra. That's all I could think about" I hoped everything went well for her he thought. "Sweet kid."

I watched the airplane fade from the sky before heading back to my Harvard residence. My head was filled with questions. I was glad Dorca's ordeal was over but I wanted her to know I understood, most of all I wanted to tell her I would still be her friend. It could never be more than that. She never let me close enough except that one night. No one knew we were together that night, no one except her and me knew what happened that evening. I guessed no one would ever know. Though it was only a thought never spoken I loved her.........

CHAPTER 15

Let's get married

After we had been back a few months mom called me to asked if I had received my invitation to the wedding. I told her I did and was looking forward to seeing the Reed family especially Glen. Mom said, they were flying in a week earlier to help Phyllis get everything finalized. She said she had been conversing with her over the months and wanted to help them make this day special for Brianna and Meldon. "I'll talk with you later son I have an appointment" mom informed me. "An appointment mom is everything alright? I asked. Everything is fine son, just my regular appointment for my hair at "Clinique Le Felicia Salon" can't keep them waiting, love you, bye." Clinique was a swank hair salon in downtown Spokane which catered to the very elite.

Mom had sent Mrs. Reed the money for Bri's wedding gown and said she had taken care of the couple's honeymoon. Mr. and Mrs. Reed had taken care of the rest of the wedding plans with the anxious groom working hard promising to pay back every penny someday. Mr. Reed had gotten him a job at the Texas Memorial Museum and he was proving to be a bright young man. Brianna and he were turning out to be good parents despite their rocky start. She worked at a local retail store and went to Community college at night. They were determined to improve their life and the family was behind them one hundred percent. Meldon had asked Glen to help him pick out a ring for Bri. Glen said he drove down one weekend from Austin and they went to the mall. "Which store should I go to? Meldon asked Glen. "Bri and I have been to them all but I want to surprise her" he added. He had saved two-hundred and fifty dollars for a down payment and said he'd get his ring later. Glen and Meldon stood talking about options when Glen's cell rang. "Hello"

"Glen man what's up?" "Whoa that's eerie, I was just thinking about you. "I'm out with Meldon buying a ring". "So, it's really going to happen man!" "You know it" Glen said. "He passed the Reed test?" I said to him laughing "that's great!" The Reeds were my backbone growing up. They were always there for me. "So, what did you pick out man, it's got to last it's for Bri!" I was excited now and wanted in on the purchase. "Where are you?" I asked. "He brought me to the local mall in San Antonio, we just got here we've been looking around", Glen said. "Listen Glen, I don't have plans to marry anytime soon since Brianna has stepped up to the plate graduated high school, working and basically getting it together. Let's you and I cover the rings." "Well that's easy for you to say Billy, but I have a few years left at U.T." "Ok I hear you. Then you buy Meldon's ring and I'll purchase Bri's. I want it to be special for them. "They shouldn't start out owing for rings" I concluded. "That works for me" Glen confirmed. Glen and I had done this a lot over the years. I knew he was good for it. "Got any idea's where we should go? He asked me". Yeah find a jeweler called Aared's. Glen knew I had money and good taste so he and Meldon pulled up in front of this posh jewelry store "AARED'S" that dripped money.

"Man, who were you talking to I can't afford this" Meldon said feeling a lot nervous. "I know Glen told him you can't yet but one day you will." "My very best friend who you will meet at the wedding and I are making your rings a gift from us" "What does he do?" Meldon asked curiously looking around. "Right now, he attends Harvard". Meldon didn't ask another question he stood silently looking around at all the sparkle that was held in that place. Glen called Billy to let him know they had arrived. "Thanks, I'll call and speak with the manager and you can call me later, pick out something nice man" I said before hanging up. I had done this for dad so many times over the years. Mom's birthday or special thank you. I had picked out all of the anniversary present's that collected dust and seldom worn. So, they knew me at Aared's. Meldon kept saying whatever you like is fine with me. Glen finally gave him some choices to choose from. They picked out a five thousand dollar set for Bri and a thousand-dollar ring for Meldon. "Glen called and gave me the bottom line I approved the selection, "you did good Glen". Meldon is still thanking Glen for having me as his friend. The gentlemanly clerk gave Glen the receipt to sign and off they went.

When they got back in the car Glen called and I talked to a very impressionable young man who I looked forward to seeing. He even promised to pay back ever cent someday. He gave the two hundred and fifty dollars to the church that next Sunday. Mr. Reed was very proud of the way this young man was turning out. His aging grandmother though feeble in years said God had answered her prayers.

Mrs. Reed told Brianna she had gotten all the details together they had planned for the wedding the date was set and the reception hall was booked. So off they went to find a dress. Mrs. Reed was relaxed for she had prayed and God was answering prayers. They went to the bridal shop. Bri was surprised at the prices. She had been looking in the magazine and figured she would get something close to what she wanted. The sales lady saw them walking in and immediately pointed them to the bargain dresses on the second floor. Mrs. Reed politely shared with her that she was only there for a fitting she had come in early that month and purchased her daughter's gown. To the surprise of Briana her mom, had got one of her wish books from her room and had purchased the Vera Wang wedding dress that was on the cover she had talked about. The sales lady whose face now was beet red apologized for the mix up and showed them the dressing room. The seamstress fitted Bri as Mrs. Reed looked on crying. "Ms is everything alright? The bewildered saleslady asked. "Everything is fine she said. "God is so good and he works in mysterious ways, she told her. The seamstress informed them that the dress would be ready for a final fitting in a week.

The Parkers were flying in a week before the wedding and staying at the Texas Hilton in downtown San Antonio. Billy would be getting in late from Massachusetts and needed Tetra to make his room reservation where they were staying. They called when they arrived and talked with Phyllis Reed who was disappointed, they were not staying at the house but understood. "What time will Billy be flying in she asked. I'd like to have dinner prepared." Mom always preferred home cooked meals to the restaurant. They always had to eat out when they traveled so it was good to have a home cooked meal. "Billy's flight comes in at 6: 00 we'll see you at 7:00 p.m. if that's alright. "I'm looking forward to it Phyllis said hanging up heading to her kitchen.

Glen had drove down the night before and was bursting at the seams to see his old friend. Hugs, embracing and tears of joy filled the rooms. It had been a long time since they came together. "It's been to long Pastor Reed said shaking and hugging mom and dad's hand. "Yes, Mrs. Reed said our children are now in college." Tetra you look wonderful, life is treating you good" she told mom. Glen and Billy after greeting everyone sat in the great room laughing out loud and catching up. "Where's the pest I asked, she'll be here soon she gets off at 7:00 and she and Meldon are coming over. I told her you all were coming and she has been asking questions all week about Washington." Soon the doorbell rang it was the couple and their bundle of joy. A gorgeous little girl dressed in pink named Suraka (Sura) came toddling in "namie namie, 'she ran over to Mrs. Reed. Phyllis picked her up and kissed her on her little cheek. "Say Hi Sura" she said looking at mom who at this point was starting to tear up. She's beautiful Phyllis may I hold her? Brianna she's a doll the pictures you sent didn't do her justice mom told her. We all sit around admiring Sura and had not formerly introduced ourselves to the groom. Meldon put out his hand to dad first, "please to meet you I'm Meldon Jenkins Bri's fiancée" and Sura's Father he added smiling, "good to meet you, young man, I heard a lot of good things about you." "Thank you, sir" and this is my wife and son Tetra and Billy Parker." "Please to make your acquaintance as well Meldon told them. "Dinner is served Phyllis said coming back in from the dining room. We walked in and sat down to a feast. The dinner rolls were steaming hot right from the oven. The Reeds had a lovely home beautifully decorated. We sat at the large oak dining table. The centerpiece was an assorted bouquet of flowers in a Laleak vase. Mrs. Reed had sliced the large roast for easier servings and smothered it with gravy. A large bowl of mashed potato sat on the opposite side of a serving dish of green beans with ham.

There was corn and a seasoned rice pilaf. A pecan pie or cherry filled for dessert. After the grace by Pastor Reed everyone dug in. We had a wonderful time reminiscing and renewing a lifelong friendship. The remainder of the week went equally as well. We got a chance to sit in on a service or two. Glen took me out around San Antonio with Meldon wanting to go. We did give him a night out and called it his bachelor party. But mom made us swear we would not corrupt this young man. 'Sir he called me, thank you for what you did the rings I mean. Glen laughing because he called me sir was feeling it too." Thank you for letting me I told him and hugged him too.

Dad and Pastor Reed built a friendship and mom and I renew a friendship that was separated only by distant and certainly what time had almost forgotten. Meldon made friendships and I too was very impressed by this young man giving Bri the thumbs up. The wedding was wonderful, the brides' maids and groomsmen were ravishing in the sea foam green dresses and accessories were out of this world. The churched was filled to capacity and Meldon's grandmother sat on the front row in a beautiful white Donna Karen gown that matched her great granddaughter Sura's dress, trimmed with sea foam green. When the key of music rang out "here comes the bride" Brianna came in walking with Billy on one side and Glen on the other. Her Vera Wang gown fully beaded from top to bottom was whispered all through the crowd. When Pastor Reed called for the rings he had to look twice, with the declaration "GOD IS GOOD!" which caused laughter from the pews. At the reception mom and dad announced their gift to the couple. "Mr. and Mrs. Jenkins will be spending a luxurious week in Hawaii for their honeymoon to the loud applause and surprise of all.

CHAPTER 16

She's fallen off the map!

In Jillian's words I was being distant that's how she put it anyway. She wanted to accompany me a few times to meet my parents. I wasn't ready for that. My thoughts are she would team up with mom, who was always getting me married to a nice girl and having grandchildren for her. Besides I wasn't ready. Dorca was the only girl I was with intimately before Jillian, and since coming here Desmond and I dated some but commitment is something totally different. Like Desmond was always saying "make sure she's the one getting rid of her cost money!" Dorca was out there somewhere if it's meant to be, I'll find her. I needed closure and to move on with my life.

It was my third year at Harvard I was feeling the pressure of deadlines, cramming for exams and case studies. I was making phone calls, searching the internet looking everywhere I knew to find Dorca. It was as if she had disappeared off the map. Since the case was all over the television every media channel broadcast it with pictures and everything. I thought just for a minute she would come back to find me. Maybe she didn't like me as well as I thought. It was probably the way I acted that night I was with her. And though it was her idea I knew better. But I fell in love. Whatever is going on with her right now obviously doesn't concern me.

I told mom and dad that I would go back to Maine and settle the property matter in a few weeks not to worry over it. I made all the arrangements with the realty company and a few weeks later I found myself once again in the state of Maine. I told myself my main objective was the property but I wanted and needed to talk with Justin the x-ray technician I had met there. Upon arrival I called Seaside Memorial "may

I speak with Justin Parker please? I asked. "Justin Parker, is with a patient may I give him a message?" came the voice on the other end. I thought if he calls me back hopefully, we can set a time to meet. "William Parker, my number is 204-6938" Parker are you related to Justin? She questioned. "No, not that I am aware she obviously knew him, just a friend. But we get that all the time "I joked. "I'll give him the message. "Click"

I drove to the realty company to meet with Lester Witherspoon the realtor on the property. I had spoken with him in great detail over the phone and our meeting was just to go out and inspect the property before making a decision. He said he had a prospective buyer and needed to get all the loose ends tied up if we were going to sell. I apologized for the delay and shared with him that mom was better after spending a few days in the hospital and she sends her apologizes too. We got into the car and drove out to the property. Mr. Witherspoon told me he had a call a few days ago from a young lady who inquired about this property. She seemed very interested but she hadn't called back and didn't leave name or number. We get a lot of those he explained.

The property set out on a cove near the coastline. Beautiful green pine trees surrounded it. It was a perfect get away place. It was a cozy little bungalow 1,100 square feet. An elegant cottage is how I would describe it. The inside was dark oak floors and white walls. In the right hands this would be a great first home Billy thought to himself. Dad had purchased the property for and investment probably never even saw the place. I looked around some more at other parts of the quaint little house. I wasn't sure if I wanted to sell it. If I decided to stay around this area it would be great for me. We got back into the car and I promised I'd get back to him. I wanted to talk to dad and let him know what I thought about this property. I was just about to stop and eat when my cell phone rang, 'HELLO" "hello" this is Justin Parker, is everything okay with your mom? He questioned immediately. "Mom is fine, she said hi by the way" I returned with a smile. I was calling to see if we could possibly meet up somewhere?" "I'm here in Maine on business and had a few hours to spare." Justin was hesitant, he couldn't imagine why I wanted to meet with him "let's see" I have an hour break at 2:15 he told me we could meet in the hospital cafeteria. "That's perfect" see you then I said. I just had enough time to get to Seaside Hospital safely without speeding across the highway. The Maine State Fair was going on and a lot of the streets were blocked off to thru traffic. The weather was perfect in Maine during early autumn. The leaves showed color bursting forth accenting the sky's blue endlessness. I thought I would definitely visit Wadsworth Longfellow's House, before going back home. Henry Wadsworth Longfellow is one of my favorite poets and it is a popular historic site. I looked again at my watch as I drove into the hospital's parking garage. Knowing how punctual a hospital persons schedule must be I quickly found my way to the hospital's cafeteria. It was a large room filled with pale pink and green chairs. Walking in I saw Justin sitting at a small table near the window. He had already secured his tray with lunch on it and had begun to eat. 'Hello Justin Parker" I said extending my hand as I walked toward him. "Hello Mr. Parker, Justin joked back with a big smile returning the hand and greeting. "Thank you for meeting me on such short notice. Do I have time to order something to eat? Or should I just get right to the point?" I asked. "No, please get something to eat the food in here is pretty good! He was enjoying a large hamburger with all the trimmings. "I've been here since 5:am so this is dinner for me. This is also my second home. Bowdoin's my first" he added. After getting lunch I sat down to eat. "Not bad" I had bought the meatloaf sandwich. Finishing I said "your name is familiar to me". Justin looked at me as if he wanted to recommend a shrink, "I thought we went over this already?" he said. "Which part sir?" Justin joked. "Justin" the Justin part" I affirmed. I know you, well I know of you I added. Is your mother's name Katherine or something close?" it's been a long time I confided. Katherine is my mom's name, who have you been talking with who would know that? Justin was feeling intimidated and uneasy to say the least and spoke louder. Who are you? He questioned. My dad is David Parker" I said to him. "Is that supposed to mean something to me? He came back bluntly. I could since he was ready to walk away." 'My dad had your birth certificate in a box of papers I found long ago." Something I remembered after our encounter a few months ago. It weighted on me after your joke about being related. With this legal mind I just had to check it out" I told him. "Thus, that conversation Justin said with him "your dad I mean" something that didn't make sense he said he was tired and was just thinking out loud. Makes sense now he wanted to know if I knew." "Kat' she hasn't used Katherine since I don't know when, has always said he was out there, but I had so many uncles out there anything she said was just another story" he confided sadly. She was always reading those business magazines what does he do? "He's a lawyer" I chose what I said carefully and prayed silently within. "Kat said she had an affair with her boss who was not going to leave his wife for her!" Justin said candidly she never hid things from me" still sounding straight forward he continued "then immediately letting her go and relocating her to another job." She's still "Kat" lives a fast life but is a good provider. I often think if things had turned out for her how different she might have been. He's probably the only man she ever loved. She says if it comes again, she'll marry it but till this day she's single. Life has not got her down though. She's always worked and provided well for the both of us. Her words Justin says, she works hard for her money. I can say this she has put away for my education. "I have the best education money can buy, that was Kat's line too", Justin smiled. Kat says if he ever wanted to find us he could". Justin had poured out to Billy what he probably hadn't thought about in years. They sat there and shared for the remainder of the hour. They had tackled a subject that could have been devastating if handled differently, timing was everything God's timing. Because of love it read like the prodigal son. Billy told Justin he was his older brother and he had grown up with his mom also. Their dad had always been a part of his life though he and his mom had only moved back together again when he was in high school. Billy shared with him his mom had opted to move away from Maine after he was born and separate herself from a hurtful situation. She didn't divorce David but lived totally separate for years. Billy was letting Justin know that his life was not a bed of roses either but he can still find hope in unfortunate circumstances. "I would be glad if you decided to visit me at Harvard" Billy added. "I'm in my third year and believe me I know about cramming for a big exam! They were both laughing and smiling again. Justin checked his watch and stood by the table. "JUSTIN PARKER YOU'RE WANTED IN XRAY! came across the intercom system. 'JUSTIN PARKER it repeated again. "Got to go Mr. Parker" he said shaking his hand. "It's Billy I told him. With a nod he affirmed and said "I'll be in touch" and rushed out of the room. I sat there for a moment thinking what had I just done? This young man was content being an only child of his mother not really giving much thought to his father. And here I come sharing that I am his brother! I hadn't even let mom know I knew! Did I say too much too soon? Time will tell.

David was so relieved when he got Tetra back home from the hospital and things had turned out so well. "Tetra he said soon after they had gotten back home from Massachusetts "I have planned a cruise for us to relax. We will be gone for seven days so pack our luggage we're leaving for the airport as soon as I return from the office today" he told her on his way out the door. She was relieved it was only food poisoning and things had turn out all right. She thanked God over and over again for his blessings. David had shared his plans with her on the way out the door and at the last minute so she knew he wasn't going to except any excuses why she couldn't go. Tetra called the Center and gave James Captain her calendar and called her office. She had not been to her job at the State since coming back from Maine and shared with the staff and co-workers she would see everyone in a week.

David and Tetra flew out of Spokane headed to Florida to board a Carnival cruise line ship from Miami to the Caribbean Sea. They walk on board the M.S. Holiday vessel with many, many other passengers boarding too. David and Tetra found their way to their cabin on the Empress deck. "Here it is!" David said putting the card key in the door. They were soon followed by Arnold Hodgson the steward who had been assigned to their cabin's floor bringing in the luggage. Tetra had made plans for she and David to walk around the large fifteen story ship and take in a show for their first evening on board. They showered and got dressed in very casual attire and with program guide in hand walked out to get involved in the events. "Excuse me!" a purser said as he scurried about trying to find the owner of luggage he was carting around. Stopping on the promenade deck in the Tahiti lounge Tetra and David sat at one of the quaint little tables and after ordering two virgin Pina Colada's with lots of colorful umbrellas, they enjoyed the moment. "Thanks honey" Tetra shared this is just what I needed a get away from it all for a while". "You're right we do need to take the time out for ourselves," she added. "Thank you for not protesting" David teased holding her hand. David was so afraid that the news regarding Justin would send their relationship into a tailspin. He loved his wife and he wanted to share his thoughts with her but didn't know how right now. If it came up, he would maybe? David reasoned I'll take it one day at a time.

David had made reservations at the Blue lagoon lounge for dinner but first they had a full day ahead. Thirty minutes after they had sailed there was an announced lifeboat drill. All of the passengers hurried in an orderly fashion to the top deck of the ship and followed instructions including putting on lifejackets for each one's safety. After satisfying the coastguard and a command performance by all passengers they were well on their way. No one lacked a place to go after the drill. As soon as the drill was over "the full casino will open till 3:00 a.m". came and announcement loudly spoken over head for all to hear. "Featuring blackjack, dice tables, roulette and of course slot machines! "David I'm not much for this let's find something else" Tetra said pulling him by the arm leading him to the American deck. "Now this is my speed David said taking Tetra around her waist to the dance floor. The American Lounge had and orchestra playing and other couples danced or listened to the mellow sounds of the music. "My David, you still have that college charm I fell in love with" Tetra flirted as they moved around on the dance floor. There were other couples some much older than David and Tetra enjoying one another's company on the floor. One couple was celebrating their fiftieth wedding anniversary and seemed to be dating for the first time. After they had danced for a while, they headed back over to Rick's Café for pre-dinner cocktail music. They sat and talked with other passengers from other areas of the United States and the world. This gave them an opportunity to meet fellow shipmates early in the cruise. This was absolutely wonderful Tetra exclaimed. There was a disco deck. There were comedy shows. There was jackpot bingo and a late-night buffet every night. David and Tetra was having so much fun, they saw themselves doing what they did in college staying up late and laughing a lot. They swam in one of the three swimming pools, toured the islands on each assigned port stop. They were having so much fun. David beat Tetra continually in shuffleboard "just one more game! She'd say. Eveningwear was formal and they dined out in the Seven seas dining room. The dining room décor was fabulous. Beautiful ice sculptures nightly and crystal goblets and glasses in which to drink from and lots and lots of foods from all over the world. They sat at the table with two other couples each night David in a tuxedo and Tetra in a designer gown. They became good friends. The couples shopped together at each port of call and took in many of the shows offered on the ship. They all went sight-seeing through the towns along the way. St. Maarten, St. Thomas, and Nassau it was awesome. Mable and Doshe' and older couple who they spent time with kept them in stitches of laughter. Doshe' was your typically tourist LOUD prints on his shirts and outrageous hats. One day as they shopped in one of the ports someone commented on the couple as they stood looking in one of the shops windows. "Hi, I was just telling my wife who has been complaining after we climbed up those set of stairs over there about how well you two look at your age and you seemed to be having so much fun," he said respectfully. Mable who had been complaining about her husband Doshe's attire just smiled and introduced herself and then her husband. "Thank you, she said politely, my name is Mable and this is my clown Doshe. David Tetra and the other couples laughed so hard they were crying. They shared their laughter with the couple who started the conversation and it became hilarious. No one was offended Doshe laughed too. He was a standup kind of guy.

My parents had a wonderful time on their cruise. Mom shopped at the stores on board and had her hair done at the beauty salon she told me. Dad visited the gymnasium got in on a talent contest with some other fellow shipmates and sang old tunes to reminisce by. As they said their final goodbyes at a late-night dance on the lido deck of the large cruise ship to a Calypso band FOR EVERYONE'S ENJOYMENT AND PLEASURE their seven-day cruise had come to an end. David had not got around to sharing his concerns about Justin. Frankly he was having so much fun with his wife and they were bonding and making new memories with lasting qualities. There was so much still they could have done so they would have to do it again next year they reasoned.

CHAPTER 17

Forgiven

David was still thinking about the awkward moment riding home from Maine to Massachusetts with Billy and Tetra. Moments were tense when it was obvious that he and Billy were trying to avoid talking about Justin the x-ray technician at the hospital. "Good morning dear" David said to Tetra as she walked into the kitchen. "Coffee? he asked. "Yes, thank you dear," replied Tetra. "How are you feeling?" he again questioned noticing her extremely happy mood these days. "I'm great Tetra exclaimed, that cruise was just what I needed! It was wonderful I have been on cloud nine since we got back. "Oh, is that what I've been enjoying David said coming over to hug her and gently kiss her lips. "I'm going into the office today, why are you asking all these questions? She smiled. "Just wanted to know if dinner out was a possibility? David asked. "Well paused Tetra "I was going to surprise you and cook your favorite southern dinner tonight, pot roast smothered in gravy and mashed potatoes with sweet potato pie for dessert". "Buuutt a girl would have to be out of her mind to turn down a dinner out! She explained "Can I get a rain check on that meal?" David quickly asked. "Sure, dear anytime, Tetra said and reached over and kissed his forehead. "Then 6:30 p.m. at Freigo's David added, should I pick you up Tet?" "No that won't be necessary I have lots to do before then I'll meet you there, she informed him. Freigo's at 6:30 p.m. she thought then I'd better wear something fitting. She kissed David again and said I will see you tonight and ran back upstairs. She dialed her salon to see if they could possibly fit her in. It wasn't her regular appointment time "For you no problem! Quince her stylist told her. It had been a long time since she prepared herself for an evening out. On the cruise they dressed in formal wear but there were other couples there too. She wanted to look special for whatever reason her darling husband had asked her out with him this evening. She had gone out with David but nothing like Friego's in a very long time. Tetra and David were always going out when they were dating and even before Billy came along. They traveled a lot. She couldn't travel as frequent "No! She said don't want to think about that, new start here we go". She watched from her bedroom window as David drove out of the driveway before heading to the shower.

David drove to work hoping for the best night ever. He prayed and asked God for the right time. He hoped for the best in this situation. He wanted to talk with her regarding their stay in Maine. She said she had forgiven him. Now this was still causing concern in David's mind. David had been giving lectures to some of the groups at Mt. Nebo about forgiveness. He offered to do it simply as he puts it because he knew to the core what it means to be forgiven and restored by God. He often quotes James 5:15 and a prayer of faith shall save the sick and the Lord shall raise him up and if he have committed sins they shall be forgiven. David had accepted God's forgiveness, Tetra and Billy's forgiveness but he was struggling forgiving himself. God was changing him continually from the inside out and he knew it. He thought differently sure acted differently and conducted himself differently with his co-workers and the rest of his staff. Many liked the changes; others said just a phase it to shall pass. After a few years they conceded and asked which gave him an opportunity to witness. He made reservations for a private room off to one side of the posh establishment Friego's. Friego's was one of the elite places to go for anyone with prominence, prestige and might I add money! when visiting Spokane. Tracy Chapman was performing tonight and he knew how much Tetra enjoyed her soulful sounds. They hadn't seen her perform since he and Tetra saw her perform in concert at London's Royal Albert Hall a few years ago. He had talked her into going for her forty-seventh birthday. He thought about this evening all day. He felt like a young man on his first date. He had gotten there earlier and made his presence known to all. Everything was set in the private dining room and he sat listening to the soulful songs of Ms. Chapman. David viewed her from his reserved seats in the establishment. Tetra walked in the vision of loveliness. She was wearing a black strapless taffeta McClintock gown that hung the curves perfectly. Her sheer nylons gave a shimmer to her very shapely legs as she walked toward him in a pair of beautiful sequined ankle strapped heels finishing her look. She thought it's been a long time since I pampered myself. I always dress well for church or work usually business attire. I want this to be special. She had her hair pulled up in a French roll, with tiny ringlet curls hanging on either side. "Been waiting long?" Tetra asked. "Not long; but you're sure worth every minute I did, expressed David. He got up and pulled out her chair, okay! David asked making sure she was secure on her chair. "Tetra, you are a vision", he repeated again.

They sat and listen intently to the soulful sounds just talking and enjoying one another. It was as if the years had roll themselves back and they were two young people getting together for the first time. After about an hour "hungry" David asked, yes dear let's order. He nodded to the waiter who was standing near the door. Soon he came back rolling in a large covered cart. He placed a tray of crushed potato skins with smoked salmon caviar and chives in front of them to get them started. The table was draped with a white Italian linen cloth and beautiful embroidered napkins. The gold silverware complimented the setting beautifully. The Curried Cauliflower and apple soup with Cilantro cream were a favor dish of theirs. "Good choice" Tetra added as the waiter placed the main dish of roast pork shoulder with pecan crust to finish off the meal. Before leaving he removed the chilled wine from the ice container and carefully removed the cork and poured a small amount of Dom Perignon champagne in David's goblet. He sipped and gave the nod for him to continue pouring the champagne. This was a special-order Dave told her just for you. "Thanks, she said smiling knowing he meant there wasn't any alcohol in it. He turned and poured a wine goblet for Tetra. Dinner was wonderful, food was great and light conversation, was pleasing. "That gown adorns you" David said. "Thank Jessica McClintock she's a great designer Tetra informed, but David enough about the gown, "What brings us to this evening?" She asked lovingly "I truly thank you for a lovely dinner and Tracy too couldn't have asked for a better evening. But why are we here other than you care? she said softly holding his hand on the table. "I have sort of made a discovery David shared nervously, he did not want to ruin this evening. "Sort of "Tetra pulled back. David had started now he couldn't turn away; "I realize this is a very touchy subject with us but I think we have come a long way". 'Tetra didn't wait for David to continue she asked, "Where are you going David?" She questioned expecting her heart to be broken again. "No Tet that's not what I'm saying. Remember a few months ago when you were sick in Maine". She nodded "go on" "Well Billy and I found out that the young man who cared for you was Justin". Tetra stopped holding his hand, everything stopped the world seemed to stop. The room with the now soft orchestra music playing stopped from his hearing and for a moment life ceased to exist for David. At least that's how he felt. What was she thinking? Did she even know who Justin was? Finally, after what seemed to be an hour Tetra spoke "Justin turned out to be a fine young man didn't he? She said softly. David sat silently he wasn't going to touch that question. "You knew! he finally said surprised. "Not until the day he came to x-ray me". The cute little nurse called him Justin and I put the rest together". "Funny how things happen" she said. "He's grown so much since I saw him the day Billy and I left Maine". David said nothing.

"David" she continued "when the birth certificate came to our home, I was devastated to say the least 'but through the hurt I was able to think clear enough to check it out. "I wanted to make sure this was right. I had heard all the whispers in the office. I didn't want to believe it I knew it could be true" This was my family and we had just started our life together". Tetra now had started to shed tears but held back making a joke about her mascara. "He's your son David, I went to our lawyer that day and made sure he never wanted for anything no matter where he went." When Katherine was visibly gone from your secretarial pool it was little left to imagine." Katherine probably thought it was from you, I didn't care I was thinking with my heart not my head. I was thinking as a mother who loved her child." "I took Billy over to see him before we left for Spokane. He doesn't remember they were both to young. "He wanted the little red hat Billy had placed on the top of the car which fell as we drove away. Looking back in the rearview mirror he had picked it up and placed it on his head with help from Katherine and waving goodbye. I had told her that whatever happened at this point was up to you. I gave her Jane's card and drove away."

David was speechless for the first time. He never knew how forgiven he was. He reached over to hug Tetra because he needed it. "David, she explained "I know you have changed in a lot of ways. When we were married, that's what we were just married. It didn't change you. I thought stopping my education after attaining my master's degree to be with you more would change you because you whispered that in my ear. It didn't change you. You still did the same things you did before we were married. I tried to change you but it took God to change you. I trust and believe now we are committed to making this marriage work. I found out that beautiful elaborate weddings, hideaway honeymoons and a diamond ring as big as Texas is great it's good that's all it is and it soon passes. Committed is forever unconditional no matter what. She reached over and hugged David "this is a no matter what" she added. And I'm not surprised he's a good kid. I often prayed for him too. I prayed he'd be the best at whatever he decided to do she ended looking in David's face. "Thank you, Tetra for caring and loving me outrageously David said holding her hand to his face. David whispered I love you Tetra in her ear and added God knows I didn't deserve you. And they danced the night away in each other's arms......

CHAPTER 18

Let's celebrate

James Captain called me to inform me of a celebration for the now Dr. Cornelius Hathaway. He was trying to get all the members past and present to attend this gala event. Please let anyone you speak with know of the event he told me. James was sending out over 200 correspondences to past members no longer in this area. "We have got CeCe Winans as our featured performer she's one of Pastor Hathaway's favorite gospel singers" He continued talking filling me in on all details. "Chelsea Parson-Mayor says she will be available, she sings for the white house now you know" "that doesn't surprise me," I said. I did see her performing on television the other day". It was a memorial for the fallen soldiers, she sang the Star-Spangled Banner." The years sure have been good to her she now looks as beautiful has she sings. Both shared a laugh in agreement. "That or either married life in Washington D.C". I said to him. James asked "have you heard from Tyler? No, someone said he moved to St. Louis. "I'll call his Mother and I'm sure she knows" James replied. "Well keep me informed I said and hang in there" I'll talk with you soon". Hanging up the receiver thinking what it would be like to see Winnie. It had been two years since she said she'd return the visit. Even though we talked now and then it would be good to see her. Melissa Eldrige, especially Tyler Parson and all the others. I would always make it a point to visit the church while I was home visiting Mom and dad. Many of the members my age had moved from home, gone off to college or the military. Some married and relocated. So, I'm looking forward to see what God brings together.

Dr. Hathaway was known all over the world. I watched him every day on television at Harvard. Some of the programs I'd have to record and watched later. I was also willing to share stories of growing up with him with my friends and the Harvard elite, those who weren't tired of listening. Dr Hathaway traveled more now doing lectures and seminars all over the United States. Staff on this project alone mom said was one hundred plus folk busy working to bring success to this one event. We are always glad when he's back home, in Washington State blessing us once again" Mom told me. Dr. Sean Edinberg is also one of our pastors and does a fine job when pastor's away". But make no mistakes mom said we love our pastor. James called me later in the week and asked if I would prepare a speech for the occasion.

I boarded the plane that night before the big celebration at Mt. Nebo. We were honoring a true man of God and I arranged my schedule to make it happen by being a part of it. I called dad so that he could pick me up from the airport, another car in the driveway we did not need. So, I didn't bother renting one for this stay. Mom was still helping get things done at the church. She worked with Ms. Pollie who should have given her spot to someone else now and retired, she said in Pollie fashion, God wasn't ready for her to retire and she wasn't either. Mrs. Hathaway made sure Ms. Pollie was included in all office decisions.

Dad sat in front of the airport door. He arrived just in time so he would not have to park so far out he told me. I phoned to say the flight was on time, so a quick stop to a baggage claim and out to the passenger's waiting zone where dad was waiting and off, we went. We talked about school, how things were transitioning from the office move for him on the ride home. Dad shared with me about the night out with mom and that he had told her about Justin. 'How did that go? I asked. "Very well dad told me. Your mom is a remarkable lady!"

"That's great dad I added, I always knew that. "Oh, by the way. I went to Maine and saw the property you have for sale." I like it! It would be great for me if I decided to stay in that area," I shared with him. "Oh, are you planning to stay in that area? Something or someone I should know about? Dad questioned. "Dad you're sounding like mom now" "it's a very nice little cottage, have you seen it? "Only on paper, but it's your call just let Witherspoon know what you intend to do" he finally told me. "Saw Justin while I was there, we talked, it went well, only time will tell" dad I'll keep you informed for right now that's all I can tell you." Dad didn't mix words he said, "your mom's okay, everything seems to be going well. We're all getting to know each other again. I trust everything goes well with Justin but I'm looking out for you and Tetra" David confirmed. Dad and I turned into the driveway. There wasn't much time to sit and relax, I had taken a late flight in and had only enough time to shower and change and get down to the church, I was meeting James there to go over the program for the evening.

I drove down to the church. Dad was letting me use the Navigator while I was there. It's a lot different than driving my little car which by the way was making the rounds with the girls at the Harvard campus. As I pulled in the church lot there were two limousines pulling in behind me. Just for a moment my heart skipped a beat. Could it possibly be? No, it was CeCe Winans and her entourage. David was sitting at home in his study looking at pictures Tetra had used to decorate his shelves. The smile caught his eye. That smile looks familiar, suddenly the doorbell rang. It was a special delivery carrier with a letter that needed a signature. David signed for the letter. It was for his son Billy. He looked at the envelope and called him. Ring. Ring. Ring, looking at the number flashing it was his dad. "Yes, dad what did I forget? I quickly asked, knowing dad doesn't usually call unless it's important. "You got a certified letter son." I signed for it. It will be here on the table in the entrance area. O.k. "Sounds great dad, I'm kinda in a hurry the guests are starting to arrive thanks, see you soon" I told him hanging up because someone was yelling my name. I stood watching all of CeCe's people file from the limo's and go into the auditorium. We had assigned each performer rooms to store their belongings in. Soon I heard "Billy! little Billy Parker. It was Mrs. Ann and her daughter I guess, was pushing her in a wheelchair. She had aged but her voice and her spirit were as strong as ever. I reached down and hugged her. "My you've grown into a handsome young man". "Always knew he would' she said looking at the young woman pushing her wheelchair. 'This is my niece Mary Ellen." "Hi I said I'm William Parker or Billy is fine. Mrs. Ann was my favorite teacher in the whole wide world and still is I told her patting Mrs. Ann's hand as it rested on the arm of her wheelchair. "See I told you he was a good kid" she continued. "It is good seeing you Mrs. Ann and nice meeting you, Mary Ellen I'll talk with you both later I replied moving away to go into the Center to look around and make sure everything was in place.

The Center was not yet open though they had set aside a time when everyone could go through it if they choose to see the facilities. "Why

Bill-e-e Parka" using the southern voice, she loved for stage. It was Erica Hathaway, "Winnie". She ran over and hugged me. 'Look what life has done with you, she delighted "how's my Harvard man? She was still Winnie I wouldn't expect anything different. She wore a black business suit right off the pages of "O" magazine. She was now Councilwoman Erica Winfrea Hathaway-Reaching. "You're looking great Winnie is Wyston going to be here? "I don't know! Winnie exclaimed. "Is Dorca going to be here? She came back, "what happened to her anyway? Just then James came running in "take your places we're ready to start. Winnie and I ran back to the church that was adjacent to the Center connected by a long hallway. "See you later late-night swim?" I asked her. "Sounds wonderful" Winnie said and walked out.

The orchestra started playing. The lights were lowered everywhere except the stage. It was a celebration fit for a king. The Lord was praised and lifted up. The choir was glorious. Chelsea sang as angelic as ever the years were kind to her. She was not only beautiful inside but her outside certainly had changed. She had married a Representative of the House. Looking at her now I saw the beautiful swan she had become. Ms CeCe Winans brought the house down singing many of her latest recordings and I somehow found the words that brought everything into perspective and sharing this night with so many of my friends was memorable. Dr. Hathaway ended with closing remarks and prayer. The auditorium was in an uproar for the LORD.

CHAPTER 19

Does she exist

I was running around getting last minute things in my luggage. I wasn't staying long this visit I needed to get back to Massachusetts and my flight wasn't going to wait for me. We had stayed up late after the celebration entertaining some of the members and friends from Mt. Nebo who had come by after the service to fellowship and have dessert with us. Everyone was gone by 12:00 pm except Winnie. She and I sat in the great room talking about future plans and past experiences. She shared she had failed terribly with marriage. Aaron Reaching who never wanted her to be so outspoken felt hidden behind her personality, and he refused to understand why she didn't want to yet have children. She was upset she had agreed to a very small wedding only immediate family to satisfy him. Her answer was she had too much to offer that needed her undivided attention. She knew he felt that way before they married but was determine to change him in the name of love. Just never happen. Bitterly they parted friends.

I asked Winnie after sitting and talking for about an hour. "It's late but the offer is still on "late night swim. 'Whoa! this is something Winnie had longed for Billy Parker to herself. She remembered back to their early dates when she had to ask him, now he was asking her. She knew if she would ever have him this would be the time. It was right it felt right and why not they were bought mature adults, what could a little swim do. "Sure, that sounds wonderful" she repeated the same words as earlier that evening in the Center.

They walked out to the pool house and both put on bathing suits. He had put on his trunks, and was waiting near the shallow end dangling his feet in the water. As Winnie walked out, he informed her "the water isn't too cold come on over!" She was wearing a two-piece orange stripped bikini and she looked fabulous. She took her tote that was filled with her clothes she was wearing and put them on a lounge chair near the outdoor patio sitting area walking over toward him, swaying her hips from side to side. "Are you sure Billy about the water temperature, you're always playing games with me?" she asked. I was breathless as she came over and caught my hand and touched her toe in to test the water. "This is not how I remembered feeling about Winnie, she was stirring up passion in me and I liked it. No, I told myself you're rushing things. This was just a friendly swim. I have Jillian back home what was I thinking. She put her hand on my shoulder to secure her entrance into the water. I put my hand on her tiny little waist and brought her in. And before I knew it, I was embracing her so close and staring into her eyes. She smiled and my lips met hers. She wasn't trying to stop things and I wasn't holding back. We enjoyed what was happening and neither onc held back our feelings at this moment. After our kiss Winnie swam to the other end of the pool. I stood in the shallow end of the pool coming to reality of what just took place. She swam over to me hugged me and kissed my cheek again. Got out of the pool, picked up her tote and left after drying off as not to drive home dripping wet, she said. She made some impression on me. "See what you could have had, or it's there but I'm not going to give it to you. You'll have to earn it. "but two people like Winnie and I "nope" would never work. Though one thing for sure she as potential and she's a great kisser!! "Got everything Billy?" mom said rushing me out of the door. I shook my head from thinking of last night with Winnie. "You're going to miss your flight she told me rushing me out of the door to the car. As I buckled my seat belt and was set to go. My cell phone rang. It was in my backpack I had just hurriedly thrown it in the back seat of the car. Mom stop backing down the driveway and I got the backpack out of the back seat and answered the phone. "let's go mom I said, "what" came the voice on the other end. I'm looking for Billy Parker. "I'm sorry this is Billy Parker may I help you? "Billy this is Justin" the voice said. What are you doing? Did I catch you at a bad time?" He asked. "No! "I'm trying to get to the airport been visiting my parents what's up?" I replied. "I was coming your way tomorrow got a few days off thought we could talk again." Justin explained.

That sounds great! What time are you looking to come? Around 4:30 p.m. tomorrow he stated. "That's good look forward to seeing you I said.

"Mind if I bring a friend?" Justin asked again. It's a long ride you know" okay with me drive safe I told him. Mom and I were now driving up to the airport. I gave her a hug and kiss and went in to board my flight. My flight wasn't bad. I slept all the way. I did think about Winnie, who probably by now had forgotten I even existed.

As I drove the next day down the campus pass Currier Hall to my residence it was about 2 pm. I knew I had time to get another nap in before Justin came. I asked Jillian to meet me at my house to help me entertain my guest who was coming in from Maine. Justin and his friend arrived in Massachusetts at about 3:30. They called me from Harvard Hall for directions to my home. I gave them direction to my townhouse and they were there in no time. "Come in please I said opening the door for them to enter. I then asked how was the drive up?' 'Not bad, said Justin, this is Ariel she works with me at Seaside Memorial". "Hi Billy she said extending her hand toward me. "Make yourselves at home I told them we're all family. "What can I get you to drink? Or eat? "All sounds good Justin said we didn't stop just drove right through from Maine." "Great then I said we'll eat" Jillian had fixed her favorite dish she always made to impress me. Pepper steak with large baked potatoes. Jillian boasted this was her specialty. It was all right I teased her. "Soft drinks are in the frig everyone help yourselves" I said. We all sat around eating and chatting about each other's careers. Jillian and Ariel gathered the dishes and went into the kitchen to put things away. Justin and I sat on my Italian leather sofa looking at photo albums mom had put together. They were great conversation pieces. "Great pad man" Justin acknowledged looking around in Billy spacious townhouse as their conversation continued. Jillian came from the kitchen with two cups of Chai Latte "great to help you relax after a long day. She said. "What is it? Justin asked as Jillian handed him the cup. 'Sweet blended tea, not bad thanks babe". Justin soon found a picture of me wearing my red cap, "Cool cap Billy," he said smiling and pointing. I had one just like it! Justin reached into his pocket and pulled the photo from his wallet, "see cool!" I shared with him that mom had told me about the cap. "You wear it well I added rubbing his blonde wavy hair. We sat and talked for hours reminiscing about the times and getting to know each other better. We had a wonderful time over the next few days. We found we had some of the same interest. We shared with each other stories growing up. He asked me about dad. Nothing prying. Just what kind of man he was? What kind of things does he like to do? I'm sure he was only trying to find the other part of his make-up. And that was all right with me. I helped Justin bring the luggage in from the car and put it in my guest room. We all sat around talking and playing a game of monopoly that first night. After a few hours the girls finally conceded to go to bed and we soon followed. We all had a great time over the next few days. The girls even got in some shopping.

Our days together went fast. As Justin and Ariel were preparing to leave, he asked me. "What are you going to do after graduation Billy? Justin was starting to like having and older brother. He wanted the relationship to grow. I liked having a little brother too. "I'm not sure what life holds I said and I have less than a month before graduation to think about what happens after that. But I know I want you in it, little brother, again smiling rubbing Justin's head affectionately.

My it feels good to finally get pass the family secret regarding Justin, my younger brother. For years he was the riff that tore my family apart. My father is a great man and my mother is a dynamic lady. And though our cultures of dad being Caucasian and mom Black are reunited and now I had discovered my Caucasian brother. Talk about mixture in a family. But we are working to put it all together with loving and caring for one another. Glen Reed is my very best friend and the brother figure that I grew up with. We share a common bond of never ending friendship. We are inseparable we are buds. Our families were joined long ago as neighbors living across the street from one another and the love is shared to this day. Everyone was preparing to come to Massachusetts for my graduation since mine was two weeks after Glen's. I had gone down to Austin by myself. I didn't know mom was meeting me there. I sure couldn't miss Glen's day. The whole Reed family was coming to share my day and I guess I was really looking forward to seeing them all especially Glen. I didn't get a chance to spend a lot of time with him in Austin the family had planned a trip to Hawaii for him. Mom and I shared Glen's graduation from college visiting with our dear friends before returning home. Bri bragged about her honeymoon to Glen. And he hinted to his parents. Mr. and Mrs. Reed made it a surprise for his graduation. We all planned a big celebration for the both of us after mine graduation. Bri and Meldon were keeping in touch sending updated pictures of Sura and the family. It took her a little longer to finish community college she wrote with working to help her family income but she did it and has enrolled in U.T. San Antonio to expand her studies. Meldon had progressed at the museum working in Zoology and is taking night courses at their church's bible college. They are staying close to the Reeds so that Sura can enjoy her grandparents more. They too have been blessed and openly share their testimonies and struggles as a young couple. She wrote us that Meldon's grandmother passed away right after Sura's second birthday. And she left victoriously just as she lived. "You did it, man, I said to Glen calling to let him know I had gotten the message that the family was coming and I was elated. "Who would think a mischievous Black boy from Washington State could achieve such greatness" I kidded. "I'm so proud of you! "Dido we did it, Glen added. "How was Hawaii?" I asked to Glen's laughter. "Beaches, beaches, beaches! Girls everywhere you and I must make a return trip" he suggested. "Let's talk soon. Over the years Glen and I had shared a lot of hurts frustrations and accomplishments. We knew of the girls we knew we weren't ready for marriage and we certainly knew we wanted to succeed. Glen had graduated with a degree in engineering and was headed to Cape Canaveral in Florida to work for the John F. Kennedy Space Center.

CHAPTER 20

The letter

It had been about six months since I had flown to Spokane. Mother understood I was finishing up and getting prepared for graduation. Mossy had won Desmond's heart and they were getting married before graduation and moving to Kansas to take over the family law office. His grandfather was retiring. 'Billy you have a standing offer to be my partner in the firm "he'd always say. "Thanks man I'll keep that in mind if life takes me in that direction" I told him. Mostalgia Filta was from Yugoslavia and Desmond was a Black brother. We would always tease them about their nationalities. Jillian always said, "Mossy's going to have the most beautiful children".

Winnie had called a few times but her letter she sent shared her true feelings. She was glad we had final got around to a choice between us. She informed me she was rebounding from her failed marriage and needed attention and to know she was still wanted. She wasn't going to use me just to get over Aaron. She still cared for me and maybe if our paths crossed again the ending might be different. Love Winnie. Last I heard Councilwoman Winfrea Hathaway of Connecticut was laying down roots, making a great impact in the political arena.

Justin says he looked forward to seeing me again for graduation. He enjoyed his visit and hoped that our relationship continued to grow. Ariel and he were engaged and to leave a date open in life to be his best man. Mom retired from her director's job with the state and now works from her home. She developed a program at the Center for under privileged children that was making a great impact in the community. They were so looking forward to seeing me for graduation and meeting Jillian whom mom had talked with several times over the phone or asked about when she didn't.

Even with all this love going around I still tried hard not to get attached to Jillian. I thought I would marry a Black woman like mom even though mom never made a difference between black and white. Jillian was beautiful I fell in love with her personality first. She does have brains and can hold an intelligent conversation. Her long curly hair has led to many a discussion about her heritage. She was growing on me I liked her companionship. But I was not ready for marriage and share it over and over again. She had me downtown Cambridge in one of those weak moments looking at rings "we're just looking at someday" she'd say. But her clock was moving so much faster than mine. I had given up hope of finding Dorca Williams. Seems she had given up on me and found someone else to spend her life with. Why hadn't she called? Why was I saving myself? That one night can't be what I'm holding on to! She's obviously moved on. Jillian was the closes thing to love in my life right now. And as far as I knew I loved her!

Desmond called to run a case by me "Freeman vs Capawits remember the forgotten letter Desmond remarked. Suddenly a light came on "Des, man let me call you back gotta make a phone call. I didn't wait for a response just clicked and hung up the line. Ring, ring Ring. Hello, mom said hurriedly answering the phone. "Hi mom I returned the greeting. "Are you alright?" She asked "I just spoke with you last night" "I'm fine mom, I'm just fine" I continued "remember the celebration at the beginning of the year sometime in May when I was there. A certified letter came for me. 'Do you still have it? I asked anxiously. "A letter?" "What letter, Billy? I don't know about a letter!" mom insisted. "Dad signed for it" I again said. "I don't know about a letter Billy I'll look and call you back" mom replied. "Maybe Ms. Laine can help is she there, mom?" Ms. Laine came in two or three days a week and would help mom clean and cook. She would even help when mom and dad gave large dinner parties with other staff assisting. "Billy I'll look right now and call you back", Tetra again insisted. Ms Laine had put the letter in the letterbox inside the large clock until Mr. Billy as she called him comes to get it. Before Tetra could call him back the phone rang. "Mom did you find it? I questioned hoping for the answer I wanted to hear. Calm down Billy I have it right here. "Who is it from mom? 'Let's see Edith Williams" son isn't that Dorca'

William's mother the one that was on television news?" mom asked. I didn't answer I really didn't know. I knew what we had heard but still wasn't sure. "Mom overnight it to me please?" "It's important "thanks mom" I was covering for my future. Later that night I called Desmond back and explained my swift departure and discussed the case with him. Jillian's parents were coming up for graduation and I had opened myself to meeting them for the first time. I was willing to talk about anything with them except marriage. Jillian knew this so there wasn't a problem. I liked Jillian a lot sure I could even love her. What I felt for her was my description of love. What we had was the closest thing to love I knew right now. And for the most part I was faithful to her. We had been an item for 3 years. I went out by myself sometimes or with Glen and Desmond. That is before he fell in love with Mossy that works for him, I'm not knocking it. Jillian always hated Glen's visits and was glad to see him leave. But that unresolved issue with Dorca was lurking in my mind. Why was Dorca's story so unsettling? I thought it was over! Finished? Was she somewhere? What was going on? Maybe the answer is in that letter can't wait this is going to be a long night.

I had left instructions that all mail was to go to Adams Hall to assure I receive the much-anticipated letter. All day I thought why was she writing me? How was she doing? Had Dorca been out to see her? I was working part-time at a law office in Cambridge getting some practice in before graduation. Three years to the bar was still in front of me and I sure didn't have plans to stay here. As I drove back to my residence, I stopped by Adams Hall to pick up the mail. My heart leaped when I saw the envelope addressed from mom. I wanted to read it in private and in a quiet place and by myself. I went over to Harvard's large library. I'd surely have quiet there. Jillian was at my house. So, entering the large library I found a place over in the corner and sat down and opened the letter. It read:

Dear Billy Parker, you're probably wondering why I'm writing. I tried hard to raise Dorca but something went terribly wrong. I'm Dorca's grandmother, her mother's mother. I allowed Dorca to grow up never accepting who she really was. The Demato's were good people to us, a little different in lifestyle but she never wanted for anything. We always had the best of everything they saw to that. Mrs Demato a nurse who was grieved when Faye her mother died in childbirth took her death very hard. She always thought there was more she could have done even when doctor's shared saving her was hopeless. Mrs. Demato contacted me because she wanted to keep Dorca. Since Faye had not made provisions for anything, they were going to put her up for adoption. They would make her a ward of the court if I didn't step in. Mrs Demato contacted me. She came to know Faye through her husband. He apparently had her name in his little black book she had mistakenly found in a suit pocket. And apparently Faye knew him that's how she came to be in that hospital. She had my name as next of kin and though I had not seen Faye in ten years at least, I knew she was my daughter. I had failed terribly with Faye and didn't want another child to raise. Not at my age and besides I could not provide for myself on a nurse's salary let alone a newborn. My old man had left me with a pile of unpaid bills. She said that I could live with her and let her raise Dorca has her own. She may have had suspensions of who the father was she never said. Victoria explained she and her husband had tried having children but were not successful. They spoiled Dorca giving her everything toys, clothes, sending her to the best schools. I came across as mean and selfish when I spoke out but I could see what it was doing. As Dorca grew older her demands on them were sometimes outrageous and ridiculous not to mention the tantrums. I told her I would leave if she didn't stop harassing her parents, the Demato's. And I let her grow up never really knowing me has her grandmother but her mom's maid. Small children don't see color. Dorca of course was lighter than I. And since Faye never had the opportunity to put the father's name on the birth certificate we never knew. Mrs. Demato loved her but couldn't take away the pain she said of always being questioned about her little baby girl. Dorca always threaten to hurt them as she got older when she didn't get her way. The Demato's were not young people. Though I never thought she would. Dorca also told me one day in anger she was letting everyone know she was adopted. I couldn't tell her the truth I had made a promise to Mrs. Demato. I was just her live in Nanny. I knew she was beginning to realize she was different. But only in color the Demato's never made a difference. They had some friends that were mean and off color but not all of them. Most of the people in the Demato's circle had children and nannies. Dorca was a quick learner. I found out from one of her little friends at a sleepover for her thirteenth birthday other stories she was telling. She got angry with her friend and never invited her over again. She made up stories all the time. I'm sure you have heard your share. Poor Mr. Demato, his precious little Dorca she had him wrapped around her finger. He didn't agree to her always spending time with Grover. Who loved to walk with him in the morning so that Dorca would come and read to him in the evenings? There were many times I had to go over and with force bring her home. The Demato's were quite a few years older than I. Vickie would have Mr. Demato send me off for days or a week at a time when Dorca got older. They wanted her to be more independent they said. And said I was over protective. After we had been together for a while one evening Dorca in a fit of anger stated "I'm getting older and I want need you, old lady!" she sounded just like her mother Faye. When Mr. Demato suggested getting Dorca a car I protested. I liked taking her to school and picking her up. I hate to admit it but I felt like I was giving Faye back some of those lost years. She liked you Billy a lot. She was very smart and as you know over achieved in all subjects. I taught her how to read myself Edith wrote. I could be sure she was at school if I took her because she loved to learn. She is an intelligent girl. But sneaking around as she had started doing had worn on all of us. She had the Demato's around her finger and she knew it. She came home and heard Mrs. Demato and I talking to Richard her husband about Grover and what I had caught him doing. That night Dorca came to my room in the middle of the night and told me I was lying and out of line. The next day Richard and Vickie suggested I go to the country for a while. I really don't know who killed the Demato's "I didn't do it." I'm writing from a cell on death row. I've been here for years and have not heard from Dorca. But I confessed to cover because I feared Dorca had done it. I am frightened of dying! I helped spoil her but I don't deserve to die for something if I didn't do it. I've been here for years waiting my death sentence. Dorca is still out there. There may be hope for her anger she's built up for me. She says she didn't do it. And I really don't know but she did threaten to hurt others if I didn't confess because she hates me and believes I did it. I failed with Faye and now Dorca. After what happened to the Demato's I wanted to die. Even though they hurt me badly I didn't want that family hurt. They didn't deserve to die either. I don't think she would hurt your family. She liked you. She called and asked me to pick her up from your house that day because I promised to confess so that this media circus would stop. I was so afraid she had done it. She had everything planned out and promised to stick by me until it was over and I was freed.

Dorca said you would be with her always. I don't know what that meant. Maybe she's there with you now. Then it's her word against mine. Please be careful. It seems all those years I was trying to teach Dorca from my medical books trying to get into her head. In the end she got in mine. You're the closest person to Dorca, just the mention of your name changed her mood. I was hoping she would change for you maybe she did. I have only a few months and I will be gone for good. Dorca learned very well from those psychiatric books. I think she manipulated us all. She told me about the bible you gave her I read it too. God Bless you Billy Edith Wright Williams

Tears streamed down my face "my God, my God what am I to believe? Who am I to believe? Please God help Dorca wherever she is. Was Glen right all those years when he said you were trying to talk to me? Please help Edith in her state if you can now! God what must I do with this please help me? I don't know what to do. Did she set me up prom night? I sat there numb and confused. Did Dorca do this or is a sick joke of Edith to spite Dorca? Help Lord please help me!! Did Dorca plan this? I REALLY DON'T KNOW WHAT TO BELIEVE!

I WALKED IN Jillian had cooked dinner and wondered why I was so late coming home. She was so worried and concerned because I had not called her. Jillian said mom had called and informed me that Mr. Grover was on the news. Someone was doing a report on muggings in the area and his name came up from a previous ran story years ago. He was apparently seriously hurt while out walking one night in the park by a mugger and was in critical condition for months before dying. She was sure they would rerun the story again later. I told Jilly I had stopped by the library to do some research on a case. She could see I was bothered by something. It was obvious I was searching for the words to complete my thought. I sat down with my head in my hands hoping not to have to answer any questions." Oh, said Jillian this package came for you today! still trying to get a smile from me. Someone knows where I live, she said, continuing to smile. It is addressed to Jillian McFinney, Radcliff Residence Cambridge Massachusetts. I sat on my sofa thinking how much more before this is over?" I have all this family coming in a week or so and now this. "What's going on? I thought. "Billy did you hear me? she repeated a little louder. "This package came for you". She handed him the package it was wrapped in a bridal floral wrap. "Someone knows something" she said thinking Billy was trying to trick her. "Is there something you want to ask me?" Jillian teased tugging at his arm. He ripped open the package. He was angry he was hurting and he didn't know what was coming next. "Billy what's wrong?" Why are you tearing that package like that? ""Who is it from?" she continued to ask questions that he didn't have answers to. "Jillian, I don't know and please don't ask me any questions! I yelled. She knew from my tone I meant it. He pulled off the remainder of the paper to expose a box about 7X10 in size. There was no return address but a small card fell from the box top which read: if you're getting this package Edith is no longer with us. "I sat thinking could I have changed the outcome if I had read this letter months ago when it was sent to me. "Why had I forgotten it "Lord are you in this?" "Why hadn't I listened like Glen said. Jillian sat next to him and said nothing she was upset about the way he had responded to her. He reached over and hugged her so tight and started to cry. A grown man but he was crying. The package he was holding fell to the floor. "What's wrong Billy? I picked it up from the floor and with trembling hands I opened it. Inside was a small child size bible. "it looks quite old Billy, whose is it? Jillian asked. Jillian took the bible from my still trembling hands and opened it to the first page which read: To my kindergarten friend, Always Dorca. Billy had been crossed out and inscribed now in its place was DORCA.

What does this mean? Jillian asked. Not knowing what the future held and holding on to Jillian with hands shaking and heart pounding as she listened, he shared his past with her.

Billy had to somehow come to grips with this past that haunted him. Jillian wasn't going anywhere, that was her words and this girl would just have to get over it and move on! Billy's past and future had finally met up with each other and as best he could he tried dealing with it. He was not sure that he wanted to be with any woman again. He did not want the responsibly of having something happen to her! Billy had many times stood holding the letter in his hand. He had not even let Jillian read it. Questions so many questions kept going through his mind. There is not a lot I can do with this letter Billy thought to himself frustrated from tossing and turning another night. He reasoned "not until I find Dorca whom I have been looking for so many years can I find answers." Why would someone send a package to Jillian?" Someone knows what's going on.   I can't live with these questions. I'm going to talk to my dad the first chance I get. I've got to, Billy sighed.

CHAPTER 21

Congratulations & gondola's

Spring had sprung and all the family was gathered to celebrate and be a part of William J. Parker's graduation day. He was determined not to bring up the package he had received weeks ago and asked his girlfriend of three years Jillian McFinney to do the same. He had prayed that God would direct him as to what needed to be done. Certainly, he would talk to his parents David and Tetra Parker but not today. Since it was really too late to save or talk to Edith Williams a former maid who had been executed for murder and according to the letter Dorca's grandmother confirming the story was out. What if it turned out that Edith did do it? What then? Will he once again drag Dorca his long-lost friend from grade school through another horrible ordeal of questions? He had called and was told the bible was sent from the facility where Edith was housed to an address somewhere in Cambridge. He was still looking for that information. So again, Dorca was cleared. When did the name change occur in the bible? What would prompt Edith to change it? Was it, Edith or Dorca who changed the inscription in the bible? It had accrued to him Dorca had written him a lot of notes that he would have kept. But they would have been stored so deep or thrown away by now. He had nothing to compare it with. Let's just get through Harvard he thought, no let's get through this week, no this day. Then I can get away and clearly think about this matter and certainly about my future. For some reason it wasn't going away. His plans now were to leave Massachusetts but where would he go?

"William John Parker" as his name was announced across the microphone at a graduating class for the second time in his life. His family and friends looked on with pride as he received his B.A. Degree in

Law. Glen his childhood friend forever stood and applauded has "Billy" stepped across the stage to receive his degree. Much to the surprise of the stuffed shirts seating across the stage looking on everyone in the audience joined in. Which each graduate greatly deserved.

The coeducational class wasn't missing Ms. Jillian McFinney as she walked across looking out to smile at her mom and dad with delight. Her friend Kelly had come to share her day also. That's what Billy thought until he met her. She had come down from New York with Jillian's parents.

"Let's go over to Hollis Hall and mingle and meet with the other graduates" I said giving a high five to Desmond Owens and a big hug to Mossy. Desmond was my roommate through college and he and Mossy had just gotten married last week. Both had received their law degree's with honors. "Man, the hard part is over", Desmond confided the next three years should be a piece of cake". "Mossy take good care of him he's a good man" I turned and told her. "Thanks Billy you are too" she said with a smile. We walked over to Hollis Hall they had set a very large banquet for everyone including the family and friends we had invited to share the occasion with us. I wanted to be around people. I didn't want any idle time to think negative thoughts. And I certainly didn't want to be around anyone who wanted a commitment from me right now. Mom and dad hugged me and of course she cried. "Very proud of you son" Mr. Reed said in his deep voice. Mrs. Reed hugged me and said she was very proud and was praying for me. Justin my estranged brother who I had come to love congratulated me and said he was so glad he came but couldn't hang around long this time he was in the middle of finals and the hospital never closed. I sensed he was a little uneasy with the others. We joked about the hospital never closing and I introduced him to mom and dad. He talked with them for a bit and dad wished him well with his studies. I'm not sure he really knew what to make of the whole thing but we got through it. After an hour or so he headed to the airport for home. Jillian ran over and caught my hand to introduce me to Kelly Lipsney her friend from New York. I had met her mom and step dad at my house that night before. Mom and Mrs. Reed made a great dinner for all of us. Everything seemed to go well. My parents, the Parker's, "the Reeds" Glen Reed's parents our dear family friends, his sister Brianna and her husband Meldon Jenkins and their little daughter Suraka.(Sura) Jillian and her parents Roger and Frances Fleming. We all had an enjoyable time with of course Glen making everyone laugh.

This day was over to soon and everyone was clearing out of Hollis Hall. The beautifully decorated room and tables covered with large flower arrangements and food was a fond memory. I thanked the entire Reed family for coming. Sura had now joined us. She was with a sitter earlier. One of Jillian's neighbors whom she knew well had a young son and she opted to keep Sura for us while we were attending the graduation. After returning from the graduation mom and dad congratulated me and the other' of the class of 1988. And said they would be leaving soon and heading back to Washington after a long weekend. All the Reeds left. Only my buddy Glen remained with me. Jillian knew Glen was staying for a few more days and was being very clingy. She knew we were planning to see the sights while he was here, I had shared all this with her prior to today. I wasn't sure what she had told her parents but her friend was definitely getting the wrong idea. "Am I the bridesmaid? she asked after catching me alone gazing into space. I had walked away and was standing alone in Hollis Hall thinking. "excuse me "I said, "do you know something I don't?" I was smiling knowing I really needed to talk to Jilly. Jillian was taking her parents sight-seeing around Cambridge. "Aren't you going with Jillian? I asked pointedly. "I'd rather go with you" she said. Soon Jillian came over and said she was leaving and kissed me. 'Let's go Kelly I don't want to leave you". "Bye Billy" Kelly replied walking off behind Jillian.

Alone at last Glen and I couldn't wait to check out the sights of Cambridge. I knew enough to know that I would go in the opposite direction of Jillian's tour. Glen and I would finally be able to talk. I needed questions answered. On our way back to my residence we stopped by the newlywed's place. They were finished packing and ready to pull out. "Man, the offer, remember the offer Desmond repeated to me. I reintroduced him away from the crowd again to Glen. "Man, I feel like I know you I've heard so much from Billy about you Desmond told him "Congratulations I heard you did this a week ago" that's great man. This is my wife "Mossy". "Mossy? Glen said with his eye brows up. It's easier than Mostalgia" I told him. "Ooo.k" Glen chuckled. "Mossy it is! Please to meet you' Glen said. Everyone laughed.

Glen and I watched them drive away from the campus. "Glen next to you" Desmond" I said wiping my hand across my eyes to prevent tears that were forming. Desmond was going to finish his three years in Kansas and work in his family's law firm with Mossy at his side.

'So, Billy did you stand up for your man Desmond? Glen asked. "You know I did" I would go to the ends of the earth for that brother" I told Glen but he knew that anyway. He and Mossy had decided to marry at Holden Chapel. It was a small intimate gathering of his family and friends. "Jillian's waiting her turn, Glen mocked. We had stopped back at the residence to give Jillian and her parent's space. Actually, he didn't want to run into them. "Don't start Glen, I told him lets go. "I see why Jillian wants to grab you!' Glen said as we got into the car to drive downtown. I had traded up for some new wheels. "She's really trying to get me man, I confided. I really like her. She's been there through some tough times but I'm just not ready for marriage. Especially after that package I received last week I told him. "A package" Glen said. I proceeded to tell him the story of the letter and the bible. "Dude I mean man what are you going to do? I'm not saying I told you so, but I told you so! "That girl has been a mystery since elementary school when they tossed me from that Rolls" he laughed. "So, you still haven't heard from her?' "No not yet" I said "That may be a good thing man, count your blessings". "Man, you need a change turn your life around" I let him continue to talk, cause somehow it was making me feel better. "You said the package was sent to Jilly?" How did that happen? It's spooky man! "Something's not right, you need to find her whereabouts for closure on your part and get on with living". "Man, I'm going to remember you in all my prayers", he closed joking. Glen laughed and joked a lot but if he says he's praying for you thank God for it. Downtown Cambridge Glen spotted some honeys at 6 0 clock he said in his street language. I looked to see a couple of girls as we were pulling up to ride the gondola.

We were going for a gondola ride under the famous bridge of Sighs fashioned after the famous bridge in Venice. "Hi" Glen yelled "would you like a gondola ride? "Sure, one of the girls yelled back as we pulled up to park the car near the pier. "She walked over extending her hand "hi my name is Lexia and this is my sister Lena. Looking at them you could tell they were cut from the same identical cloth. Lexia immediately fused to Glen and they seemed to complement each other's personalities. She grabbed his arm and walked toward the gondola. Lena and I followed. "I'm William I told her and you're. I paused so she continued with

'Lena". She was quiet and cute and appeared to be very down to earth. Both twins did for that matter. She was slim and tall with blue eyes and tanned mocha skin and a sexy short crop cut hairstyle. Definitely model material I'd say. She confirmed my thoughts as we rode down the river. They had just finished modeling school in New York and were moving to California. They were here in Massachusetts to see their friend in the live performance of the "Lion King" showing for two nights here before going on. "How did heaven know to make two goddesses", Glen said. He was right looking at them you couldn't go wrong with either choice. Lexia wore her hair a little longer with a flip to draw your eyes into those gorgeous blue ones. About a half a mile down the river Glen and Lexia was all over each other. "Man slow down! I told him handing him a small package from my jacket pocket. Glen looked at it and laughed throwing his head back, "thanks man" and put it in his pocket. The girls sensed the moment and we all laughed. It was obvious we were all mature adults out to have fun. Lena and I actually found out some things about each other. If Glen and Lexia did it's a surprise to me. Lena and I kissed lightly has we passed under the bridge as go the custom. After exchanging numbers we promised we would get together the next day. I have no idea what I was thinking. Jillian's parents were still in town and of course there was still Jillian. We were going to accompany them to the show that was here from New York. Glen and I took them to dinner and over dinner conversation Glen decided he'd get a room at the Hyatt for the night. "I'll call you in the morning Billy" Glen said after I had taken him and the twins to the Hyatt so that he could reserve his room for the evening. I took Lena to her room at the Sheraton and against what I was wanting or feeling I said good night and went home. "It was about 1 a.m. Jilly had left a note saying she'd see me tomorrow and would like me to join her parents, Kelly and herself for dinner out tomorrow night. Her parents and Kelly were returning to New York the next day.

"Hi mom how was your flight home" I asked calling the next day. I had gotten up early expecting Glen to call after he woke up and realized the situation. "The flight was fine son' how are you doing? She asked. Your dad really enjoyed Mr. Reed's company seeing you made yourself scarce. Is everything all right? Son what was that letter about you had me send last week? "It was nothing, things are fine mom, I just had a lot on my mind these days" I just need time with my buddy Glen that's all" I

added. "You two better be careful' she said give him my love". I will mom"
"Well I'm glad to hear things are okay. What's going on with Jillian, she
seems to see something you haven't voiced yet?" Tetra questioned? "That's
true mom, Jillian's a nice girl and I like her a lot but I'm not ready to settle
down or get married. "Well Billy you make sure you know what you're
doing dear" Tetra added. "Yes mom" I agree "Billy be gentle she is a nice
girl" Tetra repeated as only she could "love ya, I'll call ya soon mom bye!"
I said hurrying her off the phone before she asked any other questions.

Ring! Ring! hello, I said answering "hi hon" it was Jillian she was
sounding so sweet. "Good morning how did you rest last night? She asked
"just fine Jilly it was a long day" I said. "Where's Glen? He's probably still
sleep I said continuing to talk. She had already formed her opinion about
me spending time with him. This wasn't the first time but I was not about
to open up a can of worms. "What's up Jillian? I finally asked it's early."
Did you get my note she asked bluntly? "Yes" I said. "And you'll be here
what time, she asked assuming I was going. "Dinner reservations are at 7o
clock downtown at Shambarger's." There was a very long pause from me.
She was waiting for an answer. I told myself it's early! calm down. "Well,
what time Billy? I need to tell my parents you'll be here." she persisted as
if someone was standing over her shoulder. "Let me talk to him Jilly"
came a voice from the other end. "No Kelly!!! mind your own business"
Jilly said sharply. "Sorry, just trying to help" Kelly replied. They sound
like they were arguing back and forth. Finally, I said "Jillian I'll see you at
7 o'clock and click I hung up the phone. I remembered what mom said,
but I hung up the phone feeling pressured. I knew a lot had to do with the
letter and package and of course the twins Glen and I had met yesterday.
I was taking it out on Jillian because she wanted to be close. I dialed 606-
4983 "hi" may I speak with Lena? "hi this is Lena" the voice came back.
"This is William we met yesterday at the bridge. "Yes, I remember couldn't
forget you that easy she told me. You're up early couldn't sleep? Quite the
contrary, I slept very well, sweet dreams" I said. "Well that's good" Lena
remarked. "I thought I'd call you early, I started out saying "because I
have to change our plans". "I understand last minute" she came back
softly sounding disappointed. I felt the need to explain to her why my
plans had changed. "I have friends who came up for my graduation and
we're going out to dinner." I should have left it at that but I kept talking.
"I would love to keep in touch" I explained. "Thanks for the call" she said

as if she knew or expected this turn out. I hung up the phone and went in to the kitchen table to have breakfast. Quickly gulping down my last cup of coffee and rushing out the door heading to the Hyatt to pick up Glen it was nearing 11 0 clock. I stopped at the desk to inquire his room number not thinking to call. "Glen Reed's room please? I asked the clerk behind the counter. "oh, Mr. Reed's room, he recognized the name right away. "How can I help you? he repeated. "I'm here to pick him up. "Has he checked out yet? I questioned. "No! Mr. Reed has decided to stay with us through the weekend, "would you like me to ring his room? He then asked politely. "Please thank you" I responded. "Hey man, sorry I didn't call, but Lexia and I decided to stay the weekend, you understand" he said laughing. We do have a lot in common" he continued. To which I responded "oh, you two are actually talking" just call me tomorrow bye" I joked and left. I went back to my residence and got back in bed. I needed to be rested for this night. I also needed to reflect on what direction to head. If Jillian would just stop pressuring me for marriage, I could just leave things alone and continue on the same way. I like her even love but marriage 'No!" I remembered so vivid mom and dad. God allowed then to reunite after long years of hurt. I didn't want that for Jillian and I sure didn't want it for myself. If and when I marry it is going to be right. It was approaching 5:30 p.m. and I had just started moving around the residence after lounging most of the day. I pulled Lena's phone number from my pocket and began programming it into my cell phone. 606-4983. "it's ringing, I didn't mean to call it, Maybe she won't answer. I'll hang up! "hello" she said. "hi, sorry about that, I was programming your number in my phone didn't want to lose it" I told her "and it accidentally rang bad timing" I said. 'No not at all, I was sitting her thinking about you and contemplating calling you" then she added "you were brave enough to follow through". She knew what I needed, she was stroking every ego I had and I bought in. We must have talked about an hour before being interrupted by Jillian calling to confirm my arrival. I clicked the call waiting back over and told Lena we'd talk again soon. I hurried and showered and quickly dressed. I figured the sooner I get this evening started the sooner it will be over. I put on my Larenzo Banifi shoes and the Andrew Marc of New York outfit for this occasion. I was definitely into fashion Jilly brought that in with her New York influence. I soaked it up like a sponge. We were going to dinner but I knew they were really sizing me up. Be nice I kept saying, God does not like ugly! We were going to Shambarger's Restaurant a very elegant place. I rang the doorbell at Jillian's. Kelly opened the door. "Hi' Billy reaching around my neck and hugging me. With everyone looking on I quickly returned the greeting saying "hello". Thinking to myself this girl's got nerves! Jillian, I noticed was standing a way down the narrow hall of her small residence still very near campus. I had moved not far from her but my townhouse was very spacious in size. She had hinted a lot over the years about moving in especially after Desmond moved in with Mossy. But I somehow convinced her it would spoil our future plans. She stayed there most of the time anyway. I spoke with her mom and step dad who was sitting on the oversized sofa at one end of the room. 'Hello" I said as I walked in. "Billy, you look very nice", her mother said to me. "Yeah GQ" Kelly said standing near me rubbing down my arm. 'I stared at Kelly and said "thank you to Mrs. Fleming Jillian's mom. Jillian walked over and hugged me and lightly kissed my lips. "Hi" she said and proceeded back to finish up wherever she was doing in her room taking Kelly with her. "Something to drink son before dinner?" Mr. Fleming asked. No thanks sir I'm fine for right now. "Jillian told me he was a vice president for a information services company? I asked making conversation. He and her mom had been married for about ten years. Her real dad had left her mom for a younger woman doing his midlife crisis when she was in her teens. I love my dad but he's been a nice replacement she said. He talked a lot about the workplace. He loved golf and was an, avid golfer. I shared with him what little I knew about the game. I had been a caddy at Pebble beach one summer for my roommate's dad Mr. Owens. We shared lots of golf stories. 'Sit down, sit down son" "You know women are never on time", he said very candidly in front of Frances his wife. "How can you say that Roger when I'm sitting right here", she commented. I have been ready! "Well Frances there's always a first!' he said while sipping on homemade margarita from Jillian kitchen. "That's sure true in Jillian's case" I said to ease the tension building up. It calmed Ms. Fleming down, recognizing every case is not the same, certainly not hers. Kelly, stuck her head from Jillian's room and asked where Glen was and why hadn't he come? "Against everything I felt I told them Glen had his own room downtown. And I hated she had asked. I knew Jillian had probably put her up to it. But Jillian would have suggested we go and get him. She was always playing matchmaker. "Well Billy what plans do you have now that you're well on your way? Jillian's step dad Roger asked still sipping. "Mr. Fleming", I said, he quickly came in with "call me Roger or dad" and laughed. "Roger, I said I have 3 more hard years before I fully reach another goal, I have set for myself'" I began. I had spent all day answering this question in my mind. "I'm only twenty-two years old and I still want to travel and see the world before really settling into life as we know it" I told him. Jillian's mom Frances had now joined Roger sipping on a drink feeling uneasy about all the questions Roger was posing. And Jillian had not emerged from her room. "Billy, right? you appear to be an intelligent young man, I listened as they announced the honors associated with your degree, very impressive!" he told me. I thanked him thinking we were on the same page now, when out of left field came "didn't hear you mention Jillian in your plans, is she in your future son?" He stopped and now both where looking at me. I felt pressured and knew it was going to be a long prelude to dinner. I stood up and removed my camel color overcoat and draped it over the arm of the chair where I was sitting. "It gets chilly at night in Cambridge I said as they continued to look at what I was doing "Mr. Fleming, Jillian and I have been together for about two or three years I think" I shared with them. I knew exactly how many I was getting my thoughts in line. "Three years" Mrs. Fleming added. "Okay. I said three years", I wasn't happy right now and you could hear it in my voice. "I like her a lot you have raised a beautiful daughter I told them. I could come to love her BUT". Jillian came swiftly out of her room with Kelly laughing within inches behind her. "Let's go Jillian said we're going to be late our reservations are for 7 "o" clock she was rushing around as if she heard nothing that was being said. But Kelly's reaction was she heard it all and didn't like any of it. "Mom you and Roger ride with Kel and Billy and I will lead in his car. Okay let's go. As soon as we were in my car my cell phone rang it was good old Glen." "Billy man where are you? He asked "I'm out with Jillian and her parents" I said looking at her so she'd know who I was speaking with, but it didn't seem to matter and Glen sure wasn't the one to help matters. "I'll talk with you later man" I'll tell Jillian you said hi" I added. Bye. Jillian wasn't impressed by the call so I decided real was where she was and asked. Jillian did you hear what Roger asked me at your place?" "Yes, Billy I heard it all and so did Kelly" "Kelly, what does that mean, I'm not trying to impress Kelly, I'm not trying to impress anyone and you know me" I confided very pointed. "Kelly's so false she's here to see what kind of relationship I have. I was always second to her and if she thought I had something she couldn't have, if she wanted it was part of her game" she explained. Somehow, she had convinced herself that things would have gone differently if Kelly were not here. I had got caught up in a mind game. I continued to listen. 'YOU SAID YOU DIDN'T LOVE ME! what am I supposed to make of that? Jillian yelled. "It's not that I don't love you, it's not a marrying kind of love I told her. Jillian this has nothing to do with you. It's me I'm not ready for marriage" I said pressured to come up with an answer to calm the situation. 'You're older than me, by a few months but I would think there's other things you have planned for yourself' I replied trying to get her to see things my way again. "Billy, you've promised me this for three years" What? I asked, Well, we've been together for three years will you ever marry me?" she asked. I looked at her and just sighed, "I don't know Jilly. I can't say right now but I do care a lot and as much as one can I love you. I told her gently stroking her hair as we drove up to the valet parking. "How can you say you love me, but not enough to marry me?'" it's because of that girl the one who sent the book isn't it?" she questioned now in tears while we stood waiting for an attendant to take the keys. Jillian wasn't happy and I couldn't find the right words to say to her to change her mood. When all she wanted to hear was "will you marry me?' Jillian was silent as we continued into the restaurant only speaking to say" McFinney party of five" she told the maitre d standing at an elegant podium trimmed with gold inlays. 'Right this way' he said. We walked in and sat at a round dining table. A red damsel cloth draped over the edge causing a ripple effect around the whole table looked very chic. The circular table was perfect for conversations where everyone could join in. Kelly was trying to flirt with every sentence that she breathes. Bragging about her clothes and Mr. Right whoever he was. Kelly I found out was a fashion consultant at some large department store in New York. She traveled a lot in her work. Jillian pretended all night that she was having a wonderful time and the conversation we had on the way over never happened. Roger kept trying to get me pinned down to something that resembled marriage. Drinking what I considered one to many. Frances was put out with the whole thing. She thought she came down to make wedding plans and tonight was no time for me to change my mind. I was not going to be pressured into marriage to satisfy anyone's ego and Jilly knew that. If she didn't know then she knows now. I was very nice to everyone at the table. Dinner was served and prepared very well. I would return again but in different company. With everyone at odds we managed to be civil and get through dinner. Jilly realized how silly this was and this is something she and I should have discussed alone not an issue to be forced.

Mr. Fleming conceded by saying they were leaving tomorrow morning and you and Jillian can decide what you're going to do with your lives. Frances didn't comment. "That's a good idea" Jilly said, "very good idea" I added. I don't know how we got to that moment. I don't know why they thought we were ready to make a commitment lightly over dinner. But any way we got passed that point. Jillian had talked to Mossy and I guess had a preconceived notion, two different cases entirely. I told them it was a pleasure having dinner with them, I apologized for not being able to give them what they wanted but it was our life. Roger understood, Frances didn't comment. Jillian knowing it was all her fault was glad I didn't get up from the table and leave. The same arrangement was made going home. Kelly drove the Fleming's back to Jilly's and Jillian rode with me. She was holding my arm and talking sweet until her decision to stay the night at my house was spoiled. She was making me the bad guy. She's stayed several times at my place but not when her parents were in town and once again, she knew that. "Just take me home! She snapped "I'll be over first thing in the morning! she stammered Jillian was not happy. "Is that a promise" I teased I expect breakfast." She was wrong in what she did. I'm no saint but she made me hated by everyone at that table. Except of course were friend Kelly. Things got a little rough but I kept my word to my mother I was nice. After riding around to calm her down somewhat I drove her home. She got out of the car slamming the door. When we pulled up Kelly was finishing up packing her luggage into the car. I waved and drove away. She had driven up from New York and wanted to leave very early to avoid traffic she said. "Jillian what are you doing home? I though you and Billy had a lot to discuss". "Your mom is very disappointed with you". She thought this was a sure thing for you. For that matter so did I but don't worry Jilly your secret is safe with me" she mocked. 'Shut up Kelly, your fashion consulting job is safe with me too! Jilly remarked. Kelly was now mad at Jillian's comment. "He must have company?" and you don't want to say!" "No Kel that's not it, take me over there getting in on the passenger side of her car. Kelly drove about five or six blocks to Billy's townhouse. "He doesn't live far from you Jilly" Kelly said looking around the area. Billy had arrived a little before they pulled up. They sat and watched him enter the dark residence so she knew no one was there. Jillian sighed "let's go you see he's alone" Are you satisfied? Jillian scowled. "Are you sure Jilly?" Kelly asked. "I'm sure let's go! I'll be over first thing in the morning," she said. "What if he's sleep?" Kelly inquired. "I have a key, showing Kelly her key hooked to a ring of keys. They drove back to Jillian's and made ready for bed. Jillian had a hide abed she used for these occasions in her living room. She and Kelly put bed covers on it and after talking for about an hour mending their odd friendship Jilly went to bed. The Fleming's were sound asleep in the guest room especially Mr. Fleming it was a long weekend for him. It was about an hour after Jillian and Kelly had said goodnight to each other that Kelly went to bed unhappy. She had not convinced Jillian that someone could have been spending the night at Billy's. Jilly left her keys hanging on her key hanger near the door as not to disturb anyone looking for them or rummaging through her purse. She was taking her parents to the airport in the morning and lost keys was the last thing she needed. Billy had gotten home after letting Jillian off giving her something to think about regarding their relationship. He would have to pray about his behavior tonight and ask for forgiveness. Billy knew he was not attending church as often as he should but he did take the time to read his bible and always prayed and asked for forgiveness every night. After getting from his knees he called Lena. They talked and he planned on seeing her before she left Cambridge. He went to sleep with sweet dreams. Billy was sound asleep when he heard someone coming through the front door besides Desmond who had moved away to Kansas Jilly had the only other key. So, he listened attentively. The house was pitch black focusing he could see a woman's silhouette coming toward him. "Jillian what are you doing?" he asked her "I'm alone Jillian this is foolish once again" he repeated. The figure said nothing just stood over him." "Jillian, I smell your perfume, you wore it earlier tonight. "Jillian! and besides you're the only one with a key". Jillian you're not fooling me" I told her. He sat up and grabbed her onto the bed. "Jillian what do you want from me"? I care, I care a lot okay Jilly I love you" I finally conceded. I knew she loved me it was late. I reached to turn the light on next to my bed. The figure I was now holding in my hands pushed it to the floor. 'I was getting mad" and tired of playing this game. Okay Jillian I know what you want! You want me to show you". We had solved a lot of our issue's the last six months conceding this way. She nodded her head. I gently kissed her neck and face and then I kissed Jillian. The figure responded like she wanted me. It was so different than the kisses just to get it over with. It was passionate she had not been like that in a while, months, a year I know for sure. She was her old self. Maybe because she feared losing what we had. I don't think I was ready for our end either. I really didn't know what I wanted. She turned and I turned. All of a sudden, I forgot she had invaded my space. I was on fire and so was Jillian. I wanted to stop and talk to her after that passionate kiss but things moved quickly and it was too late. One thing for sure my Jilly was back!! I didn't realize how complacent we had become with each other. I embraced her after it was over and removed myself from my bed. Walking to the light switch near the door "click" I turned to see Kelly sitting on my bed! "What! what! how did you get in here? I asked shocked. "you let me in Billy, don't you remember? was her response. She got up and put on her clothes that I had removed and left. I sat there on the side of my bed and couldn't cry. I did feel bad for Jilly. Her friend had betrayed her. "Will she tell her, or will I?" I stood in my shower for about forty-five minutes going over what had just happened, dried off, went down stairs checked my door securing the lock and returning to bed.

"Good morning sleepy head" was the voice I woke up to. It was Jillian's sweet voice standing over my bed she had just come in from taking her parents to the airport. She said Kelly had left some time during the night and left a note saying goodbye. She lay beside him on the bed and kissed him on his cheek. "What do you want for breakfast honey? she asked rolling from the bed to go downstairs. Just as she moved away heading downstairs toward the kitchen the doorbell rang. She walked over peeked out of the window that viewed the front door and ran downstairs to open it. 'Good morning" I could hear Glen's voice "good morning" Jillian returned the greeting. I sat up in bed thinking is he alone? He wouldn't bring Lexia here? Is he by himself? I can't take much more! 'GOOD MORNING" I yelled from upstairs. "Where's Billy? Glen asked knowing sometimes I use the guest bedroom downstairs. Jillian returned the good morning greeting. She also liked how Glen's tall slim framed looked in his clothes, I heard her say. "Nice outfit she told him.

"It's from my MJ collection thanks though" he replied. "You're cheerful this morning good night? Glen asked her. "Nothing special, landed on my feet after that disastrous dinner. I'm sure he'll tell you" she added. I just got here this morning" Jillian confided. Glen didn't say anything he stood looking for the direction Billy might be in before making his next move. "I must see my man! he said heading to the room. "Are you joining us for breakfast? Jillian asked wanting to make enough for everyone including him if he had plans of staying. 'Why not, then I can hear about the dinner from both of you "Glen remarked. Jillian cringed she didn't want to go through that again. "Billy's upstairs she said and headed to the kitchen to prepare breakfast. Even though there was piled carpeting on the stairs you could hear Glen coming, If not from his feet his mouth constantly moving the whole time. "Billy! Billy!" he teased as he came into the room. "Whew! I said he's alone. Glen was casually dressed wearing an outfit from his "Michael Jordan Collection" "I like that look man, did you bring me one like that? I asked him as he entered the bedroom. We sent each other clothes we thought were exclusive. "Not exactly" he told me "but I bought you something from the collection I think you'd like" That's cool" I said reaching to shake his hand. "Good morning anyway man. "Jillian sure looks bright eyed and bushy tailed," he added waiting for a reaction. "She just came in this morning' I replied throwing my legs over the side of the bed to get up. "Are you staying for breakfast I'll let Jillian know? "oh, I told her on my way up" she's a good woman Billy" Glen confided You otta marry her", he said laughing and falling on the bed. "Jokes" Glen I said "you're full of jokes" Well I missed you last night!" Glen mocked "Yeah I bet you did! I said knowing Glen could take care of himself. "Lexia said hi" he added. 'SHHH" I said Jillian has very good hearing" "We've got to get away tonight and talk when are you headed back to Florida? "my flight leaves out tomorrow morning Glen informed me. Cape Canaveral calls. 'Glen do me a favor and keep Jilly company while I shower and get dressed. And Glen don't you dare!!!! "I know man, I know Glen replied laughing.

David Parker was home relaxing from his return trip from Cambridge. Tetra had went shopping and he was sitting at is large oak desk in his home office looking over some briefs he had brought home for review. He had left the double doors opened so he could hear when Tetra returned. He went across the hall to the game room to get a Perrier from the small refrigerator before starting his review of legal documents. 'RING, RING, "hello" "dad what's going on?" I said taking the time to call before my shower. "Son, how are you doing? settling down after that big day" he asked. "Glen is still here but as much as I can you know" I replied. "Mom home? "Not yet son she went shopping, do you need to speak with her?" "No not really, I do plan to come soon though dad" I said. "How's things with Jillian? dad asked. Things seemed a little tense at dinner the day before graduation", he confessed. "Dad that's a story I'd love to tell you. You might help me understand" I said laughing through each word. "Well I don't know if I'm the one to give advice I hope so son I'll try", his dad said being honest. "Hold on son, running back to the kitchen putting the Perrier on the center island of the enormous kitchen and walking over positioning a tall bar stool on the other side of the counter. He took a glass from the cabinet over the sink and poured the Perrier into it picked up the phone receiver, sat to get comfortable on the stool and said "o.k. son I ready let's talk." Billy started with the package he had received the week before. He told his dad he had received the bible he gave Dorca years ago in elementary school. He shared with him about how the name had been changed in it from Billy to Dorca on the bible inscription. And to really make matters worse it was sent to Jillian. I don't know how that happened, he said. "Go on son, David was listening intently. "dad the letter, remember the letter you signed for months ago, I had mom overnight it to me last week" "you just got that son, what was in it?" I didn't tell mom this dad but it was from Edith Williams, she knew that. But I didn't disclose any of the contents with her I wanted to discuss it with you first I told him. Edith was confessing to be Dorca's real grandmother and she confessed and" "hold on Billy fax me a copy of the letter as soon as possible I'd like to read it for myself'. Then we can decide from there" David told him. "Sounds great" it's in my safe deposit box I'll get it Monday when I return to the office". And on a lighter note I said laughing I've got girl trouble" "girl trouble" David repeated, "yeah Dad to many" I teased. Dad and I laughed together it was good for us both. I shared the story of Jilly's friend Kelly and Lena. I liked Lena I just want Kelly to go away" I confided. "Well son be careful, their easier to get than to get rid of and unfortunately, I speak from experience. And on advice to you change your locks or move" he added smiling. Dad and I hadn't really talked like that since I left home for college. I thanked him for being there for me and son regarding Dorca and that letter I'm not going to comment at this time. We will keep this from Tetra until we find out what's going on. I sure don't want her worrying needlessly. David laughed but he was concerned for his son. Billy I'm going to pray and you do the same" he told him. But I will call you back soon. And we'll talk again. "I love you son and I'll give your love to your mom when she arrives and son enjoy life have fun and be safe" David dad told him. I will dad goodbye" David sat in the kitchen for a while thinking about their conversation. Tears had formed in his eyes and started rolling down his face. He was thinking this was happening to Billy because of him. All the sins he had committed. If only he would have been there for him growing up. "Dear God he cried out!" rescue us David pleaded. Deliver us from this dilemma. He reached and got a paper towel from over the sink took his water glass and went back to his office across the hallway that faced the kitchen. He sat in his office study looking around at the memories and accomplishments Tetra had displayed so elegantly on the walls. Sitting in his leather executive chair David realized how quickly the years had gotten away. He had graduated Yale in 1972 with his BA, and later attaining his master's in law with his successes as a businessman later. He thought about how he was in college, and how Tetra stood by him when he didn't deserve it so many times. He looked at the pictures of Billy's life over the years it filled him with regret of not being there. Turning to his desk his pen rolled off the desk and onto the floor under the desk. I'll move it later he thought. He opened one of his desk drawers to get another pen and saw the drawing he had placed there years ago. It was a drawing that was given to him by a young child he had met while trying to find Tetra and Billy at a hospital. He began to remember when Billy was that age. All the pictures he drew for him. He somehow wanted him that age again so he could protect him. He folded the child's drawing again and placed it back into the drawer. Those precious years had slipped from him. He sat silently praying for Billy and their conversation. Justin hadn't caused a riff. It was awkward seeing him though thank God for Tetra's understanding. Justin was kind enough to let Billy have his day with us David thought. Justin did make himself scarce at the graduation. I think he felt the awkwardness too. Your mistakes never go away, but thank God he forgives them. My son needs me now and I don't know what to do. Lost in thought he heard "hon, honey; I'm home Tetra yelled coming in with her arms filled with shopping bags.

David startled, jumped up from his chair and bumped the picture of Billy and Dorca that was sitting in a frame on the bookshelf knocking it to the floor and breaking the glass. "My God what's happening Tetra yelled running in from the hallway. David calming her down and coming to grips with the moment said; "I accidentally knocked over one of your frames Tet" we're going to need a new one". "No problem she said gently hugging and kissing David after knowing the problem. She went into the kitchen closet got the broom and dustpan and began sweeping up the broken glass. David placed the picture on the desk. That girl has a smile that's unforgettable" David told Tetra. "It always seems to be trying to say something. "Yes, she does, Tetra agreed, "but I hope she is out of Billy's life she replied not knowing the conversation Billy had shared with him. "Billy called he's visiting soon" David shared with Tetra. "Good" maybe he'll get some rest" Tetra didn't know the half of it and he was not the one to tell her David reasoned. David looked again at the photograph. Her smile looks so much like the young lady he saw in Maine he thought her hair was different but her smile was a perfect match. We all have doubles he conceded. Besides she had a small child with her that surely couldn't be her. But we had to find Dorca and bring closure for all of us especially Billy. 'Honey Tetra asked, mind if we go out to dinner, I really don't feel up to cooking after that long weekend we had and after Mrs. Laine helps me with these packages, I've given her the rest of this week off'. "Tetra if you're asking, I'm up for it, I'll even make reservations, got any particular place in mind he asked. "Just pick one" she said leaving the study with her arms filled with packages. "Just pick one".

CHAPTER 22

A night to remember

I quickly showered and went downstairs to meet Glen and Jillian. Jilly was putting my omelet on the plate it was still hot. The toast hash browns and jelly was in the table's center and I got the glasses for juice or milk. "Jillian did you make coffee? I asked "yes how many cups do we need? she asked taking them from the cabinet. She poured coffee for all of us and put the coffee pot back on the counter. "Jillian you're spoiling my man", Glen teased. Do you do this all the time?" "Only when he lets me" Jillian answered. But he does return the favor. "Eat you guys. I said the food is getting cold" And with a quick grace over the breakfast meal we began to eat. After we had finished Glen and I helped Jillian clean the kitchen and put the dishes in the dishwasher. "What's on the tube? Glen asked. After a meal like that I just want to kick back and enjoy it." I located the remote and we sat around watching old movies, game shows and making small talk in Jillian's presence. I liked Jillian's company but she was smothering me and this weekend I just wanted to be with my boy! Glen and I just sat around doing the man thing and she just stayed right there under me. "Remember Billy when television used to sit on the floor Glen said looking at the wide screen hanging on the wall. "Yeah man technology has come a long way," I said. Jillian loved board games of any kind. Glen and I played scrabble with her and turned down monopoly. We'd played that game all night before. She was in heaven and Glen and I had other plans. I was enjoying her company sharing it between her and Glen. So that later I hoped she would understand. But Jillian wanted to be married and have a white picket fence and I couldn't give it to her now. Glen looked at his watch it was 4pm and he had been there for a while well most of the day. "Billy man thanks for everything breakfast and lunch was great guys" but I have some things to do and finish getting packed I leave tomorrow for Florida. Jillian ears perked up. She liked Glen but she liked him better in Florida. Tomorrow not today?" Jillian teased. "no Jillian, Billy and I haven't seen all of Cambridge yet" Glen teased back "Do you think that's possible? He added to get a reaction from Jillian. "Billy's a grown man even though he doesn't always act it, she said knowing she would love to have control of all aspects of him but really didn't. Jillian had made me look bad in front of her parents on our first official meeting and her so called friend Kelly. I was not going to let her steal this weekend with Glen from me. "Jillian, I respect you and thank you for all you've done today but I really would like to go out with Glen tonight, I told her before he heads back to Florida. "Just you?' she asked. Yes, Jillian we have a lot to talk about, men talk" I teased standing behind her hugging her around her tiny waist. Glen now trying to defuse what he started "I have enjoyed the hours I spent with you today Jilly also and I'll get him back in one piece I promise" he said to her walking over giving her a big friendly hug. Glen turned to leave "I'll meet you at 6:30 bro" later "Later Jillian take care "hugging her has he went out the door again. Jillian liked Glen she just wanted him with a steady girl or better a wife. He and I together single was dangerous and she knew it. I knew this conversation with Jillian and I wasn't over.

Jillian wasn't happy that I was going out alone again with Glen. I had spent the whole weekend with him what about her? I had shared with her earlier this month that Glen was coming for graduation and that we would be spending time together since we hadn't been out with each other since Glen's sister Brianna's wedding. So my attitude to this was she'd have to get over it. "I'll stay here tonight Billy' Jillian finally said. "Why Jillian" I'll probably be in late". She didn't say anything else she walked over and gathered the glasses from the crystal coasters and went into kitchen washed them put them away and went and sat on the couch under a soft velvety throw blanket watching television. I looked at her and went and sat next to her Jilly you can't keep doing this to yourself. I'm not ready for marriage" but babe you are welcome to stay here." Somehow this said to her I was still going to just not tomorrow. I called to let Glen know I was on my way. I had put on my chocolate brown Bill Blass suit with matching brown Stacy Adams shoes. Jillian insisted on picking the tie for the outfit. A quick stop by the coffee table where Jillian was holding my platinum watch with the alligator strap, I was ready! "Jillian I'm off, she had walked in the guest bedroom to get a pillow or something. She walked out holding out her arms. "You look and smell good enough to eat! she said "Obsession one of my favorite fragrances on you. I'll be here when you get back" she cooed. I remembered when that would send shivers up my spine. "That's sweet I told her embracing what was. She held on and I found a meaningful kiss to leave her with. She loved me and as much as I knew I loved her too. I knew it but I couldn't let her go through what mom did. "Goodnight" and out the door I went. I had traded my Ford Mustang for a silver S type Jaguar. Jillian stood watching from the window as I left for the evening. I rounded the corner and dialed Glen's cell phone "Glen, did you get tickets for the show? "Everything is covered man where are you?" "on my way". We were going to see the Lion King live from New York. Lena and Lexia has a friend performing in it and he also had provided us with back stage passes. Lexia was already with Glen. So I went by the Sheraton Inn to pick up Lena. I entered and called her from the front desk. "I'll be right down she said. I sat in the high back chair in the lobby waiting for her. "Let's go she said. I turned to see legs, legs, and more legs Naomi had nothing on her. She was wearing Sergio Rossi laced high heeled shoes and black tights. When I got to her face, I could see her hair was tastefully messy in a funky hairstyle and her bodice was draped in a black silk georgette lace-up blouse with puffed sleeves. "oh, my was I feeling guilty!" "Not" My obsession cologne had better be working overtime. Good evening pretty lady" I greeted her "hi Billy" she said sounding so inviting. The plans were to meet Glen and Lexia at the small coffee shop across the street from the theater and pulling up everything so far was going well.

"Ring, ring it was Jillian's cell phone she always leaves it on when she stays at my residence, she told me. She didn't want to give certain friends of hers my number. "Hello" she answers "hi' Jillian this is Doris your neighbor, are you busy? "Hi Doris, no just sitting watching television at the moment". What can I do for you? Jillian asked. I was wondering if you could keep Davie for a couple of hours. I have a test in one of my evening classes" She replied. "I'd loved to Doris I'm just sitting by myself." Should I bring him to you?" Doris asked. I'm not home right now I'll be by in an hour is that okay? Jillian asked. "That's perfect if it works for you" "see you then Jillian said. Doris Wright was Jillian's neighbor. She came a year after us and she was taking some night courses to make up units she said for getting started late at Radcliff. She also went during the day when her son David was at school. Her parents had paid her tuition and she was taking full advantage of it besides Jillian liked his company. He was a very active three years old and I think Jillian liked to practice with him. She took him shopping and to amusement parks and birthday parties. She spent a lot of time with this little guy at her house and mine too. She loves it when I tease her about being jealous of him. Since Jillian was going to be at my house that's where Davie was going to be also. She went to the store and got some special snacks and juice for them to enjoy for the evening. "Oh yes popcorn" Jillian told the clerk has she purchased the groceries for the night hurrying over to the shelf getting a box of buttered popcorn. Before going back to Billy's house, she stopped at her house and got the games she had stored in her closet they usually play with to keep him entertained for 2 hours. Then on to Doris's across the street "Knock knock walking up to Doris's home. "Come in" Doris replied. Jillian took a liking to Doris also. She admired the fact she was raising her son and not giving up on her education. So, Jillian would help where and when she could if Doris would ask her. It was not often enough Jilly would say. "Thanks Jill, I'll be back in two hours should I pick him up at your place? she asked. "I'm going to be at Billy's she said so I'll bring him home" Jillian informed her. "That's fine. They had done this so many times over the years. I watched this little child grow up with Jillian. She was going to miss him when she returned to New York. They got in the car and off they went. "Ring, ring," Jillian, this is Kelly, how are you? "I'm fine" Jillian replied. "Just calling to let you know I got home safe and I enjoyed my stay" Kelly added. "That's good, Kel is there anything else I'm kind of busy" Jillian told her. "I left a message on your home machine". "Are you at Billy's?" "Yes Kelly" tell him I said hello". "bye Kelly" Jillian said pressing the button to disconnect. Jillian and Kelly had met when the two of them worked a Macy's in New York. They were in constant competition in everything. Kelly is vindictive and befriended Jillian because she had more money than the other girls in their high school circle. "That's Jilly's story" And she saw she could easily manipulate her. And that's Billy's story" Though they are total opposites Jillian is always kind too her. She says she knows the real Kelly! Well after the other night he knew the real Kelly too. "Come in Davie," Jillian said opening the door to Billy's home coming in with her arms filled with goodies for the evening. Davie ran right in and made himself at home. Davie and Jillian knew the layout of his place better than he did. They had been there often. A few times he's come in and stepped on a toy or picked up a teddy bear from the sofa more than once he'd admit. Jillian was going to make someone a good wife and certainly a good mother. I had warned her of how attached she had gotten to Davie. She would always say they're not far from New York I can always come and visit. Jillian was ahead of the game contemplating a job offer in New York but was waiting to see what Billy's plans were. She was doing everything right in his book! Why didn't he want to get married? Only he knew! He would not and could not allow her to be hurt, because William Parker was not ready for marriage. Jillian and Davie played for about an hour before he became sleepy. It was eight 0 clock and nearing his bedtime. She wiped him off and put his little pajamas on him and sat him on the sofa next to her under the big fluffy throw. She gathered all his things and sat them by the big armed chair. It would still be another hour before Doris returned. She turned the channel to cartoon network and after two or three cartoons Davie was fast asleep. She looked at him and covered his little feet with the warm throw and put her arms around him so he would feel safe. Time went by quickly.

Jillian sat looking at old movies on the television. She had taken David home and was trying to find something to occupy her time until Billy returned. She went in the kitchen and made a large banana split from the snacks she had purchased for Davie. "Lots of whip cream and nuts' she said to herself has she stood looking at the clock it was now 10: 0 clock. She ate every bit and knew she would surely be hitting the gym this week. Again, on the sofa she tossed and turn trying to stay awake but she was truly tired especially after that work out with Davie. Conceding she went up showered brushed her teeth put on her pajama's looking at the clock "11:30 pm she thought maybe he will be home soon and headed to bed.

Billy and Lena left the car with the valet and headed to the coffee shop. Sitting right in front of the quaint little shop was Glen and Lexia. "Hi' guys they said as they entered "lattes before the show?" "Sounds great" I said ordering for Lena and I. We pulled up two chairs to the small little table where Glen and Lexia were sitting. They had to stand allowing the chairs to fit. I gave Glenn a nod on his attire from "Cole" and Lexia was wearing a small black sweater with her mid drift showing complemented by a black skirt hinting to her knees. It fit the curves tastefully and her black Giorgio sandals were striking as she stood to allow us to pull the chairs closer. 'Sis what's happening" she asked looking at Lena. "We're all packed and ready for California. Phillip called we fly out tomorrow at noon" she told her. "That's wonderful Lexia said "I've been waiting for this day all my life!". The four sat talking and enjoying their latte mixtures before the show. The girls shared about their journey from Brooklyn to New York and now LA. "I'm letting nothing stop me Lexia said. I'm ready! "Good luck to both of you two ladies" I said holding Lena's hands in acknowledgement. Billy and Glen could sit and not say much but say everything with their actions to each other. They had learned to communicate with one another without saying anything. Soon the couples got up and went across the street to the theater. The show lived up to its billing. It was great! They went back stage after the show to meet Lexia and Lena's friend 'Larry' and got an autograph from him. He ran over and hugged them. "Those outfits are to die for girlfriend" he said as only he could. But unfortunately, he seemed more interested in Glen and I than in them. Again, we all had a good laugh after thanking him for the autograph and heading out to party. After the show we walked out and waited for the valet to bring the cars around and off we went. We guys had found a wonderful night spot called "Omega's. It was a perfect place with a mischievous atmosphere. It was very retro and very funky. "This is hip, hot and totally GQ Lexia voiced. Let's go in" dragging Glen by the hand. They had everything in one place we drank sociably, mingled and danced the night away. At 1:00 am we went over to the restaurant that was adjacent to the posh establishment and had dinner. I was enjoying myself. I had convinced myself not to feel guilty. I felt I needed this. I had been under a lot of pressure, with finals and then that letter and package. I didn't want to think about any of it I was just letting my hair down. Jillian and I didn't go out a lot anymore like when we first met. The only difference I thought with marriage and our relationship is that there wasn't a ring. We sat at home a lot. Glen could dance and I loved to move around on the floor. He surely had found a partner with Lexia they stayed on the floor most of the night. Lena was an excellent dancer too and me oh! I wasn't bad I could hold my own. After a few dances they sat in a booth talking, Lena with her head on Billy's broad shoulder. He put his hand on her face and stroked her cheek. "Tired?" he asked her "a little" she said. "I haven't done this in a long time I really enjoyed it" he added. Glen and Lexia hit the floor one more time before announcing they were leaving "we're out guys" Glen announced. I gotta get up early he confided. Throwing his Kenneth Cole jacket over his shoulder and his arm around Lexia they headed for the exit. Lena and I wasn't far behind paying for dinner leaving a sizable gratuity and on our way. To our surprise Glen and Lexia was still waiting for their car. Seems everybody was coming out now at the same time and every valet was busy moving cars. It was close to 2am or maybe 3am. I was glad I was able to spend time with Glen. He and I hugged in boy fashion as we all ways did and we whispered in one another's ear "keep praying" that's from our upbringing.

Jillian woke up again and walked downstairs to the kitchen to get some water a quick trip to the bathroom and back upstairs and jumped back in bed. She did notice it was 1:30 am and Billy was still not lying beside her. He was still out with Glen who thank God was leaving tomorrow she thought has she closed her eyes again.

The couples had secured their cars and headed in the direction of a goodnight's rest well what was left of it. Billy drove up to the Sheraton and parked his Jag in a secure space. "I'll walk you up" he told Lena. Is that "okay?" he asked "That's fine I'd like that, she replied. They walked in arm and arm laughing and talking about their wonderful evening quietly all the way to the elevator pushing the button for the fifth floor. "We're here" Lena said walking off the elevator room 511. Taking the door card from her purse and putting it into the lock "click the door opened. "Coming in" she asked holding him by his hand. "If it's alright with you" he remarked. Seductively she said "please come in" smiling and pulling him into her grasp......

CHAPTER 23

Confronting Katherine

Justin was so glad he had finally got a chance to meet his father David Parker, his brother Billy Parker who found out who Justin was by an accidental meeting when Tetra Billy's mother was in the hospital in Maine for food poisoning. Billy remembered Justin's name from a birth certificate he had found under his father's bed years ago. After making a phone call to Justin and meeting with him. It was confirmed that this is his younger brother. Billy and Justin had different mothers but the same father. Whoa! That is a lot to think about Justin thought. Billy was glad he had found Justin and began immediately building a relationship with him. Justin was glad to have an older brother. And finally answer a lot of questions he needed answers too. They had exchanged phone calls and visit's over the months and had learned some things about each other. Justin had just attended Billy's graduation and he certainly liked having an older brother to share interest with. He had taken Ariel his girlfriend to Cambridge to meet him too. They were building a relationship that was flourishing daily and Justin still had not shared with his mother Katherine Heller about it. "I KNOW I WILL HAVE TO TELL HER SOMEDAY, BUT HOW? Justin sat in the campus parking lot after class and reminisced over the past months. As he drove out of the parking lot leaving Bowdoin College on his way home one day, he decided to call Katherine his mother. "Ring, ring, ring, hello, the voice came across the line. "Kat this is Justin are you sleep?' he asked because her voice sounded groggy. "Yeah I just got in from Mardi Gras in New Orleans" a little why?" Katherine asked him. "I was thinking of stopping by. I have the day off and wanted to talk with you" Justin replied. "Well is it important Justin?" "Maybe not I'll talk with you later bye," feeling a little neglected he pushed the button on his cell phone and disconnected the call. He readied himself to exit the freeway and go in another direction toward home. "Ring, ring, hello he said, "Justin are you coming by?" Silence he didn't say anything. "Justin Parker I'll see you in an hour! Katherine said then hung up. An hour? Justin wasn't an hour away. He decided to head to Kat's house going slowly since she had stated about an hour. He drove on and took the exit off to Valden Creek. A neighborhood filled with track homes three and four bedrooms. He had grown up here and watched all the newer homes constantly being built around them. He passed the high school where he went just 2 years ago and now, he was a college man. He had lots of time and decided to go in a different direction to see the elementary school. With time to waste he turned the block. Down two more and there it set off to the right. It looked so tiny. The district had kept it up pretty well despite budget cuts. He parked his car on the side near the playground and got out. He walked over to the small swing set. His legs were much too long to even swing. It made him chuckle. This is where life started for him, he thought has he dangled his legs so close to the ground. Justin sat there reminiscing over his life. He sat looking around at the small playground that used to be so enormous to him. Sitting there his mind wondered over the years. And time had went swiftly "oh my I gotta go" he told himself looking at his watch. Has he rounded the corner to Katherine's he saw a car leaving, "Oh he thought that's why she said an hour". Katherine was still a single woman with a very active life and he knew it. She loved and cared for her son, who since growing older had made a life separate from hers. He had moved into a small apartment close to campus with his girlfriend and though he never said wasn't pleased with her lifestyle. Walking up to the door knocking "Kat, Kat, Justin said again seeing the door was ajar. "Dan is that you?" came a voice from the back of the house. "No Kat it's Justin" walking in and closing the door behind him. Clearly and hour was not enough time. Katherine came walking from the back with her long silk gown and pink bunny slippers on. Her hair was frizzy all over her head. "Come in, come in Justin she said heading back to her room to make herself more presentable he hoped. Justin headed to the kitchen to make coffee because it was obvious, she would need it. Emerging again from her room she had a luxurious satin robe that hung to her ankles and her hair was now pulled back in her signature ponytail and of course her bunny slippers came too. "Hello son, how are you? she asked walking over to him to hug and kiss him. "I'm fine Kat, how are you? Justin replied heading to the kitchen to get the coffee. "I made coffee for you". "Thank you Justin I need it" she confided. They sat in the den and shared coffee and light conversation. Katherine explained she had gotten in at about 1:30 am this morning from vacation in New Orleans and needed another week just to recuperate from it. "New furniture Kat? Justin asked looking around the den. "Oh yes I'm having the whole house redone eventually she told him. "That's good it still looks nice in here, he told her. "I know but it was dated" Kat confided. I don't think I've changed anything in here since. She paused oh! I don't remember when," she smiled. "How's school and work? Katherine asked running her hand over Justin's wavy hair. "Kat, everything is fine" he said "are you sure?" she asked "something seems to be on your mind." she added. "Oh, hold on", Katherine said "one minute" getting up from her soft comfy chair and going to the room to get her purse. She sat back down and handed him a check as she did every month. "You could have sent that Kat like you always do, that's not why I stopped by" Justin replied. "Well you're here and besides stamps have gone through the roof" she joked. "Thanks Kat reaching over and hugging her. She had a good job working in the school district so she made sure Justin didn't need for anything. And besides he was tired of fighting a losing battle with Kat when he refused to take the money. Tetra Parker had set up a trust fund for him at the time when she found out about him. But until a few months ago Justin never knew who she was or what she had to do with him. Finding out he was her husband's son she had her lawyer take care of the matter Kat had told him. Katherine had shared everything with him after he was old enough to understand. She had offered the trust fund to Justin when he became eighteen on his graduation day but he chose to wait for it after he received a scholarship from the high school he attended. He was aware of how much it was but had bigger plans for it like medical school he told her. "By the way Kat" here's my new cell number" he said and handed her a small piece of paper. I don't want you to panic when you can't get me". 'New number, "I'll program it in my phone later" looking around she said, "mine is in my bedroom." Justin got up and went into the kitchen after refilling Katherine's cup for the second time. He opened the refrigerator and made himself a ham sandwich and returned to the den with sandwich and soft drink in hand. It was noon. "Can I get you something Kat? He asked. "No Justin I'm fine some rest is all I need, pulling her legs over the large ottoman sitting in front of her. Justin took a bite from his sandwich, chewing with his mouth full, he said "Kat I met someone". What Justin? "Don't talk with your mouth full" she replied, still trying to correct a much talked about behavior. Justin repeated, "I met someone" "who Justin where's Ariel? thinking he was referring to a girl. "No!' Justin told her, 'I met William Parker". After a pause" "William Parker you mean Billy Parker!" she asked surprised. "One in the same" Justin replied still finishing up his sandwich. "How did you find him? "Well actually he found me or we happened upon each other" Justin confessed. "Last year his mother was in the hospital and my name came up. I had to x-ray her and Billy put two and two together." "LAST YEAR JUSTIN! How long have you known about this and what happened to Tetra? She had now taken her feet off the ottoman and was sitting up looking directly at Justin. "Is Tetra alright? Kat asked concerned for she was. They had both went after the same man. She reasoned Tetra had the upper hand. She was already engaged and eventually married David Parker. But Katherine was in love and didn't want it to end. "Mrs. Parker is fine I just saw her two weeks ago" he told her. "She was here last year looking at property and got food poisoning but she's fine now" Justin confided getting up to take his plate in the kitchen. "A week ago! Katherine repeated" "Yes Kat at Billy's graduation". "Billy's graduation!" Katherine was repeating everything Justin said for she was surprise and a bit shocked at what he was telling her. "Billy invited me to his graduation" Justin continued "he graduated from Harvard University in Cambridge and he flew me down to be a part of his big day" "Billy graduated from Harvard! Not far from here! is that where they live?" She asked curiously. "That's where Billy lives, he has a nice pad too Justin added. "So, tell me, tell me? Katherine was now intrigued and didn't know what to ask. "Kat, Justin began, "Billy called me back after Mrs. Parker was released from the hospital, she was only there three days". "About a month later I guess he wanted to meet with me. I had teased him about our names when we met in the hospital about being related, and it piqued his curiosity" "He's a lawyer you know! He told me he had found the birth certificate you had sent to his father's house and the rest is history. 'Did he ask about me?" "Well Kat he asked if Katherine Heller was my mom to confirm it, yes I guess he did" Justin told her. "And after I called him back, he invited Ariel and I to visit Cambridge to which we did about three months ago". "Justin you never told me" Kat replied sitting now wiping her tears. 'Kat you're always so busy and besides I didn't know how you would take it," Justin added, "and I like having a big brother!" "Did he mention David?" she finally asked. As caring as he could Justin held her hand. "David and Mrs. Parker live in another state Kat, they live together." Katherine looked up at Justin. When Tetra left years ago, I thought things were over between them" she confessed. Then David left and sold his big house in the Hampton Hills about four or five years ago then he left. I guess he chose her again" she confided to her son. Justin was feeling Kat's hurt but he didn't want it to come between his relations he had built with his brother. He stood for a moment and embraced her. "Kat, he showed me the red cap picture of him and I showed him mine, Justin finally said. Katherine smiled remembering that day fondly. "That's good, that's good wiping her eyes and patting Justin on his hands. She stood up walking around in her den "they're still together" she said quietly to herself, I didn't think he could love anyone that much! "They seem to be very happy" Justin told her. We had a very good time at Billy's house. Everyone was there. "Did you talk with David? 'Yes, I did I talked to both of them he and Mrs. Parker they wished me well in my studies." Justin was now standing and feeling very good about his accomplishments in life. "Kat, these people have been nothing but nice to me, I like them and they like me" Justin said feeling justified in his situation. But, that's your father Justin, they should be nice! Katherine said feeling left out. Forcefully she asked? "Did he even acknowledge the fact?" "No, not really, but I was there! Justin replied. "I understand that things don't happen overnight, right Kat?"' "I have Billy in my life now and he acknowledges me." I know it will probably take David a lot longer if he ever does at all" but that's alright I have Billy and for now that's enough." Justin stood up to leave "I have the day off from the hospital I'm going home to study" he told her and thanks Kat" referring to the check she had given him. 'TELL ARIEL HI" Kat yelled out the door behind Justin who came back to the door to acknowledge "David's a nice man mom" bye and got in his car and drove away. Katherine sat in her living room after Justin left. She was glad Justin had finally got a chance to meet David his real father. What he said about things not happening over night was right but she didn't want to accept it. Truthfully over the years none of the other guys had added up. No one since David had stolen her heart. He was her real first love. If only things would have worked out she thought. Justin had taken meeting him better than she had envisioned. He was a bright young man so much like David she remembered. She was a goggled eyed young girl like all the rest in love with her handsome boss. She was in the secretarial pool. Quickly moving up to executive secretary and then taking traveling assignments to the envy of the others in the large office pool. She fell in love! for him until now she thought Tetra Raleigh was just another notch in his belt. She knew he was engaged to one of his college mates. But that didn't stop Katherine she had beat a lot of odds in life. David was a big tease and would always flirt with all the women in the offices. Katherine thought no one in her right mind would turn him down. She probably wasn't the only one. He wined and dined her on their traveling meetings and told her she was special. He was perfect after all his family owned the business and others statewide. When they announced in the office about the wedding Katherine was devastated. Soon it was apparent that he was getting married to Tetra Raleigh after she came through the office showing off her large flawless diamond engagement ring. Katherine was furious and decided she was going to get pregnant. She had met David's dad and surely this is not what he wanted. Marrying out of his race was unheard of. On her next business trip with David she put her plan into action. Knowing she knew how to get what she wanted in their alone time together, thinking that would end the talk of marriage. She never complained about what was happening. She politely played the other woman until she got what she thought she wanted. But it didn't and she was left alone with a child and unfortunately a new assignment. Katherine went back to her bedroom crying throwing her bunny slippers aside of the wall. She lay down and went to sleep. She should have been happy but she wasn't....

CHAPTER 24

Safe

The chill was still on the morning air when Billy left the Sheraton Hotel parking garage.

He had bid Lena Morgan a safe journey and success in her new endeavor and left very earlier in the morning. With hugs and kisses he said goodbye. Walking passed the hustle and bustling of patrons arriving through the main lobby of the hotel he made is way out. Outside he put his overcoat on and noticed he had forgotten his tie. The tie Jillian had picked for him to wear. Go back "no" it will be a small thing in what he's going to face coming in at this time Billy thought. Directly in front there were vans loading and unloading passengers bringing a new start to what seemed to be a busy day already, a nod of "hello' to the bellhop and on across the street to the secured spot where his Jag was parked for the night. Handing the attendant his parking stub securing his car and off he went. Billy located his hand-held cell phone in his center compartment console immediately noticing all the messages from Jillian. As he drove, he listened to every message after the third or fourth one they all sound the same "bleak", the last one came in at 1 :30 am and it was now the next day. He put down his cell phone and called Glen from his car phone. "Ring, ring" "hi guy" are you still living? Glen teased. "I'm on my way home now it's 8 am here, did you get off ok". I asked knowing he had and early flight. "Yeah man I slept all the way. My flight left out at 6am. Good flight though just touched down and hour or so ago". It's just 6am here in Florida so I have a little time before I head into the office" Glen replied. Continuing our conversation Glen commented "coming from that weather to this humid climate ain't no joke! with a smile in his voice as he said it. You'd better have you wardrobe to-get-her for the change! he added. "Glen man, do you think you'd ever see Ms. Morgan I mean Lexia again? Billy asked. "Can't say she was a fun girl out for a good time and we sure did that" But I don't know man what about you? Glen asked. "I'm not sure, maybe the same day to day, Lena definitely seems to have her head on straight" I told him. "I'm headed to Jillian right now who is in my house and probably in my bed!" "Man what? She's at your place? Glen questioned somewhat surprised. You know it!" I said "Man this sounds like the girl is seriously in love with you!" You had better be careful! Glen warned. "I know she is and she wants to get married and I don't" I confided. "California is a long way from Cambridge so if you get through this day maybe?" No! If you get through this morning CALL ME! Glen mocked. "Man, for real though, I truly enjoyed our time together" Glen added and I hope things work out between you and Jillian. "Me too man, me too. I expressed. "Be careful and take care of yourself we will talk soon bye "Glen said, disconnecting his phone. And with that I was pulling into my driveway. Jillian's car was parked out in front so there was no doubt she was still there. I got out threw my coat over my shoulder and looking up at the window that looked out to the street to see if Jillian was watching. I had thought about going to her house and sleeping but I couldn't continue to do this. I would have to face it and hoped it wouldn't hurt her to much. I really didn't want to hurt her but I don't want to get married either. Putting my key into the door I walked in looking around. I didn't see Jillian. I took a quick survey around downstairs. Then I heard something upstairs. With overcoat over my arm I headed up the stairs "just get it over with" I thought. The noise got louder as I got closer. Entering my room, I realized it was my shower, and Jillian was in it. I hurried back downstairs and quickly undressed throwing my clothes on the chair in the corner of my guest bedroom totally out of character. I took good care of my clothes. That will show her how tired I was I thought. I put my cell phone in visible sight after clearing all the messages on my side bed table and hurried to the bed and lay down. "Ring, ring" looking at the caller ID it was Jillian. I used a gruff morning voice and answered "Yes Jillian" "Where are you Billy?" she said sounding put out. "I'm in bed" I answered knowing this was not sounding good to her. "What! Whose bed are you in? She had started to cry. "Billy why do you, you know I love you! she continued." "Jillian, it's too early for this! I said sounding stern, knowing that this was all going to work for my good somehow. "I'd like to go back to sleep now" I said. She went into hysterics "don't you dare hang up this phone! I hate you! I hate you! "WHERE ARE YOU BILLY" she screamed "O.K. enough I told myself "I'm at home Jillian where are you?" "You're not home. I'm here at your house". "I know! you were sleeping like a baby when I came in so as not to disturb you, I went into my guest room." I lied with all the sincerity I could muster. I knew I would have to ask for much forgiveness on this one. But she wouldn't understand the truth right now. I convinced myself. Jillian came running down the stairs and into the room where I was. She looked at the clothes all mused on the chair and floor. She was still wiping her eyes they were red from crying. I felt bad, I felt her hurt. I can't continue to do this to her she, didn't deserve it. And I knew it. "She ran over and began pounding on me, and laughing. "You got me good!" she said. I had you lying up in somebody's hotel" she confessed. "Billy I ought." I pulled her in and kissed her passionately. She loved me back. She laughed and I laughed at the joke I had just played on her but inside I knew it was not a laughing matter. "Billy, I find nothing funny that you did this to me, she joked "you had better be glad I was not awake when you came in Mister!" lying beside me on the bed still fresh from her morning shower. "Breakfast for my night owl" she said mocking. "If you have time Jilly, you don't have to bother" I replied, I did, I really felt guilty. She reached over and kissed me again "I have time "French toast alright? She asked rolling out the other side of the bed and heading to the kitchen. "Jilly, I called to her "hold on I'm drying my hands I'll be there in a minute" she called back". "Yes" she sighed standing in the door with her arms up as not to dirty her hands again. "I love you" I said. She turned smiling as if she had just slept with me all night. She accepted that weak story. It didn't even have legs to stand on "alibi" there wasn't one. It was obvious Jillian was in love with me and for four years she was the only one, well she was the main one. God had given me another chance with Jillian. I thought, I had tried to listen to the small guiding voice but to do or not to do had gotten switched and twisted around I didn't know what direction I was going. There was only one thing I was sure of at this moment and that is I was home and in my own bed. After Jillian made breakfast, she left for her office kissing me and going happily out the door. She was working in town for Laney Mcormick and Fry. She was training with lawyers in her field of study. I had gotten out of bed kissed her as she left and sat at the table looking at the Cambridge newspaper and enjoying my last bite of French toast Jillian had prepared. I had placed my palm pilot on the coffee table after checking my schedule for the day. Suddenly my reminder buzzer went off. I walked over to check. Looking it read "fax letter to dad" "oh yes I thought I must get in a little early so I can go by my safety deposit box and get that letter to dad, gazing down at my watch. I removed my dishes from the table and ran upstairs to shower and get dressed for the day. As I stood in the shower I thought about Jillian? How she had talk to my mother and learned how to cook most of my favorite dishes. Some still needed work but she continued to try. The breakfast she had prepared this morning was great. I guess you could say very close to "Tetra Parker's" he smiled. Quickly finishing my shower and starting to get dressed I noticed Jillian had hung my clothes that I had purposely tossed in my guest room from the night before. I wonder if she noticed the tie was missing, I thought. She had purchased one of those tie rack things that when you push a button a rod would circulate around until you find the tie you wanted. Just like in the dry cleaners she told me. So, to answer the question I'm sure she's noticed it she just as not said anything about it yet. I pulled my wool double-breasted suit by "Abboud" from my closet and silk tie "Perry Ellis" replaced the platinum watch in the armoire and put on the signature series a few sprays of 'Joop' for the ladies and briefcase Monday and off I went. Dialing from my phone I called mom. "Ring, ring," You have reached the Parker residence came the answering machine. I hung up and said she's probably at church or out shopping I'll call her later. He had already tried her cell phone several times. Turning his radio up louder he rode into the office with Take Six and Shirley Caesar singing in his ear on his favorite gospel station. He had gotten a jump on Jillian in his career. The fact is he had started with another firm a year before graduation so he was now helping prepare minor cases and overseeing a few major ones. Billy was in private law or civil law someone might say. The firm he worked in handled a lot of their case matters out of court. He looked for the day when he'd take on that big case. But wasn't hurrying the process he'd wait until after he passed the bar exam. Walking into the Stellar Building in Cambridge where the firm was located on the tenth floor had become a routine. But first a stop by the safety deposit box area located on the first floor. Pass the security desk badge in. Behold! Shelves and shelves of boxes, looking and going straight to the area where his box was located in the secured area box 1144. Putting in his key and pulling out the safety deposit box taking it over to the desk to sit down and find the letter Edith Williams had sent him. He hadn't looked at the letter since he put it in there weeks ago. After he had read it over and over again, he brought it here for safekeeping. He was glad he had finally spoken to his dad about it, because he needed advice on what to do if anything. Looking through his important documents and papers was a picture of him and Jillian. "How did this get here? he thought. The picture was of him dressed like a clown. Jillian had talked him into taking Doris Wright's little boy to an amusement park and they had lots of fun with face painting and dress up. He dressed as Bobo the clown. It made the child laugh and it was fun he remembered. Shaking his head, he put the picture back in the box. He guessed it had got accidentally placed between some legal papers he had been working on from home. 'Here it is" he said finding the letter and putting it over to the side near his briefcase. Putting back his deposit box, grabbing his briefcase that now contained the letter, pass security and up to his office. "Good morning Mr. Parker" "good morning Andrea". Good morning could be heard by everyone as each entered into his work day." Good morning Bill" good morning O'Rielly ready for the meeting? "I am, I am' I returned the greeting. Monday's are usual one of the lighter days around here in the office. Walking into my office and sitting behind my desk I pulled the letter from my briefcase and began to read it again: Dear Billy, you're probably wondering, I read it to the end. Getting up walking over to the fax machine located in my office I dialed dad's fax number. After making a cover sheet I faxed it directly to his office. 'Sitting back down I called to let him know it was faxed. "Ring" "Ring" Mr. Parker's office. "Hi Verla is dad back from lunch yet? I asked. "Oh, hi Billy, how are you? she asked, "I'm fine just looking for dad. Verla will talk your head off in the morning. She was a very nice southern lady who worked the receptionist desk for the building. Mr. Parker, just went up a few minutes ago, would you like me to page him for you Billy?" she replied "I'll call up to his office again, thanks Verla" and have a good day' I told her hanging up. I called back on dad's private line again. "Good morning son" "good afternoon dad how was lunch?" "It was good, business lunch he replied "We got some good things down on paper" "I got the message you left for your mom" he went on to tell me she's at a women's convention in Dallas." "Go mom!" I said. She and at least a hundred women I know went down to support first lady Hathaway. She is teaching a session on "A woman God can use". And I understand that first lady Reed's session is 'Power and Praise." She's coming in from San Antonio with her group". "I spoke with her briefly yesterday she had just got there and everyone was settling in I'm sure I will talk with her tonight" he concluded. "Dad do give her my love," I said. "I will son I will". Mom was such an independent woman dad told me before they were married. That was one of the things he admired about her. He even went against his family to marry her. Marrying out of his race they say was unfounded but he loved his independent Black woman then and he loves her now. David was glad she had started going again and asserting her independence and openly expressing her love for God which both shared. "Dad I faxed that letter to you we talked about did you get it? Looking over at the fax machine, David got up "it's here I have it in my hand" I'll sit down at home tonight and read it and get back to you in few days" he said. "Sounds good dad". "Other than this son how's everything else? Dad asked. "Dad its Monday things are back to normal as they can get" I replied. "How's the women problem you're having?" he said laughing to lighten the conversation. "Well dad you know that Parker charm!" I teased back. 'Yeah" "Love you son, got a meeting to prepare for you take care and I will talk with you soon." O.k. dad love you too bye." I sat at the desk and thanked God for my parents. I was independent and self-sufficient but I sure needed them and were glad I could reach them when I did.

Jillian's birthday was in a few weeks and I had not thought of anything special for her. I knew about a bracelet or necklace. I had pretty much run the gamete of those kinds of things. Short of a ring I had purchased everything else in the jewelry line. I just wanted to surprise her and let her know I cared. A weekend in New York I thought, she'd love that! We could even take in a game. I'll call and have dad set it up. Just a relaxing weekend, just she and I would be a perfect present.

After my day at the office I went by the car wash and home to park in my garage. I had left it out the night before and nature wasn't very kind to it "those feathered kind". Glen had left a message for me when I got home so I called him back told him that incredible story he laughed and unfortunately, I laughed with him. He gave me a nickname of wild Bill "our joke he told me" you dodged a bullet man." After saying we'd talk as we always did and Glen was glad that I was o.k. I went up to change, unwind and relax.

Jillian had classes tonight so I knew this was truly a relaxing night for me. I put on my sweats and put a frozen dinner in my microwave. "Mom would have a fit if she knew I was eating like this! I thought to myself smiling. I didn't feel like cooking and sense it was only me, "Hungry man" here I come. I tuned the television to one of those reality shows and waited for the bell on the microwave to ding. "Ring, ring" "looking at my caller ID unknown, "hello" I said "hi Billy" "Lena, how are you?' 'DING' "I'm fine I just got settled in and I thought I'd call you" she said in her soft voice. "That's nice, how was your flight?" I was making small talk surprised she had called back so soon. "The flight is wonderful. The accommodations are fabulous and the view from this penthouse is spectacular she told me." I said, "it sounds like everything is going well, that's great!" "How is Lexia?" she's out already on the beach' Lexia's not wasting anytime, she confided. "I called to give you my number here because I do aim to keep in touch Billy!" she affirmed. 'That's wonderful, I was thinking you had forgot all about me when you stepped on that plane", I told her. I was starting to feel my Casanova side creeping in. "Forget you William Parker! not in a million years!" we must have talked an hour concluding to call each other frequently. I even promised a visit. I'd have to wait and see about that one I thought to myself. Lena aroused passions in me that I hadn't felt for a long time. And has much as I cared for Jillian, Lena was going to be a hard one to let go of and I don't know if I really wanted too.

CHAPTER 25

JFK Space Center

The next day from my office I called Glen to tell him about my plans with Jillian and see if Lexia had called him. Not getting an answer I called and left a message in his voicemail at his office. Glen worked at the mission control center of the John F. Kennedy Space Center in Florida. He as part of a crew has the major responsibility for planning the space shuttle launch, orbit, and reentry maneuvers. He shared with me he also helped to establish a daily plan that enables the crew to accomplish its flight objectives. He and I talk often. Glen had shared with me the last time we talked that NASA was launching a satellite soon and he would be very busy getting things ready. Since starting his job, he had found it very exciting and he says he is always learning something new. Interfacing with a lot of the high-ranking brass from the military and many political figures day to day keeps him on his toes. All business, so to speak with Glen during business hours, he was a totally different Glen when you would meet him out socially. He was equally the gentleman intelligent, and polite just relaxed and suave. He shared recently he had been chosen on the committee at NASA to develop the tracking and communications network for the space shuttle program also. This brother had it going on. When I visited him after he had been there for about a year he gave me an extended tour of the facilities. "Bill you called" he asked calling me back "sorry it took so long meeting with the brass" he said "what's up? Hi guy, just touching bases with you, I replied. "Lena called to say that everything was going well and gave me her number there in Los Angeles". "That's great" he said I haven't talked with Lexia "but that's alright, I've got my hands full here!" he said laughing regarding women. Glen and I didn't have a problem with meeting or getting women but getting rid of them was another story. Glen had this one that was stalking him. She would sit out in front of his deluxe townhouse every day. She knew and talked to all his neighbors telling them she was his girlfriend. "He finally pawned her off to one of his high school buddies in Austin and never went to that restaurant where she worked again. "I don't know yet what will come out of this encounter with Lena I'm thinking of paying her a visit in sunny California" I joked. "O.k. wild Bill he said laughing". You escape a bullet once already teasing about our night out in Cambridge. "No, but seriously "I'm taking Jilly to New York in two weeks it's her birthday" I told him. "That's right, he replied, my sec would have reminded me. Haven't missed sending her flowers in three years" he added. "Let me know when I can stop" he joked "I'm trying to keep you out of trouble" he laughed." Glen liked Jillian and thought she was a great girl he just knew me to well. He always sent both of us cards or flowers for our birthdays and other occasions. Thanks to his secretary's reminders. "Now you will let me know when I can start sending those flowers"! I mocked "Deal! Glen laughed. "You must let me know when one stays around long enough though!" I told him in our friendship loving way we talked with each other. "Man, I gotta go" good talking with you and you have fun with Jilly she's a good woman" Glen reminded me hanging up the phone. Jillian was spending the morning with Davie. She liked playing mommy and it gave Doris some time for herself. I called and asked her to meet me for lunch at "Ante Pasta" an Italian restaurant not far from my office. She agreed and said she'd see me a 12:30pm. Jilly had her morning with Davie mapped out. She had Disney movies and popcorn and games always around the house for him. He was becoming attached to her and her to him. She dressed him in a suit with a cute little bow tie and took him downtown to a photographer and had pictures made of the both of them together sharing the proofs with of course Doris and later with me. "These are very nice Doris said I'd like to have one of these where Davie's by himself" she remarked.

Oh! Jillian stated, looking at her questionably? "I'd like to send it to my mother she said. "Oh, I see, Jilly replied putting the proofs back in the envelope. Doris Wright was very scarce when I came around. I hardly saw her at all. Most of the time she was walking back to her house with Davie. I thought her behavior was strange until Jillian told me she had a scar on her face that she was embarrassed about. Jillian said "it took her a long time to show even me" she confessed. It only happened by accident one day I came in and she didn't have time to reach her scarf to cover her face. That's how they became better friends Jilly went on to say. She said it was from and abusive boyfriend and so she had a thing about men. But confided in Jillian she thought I seemed nice." thank God, she didn't seem like someone you wanted as an enemy.

I looked at my watch and hurried out of the building walking briskly down the street to get ahead of the afternoon crowd. I wanted to get to the restaurant and secure a table before the lunch crowd ensued. I requested a small table next to the window that looked out to the busy street of Cambridge and sat waiting for Jillian, ordering up two latte's for Jilly and I. I waited looking over the newspaper that was near in a holder by our table. We always enjoyed that togetherness we shared over coffee even in college. Looking out onto the street with the autumn leaves covering the sidewalk I saw Jillian walk by. She was wearing a red leather thigh cut jacket trimmed in black and white checks with a black and white checked knitted hat. Her black shirt barely showing below her jacket matched the black tights and knee-high black boots and gloves she was wearing. In she walked with this big smile on her face. "Hi sweetheart", walking over and gently kissing my lips while taking her gloves off to sit down. She was glowing! Davie could always put her in a good mood. "Hi to you" I said "and what has made your day so bright?" "Davie is so cute" she insisted "The photographer talked about him being a model!" he's so full of personality wait until you see the pictures!" she said with excitement. I showed them to Doris earlier". After getting her to sit down and settled from her morning we ordered our lunch and talked. Jillian was heading to her office when we finished our lunch. She was meeting with one of the attorneys from the firm in New York who wanted to hire her and give her a corner office with view of Trump towers. They were very impressed with her resume and her shared work she had done for them with her now firm Laney, Mcormick and Fry directly around the corner. Jillian sat down taking off her red jacket she was all business. Her black suit with the short-cropped jacket surely would make a statement with any male or female attorney. (She was certainly giving Boyle a run for her money) "I will be by around 5:30 or 6:00 0 clock she said I need to stop by my house first and pick up something. "It's not Davie is it" I said. "Nooo," honey just going to change into my jeans for comfort" she added.

I went back to the office to finish up for the day. Desmond had called and left me a message so I returned his call. "Desmond, how are you?" I asked glad to hear from him. "I'm settled in and there's lots of work, grand-dad hasn't done anything with this office since 1902" he said jokingly "Mossy is out right now looking at computers!" He continued. "Just funning, things are coming together he said. "Found a bright energetic young attorney to join my staff' until you come on board" he told me. "Yeah right" I said. "No really man there will always be a spot for you here you know that!" "Thanks Desmond man that's good to know". "Speaking of Mossy how's she adjusting to Kansas life?" "She'll be fine once we're in our home," he said. The weather caused a delay in the building but we should be in before Christmas" he reasoned. He sounds relieved. He had shared with me earlier about the tight quarters they were in. And the stress it was causing. Some of their things were still in boxes and in storage he had confided. "But how are things with you and Jillian? No wedding bells yet?" he teased. "Well you know if Jillian had her way we would have married before you and Mossy' I said laughing. "I'm taking her to New York next week for her birthday, and if I get out without the talk of a ring, I may consider it" I joked. "Man, thanks for the call and give Jilly our love" Desmond told me. "I'll do it bye. I had several briefs to get to the secretary so they could get typed and sent out. I sat down and got lost in my work. The time went quickly. I had asked that all my calls be held unless they were extremely important or family, all the receptionists knew that. Looking up I noticed it was 5: 15 pm and almost everyone was gone from the building. There was usually a mass exodus at 5 "o" clock. I had been so busy in my office with the door shut I had missed everything, quickly putting everything neatly away grabbing my briefcase coat on and headed out of the office bumping into Heidi the janitor for the building starting her shift. "Yello Mr. Parker, she said "I'm apologize for being in your way" she told me with her strong Spanish accent. "Not your fault, don't worry see you tomorrow" I said continuing out the door.

When I arrived, Jillian had already gotten there and started dinner." Hi' I said walking in sitting my briefcase near the staircase. The desk I worked from was upstairs. When I'm working, I don't want to be disturbed? I took off my overcoat and hung it in the large coat closet near the front door. "Hello sweetheart," walking in the kitchen to kiss her. "How was the rest of your day?" she asked. "Not bad busy but I can handle it" I teased. "What's for dinner?" I'm trying out a southern dinner she told me. She had gone to the store and bought chopped mint leaves, and lemons for lemon juice, curry powder cumin and coriander. My kitchen was turning into Tetra Parker's kitchen. "Well I thought if it doesn't turn out there is always Swanson's in the frig. I went upstairs changed, showered and let her do her thing. She was turning out to be a regular little Martha Stewart has she mixed all the ingredients for our meal. Jillian's country chicken and 'seasoned rice couscous" with baby green beans was worth a second helping. I helped her make us strawberry shortcakes with lots of whipped creamed for dessert. She was so proud of it and I was so proud of her too.

CHAPTER 26

Anxiety is not of God

David walked into an empty house. He had not done that in a long time he really missed Tetra. She would be coming over to him or he would be walking over to her for a kiss and hug after a long day at the office. He put his briefcase down in his study and went into his great room. He was going to watch a few of his favorite shows including a game. David had a late lunch so he figured he'd snack something a little later and go to bed. After going up changing into some clothes for relaxing he came back down to the great room to watch the game on the big screen television. In his large reclining chair, he put the phone receiver and remote in reach as not to be disturbed getting up, tuning the channel to the basketball game first before settling in. David had attended so many games as part of his job early on that now he just enjoyed sitting home watching a game every now and then without the crowds and fan fair. Of course, was a season ticket holder. He had his favorite teams and players. Some were even assigned to his agents. Nowadays he and Tetra frequently went to regular games but liked the playoffs games and rarely missed rooting on his favorite teams. With his evening Perrier next to him on the table he was set to watch the Spurs and the Lakers. "Ring, ring, "hello, David said answering he never looked at caller ID "Hello" "hi honey" Tetra said "oh honey it's you" David replied sitting up turning off the set as to give her his undivided attention. "I miss you" I didn't realize how big and empty this house is without you" he went on to say. "Dear I miss you too and I can't wait to get back to you and my bed" Tetra told him. "Oh, it's the bed you really miss" David teased. After they enjoyed a laugh with each other it was obvious they really missed one another. "Tetra asked "what did you have for dinner David? "Tet I had a late business lunch so I figured I'd have something a little later before I turn in" he told her lovingly. "nothing to late Dave it will upset your stomach" she added. Okay dear, he replied. Are you having a good time? "Wonderful time and a glorious time in the Lord! I'm being renew in my spirit and refreshed!" she said enthusiastically. "How did Phyllis say Wallace was doing?" He asked making reference to the Reeds. "She said "he's fine and Glen was down last weekend and spent a few days with them". "That's nice the boys have grown into some wonderful young men" David replied talking about Billy and Glen. "Speaking of young man have you spoken with Billy since you've been there?" David asked Tetra. "I got his messages, Tetra told him. I planned to call him later I have a few hours on our next break and I'll make it a point to speak with him" nothing wrong is it?" she asked

"No nothing that I'm aware of but I do think he misses you!" David replied. "I'll make a point to call him!" "And honey are you alright?" Tetra asked sounding concern. "I'm fine, just can't wait for you to come home it's been a long week" David confessed. "For me too dear, I love you and I'll see you soon" she said lovingly. "I love you too bye". Goodnight dear". Tetra hung up the phone and got down on her knees and thank God for what he has done and continues to do in her life. She prayed for her family and her church and specifically prayed for her companion lifting him up to God.

David smiled from within he was glad to hear from Tetra. It somehow shortened the week. "Thank God he said, reached for his remote turned on the television and continued to watch San Antonio beat up on Los Angeles.

"Ring, ring "I'm glad this isn't a playoff game he thought answering the phone. "Hello,' "Hello dad". How are you doing? Billy asked. "I'm fine now that I've heard from your mom" David said with a smile in his voice. "That's good I was just checking on you, I know this is your solo time! Making sure you were holding up" I teased. "I'm doing fine son. How are you? Staying out of trouble I hope?" that's what I told your mom anyway!" David added. "Yeah dad no problems there, thanks for looking out though!" I added. "Dad I have been trying to get tickets to a Knicks game for Jillian's birthday this weekend "no luck! He told him. "You headed to New York son?' that's a great present! Anderson has a sky box there shouldn't be any problems getting you two in" David added. "Dad that's good, but I was trying to get in the action close to the floor" Billy confided. "And you need Saturday's game" David asked. "If possible dad," "I'll see what I can do" David replied. "Dad? when will mom be home" I asked. "Billy your mom will be home Friday night in her own bed with me! he said. "I miss her too dad" I told him. Okay on the tickets then, thanks dad I love! I love you too son goodnight". David finished watching the game. The Spurs clinched a spot in the playoffs. David turned off his set and went down the hall to his study and got the letter Billy had faxed him. Now I'm unwound from this day I can think clear regarding this letter. He took the empty Perrier bottle to the kitchen to dispose of it. Looking into the freezer of the refrigerator Tetra had made some homemade frozen chicken pies. She will approve he thought putting one in the oven setting the timer button and going back to his study. He sat down and took the letter from his case and read: Dear Billy, you're probably wondering why I'm writing. I tried hard to raise Dorca, but something went terribly wrong. I'm Dorca's grandmother, her mother's mother. I allowed Dorca to grow up never accepting who she really was. The Demato' s were good people to us, a little different in lifestyle but she never wanted for anything. We always had the best of everything. They saw to that. Mrs. Demato a nurse who was grieved when Faye died in childbirth took her death very hard. She always thought there was more she could have done even when doctors shared with her it was hopeless. Mrs. Demato contacted me because she wanted to keep Dorca. Since Faye had not made provisions for anything, they were going to put her up for adoption. They would make her a ward of the court if I didn't step in. Mrs. Demato contacted me. She came to know Faye through her husband unfortunately. He apparently had her name in a little black book she had mistakenly found in his suit pocket. And apparently Faye knew him. That's how she came to the hospital. She had my name as next of kin and though I had not seen Faye in ten years at least I knew she was my daughter. I had failed terrible with Faye and didn't want another child to raise. Not at my age and besides I could not provide for myself on a nurse's salary let alone a newborn. My old man had left me with a pile of unpaid bills. She said that I could live with her and let her raise Dorca as her own. She may have had suspicions of who the father was but she never said. She explained she and her husband had tried having children but was not successful. They spoiled Dorca giving her everything toys, clothes, sending her to the best schools. I came across as mean and selfish when I spoke out but I could see what it was doing. As Dorca grew older her demands on them were sometimes outrageous and ridiculous. Not to mention the tantrums. I told her I would leave if she didn't stop harassing her parents the Demato's. And I let her grow up bitter and never really knowing me as her grandmother but her mom's maid. Small children don't see color. Dorca of course was lighter than I in skin tone. And since Faye never had the opportunity to put the father's name on the birth certificate, we never knew who he was. Mrs. Demato loved her but it couldn't take away the pain she said of always being questioned about her little baby girl. Dorca always threaten to hurt them when she was disciplined or didn't get her way The Demato's were not young people. Though I never thought she would. Dorca also told me one day in anger she was letting everyone know she was adopted. I couldn't tell her the truth I had promised Mrs. Demato. And I was just a live-in nanny! I knew she was beginning to realize she was different. But only in color the Demato's never made a difference. They had some friends that were mean and off colored but not all of them. Most of the people in the Demato's circle had children and nannies. Dorca was a quick learner. I found out from one of her little friends at a sleepover for her thirteenth birthday other stories she was telling. She got angry with her and never invited her over again. She made up stories all the time. I'm sure you have heard your share. Poor Mr. Demato, his precious little Dorca she had him wrapped around her finger. He didn't agree to her always spending time with Grover who loved to walk with him in the morning so that Dorca would come and read to him in the evening. There were many times I had to go over and with force bring her home. The Demato' s were quite a few years older than I. Victoria his wife would have Mr. Demato send me off for days or a week at a time when Dorca got older. They wanted her to be more independent they said and I was over protective. After we had been together for a while Dorca in a fit of anger stated "I'm getting older and I want need you old lady!" she would sound just like her mother Faye. When Mr. Demato suggested buying Dorca a car before she finished high school I protested. I liked taking her to school and picking her up. I hate to admit it but I felt like I was giving Faye back some of those lost years. She liked you Billy a lot. She was very smart and over achieved in all subjects. I taught her how to read myself Edith wrote. I could be sure she was at school because she loved to learn. She is an intelligent girl. But sneaking around as she had started doing had worn on all of us. She had the Demato's around her finger and she knew it. She came home and heard Mrs. Demato and I talking to Richard her husband about Grover and what I caught him doing. That night Dorca came to my room in the middle of the night and told me I was lying and out of line and the next day Richard and Vickie suggested I go to the country for a while. I really don't know who killed the Demato's "I didn't do it." I'm writing from a cell on death row. I've been here for years and have not heard from Dorca. But I confessed to cover because I feared Dorca had done it. I am frightened of dying I helped spoil her but I don't deserve to die for it. I'm sick I've been here for years waiting my death sentence. Dorca is still out there. There may be hope for the anger she's built up for me. She says she didn't do it. And I really don't know but she did threaten to hurt others if I didn't confess because she hates me and believes I did it. I failed with Faye now Dorca. After what happened to the Demato's I wanted to die even though they hurt me badly. I didn't want my family hurt. They didn't deserve to die either. I don't think she would hurt your family. She liked you. She called and asked me to pick her up from your house that day because I promised to confess so that this media circus would stop, she told me. I was so afraid she had done it. She had everything planned out and promised to stick by until it as over and I was freed. Dorca said you would be with her always. I don't know what that meant. Maybe she's there with you now. Please be careful. It seems all those years I was trying to teach Dorca from my medical books trying to get into her head. In the end she got in mine. You're the closest person to Dorca, just the mention of your name changed her mood. I was hoping she would change for you maybe she did. I have only a few months and I will be gone for good. Dorca learned very well from those psychiatric books. I think she manipulated us all. She told me about the bible you gave her I read it too. God Bless you Billy Edith Wright Williams.

David threw his head back and closed his eyes when he finished reading the letter. The timer on the oven had buzzed a while ago. "Thank you, God. for protecting my family especially my wife and son who grew up under her watchful eye David thought out loud. If this is true this young lady is sick and truly needs help. I need to find her he again thought. She really holds all the answers. I wonder if she knows about this letter. We have to be careful. Billy has to be careful. I'll have an attorney advise me on this matter. But I'm going to start turning up every rock until I find her. She has to be out there somewhere. The confession closed the case but if Edith Wright didn't do it who did? I will call Billy first thing in the morning. This can't be sweep under the rug we have got to investigate. David prayed before he turned in. He didn't have much of an appetite for eating after reading the horrible letter. Needless to say he went to bed alone and tossed and turned all night.

CHAPTER 27

The conference

The conference being held at Reunion Arena in Dallas was rich with spirit and love. Tetra walked into her room at the Reunion Hotel rejoicing but tired from a full day of praising the Lord. She had purchased some books and had obtained lots of informational literature along the way. She put everything down on her bed and removed her shoes and flopped in the big chair near the window. "What a day!" she thought. She was meeting with some of the other women from her church for dinner in three hours but for now she was getting some rest. Looking at the king size bed she had requested with its big fluffy pillows calling to her she decided to take a nap. She removed her jacket and laid it across the chair and moved over to the bed. Her cell phone fell from the pocket. "Oh, that's where it is"! she had been looking for it earlier that day. Putting it on the bedside table she laid down. Then she thought this is a perfect time to call Billy. Checking her watch, the hour difference, he should still be at the office she thought I'll try him there. "Ring, ring, "Obermeyer, Finswick and Hannagan" how may I direct your call came the voice on the other in. "William Parker please" Tetra asked. "Mr. Parker I'll ring that for you" ring "Good afternoon this is Mr. Parker" "Hi Billy" Tetra greeted her son. He had a year left before the bar and he is still Billy to his mom. "Well hi mom and how's my favorite girl in the whole world!" he replied. "I miss you too" Tetra told him. "Having fun, you know enjoying yourself' I asked. "I am, I am" and how are things with you son?" "Things are good mom. Jillian and I are going to New York for her Birthday this Saturday should be fun!" he explained. "Have fun but be safe" Tetra said with motherly concern. "We will mom" Billy said assuring her. "I talked with dad a lot since you've been gone, he misses you" I confided. "I know I miss him too. I miss you both when are you coming to Washington to visit and rest at home?" Tetra asked. "soon mom, soon" I added changing the subject quickly. "You will be home tomorrow?" I asked affirming that was her arrival time. "Yes, your dad is picking me up from the airport and I'm going straight home!" she told him. 'I love you mom I have a meeting we will talk soon" he told her getting up from his desk "I love you too son bye" "bye mom" I said rushing to another part of the building for a staff meeting. While I was away from my desk an airmail express package came for me. The receptionist signed for it and placed it in my chair. I had no need to stop in my office on my way out. I walked by looked at my desk and clicked off the light and went home for the evening. This was one of Jillian's school nights at Radcliff so I was alone again. "I had talked to Lena earlier that day from my office. She was trying to get me down for a visit to LA. to pick up my silk tie I had left in her hotel room. I shared with her I was very busy at the office but I'd keep it in mind hanging up and I soon settled in for the evening.

Looking at some briefs I had brought from the office my telephone rang. "Ring, ring" hello I answered, "Hi guy what's happening? The voice returned was Justin. "Hi Justin, things are fine how are you?" I asked. "Working and studying you know the drill!" Justin said smiling in his voice. "How's Jill? Ariel says to tell her hello" Justin added. "Jillian's good I'm sure she sends her love to you both too" I told him "Just had a few minutes and I thought about you" Justin said really sounding like he meant it". "I'm glad you called we will have to get together again soon, maybe take in a game or something with the girls or by ourselves", I shared with him. "Billy that would be great man! I have been telling my friends about you, I hope I have bragging rights?" Justin hinted. "You are my little brother!" I said, "can't stop you from talking!" I continued laughing and teasing with him. I asked about his classes and his professors at the college, about his major and of course things at work. I talked with him as brother to brother. I was genuinely interested in his success. Justin was so proud of Billy. For the first time he had someone other than Kat to look up to. Someone who cared about his well-being and he felt good. Justin thanks for the call, feel free to call me anytime and I will do the same o.k." promise? I asked. "I promise?" Justin said hanging up the phone. I made that promise more for myself than Justin. There were many times I wanted to call Justin but was afraid of over stepping my boundary. Truth is I liked having a little brother too.

Tetra had set her alarm for and hour's nap after she got off the phone with Billy. She and the ladies were spending this last evening in Dallas at Dealey Plaza downtown, a relaxing dinner, good conversation and shopping of which no trip is complete without. First lady, Phyllis Reed went along with mom. It was like old times. Sales, bargains and just got to have it no matter what the price is! the slogan of the day. Dad always says mom comes back with more luggage than she leaves with. One session of prayer in the morning, load up our luggage and head home.

David woke up earlier than usual the next day. He had tossed and turned all night and wanted to talk with Billy. He went downstairs and pushed the button on the coffee maker he had set the night before. Back upstairs to shower and got dressed looking at his clock it was 6:30 am that means it was still the middle of the night for Billy. After dressing he went down to coffee and a breakfast roll. David was feeling a little hungry but he'd get something at the office later. He sat reading his paper and the phone rang" it was Tetra saying "Good morning" and do remember her flights comes in a 1:30 Washington State time she teased I'm going back to bed. "After talking with Tetra, David still was anxious waiting to call Billy. He decided to head to the office. He had called Andersen about the game and would talk with him again later today. All he needed now was to talk to his son. Heading in driving his black Porsche in silence no radio on and no tape player he just wanted to think. David walked into his office "Good morning Mr. Parker" "good morning he returned the greeting. Up the elevator his mind was on nothing but calling Billy. He sat at his desk and dialed. "Ring, ring, ring, ring, "hello' came a very groggy voice" Good morning Billy this is dad is everything alright?

David asked. "Yes, dad everything is fine it's about 6:00 AM I usual start moving at 7:00 is everything o.k. with you" I asked. "I really need to talk with you about that letter son". David confided. Billy sat up in bed and gave this call his undivided attention those words "THE LETTER" "yes dad what about it! "Well get showered and have your coffee, I want you alert Dad told me. "We have got to find this young lady we need answers!' he said to Billy in a matter of fact tone. "Then there is reason to be concerned!" I questioned. "There is every reason to be concerned, and on alert if this is true this girl is sick and needs help" David stated. "Billy you get dressed and call me as soon as you get to the office!" "I have an appointment to speak with Rayford my attorney on this matter and I'll have more to tell you then. Son you be careful and I will talk to you soon" hanging up the phone.

I knew no need to stay in bed I wouldn't get any more sleep. "Good morning! Good morning! I heard Jillian coming in the front door yelling! She was exceptionally cheerful this morning. I rolled over and stretched then sat up putting my legs over the side of the bed. Jillian walked in "Coffee's brewing, she said coming over beside the bed standing between his knees and falling on him with a big kiss. 'GOOD MORNING" she said again. "Good morning sweetheart you're in a good mood!" I replied. "The firm in New York sweetened the salary offer!" "You want to work for me?" she teased handing him a piece of paper. "Are you kidding me Jillian?" I said looking at the six-figure salary they were offering. "Lawyers that have been working for years don't make that kind of salary". "I'll definitely consider it" I joked back. Jillian got off the bed and walked around the room, "I'm going to try my hands at grits for breakfast" she said. "I don't think I have any in the house right now Jilly, grits are kind of tricky" I told her. "I bought some the other day at the market. They sound pretty easy from reading the labeled instructions what can go wrong?" Jillian said very confidently. "Grits!" I laughed and shook my head "o.k. Tetra" I teased. "Oh Billy, your tie, your silk one you wore out with Glen I couldn't find it!" Jillian acknowledged. It's around here somewhere Jilly I'll look for it, you go cook your grits!" I said hitting her on her backside.

Jillian went downstairs and I headed for the shower. I began thinking again how concerned my dad was over the letter. I'll have breakfast and go into the office early and call dad I thought. "Oh!" that's right looking again at my electronic organizer that held my schedule. I have an exam in Rothaways class on "the legal ethics of law" this morning then off to the office. I got dressed in my dark power blue imported suit reaching for my briefcase and went down stairs. 'What do you think of this look?" I asked Jillian walking to sit at the table. "I like it! It's a new look for you" she commented. "Yes, I got rid of some of the old ties and replaced them with new ones, hope you approve." He was stroking her and also covering for that missing silk tie Lena has. 'I approve, tangerine is a good color for you" Jillian concluded. I removed my coat and placed it on the arm of the sofa. I sat down and poured a cup of coffee and began reading the Cambridge news. "Oh no! Oh no! I heard Jillian say. I looked to see Jillian trying to stir a pot of grits. Either there was to many grits for the pot she was using or not enough water for the grits she had poured into it. Either way she used the entire box and we were not going to have grits this morning. I'll get something to eat later Jillian" I said standing now hugging her to comfort her. "Are you riding in with me?" I asked finishing my cup of coffee still trying to make her feel better. She felt bad and embarrassed quickly pouring out the stiff pot of grits and cleaning the pot. "I don't know what went wrong I read and reread the instructions!" she confided as we rode together all the way to Harvard Hall. "It's okay Jilly, "I'll talk with you later, and don't feel bad we all make mistakes" I said kissing her and closing the passenger door.

The exam lasted for about 2 hours. I had put my cell phone on vibrate as not to disturb others and someone wanted to speak to me really bad. They kept buzzing me. I looked down at the screen it was my dad. I hurried through finishing the exam and walked out and called him. I had several messages on the car phone as well. Most of them were from dad too. "Hello dad" before I could finish, "son are you alright? I've been trying to reach you and Jillian for the last two hours is everything alright! He sounded hysterical. "Dad, I'm fine and as far as I know Jilly is too" I forgot to tell you I had and exam this morning before I go into the office, I'm sorry I made you worry" I explained because plainly that letter bothered him. I stood for a moment talking with him and Jillian drove up with Doris to let me know dad was trying to reach me. Jillian then explained they were going out shopping for little Davie he was starting school in the fall.

"First grade! My how time flies" I thought. This child had grown so fast. He was very young when I first met him. Barely a toddler when Jillian began keeping him. Now he was headed to school. "Dad I'll call you as soon as I get to the office. I'm headed that way now and dad Jillian's fine too" Thanks son I'll talk with you soon" David said disconnecting the line. It was clear that letter had dad really on edge I thought as I drove to my office. It's as though he thinks Dorca could be out to hurt someone namely me. This feeling was getting to me. I walked in looking over my shoulder as I passed through the covered parking garage through the lobby and up to the tenth floor. I was a little early getting in. There were a few lights on. It was close to 8::00 a.m. the day started in our firm at 9:00 am. I walked in and clicked on the light to my office. Hanging my jacket on the designated hanger behind the door and looking at my chair I saw the airmail envelope. Forgetting I didn't stop back after the meeting yesterday, I wondered how it got here." Dad is sounding strange. And now I'm feeling paranoid. Is there something he knows that is contained in the letter that I missed? I was now questioning myself. I looked around the office and saw Cooper's light on he always came in early.

Walking over "Cooper did you see you left this package at my desk? I asked. Cooper is sort of a recluse and only answered "nope" and turned and continued reading his newspaper. "I called and Beth the receptionist wasn't in yet. I was really starting to worry now. I sat at my desk and slowly opened the envelope hoping not to find still another letter. I opened it further and pulled out my tickets for Saturday's game. Relieved I laughed at myself "Wow! our seats are right behind the home team!

Feeling better now I dialed Jillian. I needed to share with her our plans for the weekend and then relax from this hectic morning. She still wasn't home. My guess is she was still out shopping so I left a message on her home phone and dialed her cell number. "Hi honey" came the greeting. "Jillian can you meet me for lunch?" I asked still looking at the infamous airmail envelope. "Where Billy?" Jilly asked. The usual place 'Ante Pasta's" it's close to the office" I replied. They ate there a lot for lunch it was middle ground for both offices and the food wasn't bad either. "Can't today sweetheart I'm meeting again with Blair Christianson, the attorney out of the New York office" she told me. Oh, I thought to myself this person finally has a name and a gender. In the past she would only speak of meeting with an attorney. I only asked you where so that I could say would love to have dinner out! you make the reservations" she added. O.k. Jilly let's say 7:0 clock at Omega's and we can do a little dancing. We haven't done that in a while" I found myself saying. Was I feeling a little intimidated by this meeting "Blair" what kind of name is that?' I thought. "Sounds great honey. "Then it's a date" Jilly replied and said nothing else. She was trying to rush me off the phone it seemed. "Where are you Jillian? I asked knowing she was still out. "I'm here at "Dr. Meloo's office he is Doris' doctor" She is in with him right now. I'm keeping little Davie company until she comes out". "He has found someone to do the cosmetic surgery she needs on her face we're excited!" she explained. Jillian was always trying to help out anyone. According to Jillian she read in O'Magazine that it would give Doris her self-confidence back and surely builds her self-esteem. I guess that was all right. Doris wore lots of fashionable scarves and dark glasses to cover her distorted face. Only when she was alone or around the house with Jillian did she ever feel comfortable enough to let it show Jilly told me.

Because of Doris's flawed face it made her appear to be an introvert around me but Jillian knew other wise and was always encouraging her. So, on that note, I guess? "That's great Jillian" when is she having the surgery done?" I asked knowing that Jillian's not telling me the whole story yet. Hesitantly she said "the Dr. is in Los Angeles and it's going to take about six weeks" she confessed. "I have to go Billy Doris is coming out of the office now." "I'll be late for my meeting! I'll see you tonight, she said quickly disconnecting the phone.

Jilly knew what my next question was, "who's going to keep Davie her six-year-old son?"

Hanging up with Jillian, I called my dad again for the third time. I had been trying leaving messages with his secretary and on his private line. I stepped away from my desk to retrieve a fax from one of my colleagues down the hall and heard my phone ringing. Walking back, I could hear my phone ringing louder 'ring! Ring! Ring! "Mr. Parker, I ANSWERED QUICKLY BEFORE IT STOPPED RINGING "How may I help you?' I asked running over to answer the phone. "Hi son" came his dad David's voice he was sounding very tired. "Dad is everything alright?" I asked concerned. I have been trying to reach you since I got to the office. "We seem to be playing phone tag." Are you sure, things there are alright?" I continued to question. "Billy I'm fine my concern right now rest with you" he confided, "with me?" I repeated. "Rayford thinks since the bible came to your new location or surrounding area that Dorca is probably in your area" David shared.

"She may be watching your every move,". "I don't want to cause and all out panic but I'm very concerned son' David warned. "I am going to go over and talk with Mr. Grover the neighbor maybe he remembers something or can share some insight on this young lady." Have you changed your locks son?' he then asked "Honestly dad no I haven't I confessed. "Well you might want to seriously consider it or maybe relocating to a secure building" he added. "There are some beautiful gated homes not far from Cambridge with only a short commute a least until you finish the bar Billy" since you're going to be in the area." David continued advising him something needed to be done. "I will certainly look into it dad," and I will call a locksmith today regarding the lock change on my doors at home" I told him. "Thanks son that will help me sleep better!" David affirmed. 'I have Rayford looking into some things extensively regarding this young lady. We have got to find her and hopefully get some answers" "She has never tried to contact you as she Billy?" "No only the bible, but I found out it was sent from the prison." I said. "O.k. we will look further and see what we can come up with." "In the mean time you be careful son" "I'll be fine dad I just need you to relax" I said again to him. "Oh, and dad I got the tickets for Jillian's birthday." "Mr. Andersen sent them yesterday, "THANKS!" "That's wonderful news son, enjoy yourself and please be safe! David told him. I love you son!' "I love you too dad!"

David sat at his desk his mind going in every direction and wanting to be everywhere at the same time. Exhausted from his hectic morning he called Verla and informed her he would be out of the office the rest of the day. He was headed to the airport to pick up his wife and go home.

CHAPTER 28

The beginning of a birthday celebration

I finished my work day at the office. Sitting for a moment I decided to call and shared with Glen what dad and I talked about. After catching up as always and a good laugh together Glen confided he has been so busy working with the launch of the satellite he's not getting out a lot these days. He stated he's trying to stay close to home". Not much socializing either" he admitted. "Bri and Meldon came down last weekend and took Sura to Disney World" She brought along a friend from her church group. According to Glen Brianna had called him earlier in the week he said to ask if he had the time to go along with them to accompany her. "After seeing her and talking with her Glen confessed, I found the time" he joked with me. She is a schoolteacher. "Bri thought she would be a good catch for me", Glen shared. "Glen's reply to Bri "was as long as no one is having prophesies of marriage we can talk! "Glen you're nuts I told him!" just keeping it real wild Bill" he said in Glen fashion. "If Dorca comes looking for me, I may come your way," I said joking of course. "Man, after that incident I had a few years ago with that girl from that restaurant I know that is not a joking matter"! but if you have to come this way you know I have your back bro. No joke!" Glen replied very sincere. 'Let me get out of here I'm meeting Jilly for dinner we will talk soon" bye.' Hanging up shutting down my computer, coat, briefcase and lots of "have a good evening to my co-workers" and out the office I went. I got in the car and drove to my favorite florist to pick up some fresh flowers for Jilly. She always liked fresh flowers on the dining table. Whistling walking back to my car with my arms filled with and assortment of tulips, delphiniums, roses and variegated Weigela flowers humming and thinking of a wonderful night with Jillian. "Ring, ring 'hi Jillian I said answering the phone in the car and buckling my seatbelt in unison.

"Honey I will be a little late my meeting with Blair lasted longer than I thought" she said. "Should I cancel the reservations?" Billy replied he was a little teed. "First lunch now dinner" he chided. "No honey don't do that I'm leaving now, I'll go home and change and I will meet you there" she suggested and then added Blair sends his apologizes." 'I didn't answer but I wasn't happy at all. I drove home to reflect before the already messed up evening. Lena had left a message on my answering machine. I truly had been avoiding her trying to stay on the straight and narrow purposely not taking her calls or forgetting to return them. I needed and ego boost. Dialing "hello" hello Lena" this is Lexia I'll get Lena for you if you tell me why your boy is avoiding my calls?' Lexia said candidly. "I wasn't aware of that, honestly it's been a minute since we spoke, I'll check into that for you" I told her "o.k. I'll get Lena" "HELLO Billy" Hello why did you put your sister on me?" I asked. "Glen's a grown man" he added. 'That's Lexia's on doing she's out the door already. I told her that could be the problem she's never around" Lena stated. "I have talked to Glen a couple of times and he stated he wasn't able to get in touch with her" Lena confessed. I laughed "wild Bill ah" well you know more about it than I do" I told her. "Well how are you doing?" I asked her. "Missing the only man that could curl my toes" she said in a sultry sexy voice. You sure know what to say" l told her. "I know what to do to" she added. Lena and I were good for each other I had convinced myself after that conversation. And very soon I told her I would be paying her a visit in L.A.

After settling down from my conversation with Lena I called and checked on dad by talking to mom before heading out the door. Mom told me dad had turned in early and was upstairs resting. "He was so exhausted and had not eaten anything all day". "And David didn't rest well last night. She told me I prepared him something light to eat and sent him to bed hopefully to rest".

Billy headed to Omega's to wait for Jillian. He wasn't much on waiting so he left around 6:15 arriving to park his car at 6:45. Walking in and getting a table near the dance floor as requested in his reservations. Right now, he was not feeling 'dance'. At 7 "0" clock he looked at his watch and then at the door entrance no Jillian! Sitting at his table enjoying a drink while waiting for Jillian he watched others moving around the floor. Some girls from the dance floor came over and asked him to dance. They had watched him from the time he came in by himself. After a couple of refusals and still no Jillian he obliged dancing again and again. Jillian walked in Omega's at 7:45 "Honey I'm so sorry our evening you planned got ruined!" walking over to the table to kiss him. "I know how much you hate to wait, has boredom set in yet?" she teased trying to make him smile.

"Oh no!" he said "thanks to those two right there pointing to two hot looking chicks that knew how to move on the dance floor. Jillian looked and turned up her pretty little pink nose! "How was your day? she asked, "I haven't seen you since this morning" Jillian said knowing she had turned down lunch and dinner hadn't started yet. I just sat there for a while letting her talk until, I felt better. After I made her feel bad about being late, I stopped pouting. She told me the New York firm was very impressed with her work and Blair would help her make the adjustment into the office. We would talk more about that later she assured me. Then she dropped the bombshell! Doris was having her surgery starting next month and she was considering keeping Davie. Or Doris would take him to her mom's in Maine she told Jillian she had option's. "But then he would miss school," Jillian sighed. So, I told her we would have to see. After she had shared her entire day with me our evening began. I asked her to dance. "Keyes song 'If I can't have you" was playing and I held Jillian in my arms. I really was feeling that she had chosen that Blair fellow over me but I couldn't tell her that "male ego Billy male ego I kept thinking. We continued dancing until the end of the song. She kissed me and said, "I miss you Billy you complete me". "I love you to Jillian" there it goes again Blair bringing out things in me I don't want to say. Not right now anyway. We sat back down and ordered dinner starting with a crumbled Maytag blue cheese salad garnished with red onions and lemon olive oil dressing with sliced tomatoes." umm, umm, good! I said starting right in because I had missed lunch. Now enjoying our conversation with each other finishing our salads the main dish sported a mixed grill beef fillet, whole shrimp, and chicken breasts, sweet Italian sausage marinated in lemon juice with sliced red peppers. "oomph" "Great meal, great company" I said looking at Jillian. I was so angry at her that I had not looked at what she was wearing. Her soft blonde hair was wisped behind her ears with a strand hanging across her eye as a tease. Her starry blue eyes and her big beautiful smile with teeth so white they sparkled, and a tiny little nose, so kissable when she flirted with you a certain way. She wore a doubled breasted tweed fitted jacket and a matching pencil skirt. And what was becoming her look black leather gloves and a tiny zebra bag with white pearls around her long neck. My girl was hot! 'Did you go home and change?' hoping Blair had not seen her this way, I asked. 'Just for you!' she affirmed. We danced and danced enjoying one another's company. We had forgotten what fun we had when we first met. Two young college students out with friends for a good time. We sat down at the table and I handed her a birthday card. Jilly loves cards. She opened it and read simply in big bold letter's Happy Birthday and I love you!" I could always trust Hallmark to say the right thing. Shedding tears she came over and hugged me and kissed me passionately with on lookers. To which I explained it was her birthday and everyone sang happy birthday to her and of course she was so embarrassed. But she could blush so beautifully. Sitting back down she pulled out the tickets for the basketball game in New York. "Oh, thank you Billy thank you! I love you so much". I was in a good mood and all was well with me. I drove to my house and parked in my garage. Jillian and I didn't have a discussion of where she was staying tonight. She commented on the fresh cut flowers I had purchased earlier before heading upstairs to finish off our evening. Jillian and I had a wonderful dinner and when she dropped my large towel robe from her wet shapely body the evening was going out in a bang! 'Pamela lee Anderson who?

David was glad that Tetra was back home. He was resting better and had turned in early even after taking a nap earlier that day. Tetra shared with him Billy had called to check on him. He's fine and was going out to dinner with Jillian. David sat up in bed looking at Tetra sleeping so peacefully on the other side of their large king size bed. He knew he would have to tell Tetra about the letter sooner or later but there were some things he needed to find out first. He didn't want to alarm her regarding Billy. He knew that is what would happen if he told her now neither of them would sleep. He got up and went to the kitchen to get a warm glass of milk to help him sleep better he reasoned. Heating up the milk and carrying it back on a tray David stop by his study home office. Putting the milk on the desk he took the picture of

Billy and Dorca from the shelf. Tetra had replaced the broken frame with a new one. He removed the picture from the frame and placed it on his office scanner. Getting it up on the screen he cropped the picture so it would only contain a picture of Dorca. Then he enlarged the photo and printed it out. He was going to use the picture to ask about Dorca around town. He then put the picture back in the frame and placed it back on the shelf carefully. His plans were to go and see Mr. Grover the Demato's neighbor. He also planned to go and talk with the old gentleman he met at the farm. David had all the names written down at the office he thought as he turned to go back upstairs. "I'll stop by my office on my way-out Monday morning". Just as he finished his thought and turned off the lights and headed back up the stairs, he heard Tetra calling "David, David she said sounding concerned that he wasn't in bed. "I'm right here Tetra" he told her coming into the room trying not to spill the warm milk. "David is everything alright?' I woke up to find you gone" it startled me" Tetra said. "I just went down to get some warm milk hon I was starting to toss and turn" David shared with her, I'm sorry I caused you worry go back to sleep" he added. David got back into bed sitting up beside Tetra. She placed her hand in his and closed her eyes and went back to sleep. David finished the milk and lay down on his pillow. He looked at Tetra's hand holding tight to his. He began to weep silently and ultimately began to pray. "Dear God, I'm coming to you realizing you are the totally sacrifice. You said I could call on you and you would answer my prayer. I ask for your guidance and your direction in this matter. Lord please protect my son and protect this family you have entrusted to me. I love you lord. You have forgiven me for so much and you have given me so much. God I now lift you up, because you have given me my family again. Please Lord help me! Lead me and guide me. I put it all in your hands. In Jesus name Amen. David laid and wept pouring his heart out to God. After a while he closed his eyes for a very good night's sleep.

Things were back to normal it was early Saturday morning and Tetra was in the kitchen making breakfast. She and David were going to have breakfast out in the morning sunshine and relax on the porch taking it easy. Ring, ring, "Good morning" David answered "good morning dad how are you doing?" I'm fine you're up early son" We're heading out to the big game in New York remember" "Yeah that's right, his dad replied.

"did mom get in okay? I asked him because I hadn't spoken with him. He was asleep when I called and spoke with her. "She sure did do you need to speak with her?" no dad I'll call later on" I told him I just didn't want you to worry" Thanks son I appreciate that "and have a wonderful time" David hung up the receiver thinking I 'didn't say be careful, that's alright he said I' have put it in the hands of Jesus and he can take care of it better than I.

Tetra brought out two trays of toast, biscuits and hash browns with sunny side up and scrambled eggs, homemade Jelly, and crispy strips of bacon. David ate like he hadn't eaten in a week. I missed you Tetra, I'm glad you're home, and I'm glad we're together, he said reaching for another homemade biscuit, gently kissing Tetra on her cheek to affirm it. They sat quietly listening to the sounds of the city from their spacious wrap around porch that looked out on their beautiful lush flower garden and shrubs that surrounded the yard. They talked about the conference in Dallas Tetra had just returned from and David caught her upon things going on at the office. He knew he would have to tell her about the letter and what was in it. But for now, he just wanted to relax and enjoy his wife. "This is a wonderful day David" Tetra expressed. I'm enjoying it "I am too dear!" David confided. "I really needed it after this week and he added I missed you honey! The two enjoyed a much-needed rest at home. And after a light dinner in the evening they turned out the lights for another good night's rest.

David and Tetra was up early Sunday morning finishing up their orange juice and coffee and heading out to Mt. Nebo. Taking a class together on "Growing in Christ" was fulfilling. They were really enjoying all the newness that was being shared through this study and were meeting other Christians who were learning and growing as well. Their Sunday ended with a rich high praise worship service lifting up Christ. The choir ministered through chosen songs that uplifted their hearts and spirits. And Dr. Hathaway in a very understanding kind of way taught the word enriching their hearts even further.

At home Tetra shared with David some of the pieces she had bought on her shopping spree in Dallas over dinner. Besides a new suit for the spring from Finnegan's Boutique" she had purchased a lace chemise nightie in his favorite color. She surprised him by clothing their king-sized bed in Charmeuse satin sheets in a smoke blue silk and lighting a fire in the double-sided fireplace with scented candles surrounding their bedroom for an intimate relaxing moment. The soft sounds of music greatly attributed to the mood of the evening. David and Tetra turned in for still another very good night.

CHAPTER 29

New York City

Billy and Jillian arrived in New York and checked in their rooms at the Waldorf Astoria Hotel. They had decided they were going to do everything just like a native New Yorker including hailing cabs. Outside the airport Jillian secured a cab they soon arrived at the famous Waldorf Astoria safe and for the most part sound. The flight from Cambridge was short and sweet not much time to sleep before landing down in New York City. Billy was looking forward to a long nap before the basketball game in Madison Square Garden so he didn't waste any time getting their luggage and headed to the hotel. He wanted this birthday to be very special for Jilly and planned to spoil her the whole weekend. Things had been going well since their makeup before coming to New York and he was feeling the love. Jillian's parents lived in Manhattan and they were going to see them before they left New York, but these first few days were to be there's exclusively. They knew it was going to be a very busy two days. They had planned to take in many of the sights. Jillian was glad Billy finally came to New York City and couldn't wait to share him with the 'Big Apple'. A native she knew her way around and wanted him to see where she grew up. They were finally here she thought looking out her 20th floor window at the New York skyline. So much was planned, a week of shows on Broadway and shopping of course. They would certainly visit the Statue of liberty in the New York Harbor and many other sights before returning to Massachusetts. But tonight, is the Big Game at Madison Square Garden and they were excited? Their seats were directly behind Patrick Ewing and the entire Knickerbockers team. Jillian looked over at Billy who had now flopped on the big over size bed to sleep. Their flight left out a 5:30 am from Cambridge getting up early to catch their flight not to mention the late night they were feeling kind of tired. After having stayed up late the night before dining and dancing both needed a nap. Jillian lay down but decided against sleep and opted to go shopping down on the main floor of the hotel. First, she purchased some jerseys from the N.B.A. store located in the lobby (Patrick E. for her M. J. for Billy) She knew she couldn't go wrong with that one. Even New Yorkers loved Michael Jordan.

She walked around browsing in some of the other high- end shops. Shoes, handbags, and hats any and everything you wanted or needed were available. She knew she would be doing lots of shopping so she packed light for the trip knowing the flight weight on the plane trip home would make the difference. After looking around for about an hour she went back up to her room to wake Billy. He was already up when she got back and wondered where she had gone. "I was just getting ready to dial you" where did you go? he asked before looking at the large shopping bags she was carrying. "I went down to the first floor and got us some jerseys for the big game!" Jillian said enthusiastically. She was going all out she loved the game but really didn't understand certain aspects like traveling or when the referee called a foul on her favorite player Patrick. Jilly was a fan to the very end. She spread the jerseys out on the bed "I know you purchased M.J. for me!" Billy said. "You're right! 'This game is all mine!" Jillian said throwing her Ewing jersey over her shoulder "bring it on". Our plans before the big game tonight were to go and visit the Statue of liberty on Ellis Island. We decided on the subway this time rather than a cab so we made our way to the subway. Jillian had shared stories about the overcrowded sub stations and so I thought I was prepared. Walking along the street heading to the subway there were many immigrants spread out along the sidewalks. And all the glamour you hear about New York City had somehow faded. Who would know that they had slums and air pollution and traffic jams? "Is this what you wanted me to see?" I teased as we hurried to get the Ellis train to the statue. "Oh, don't be funny Billy", Jillian expressed New York is a very exciting town!" "I'm waiting Jilly I'm waiting". Soon they were loading in the crowded sub train and on their way. After the third train they were headed too their final stop the Statue of Liberty holding on to the rails of the sub train for dear life. It was standing room only. At the stop that proceeded ours a seat became available. Jilly quickly sat down to relax when she heard "NEXT STOP

STATUE OF LIBERTY". Standing up for a quick exit from the still over crowded train Jillian was motioning to Billy who was pressed between several people with the same destination in mine. He was holding on to his tourist look "his camcorder over his shoulder. 'THIS IS OUR EXIT" she yelled out to him. The train stopped and everyone pushed forward. Jillian went out first and soon Billy followed. They held each other's hand relieved and walk toward the famous statue." "And this is what you want to come back too?" he asked making reference to the law firm whose offer she was considering. "Billy you really get used to it" she told him. "It becomes second nature. As we walked up to the statue I asked "What do you think she weighs? "Who?" Jillian asked missing what I was asking. 'The statue silly" What are you thinking about?" Jillian had for a moment start thinking about the firms offer, she confessed. But this was their time alone and she and Billy promised to leave all business matters at home. "What kind of question is that?" Jilly asked. "And you have graduated law school and only a year left before the bar!" he added "one might question?' They stood in a long line waiting for the elevator. Each time it was too crowded to enter. Jillian and he decided to walk. Realizing there were 168 steps in each stairway to reach the top they would surely be using the rest seats on every third turn of the spiral. At this rate they would get back to their hotel just in time to go to the big game. They were going 150 feet in the air to the Liberty's crown that housed a twenty-five-windows observation platform. "Billy you see I told you we would need water" pulling a bottle of water from her large purse. "Thanks Jillian" he said, "you think of everything" As they continued upward to the statue's crown enjoying one another's company. Surprisingly it did not take them as long as they thought to get to the top. Billy's weekly game of tennis was paying off and Jillian made her way to the fitness center in spite of her already tiny frame "to stay in shape and certainly muscle tone" is why I return every week she tells him. They passed many of the couples they met at the beginning of their trip up who had to sit longer before continuing to the top. When they got to the observation tower, they could see all over the Bronx, Brooklyn, Manhattan, Queens and Staten Island. "Over there is where my office will be!" Jillian explained "in the financial district on Wall Street" The New York stock exchange is over there also" she added. "It sounds like you have already made up your mind about the offer?" I replied. "I haven't decided not to," Jilly said walking away to look out of another telescope. "Look Billy Rockefeller Center on Fifth Avenue maybe we can take in a show there!" she was very excited she had gone to a lot of shows there. Her mom was a theatrical buff and loved theater. "There is a possibility" I affirmed trying to keep things in perspective. Billy didn't like the fact that Jillian had made up her mind and had not shared it with him. But nothing had been confirmed so, he'd live with it. "Is she trying again to pressure me into marriage by flaunting this offer in my face he thought? They stayed up in the tower for an hour talking and viewing the Empire State Building, Greenwich Village and of course across from the Rockefeller Center Is the Saint Patrick's Cathedral the seat of the Roman Catholic Archdiocese of New York. Surely, we could not visit everything in a week I thought to myself but I would not be lying if I said I saw it," standing tall looking over New York City's magnificent view holding Jillian in his arms. "Let's, ride down on the elevator Jilly remarked "It's an hour back to the Waldorf by subway train" she added. And down on the elevator they went. At the bottom Billy purchased souvenirs for friends at the office and his family. With his camcorder safely back in the bag they headed to the subway for the return trip back for the big game. When they arrived back to the Waldorf it was only an hour or so before they would start out again in a different direction. Billy decided that it was just too soon to head back to the rush of the big city. He called and had room service sent to the room and after eating and relaxing a little not to mention letting Jilly sport her Ewing jersey they held a cab for the Garden. "Madison Square here we come!"

The big game was just what they'd hoped for. The garden was filled to capacity with screaming fans. Their seats were so close they could reach and touch the players to give advice. As a matter of fact, he did and yes it resulted in two points. Jilly and he stomped to the music they refereed and yelled and screamed seems like to every cheer. But it was not to be. The Knickerbockers couldn't put the "gimme" points of free throws in the net when it counted so the Sacramento Kings won 106 to 98. Jillian wasn't disappointed she loved the thrill of the game and both had a wonderful time. We made our way through the thousands of fans and people pushing to get out of the stadium. We hailed a cab after about 45 minutes of waiting and went back to our room showered and crashed. "Happy Birthday Jilly" is the last thing I remembered.

I got up early the next morning and stepped out of the room and called to make reservations for the evening leaving it on their recorder requesting a confirmation. Jillian was still lying in bed fast asleep. I called down and ordered room service for 10: o clock I knew we should be up and moving by then. The plans of the day were the Bronx zoo spending the day enjoying the animals. This was one of Jillian's favorite places to visit with her parents while she was growing up. She remembers seeing her first giraffe "dad's he so tall will he ever stop growing? "she asked him. Her stories of the zoo go on and on. Back in our room I noticed Jilly was still asleep. I walked over and took my luggage down off the rack in the closet. Opening it I pulled out a little black bag that contained my toothbrush, and other toiletries. Moving them around I said to myself "there it is!" and put the bag back in place and placed the luggage back on the rack. Jillian didn't move she was getting some much-needed rest.

Looking at the clock and hopping back in bed snuggling up to Jillian I pulled the covers up to reposition myself and noticed the black-laced teddy Jillian was wearing. She didn't have that on when we went to bed I thought smiling to myself. I wouldn't have gone to sleep! He put the covers back on her very sleepy body straightening them on the bed and snuggled closer kissing her on the back of her ears and neck. She moved a little and laid still unaware he was causing this emotion. He began kissing her ears again and her neck and reached over and kissed her lips. "Honey" she said in a groggily early morning voice. She opened her eyes to find him starring her in the face smiling." why are we waking up so early Billy? "I'm sorry honey did I wake you?", that was not my intention" I said so innocently. "I was giving you your birthday kiss. Neither of us moved a muscle when we came in last night!" "You're right! Jillian said still not quite awake, but now aware I intentionally woke her up. She sat up and looked at the clock it was only 6:0 clock in the morning and she flopped back down on her pillow and covered her head. I tugged lightly at her pillow. "Honey it's only 6 a.m. go back to sleep!" she said pleading to him. "How do you expect me to go to sleep now that I have seen what you are wearing?" he said sitting up on the side of the bed. "You didn't go to bed like that!" I proclaimed. "Billy you were so sleepy last night if I would have gone to bed naked you would not have known it" she said smiling now that I had waken her up and she knew I was not going to be let her go back to sleep. "Honey you were so tried and worn out after that subway train and the climb up the Statue and the crowds last night you went to sleep immediately! and I snuggled in close to you". "You put your arms around me and we both went to sleep end of story" she said turning her back to him. "I'm not sleeping now he said jumping back in the bed snuggling behind her. He started kissing her face and then her ears soon he was kissing her long slim neck slowing putting his hands under the covers of the bed. Jillian squirmed from his touch. It was early but she couldn't deny what she was feeling she responded to his playful passions and started a new day in New York City.

After a very hearty breakfast Billy and Jillian left going to the Bronx Zoo. They were going to once again brave the subway. And he was ready. Sundays are totally different than weekdays. The crowds were manageable and there were available seats. So they were able to sit down on each train all the way to the Bronx the very center of New York. They got off the train near the major boulevard "here's the Grand Concourse" Jillian replied, "let's go this way. They walked along toward the famous Bronx zoo. There were apartment houses, offices buildings and stores. A little further they could see the large gate at the entrance "We are here Jillian," Billy said, taking the camcorder out of the pouch and panning the area. "Stand over near that sign Jillian please?" NEW YORK'S FAMOUS BRONX ZOO" Billy and Jillian walked slowly along the designed paths looking at the animals contained in the cages. Realizing that this zoo has the largest collection of animals than other zoos they chose paths of frequent traveled visitors as to see all that was available. Walking in they saw the beautiful flamingo's standing together some were slowly walking around the mossy grassy water eating shrimp. Their color is brilliant, Billy said. "Look how he stands on that one leg!" Jillian said while falling over trying to imitate one of the Flamingo's. "Oh, my Billy look at the monkeys they are so tiny "that's amazing how they're able to swing by their tails." The larger Baboons just sat starring back at them as they walked by. They moved on through the wildlife conservation "these species are endangered" Billy said reading the sign posted in front of the cage. "What are they Jillian asked standing down at the other end patting the head of one. "I know it's in the deer family Jillian added. "It's a European Bison" I informed her precisely standing in front of the sign which bear its official name. Moving on to another path they went to see the Orangutan. "Now he's one of my favorites! Jillian said they have so much personality, watch look at the little one hiding behind his mother". "Look! Look up that one is throwing something from that tree"! They are funny creatures" Billy added. They went on and on path after path looking at the large hippos going up and down in the water, the huge tigers romping around the cage. "Oh look he's tired" he's gone to sleep Jillian said of the big Tiger lying near the wall behind a bush. Birds, elephant, white bears, black bears and of course the humongous Brown bear. "Sharp claws Jilly like a woman scorn!" Look at all the Joey's hopping around! 'Joey's' "yes Jillian the Kangaroo' and the Wallaby over there". 'Oh, I knew that Billy, you just caught me off guard on that one" Jillian replied. "There is so much to see Billy and we have not gone to the reptile cages yet" Jillian said excitedly. Billy and Jillian got to another path "This way Billy" "No this way Jillian!" look at the leopards, and mountain lions "he's got long teeth!" I would not like to be his prey!" Jillian was enjoying herself and he'd have to admit he was too. After it got very close to lunch, they headed to the botanical garden to eat and relax. They sat relaxing, watching the butterflies frolicking through the flowers. They also watched tourist and native New Yorkers enjoying the animals as well! "How's your hamburger Billy?" Jillian asked. "IT'S GONE! I laughed finishing my coke and tossing the cup in the trash. This walking had made me very hungry. "It was good!!" We sat a while and let our food digest and headed to the reptile house and ooooooo"d!!! and awwwwdd"!! over the snakes and lizards displayed there. "This was a very good idea Jillian my cam worked over time but I got a picture of you and your family see" I teased "putting the cam up to her face displaying the monkcys!" She shoved me away playfully and we kissed. It was another beautiful day in New York City. On our way back by subway train we stopped in Central Park and did some shopping in the spacious mall. Jillian and I had dinner while listening to an outdoor concert in a park near the river. Our quaint little table set along the banks of the Hudson River. The jazz band played and some couples danced to the beats. "You're so romantic" Jillian expressed as I was purchasing flowers from a vendor walking by "I love you!" both said in unison!!!

CHAPTER 30

Too many years

David left for work early Monday morning refreshed from a restful weekend with his wife. Tetra shared coffee with her husband and kissed him good day has he left for the office. He had planned to stop by his office and get the names of the people he needed to talk with before heading out to Oregon. He drove in wondering how Billy's trip to New York was going since he had not spoken with him all weekend. He had not talked with him but he trusted everything was going well. "Ring, ring good morning" David voiced. "Good morning dad how's it going? I said in a cheery tone. "Hi son it's good to hear from you how's your trip"? he asked "it's going wonderfully well and the game was awesome please thank Mr. Anderson again for me" I added. "I will son" replied David. I continued talking to dad. "I didn't want you to worry and I wanted to touch bases with you to let you know everything is fine here dad!' "Sounds wonderful son, when are you due back?" David inquired. "Dad I'm going to visit Jillian's parents today dinner and a show at Radio City Music Hall tonight and I'm due home Friday." 'Well son I'm glad for you. Your mom and I had a much-needed quiet restful weekend I'm glad she's home!" "Me too, enjoy your day" love ya, dad goodbye". David hung up the receiver of his car phone pulling into the covered garage of his office. He'd make a quick trip up to his office go over his schedule with Verla the receptionist and his secretary informing them of his sudden change in plans for the day. Getting the names of the persons he wanted to speak with from his archives file and was out the door.

Great everything went as planned. David was out the door and on the road to Oregon. It is such a beautiful ride up this way David thought as he drove along the open highway. He loved the trees and green skyline against the white and blue cloudy sky moving peacefully in silence down the highway as he sped ahead. David didn't know what he was looking for or if there was anything to find but he had to try. He needed answers to all the questions Edith had purposed in her letter. After he had driven for about two hours, he began to look for the turn off to the Demato farm. He took out the directions and placed them upon the seat next to him. "There it is! David said turning off onto a two-lane dirt road leading down into the woods He looked around. The trees were green and had full foliage of bright green leaves on each one. There were many pine trees reaching high into the sky declining as each grew upward. Driving alone the small dirt road he came upon the farm and the large ranch style home. He drove a little further down a path that lead to the front entrance of the property and pulled his car to the side of the paved driveway and got out. Looking around he saw children playing in the yard on an old tractor seemingly to favorite it over the swing set that was visible on the other side of the large yard. A lady sitting out on the porch knitting and overseeing the children at play watched him carefully as he came toward her. As he walked up closer, she stood looking at him. "Good evening" David said walking up extending his hand. "Good evening sir" came the returned greeting. "May I help you?" it was very obvious she was from the Midwest." Are you here to see the property sir?" "No maam" David found himself saying 'I was looking for Mr. Hemley" "oh granddad" she returned. "He doesn't live here anymore he's moved back to Kansas" she said. "Got so lonely round these parts for him without Grandma Clara you know". "Oh Kansas! I see. I'm so sorry to hear that". "Is it possible I can speak with him by phone?" David suggested. "Well he don't talk much these days sometimes he has good days and something to say. Sometimes he don't. Bud says he just kinda sits around most of the time now" she told David. "I do understand" David affirmed. Before he could say anything else "Rebecca, sir is my name" I'm Rebecca" she said smiling. "I'm very pleased to meet you I'm David Parker". "Rebecca is it possible you could give me a number to try and talk with your granddad"? David lightly suggested again to Rebecca. A lady probably in her forties early fifties dressed in a farm style dress and apron around her waist. "Granddad don't have no number that I know". Then turned quickly yelling, "HENRY! HENRY! COME ROUND HERE! she yelled to the back of the house. The children that were playing came running from their play. "I DIDN'T CALL YOU I CALLED HENRY, YA'LL GO PLAY!" she admonished them. Finally, this young man maybe late twenties came on the porch dressed very conservatively "good afternoon sir" came and unexpected voice. Henry Hampster" this is my sister Rebecca how may I be of service? He asked in his very polished way. "David shook his hand and shared with him he needed a number for his granddad Mr. Hemley. He needed to speak with him about a person who had lived in the home. He told him they had spoken before. "Sir granddad Hemley doesn't talk on the phone at all, I know that may seem funny to you but this may sound even funnier he may speak with you in person". He's more apt to talk if he sees you face to face", he reasoned. "But I'll get a number for you, this is the person my aunt Mrs. Wheatley she cares for him" maybe she can be of help to you". Just a moment please," he said going into the house and coming back with the telephone number on a business card and handed it to him. 'Thank you very much!" David replied putting the card inside his inner suit coat pocket. "Did your family buy the place? David asked looking around it was still very well kept up and still looked maintained. "No sir still belongs to the Demato Family" "we justa keeping it since granddad got ill" signs around back" Rebecca said smiling. David extended out his hand and shook the young Henry's hand and thanked him for the number. He thanked Rebecca too and got in the car and drove away. They watched until he drove off the property. David walked away curious about the diversity of Henry and Rebecca. Rebecca so country and her brother Henry so polished. He got back in his car and headed to talk with the Demato family if possible. They were in Chateau convalescent hospital in downtown Oregon. Driving along David stopped and called Tetra and got a sandwich from a small roadside deli. He told her that he was out of the office on business and should be home in time for dinner. Back in the car he found the hospital's location on Plum Street. The staff was very gracious to let him see the Demato' s but neither really knew what he was saying or aware David was even there. Both were extremely polite and friendly. Mr. Demato shook his hand after every sentence wishing him well each time he passed on his continual pace around the large open dayroom. And the Mrs. just sat quietly looking at her surroundings. David soon thanked the hospital staff and was on his way. He thought since he was here, he'd stop by and see Detective Masony.

Maybe he could shed some light on this already non-informative visit. It's possible he knew the whereabouts of Dorca Williams. But since the farm was still the Demato property and her return to this area was based on that it was not likely and probably hopeless. Walking in the precinct things had changed. The dusty place was now brightened by a new staff of detectives. After a brief conversation with the clerk at the front desk he found out detective Masony had retired and move away from the area. He left his card and asked if they would pass it on to him and have him call. Soon David was back in his car and headed home. Well! I don't know what's going to come of this he thought as he drove back on the highway heading home. One telephone number anyway David thought. I'd better head straight home.

Arriving back in Washington and hour earlier than he expected David pulled up in front of the estate in Richvale were he first encountered the knowledge of that gruesome scene. The house still in immaculate condition but had been recently painted a different color than he remembered. Of course, no signs of that awful police tape cordoning off the premises. He walked over and rang the doorbell of Mr. Grover the Demato's neighbor. After a while a maid came to the door "Good evening I'd like to speak with Mr. Grover?" he said to her. "Misuier Grover is no longer with us regretfully" she told him. David looked as if to say, 'what do you mean?" "Misuier Grover passed away" she shared shaking her head while holding it down and backed away from the door. "I'm so sorry to bother you madam" he said and walked away as she closed the large door to another unanswered set of questions. David had planned to stay a lot longer thinking he would be talking to Mr. Hemley, the Demato's parents or Mansony but nothing. He was sure Grover could answer some family questions but he was gone. So many years had lapsed since 1984 life had moved on maybe Dorca had also he sure hoped she did.

CHAPTER 31

Sign on the dotted line

This was Jillian and Billy's last full day in the "Big apple" before returning to Cambridge Massachusetts. They had renewed the love each shared with one another. Things planned could not have gone better has they sat eating breakfast in the restaurant of the Astoria Hotel. "Billy I really want things to go well tonight at my parents" she told him. "I do too Jilly, I really think that if they just let this be our decision things will turn out, right." he shared with her holding her hand across the beautiful white linen cloth of their breakfast table. "I agree, she said and added, "I'm so glad we left all that business and other people from this time we are sharing together". Kissing each other in agreement they continued talking and finished their breakfast meal. "Did you call your parents to let them know what time we would be coming Jilly?" I don't want to add to anyone's stress!" I teased knowing that I had a surprise planned for the evening. "I have called and everything will be fine", she told him. "Billy I would like to go to Neiman Marcus while I'm here. "Kelly says they just got back recently from a buying trip and they brought back fashions from Paris' many one of a kind", she stated looking and hoping for yes let's go!" He didn't have a problem with Paris fashions but the last thing he wanted to see was KELLY! "I have an idea Jillian, he replied as they got up from the table after signing the receipt. "You can spend the morning and take your time trying on and looking and looking again and trying on, and getting your opinions from Kelly, and I will go and workout in the fitness room right here". And I won't rush you and I'll be right here when you return!' What do you think about that suggestion?" Billy remarked. "But I thought this time was for us to spend together" she said sadly. "We are, we have the rest of our lives" I told her "go enjoy yourself!" 'Are you sure

William Parker? Jillian smiled hugging and kissing him gently on his lips. They went back to the room she got her purse and with "remember the weight limit of your luggage" she was out the door. Jillian really wanted Billy to come but, he was right and she knew it. A man rushes you through shopping and always wants you to buy the first thing you say you like. So, guilt off here I go! she said "to the New York subway to Neiman Marcus". Billy stayed sitting in the room looking at the phone he decided to dial the Radio Station Music Hall box office to affirm the reservations for tonight's show. This was a surprise for Jillian. He had not shared it because he planned to give her something else there and was bursting about it. He totally blocked it out of his mind until the time came for his big surprise. He looked again at the small black box in his luggage and put it back. Then he thought all this walking and the subway experience was exercise enough so he ventured out on his own in New York.

Just as Jillian was approaching her stop to get off the train her cell phone rang. "Hello" not recognizing the number showing on her caller ID. 'Hello Jillian, this is Blair Christianson, hear you're in town?" he asked in his business tone. "Yes, she said putting on her very business voice surely not looking the part. She had dressed in her black jeans and a cropped white top with her midriff showing. Her knee-high bone color boots and her Burberry purse total relaxation from business. "I wonder if you could stop by, I'd like to show you the results of the work you have been doing for us". Jillian was silent. Billy and Jillian had promised no business. "I'm not really here on business Mr. Christianson, just out enjoying some shopping in New York she told him. "Please, he said call me Blair, I do understand but it would only be a moment and you could resume your shopping he suggested. She was going to Neiman Marcus that was only two blocks from the office location on Wall Street. Against everything she thought good she said "O.K" and as if that wasn't enough from Blair "you can meet our President". I will see you soon"! Blair concluded hanging up. Jillian got off the subway train and headed to the lady's restroom in the substation to freshen up after her train ride. Powered her face and a few touches of St. Lauren's perfume she walked into the financial building to the law firm. Blair was waiting at the front by the receptionist area to escort her up. "What a magnificent place" she thought as she walked in. It gave the Walldorf Astoria competition. 'Hello Jillian, said Blair walking toward her with hand extended, "thanks for making time for me" he told her motioning her to the elevator. They went up to this very large office at the end of the hallway. Looking at the name as she walked in Jillian said, "you have a very nice office" also noticing you could see all over the city from his window view. "Well Jillian this is where you will be working right on the other side of this wall" he said pointing to an equally as nice space. Then with Blair pulling some folders and recognizable papers from his desk Jillian pulled up a chair and began to listen. "May I say you looked very nice today Jillian" Blair remarked in a flirtatious tone. Jillian said nothing, Blair noticing that the compliment made her feel uneasy he then said" I mean very relaxed that shows you have another side not just work! Work! Work!" he added smiling. "Oh, I see what you mean "thanks Mr. I mean Blair". They sat down and started looking at briefs and documents that Jillian worked on initially. She loved her work and will often lose track of time because of absorption in the moment. An hour and a half-had pass when Morgan one of the female lawyers came and knocked "lunch Blair? I'm going down to the little sandwich shop on the corner that's all the time I have today" she shared in a very hurried fashion. "Morgan, he replied "this is Jillian McFinney looks like she may be coming on board with us" she's down visiting New York and I persuaded her to come by and look over some documents we worked on". "Please to meet you" Morgan Taylor" she replied extending her hand, "Jillian McFinney she repeated "please to meet you as well". We'll walk together Blair suggested and you two can converse a little regarding our work here. 'Sounds great Morgan said and she and Jillian headed down toward the elevator. "You two go ahead I'll be right behind you" Blair shared heading in another direction. What Morgan had to say about the firm was very impressive. She had been there for three years and liked the office and the people she worked with. The case-loads varied, but you are never out of work in corporate law she added. They ordered sandwiches and sat at a little table on the sidewalk outside the elegant small restaurant. Jillian now cognizant of the time thought she had better get something to eat to with only an hour left of her shopping she still had not purchased anything. She and Morgan sat and talked while eating their lunch and Blair's sandwich wrapped on the table laid untouched.

I on the other hand was having fun getting lost and finding new places to explore. Besides a lot of old abandoned buildings in some parts of New York there were others that were magnificent where the

Lincoln Center for the performing Arts was built. I sat out by the gushing waterfall out front and listened over the intercom to the Philharmonic Orchestra playing and had lunch throwing some bread crumbs to the birds. I watched a group of young men playing street ball in another park enjoying trash talk and having fun. Soon I found myself on Wall Street. I didn't know how I got there but I was there. "So, this is Wall Street' I thought to myself as I looked around at the banks and brokerage houses and of course the much talked about stock exchange building. I read the daily stock exchange rating almost every day. My dad had taught me about that when I was much younger. I spent lots of our visits learning how to read the ratings and interpret the stock market over breakfast most times. Looking at a map I had obtained from a corner newspaper stand I headed to the New York Stock Exchange on the corner of Wall and Broadway. When suddenly looking over I spotted "can't be I said Jillian was sitting down having lunch with a man. Who was he" I thought, she is supposed to be shopping. I sat on the wall and watched the two of them conversing. It was obviously someone she knew. She was laughing and enjoying herself. Could this be one of her old boyfriends? I should call her pulling out my cell phone from my pack. Then I remembered what she had told me in the Statue. The office she would be working in is on Wall Street. She wouldn't dare mix business with our time together! Was this meeting intentional or planned? I'll call her before I jump to conclusion I thought, and this will be the end of it! There's a lot weighting on this. I'm visiting her parents tonight and the little black box at the hotel holds the future. Lighten up Billy I told myself. You are drawing conclusions. Standing off around the corner but still had Jillian in sight nervously dialing. "Jillian answered. "Hello!" Morgan had finished her lunch and went back to the office and she and Blair was still talking while he finished his lunch. After talking with Morgan Jillian was full of questions and was ready to sign on to the firm after she had confirmed most of it with Blair. She'd have to shop another day. "Hi Billy, how are you?" oh just doing fine how's shopping going? "Funny you would ask" she said "I've been shopping all morning and haven't found anything I like." "Leave it to Kelly to give wrong information" Jillian replied. "So, Kelly is with you?" I asked starting to get very upset. "I saw her earlier" look Billy sweetheart, I have one more item I'd like to look at and I'm heading to the subway" she said with certainty. "So, you're still in Neiman's" trying on everything" I teased but was fuming inside. Jillian was lying to him and it hurt. "Yes, Billy I'll see you soon I love you!" she said hanging up. My first instinct was to run across the street and let her know I saw her. But I had opened myself up to her and she had crushed my heart. Boy it sure feels different when it happens to you! I thought. But Jilly never saw me with the other girls, I reasoned. It was not going to go well so I headed back to the Waldorf a different person. Jillian was so excited about all the things she had found out from Morgan regarding the firm. She was very knowledgeable in law. She had looked over all the paperwork several times. She just wanted to share this moment with Billy but she couldn't talk business not on this trip. They had promised one another. She'd figured out a way to tell him later on Jillian concluded. Billy walked to the corner heading for the substation and looked back to see Jillian walking into the financial building with the same guy she just had lunch with and he was now devastated. Jillian went back up to Blair's office to say goodbye to Morgan and thank her for everything including lunch. Blair sensing the moment that he wouldn't need to introduce Jillian to the president to get her to sign at this time she was ready if it was done right. They came back to his office. He called someone on the phone. "Now all we need is you" Blair told her looking up with this big grin on his face. Jillian had wanted Billy to know what she was doing. She wanted him to be there and go over all the paperwork with her. But Blair was right it was a great opportunity for her coming right out of law school and landing this kind of a job and at this firm. Blair pushed the proposal in front of her and with Morgan nodding Jillian signed on to the firm. "Celebrate! Blair and Morgan hugged her. She wished Billy could have been there. She shook Blair's hand and headed out of the building rushing to get back to the Waldorf and was looking forward to another wonderful evening with Billy. Blair walked over to Morgan's office and handed her a sizable bonus "well done Morgan" giving her a kiss before leaving her office.

Billy got out of the cab in front of the Waldorf handing the cabbie a bill from his pocket. "WOW THANKS! He said as Billy waved to him going inside. He wasn't feeling anything right now and just wanted to be by himself and think. He stopped by the store in the lobby and went into the elevator. He got off the elevator after riding up twenty flights by himself. You could do that during day hours at night it was different you would have someone going or coming on every floor. He took out the card key and went into the room. He looked at the bed where he had slept with Jillian. Now all he wanted was to pack his bags and leave. "Get it together Billy" he kept telling himself. "You're the man! He didn't feel like the man he was angry, hurting and felt betrayed. What was the story? Why was she lying? "Get it together Billy she will be here soon. He went in and began his shower water and started to undress. He had taken a cab back that took a half hour but Jillian probably took the subway so she would be at least an hour. He had been sitting there about forty- five minutes or longer when she walked in "honey" honey" in her playful way. Billy hurried and finished taking off his clothes and jumped in the shower.

Jillian came in the bathroom "mind if I join you?" she said reaching her hand behind the shower curtain. "I'm finishing up Jillian" you're cutting it awfully close we have to be at your parents in an a few hours" I said securing my towel round my waist before coming from behind the curtain. She wasn't getting my hint. Sweet heart we've got plenty of time and you're ready now she said making playful advances toward me. I pushed her away! She noticed my facial expression! "Sorry Jillian but we don't have time for that we're running late get showered and get dressed!" Jillian was thinking I was upset because she had cut the time to leave so close and the subway to her parent's house in Manhattan was an hour if you catch all the first trains. Many times, in the evening there is massive overcrowding on the subways. Jillian walked in the bathroom still trying to make small talk and all I could think about was let me out of here. "I DID FIND SOME NICE THINGS FINALLY she said speaking from behind the shower curtain loudly. "HONEY, HONEY, I BOUGHT YOU THAT NEW COLGNE "BLACK" BY KENNETH COLE! Billy wasn't answering Billy wasn't even listening. Jillian got out of the shower and walked into an empty room Billy had walked out.

I knew I needed to get away for a minute. I rode the elevator down to the main floor and walked into the hotel drug store and purchased some gum. Pulling my cell phone from my pocket I called Lena. Ring, ring! I stood listening for a moment. The message she left says she's out on a photo shoot and will return in three weeks. Hanging up I dialed Desmond, ring, ring, "Hi Billy." It was Mossy, "hi Moss is Desmond in?" I would usually talk to Mossy we knew each other well and had a very good relationship but right now all I wanted was to talk to my buddy. "No, I'm sorry Billy he is still at the office", is there something I can help you with?" she asked "Nothing important just need to speak with Des" I said. How's Jillian? Was her next question and I knew it, "Jillian's fine, I'll catch Des at the office bye!" Hanging up he called Glen he wanted someone to say what he needed to hear that did not included Jillian. "Ring, ring, ring "Hello "CLICK" I hung up maybe I have a wrong number a female answered. Ring! Ring! Ring! "Hello Billy came Glen's voice. "Man, for a moment there I thought I was losing my mind some girl type answered your dial numbered and I hung up" I said knowing Glen will not let female type other than Mrs. Reed answer his phone. "No, that's my coworker Gail we're her trying to figure out how to put a man on the moon" He joked. "What are you up to?' Glen asked. "Needing to run" I told him. Glen knows that's what we say when we need to get out of a relationship or out on the town. "Billy, man talk to me", I just left a few months ago and we painted the town of Cambridge red twice" Glen joked. "I'm still feeling it" he added. "How's Jillian?" "Don't ask, I'm down here with her in New York and she has got me tripping" I confided in him "Billy talk to me! "This is ya boy what's happening? Glen asked concerned. He knew Billy well and this call was so unlike him. He shared the story of his days in New York. Glen and he talked about everything. "Who is this guy?" "did you ask her?" Glen questioned. "Not yet I just want her to tell me why she lied to me about it!" Billy had moved to the sitting area in the lobby and continued to talk to Glen. "We had promised each other that this was not a business trip and we were here to enjoy each other. She was supposed to be with her girl Kelly at Neiman's shopping and" I "mind you saw her sitting having lunch with this bleach blonde "Alfonso Lamas!" "Glen thought for a moment, Bill all jokes aside I really don't know the situation as you do, I admit but before you jump to conclusion and do something you may regret give her a chance to tell you the truth." Glen was sounding like his dad and I knew this was good advice so I continued to listen. "I'm listening man" I told him. "We don't always know the truth, we often jump to situations to quickly and cause ourselves unneeded hurt and pain" "If I was a betting man, I'd give Jilly the benefit of the doubt!" Glen concluded. I thought for a minute and said, "Thanks man I'll think it through" and Glen "thank your dad for me for raising such a wonderful son, bye" Glen hung up the receiver and excused himself from his coworkers who was there in his home. He was surely giving Billy his dad's advice. He can't say what he would have done in that situation. Glen partied with the best of them but he knew his limits and somehow could pull himself back on the curve when needed. This call concerned him. This was his dear friend his brother growing up and he didn't like the tone of his call. He knew Billy loved Jillian and she had somehow broken his heart. Real first love can be that way. He took a moment by himself and prayed for his dear friend. "Dear God, please help my brother to be free from anything that is holding him except you." Help him to leave his past in the past and look to you for his future. Most of all help him to forgive Jillian so that he will be forgiven in Jesus your darling son's name I pray AMEN"

Billy sat looking at his watch. He knew the time was getting closer and he was sure she was missing him by now. He needed to get his heart back. He was caught up in the Big Apple and had almost made a decision that he wasn't ready for is what he was thinking as he continued to sit in the lobby watching couples go walking by. Then he got an idea and headed up to the second floor of the Waldorf were the retail stores were located. Jillian had finished her shower and got out looking around the room. The rooms at the Waldorf are quite large but it was obvious Billy wasn't in this one. Jillian dressed for the evening and sat waiting for Billy to return. She had called his cell phone but was only getting a recording. She looked over at his luggage he had left lying open on the bed in his hurry to leave the room. "I tell you this is so unlike Billy" she thought to herself as she put the pieces of clothing back, he still had in his luggage. Most of the things they a brought with them were in the drawers or hanging in the closet. But he kept his shaving bag, and a few other pieces still in the luggage. Jillian moved the luggage around and out fell this little black box. She screamed. "OH! OH! I SHOULDN'T! Jillian couldn't resist she opened the box to find a "five carat flawless diamond ring! "OH MY GOD! She looked and she put it on her finger and danced around the room. "It's going to happen! It's going to happen! She was on top of the world. She moved over near the bed. Then she heard Billy make a noise at the door, quickly putting the ring back in its case and putting it in the luggage. She would put it back in its pouch later. Billy walked in '" ready yet" using a now cheerful voice and attitude to match. '" I'M READY! Jillian said excited for this evening to start. '" I have decided to take a cab to Manhattan to save time okay with you?" Sure!" Jillian said everything at this moment was okay with her. '" I certainly couldn't have you riding a subway train in that outfit" he said smiling at the gorgeous Jillian. She was wearing a lush alpaca dress with a matching long coat in an oatmeal color which she accented with red crocodile print pumps with high heels showing off her very shapely legs and a matching boxcar tote. '" Just for you honey" she said coming over and wrapping her arms around him and kissing him passionately. He returned the kiss but inside he wasn't feeling it. Billy was still thinking about earlier today. He looked at the luggage he had left on the bed and walked over to it. '" Jillian will you do me a favorite?" I asked '" anything for you Billy this is our week together'" she sweetly replied still thinking about that ring. "Would you go down and get some aspirins from the drug store? I'm feeling a slight headache and I don't want anything to ruin this evening" I confessed. "I'm on my way" she said leaving grabbing her Truex handbag tote and walked out the door. I opened my luggage and immediately noticed the little black box had been moved from the side pouch of the suitcase. I took the black box and put it in the inside pocket of my suit jacket and returned the luggage back to the rack. I have got to give her a chance to tell the truth. I don't want to jump to conclusions. Finally, Billy sat on the bed with his head down and his heart hurting. "I love her".

He had grown up watching his dad make all the mistakes in the relationship. And his mom never did anything that he was aware of and was there for him when everything else wasn't. That's what he had found in Jillian and today she shattered all his dreams and her picket fence! Soon he heard Jillian coming in. She was singing their favorite song "Here, sweetheart feel better" she said handing him the aspirin bottle. Billy had earlier purchased a huge bottle of aspirins coming in that day from Wall Street. 'Thanks Jilly" he said walking over to get a glass of water. "Jillian you must be hungry did you even get lunch today?" I really didn't want to ask the questions, but I needed the truth, because I had purchased a ring for my second favorite girl next only to mom and wanted to give it to her at her parent's home. The truth Jillian! the truth I kept thinking to myself. Jillian on the other hand was thinking if he knows I met with Blair behind his back he will really be mad! NO! this is our time together she thought to herself. I cannot tell him I met with Blair! "You're right honey, Jillian explained. "I'm starving I walked around in that store from floor to floor and lost all track of time. There was no time for lunch" she said sweetly to Billy sitting next to him on the bed. "The truth all I wanted was the truth". I paused for a minute thinking she would change the story. But sadden still she didn't. "Okay Jillian I'm ready let's go" I felt sad holding her hand has she reached for her matching coat and headed to Manhattan to her parents' the Fleming's home. The Fleming's house was very nice. They lived in one of the affluent neighborhoods in Manhattan and their home exemplified it. Frances had planned a beautiful dinner and light conversations kept a smile on everyone's face. Jillian sat talking about her shopping earlier and leaving out the part that really mattered to me though I KEPT MY SMILE IN TACT. After a very lovely dinner and talking golf with Roger Fleming Billy presented Jillian with her birthday present the little black box. She was so surprised when she opened it and found a diamond tennis bracelet! Jillian, her parents and Billy sat through a show at Radio Music Hall in silence. And Jillian excused herself several times because the show was a ballet of Romeo and Juliet and she couldn't contain the tears that continued to flow even after they returned to the Waldorf. She turned her back and cried all night long. He only listened.

CHAPTER 32

Listen to the voice of God

Billy returned to Cambridge Massachusetts and poured himself into his work. He would go into his office very early in the morning. And when he didn't have classes at the University he would stay late at the office. Jillian stayed the remainder of the time in New York visiting her parents and his best guess, trying to understand what went wrong. He had asked her several times about her day in New York but she couldn't bring herself to tell him about Blair. If there was nothing affectionate going on between the two of them why the secrecy? My guess that didn't even enter her mind, Jillian's attitude was due to Billy. She didn't know Billy had seen her with Blair. She wouldn't have lied. She wanted him to be there when she signed on at the firm. But what was on her mind is that they had promised to discuss the job proposal before she signed. So, she couldn't tell him she had already signed. She couldn't tell him she planned to see Blair, after he called. She had every intention of going shopping! She couldn't tell him she had lunch with Blair when she was supposed to be shopping! If only Billy would have come along. Jilly would probably be wearing his ring right now! Jillian sat crying her eyes out. He had caught her in a lie. Everything beautiful Billy had planned for that week to him had been ruin. And as if none of it mattered, she had betrayed his trust. Not only with the meeting but his love for her she had brought miss-trust too! She thought to herself would she ever rebound from this? She loved Billy and no one else!"

Billy was working late one night at his desk when his phone rang after hours. He was tired and found himself nodding very close to sleep. Cooper had even said goodnight at least an hour ago. He was slowly but still getting out some briefs for an upcoming case. "Hello William

Parker" he said answering his phone. "Hi Billy" came the voice. His heart stopped this voice sound so familiar, it couldn't be not after all these years "Hello, he answered again trying to distinguish the voice. "Hi Billy this is Doris, Jillian's friend, came the voice. "Oh, I'm sorry for a moment there you sound like someone else I knew a long time ago"! he told her. How may I help you?" "I was looking for Jillian I haven't seen her lately is she alright?" Doris asked. "Jilly's find she's spending a few days with her parents in New York. Is there something I can help you with?" he then asked. "I don't know if Jillian shared with you about my surgery I'm having" Is it possible you could have her call me?" she asked. "Jillian did mention it Doris but I will call her and you can speak with her" he remarked. "Thank you and please tell her Davie says hi!" she added. I will goodnight". Hanging up he went to the men's room and washed his face, came back to his office and got his briefcase and coat, turned off the lights and went home. He had been home two days and it was so lonely without Jillian, her cute little smile and her way of coming up with all those recipes to cook. Billy thought about everything she ever did. Love had him and he loved her. He walked into his empty house nothing unusual about that. He'd done that time and time again. But Jillian was right around the corner or soon coming. Now he knew how she must have felt. But this was her fault, she lied he thought to himself. A lie hurts everyone involved he reasoned. He had not spoken with her since leaving New York and now he had promised Doris he would give Jillian her message regarding her upcoming surgery, can't put it off walking over to dial her mother's number "Hello' good evening Mrs. Fleming how are you this evening?' Billy inquired. I'm fine, just fine thank you for asking. She returned the greeting "And you how are you doing?" "I'm great is Jillian in?" "Jillian's still at the office would you like me to have her call you when she gets in?" she responded. Stunned, but obviously she thought I knew "Sure please have her call me as soon as she gets in" "Thanks Mrs. Fleming have a good evening". Hanging up I flopped on my leather sofa exhausted and confused. Seconds later my doorbell rang. "Ding, dong" who could possibly know how tired I am and want to visit me now? he said joking as he slowly walked to the door. "Yes, may I help you?" asking opening the door. It was Doris and Davie they had brought him a homemade spaghetti dinner and all the trimmings. French bread and Parmesan cheese with a large green salad.

"I felt so bad bothering you at the office" Doris said "I wanted to do something nice for you". So, Davie and I cooked you, dinner. Hope you haven't eaten?" She questioned. "No, I haven't eaten but you didn't have to do this. "Though I do thank you very much, do come in" he told her. She brought in the main course and while she went back to her car to get the bread and other trimmings Davie sat on the sofa and told Billy all about his first-grade class. Doris walked over with her scarf covering her face to hide her disfigurement and said "thank you for letting me do this for you!" Davie was missing Jillian and you. Before he could answer his phone rang; it was Jillian. "Hi Jillian, hold for a moment, handing Doris the phone. What Jillian and I had to talk about is going to take longer than a phone conversation. So, I handed the phone to Doris. I went over to the table to prepare my plate while Doris spoke with Jillian. They talked for what seemed minutes then she walked back over to the table. Davie had started eating spaghetti with me. "Davie has eaten already Billy!" Doris informed me. "I know mommy but I wanted to eat with Mr. Billy so he wouldn't have to eat alone" Davie said. "Thank you, David and thank you Doris this was very kind of you." and these are great spaghetti you must give Jilly your recipe" he requested of her. "I will do that for you". Doris sat down quietly on the sofa and read a magazine while Davie finished eating his spaghetti dinner. "Let's go Davie I'll get the dishes from Jillian later." Doris then turned to say Jillian will be home Saturday. "Thanks again I said. I hope I didn't sound strange at the office but your voice startled me. You sound like someone I use to know" Billy shared. "I didn't mean to bother you, thanks again! Doris replied and moved quickly out the door. "Goodnight Davie, Goodnight Mr. Billy.

After an hour or so Jillian called back "Has Doris left yet? She asked "Doris said Davie wanted to bring you dinner" "Yes! Quite a while ago Jilly but I know that's not your problem!" I was very pointed. Jillian called with a chip on her shoulder and trying to imply something between Doris and I. I wasn't going to be the one she trashed on. I was hurting too. "Jillian let's start again I suggested. "How are you doing?" "I love you William Parker and would've got me going crazy!!" Jillian confessed. I really don't know what I'm saying" she burst out. "Jillian when are you coming back to Cambridge?" I asked her. "Saturday Billy, I'm going to try and keep Davie while Doris goes to Los Angeles" she told him. "For six weeks Jillian? I hope you know what you're' doing!" I warned. "Your mom says you were at the office". "Mom said what?" "Enough! Jillian, we have to talk I'll see you Saturday" I stated and disconnected the line.

Tetra had thought about calling her son today. She had gotten up early preparing for her evening fellowship she had planned with her women's group. Realizing the time difference, she decided she'd call him later. She wanted to see when Billy had planned to visit it had been to long between visits she thought. She had Ms. Laine and other staff preparing tonight's courses and the house was filled with all kinds of wonderful aromas when David came down for breakfast before heading out to the office. "You may be safer upstairs honey" Tetra said. "I'll bring up our breakfast. Without questions David turned and went quickly back upstairs. She was having a "Women reaching women" meeting at her home and it looked to be a success. All age groups of women were invited and Tetra had been working for weeks on the menu for the night. She and Christine Guillory's group headed up the effort with the leaders of various women groups in the church. "Ms. Lanie is the rack of lamb being prepared?' "Yees, madam Parker" everything who have requested so far is being prepared or is already." "Madam you are preparing the crumb apple strudels no!" Ms. Laine asked with her strong accent. "Yes, yes I will take care of those". "Please over see everything for me Dora please" I have some things to do at the Center. If you need me call there you have my office number" Tetra said going upstairs with a tray carrying breakfast for her and David. "Good morning again honey, she said entering the room. "I didn't want you to get crushed under all that activity going on down there" she teased putting the tray on the sitting area table of the large master bedroom. "Something nutritious for you" she said pointing to the half grapefruit toast and coffee in front of him. "Thank you dear" he voiced.   David finished tying his necktie and picked up his cup of coffee. "So, this looks to be a great success" he remarked. "Well those of us who went down to Dallas came back rejoicing and wanted to share with all the women in our congregation". So yes, I'm looking for a wonderful *time*. "I have material I brought back to share that hopeful will inspire, renew, and refresh all of us" Tetra added. David sat down eating his toast and grapefruit and finishing his coffee. Tetra continued to share her plans for the evening. "I'll certainly make myself scarce tonight" David told her. "I'll probably be a little late anyway" he admitted. "Not to late, I hope. You do tend to work a bit late dear". Tetra was concerned he usual drops before he stops. "I won't be that late I'll sneak in and hide up here in the bedroom" He smiled. "Babe I'm sure you won't be detected anywhere you chose to sit in this home" I still have to look for you on occasion" she teased. They finished their breakfast and checking their looks in the mirror and headed down stairs. Tetra stopped by the kitchen dropped of the tray gave last minute instructions to Ms. Laine and kissed David and both walked out the door together. David headed to his office he was going to try and called Mr. Hemley's caregiver and make an appointment to visit him in Kansas. He walked in the office. Everyone was busy as usual. He sat down and started his day. He had several messages to answer and his secretary was standing at his door. "Mr. Parker, I have rescheduled your meeting with Benuf and Brown at l0 am today in the large conference room 4. With a nod from David she went back to her desk. David knew there were a few things he wanted to have in place before this meeting. He had been after this account for a year and contract negotiations were on going. This young man they represented had great potential and David's firms as well as many others were vying to clinch the deal. He came out of his 8:30 meeting and saw a folder his secretary had left on his desk. It was his reservations and itinerary with schedule for a conference he and his mangers were attending in San Francisco. "He had to remember to share it with Tetra. It was one of those few trips he still had to make as Chief Executive Officer lasting two days Monday and Tuesday. "'Good he thought the beginning of the week. He was still trying to find some time off soon to go to Kansas. But for now, his plate was full. "Mr. Parker what time is the manager's meeting today?" Gavin one of the managers asked passing him in the hallway. David had asked his secretary to schedule a meeting so they might discuss the trip to the Bay and field any questions are concerns needing to be addressed before they leave. "Three or four but check with Gabriella for definite time and place" he said hurrying to a vendor's meeting on the third floor.

Tetra parked in the parking lot of the church. This was a rare thing to do when services where going on there. It would be full. Only the early arrivers get designated parking spots. She looked out on the vacant lot on the east side of the building. Mt. Nebo had grown. With the exception of this piece of vacant property they owned three city blocks. Even by those who did not attend the worship services at Mt. Nebo on Sundays or throughout the week were using the Parsons Center. Tetra had put together a program with the schools in the area that now actively had many after school activities and programs for all including the underprivileged. There was tutoring for anyone wanting or needing this service for every age group. She loved the work God had called her too and prayed mightily about it every day.

As she stood there looking, she decided to go over and walk around in the lot. It would make a perfect overflow lot not far from the main building she thought. "I wonder who owns it." She knew that wouldn't be hard to find out. A call down to the City and that question would be quickly answered. She was compelled to pray and then she went into the Center and sat at her desk. Answering calls and prescreening for the use of the recreation facilities Tetra was very busy. She was setting up tutorial student volunteers from the college to aid the many members and community participants that came through looking for a particular service. It was going very well. The students loved it and they were helping others and getting college credits while doing it. Tetra had been so busy her morning had gotten away from her. "'Oh, she sighed a few quiet moments, she sat back in her chair. "'That's right let me call and see who owns that property.

She called and found out the property belonged to a Mattie Stroggins. "May I have her address please?' Tetra asked the clerk. A quick "thank you" and she hung up. Looking quickly at the address it was a little old house sitting right next to the vacant lot. It almost appeared vacant as Tetra left her office at the Center walking up to it. Funny had not noticed it before and had driven by it every day coming to Mt. Nebo or the Center. She looked around as she walked upon the rickety little porch and knocked lightly on the door. She stood for what seemed to be five or ten minutes and started to walk away. Then she heard "You finally came!" this little old lady with white hair pulled back in two large braids came to the door. "I knew you would come!" she said again. Tetra was thinking she must be expecting someone and thinks it's me. She opened the door as if she knew her or had seen her before. "Hello Mrs. Scroggins?" Tetra question because she had never met her nor seen her before. "Its alright baby come on in" she said inviting Tetra into her home. "I was wondering if you all were listening to me?" she kept saying. "Tetra looked around and it was very apparent that she lived alone and as best she could take care of herself.

"Mrs. Scroggins, she said "I'm Tetra Parker I work over at the church" "Yes, I know, I sees you all coming and going all the time. I keeps praying that God would send one of his angels to see bout me his word said he would" she told her with her heart. Tetra looked around and lying on her table was a very well used bible that lay open to the book of Psalms. "Baby can I get you something to eat or to drink? she asked. She reminded Tetra so much of her Grandmother Charlemane when she was growing up. "No maam" she answered, "I came to talk with you about the vacant lot you own next door." "Oh, she sighed "he never told me how he would get you here". And for a moment Tetra thought she still didn't understand. 'Herbert bought that land for our son a long time ago when he was a little boy" she said with her southern accent which Tetra understood perfectly. Herbert Sr.'s gone now and I have no use for it. It just sits there" she added. "I would as a member being part of the church like to purchase it for a parking lot". We have grown so large parking has become a problem she shared with her. "That's all right it all belongs to Him what we do with it should be for Him" she said and got up to get her a drink of water. Tetra noticed she was laboring to do so. So, she quickly jumped up "please let me help you ma'am." "Thank you kindly, I don't get to much help round here, she acknowledged. They sends Jean in once a week to fix me some food. And they's bring me a meal every day. But they don't stop long enough to talk. So, thank, you thank you kindly for this visit." Tetra handed her the glass of water looking at the overcrowded kitchen and the rest of the house. She made her way back to her chair and sat down. Tetra stood for a moment in her small kitchen and prayed. She felt badly, she was practically on top of the church and all the help they were giving out they had missed this precious soul of a women. "I don't get out much anymore." "I sees folks going by on they's way to church. Be wishing and praying some time they would stop and help me to go". "Herbert and I used to go there, long time ago. But the small church sat empty for many years". She told her. "When you plan on using it?" she then asked. "We want to buy it from you Mrs. Scroggins, and pave it to match the other lots we have,"

Tetra shared with her heart so heavy she wanted to cry. "Well that's alright too. Just a minute" shuffling through a drawer of papers near her "Here it is" handing Tetra a business card. 'Call my son, he'll give it to you" he knows all about it!" she said handing her the phone. Tetra had not seen one of the rotary dials in a while. Mrs. Scroggins sat looking at her "dial, baby it's alright she kept saying. "Tetra sat the heavy phone on a table covered with papers and letters, "that's alright, just pushed them to the side" she said in her soft sweet voice. "Mr. Scroggins office how may I help you?' came a secretary sounding like she was speaking from her nostrils. "May I speak with Herbert Scroggins please?" 'I'm calling on behave of his mother Mattie Scroggins is he in?" Tetra asked. "Hold on please" she replied. Hardly any time passed when "Hello this is Herbert Scroggins Jr. is my mother all right?" came a deep voice. "Your mother is fine I'm sitting with her right now" Tetra shared with her son. I'm calling on behave of the church next door. We're interested in the vacant property your family owns" she told him. Yes, yes, he kept saying as Tetra laid out the plans, she thought they would use. She hadn't talked with anyone from Mt. Nebo. God had just laid it on her heart this morning. Then he asked to speak with his mother. "Hello son, I'm fine now that God has answered my prayer. "That's wonderful Herbert that's wonderful it's what he wanted. I love you too son." She handed her back the phone wiping her eyes with her hankie she called it. Herbert Scroggins told Tetra in a loving way that's what his mother wanted prepare the paperwork and send or fax it to him and it's a done deal. He wasn't asking for any certain amount his mother told him God had already set the price. Just send him the documents and he'd get everything signed. And he will make sure everything is taken care of and sent back to her as soon as possible. Her son now lived in Mississippi with his wife and children. "Thank you, baby, she told her. "Oh no Mrs. Scroggins we should be thanking you" Tetra affirmed. "No! no! declared Mrs. Scroggins what I did was nothing. I learned a long time ago to obey my father, but it took me some time to do what he says. You heard him speak to you this morning and you acted on it today". Tetra sat there with her listening to her wisdom and her knowledge of God's written word. She shared about her days in the little church how active she had been. Her husband was a devoted deacon that had gone on to be with the Lord. Tetra even fixed them a cup of tea and prepared her some buttered toast as they continued to talk and relate to each other about God's promises. Then Tetra got an idea. The women's group tonight will have a special guest in their midst, Mrs. Mattie Scroggins not only tonight but as long as Mrs. Scroggins lived. She Tetra Parker' would personally see to it.

CHAPTER 33

Have I convinced you yet?

It was late November and Jillian had made good on her promise to keep little Davie for her friend Doris while she goes to Los Angeles for facial surgery. She came back from New York and shared with Billy about the day he saw her having lunch with Blair. "He's the Manager over the department at the New York firm" she confessed as she sat talking with Billy about that awful day in New York. She shared with him about how she wrestled with signing but then decided to accept the firms offer. She knew Blair was right. She had spoken with many of her colleague's and friend's, who were still trying to get their foot in the door. This was a great opportunity. Jillian felt so bad because she and Billy had promised each other that this was a fun trip not business. "I'm sorry honey I spoiled our time together" she sighed. Billy was forgiving of her lie but still held off giving her the engage ring. He felt the moment had passed and he needed time to forget about the incident too! Jillian had signed on to work in New York starting after the first of the year. That would give her time to prepare mentally until she passes her bar exam which was due to be taken in mid-December.

They both were very busy these days Jillian was getting Davie off to school and going to her law classes at Radcliff and still working part time in the Cambridge firm. Billy was working longer hours at the office negotiating contracts and reading and rereading a load of briefs. The few classes he had left at the university were in the evening and maybe an occasional Saturday if needed. But far the most part he had completed his study. Jillian was staying home more now. She didn't have the freedom to come and go at will. She was taking care of little David Doris's son. She really didn't mind she loved it. I said almost too much. "Hi Jillian, how's your morning?" I would really love to see you!" Billy said calling because Jillian and he had spent very little time together since she came back. "I have to take Davie to school and I have an exam that should last an hour and I'll meet you at your place about 10 am" Jillian told him. "I'll be there!" I said hanging up my phone excited to be meeting my girl. I faxed several legal documents to the courthouse and had the secretary type some others. I sat through a meeting regarding affirmative action and looking at my watch the whole time. Shortly after the meeting I shared with the receptionist that I was taking and early lunch and would be back in two or three hours. I was glad I still had this luxury as an employee for the law firm. "Whistling along to my gospel music I stopped and purchased fresh flowers and picked up two specialty sandwiches from our favorite deli. I always played gospel music when I'm by myself it keeps me grounded" I think. "Ring, ring, Hello, hi son!" hello mom how are you doing?' I'm wonderful but I'm missing you it's been a long time since you graced my presence planning to soon." Tetra asked. 'Mom if I plan nothing else you know I always plan for you!" he remarked. "Yes, yes I know she said teasing but when are you coming to see me?" Well mom I tell you I'm cramming in all my classes and work is busy though fulfilling, not complaining"." Jillian is keeping her friend's little boy and our schedules are not very flexible right now". I confided. You and Jillian can't steal a weekend off it would do you both good". She told him. "But she has her friend's little boy" I kept saying. "I don't see a problem bring him too, mom stated, how old is he Billy?" "A very talkative six-year-old mom and you know how that can be" I confessed. "I sure would love to have you all over Thanksgiving, and bring the child with you we have plenty of room" mom said persuasively to me. "Mom I know Jillian would love that we will talk and I will let you know soon." I love you son and give my love to Jillian." "I will mom, I will. Billy was rounding the corner when he saw Jillian standing out front of his house banging on the door. Seeing him pull up she stepped away and stood by her car. "Why are you standing outside? I asked walking up with an arm full of flowers. "How do you expect me to go in?' Jillian asked. "Where's your key Jillian?" right here she said showing him her key ring. "It doesn't fit!" Oh! That's right I had the locks changed, dad's suggestion he said putting the key into the lock and opening the door. "Your key is up in the armoire. "William Parker you'd better be glad you showed up when you did" Jillian said holding him around his waist walking into the house. She took the flowers and put them in a vase and Billy put the sandwiches in plates on the table. "Good you bought lunch thanks! Davie and I eat so early and we are usually in bed by nine" she told him.

"I know!" I told her "the other night when I stopped by after a law contract class you were sound asleep. And I didn't have the heart to wake you". "Did you get my note? I asked. "I did and I do" Jillian told him coming over standing between his legs as he sat at the table. She kissed him passionately and flirted in front of him with her body. "I'm trying to finish my lunch you know!" he told her responding slightly to her advances. "Okay but your loss" she said going back sitting to finish her sandwich. "Jillian mom called she wanted to know if we would like to spend Thanksgiving with her?" "That's wonderful Billy you know I would love to go to mama Parkers but I have Davie?" I know, I told her she said you could bring him too." "She really did! Oh, Billy let's go please let's go! She said running over to sit on his lap hugging and kissing on him. "You're starting to convince me!" she kissed his neck and then Jillian kissed him with her heart possessed for him her hands moving up and down his head. He grabbed her around her tiny little waist and with his hands moving all over her body things had started happening. "Have I convinced you yet?" she said teasing him with her tongue. "We are getting there!" he muddled because she was kissing him again. This time off came the top she was wearing. "I really feel like you want to convince me! he mocked. Then she moaned his name. "Biillyee!" "I know you're trying to convince me" Billy said "Let me help you!" he picked her up and headed up the stairs. Alone at last all that could be heard was "Oh Jillian" after they entered his room.

CHAPTER 34

Kansas City our new home

Desmond and Mossy had finally moved into their home. The white fluffy snow covered the ground. And the mover's truck was still stuck in the driveway. Snow was completely covering the tires of their large vans and no matter how they tried it wouldn't go backward or forward. The large moving vans delivering the Owens furniture had gotten stuck in front of the couples newly built home. They would have to wait till morning to get a snow shovel to help plow them out. So, the befuddled movers stayed the night in a hotel near Langley Estates courtesy of the Owens and Owens & MacFinney law firm. Most of their furniture for their bedrooms was already in the house and Mossy had begun putting the beds rails together despite Desmond telling her to wait until he came back from taking the men down the road. Getting assistance from the movers Desmond put together the master bed before leaving. Thanking the men for their help they all loaded into his Hummer and off they went. He drove his four-wheel drive H2 utility vehicle right through the snow. "I'll be right back Moss" and we will put the other beds together tonight if nothing else!" he told her. With all the movers out, Desmond locked the door and left to go a mile or two down the road with all eight movers on broad. "I'll be in here hanging our clothes!" Mossy yelled to him as he left. They had purchased a beautiful custom-built home in the Kansas City Hills. It was out a ways and the next neighbor was miles from them. They had built a custom home that was fabulous. It was truly a dream home taking almost two years to build. Mossy was so glad she could get everything out of boxes and spread out some beautiful pieces of art she had gotten from her homeland for their wedding. Her clothes she teased had gone out of style stored away all those months. And her coats she would trade for bears. It got cold in Massachusetts. And Kansas had snow, snow and more snow. Desmond and Mossy encountered their first impression of Kansas City, Kansas, when they went down town to purchase furniture for their new home. Mossy wanted the smooth modern look for their living room. One day Desmond while downtown becoming familiar with his new surroundings walked into Cogenhagen Furniture store in downtown Kansas City. In his casual dress wearing his blue jeans and Kani boots he had been working around his new home and walked in with a big "Howdy" smile on his face. He browsed around the store with the watchful eye of the store clerk surveying his every move. 'Finally walking over" the store clerk asked. "Is there something you want?" according to Desmond he asked in a tone that suggested he was in the wrong part of town. "Excuse me?' Desmond returned in his now I've passed the bar voice. Pointed enough that the clerk changed the tone and words of his next question "How may I help you?" to which Desmond answered "I would like to purchase some furniture for my home" he said very confidently. The clerk still questioning, "let's walk this way" the clerk said heading toward the closeouts and 30% and 50% off most items in these sections. Desmond likes a challenge so he went along for the ride. "These pieces here are great in smaller homes in the area." Looking as if to say I got cha!' to Desmond. "I'm sorry I didn't get your name sir" Desmond replied. "Scott Duncan" he returned. "Scott please to meet you I'm Desmond Owens" extending his hand out. He had now reversed the leadership role typical Des. "My family and I just had our home built in Langley Estates. "Still haven't met our neighbors do plan to on our next vacation "he joked. I'm looking for something that would cover 4,500 square feet of home area. I'm just not sure if this will do it!" Desmond stood waiting for the salesperson to show his real color. "The man stood up straight and tugged on his trousers checking his appearance with a forced smile. Desmond continued, "This establishment does have very nice furniture pieces that I'm sure would fit in some areas of my home. Maybe you can give me a call when you have had time to think about it" Desmond remarked handing him his gold embossed business card "Desmond Owens "Attorney at Law" and walking out of the store. Before weeks end Desmond and Mossy walked into Cogenhagen. He now wearing his business attire and Mossy in her designer apparel got the top end furniture they wanted that just happened to be on sale. They found no mattered what they wanted the whole store's merchandise was on sale. "Most blacks and poor whites live in the slums southeast of the freeway loop" Desmond shared with Moss as they walked out of the store. "Thus, the over kill today with the sale" she added. So, no matter what it took the movers from Cogenhagen were going to keep their promised day of delivery and so that's how it came to this. But Desmond didn't mind putting them up for the night he had gotten such a great deal on all the furniture pieces he purchased from them. Arriving back home he found Mossy curled up in her large king size bed with boxes all around her. The closet had started to come together and their toiletries were scattered on the vanity top in the master suite. Desmond looked at his watch and sat for a moment unwinding from the drive through the snow "What a relief" he said "I'm in my home at last"

Desmond was from a very prominent family. Both his parents were lawyers also. So being in a large home was not over whelming. But being in his own home with his wife was frosting on the cake he says. He knew after the move in episode his first purchase would be a snowplow of his own. And some snow ski's for family fun. They were traveling thirty miles one way to their office in Kansas City from their home in Langley Estates. Mossy would rotate her schedules going in late or coming home earlier most days. Desmond and the new young attorney they had hired would usually close for the evening. "Desmond honey, who is Macfinney? Mossy asked one day as they were setting up the office and rearranging the desk furniture. "I noticed you didn't take his name down when you put our names on the marquee outside" Mossy added. "There is no Mr. Macfinney!" he said looking at her. "Well ok Mrs. Macfinney, I know I wasn't the first female in this law firm!" she said starring at her husband. "Well Mrs. Owens you're wrong!" 'Desmond, why does everything have to be a puzzle?" I asked if it was a he, you said no! then I said she and you say no! What? or who is Macfinney?" she stammered. Desmond liked doing this he says it makes you think. "You were right saying Macfinney is a woman, but Macfinney wasn't a lawyer. Macfinney is grandma's maiden name. "When granddad opened this firm, no one would come to him because he didn't have a partner saying two heads are better than one. So, he invented him a partner in the way of grandmother who never studied law and increased his business greatly. So, it's always been here as part of this firm's heritage and family secret he smiled kissing Mossy on her forehead. 'Oh, I see she said "family secret". Mossy smiled and continued working around the office.

"Desmond have you spoken with Billy lately?" Mossy asked. "It's been months since I've talked to Jillian". I'll have to call and let them know we're in our home. Maybe they can come up for a visit?" she suggested. "That's wonderful the holidays are coming up chest nuts and cozy fire, enjoying it with old friends, let's call!" "Then looking at his watch Desmond remembered the time difference. I'll catch him at the office according to the time he should probably still be there. "William Parker" came the voice at the other end of the phone. Billy it's Desmond, how are you?" hi guy great! Good to hear from you!" I said enthusiastically. "How is Kansas?" "Cold and right now under snow" Desmond informed him but there is good news!" we're in our home!" he added. "That's great man, is it everything you wanted?" Billy asked. "It's getting there we finally got everything in Mossy is still designing some rooms but for the most part it's livable and I can find my razor!" he said drawing a smile from Billy. 'What does your holidays look like?' Desmond asked getting out his electronic organizer to check his schedule. "Going to Washington to my parents for Thanksgiving, mom's been calling so I'm taking Jillian with me this time." He said. "It's about time you make a honest women of her. Are you going to pop the questions there?" Desmond asked. Billy hadn't even thought about that after the disastrous ordeal in New York. He had put the ring in his safety deposit box and forgot about it. "Desmond, if you were anyone else, I would be offended by that, you know I love Jillian but a Mossy doesn't come along very often if at all", I told him. Desmond knew marriage was a serious thing for Billy they had talked about it in great lengths when they room together in college. "Man, I know it's your call I truly didn't mean anything by that he told him. "I know man I know". "Give my love to Moss and I'll call you when I'm headed your way" Billy concluded. "What's your address out there, cow poke! "I asked trying to make Desmond feel better about what was said because I really understood that he meant no harm. "Got it. Take care I'll call you soon bye." Desmond disconnected the line he was still holding on to the receiver. "Mossy" I feel so bad" He was sitting down in his red leather executive chair after hanging up the phone. "I want everyone to have what we have" he said looking in Mossy's face and holding her hand.

Mossy was from southeastern Europe Yugoslavia. She was not able to have her parents at their wedding but her parents would plan a trip to see them as soon as things settled down. Her younger brother and sister wanted to come and visit but because Desmond and Mossy were not yet in their home it made it impossible. The small temporary apartment space they had been living in since coming to Kansas could hardly hold the two of them. Now Mostalgia was decorating her own home with some of the beautiful items she had brought with her from her country. She and Desmond went for a visit before the wedding to meet her parents who for health reasons couldn't travel then. She had brought back several gifts from her homeland. Most were wedding gifts from family and friends in Europe. "Desmond" will you please help me place this," she asked as he sat reading the Washington Post news. It was a print of religious writings she had beautifully framed and was trying to place it on the wall in their home office. After what seemed a long time and still no answer Mossy asked again. "Honey are you coming?" she repeated. "Yes, dear I'm getting the ladder because I know you're going to move this more than one time. "Did you write your parents and let them know we were in our home?' "Yes, Des and Dalmatia and Slovenia are very anxious to come. That's great what did you tell them?"

"I'm trying to get the house together Des, and then we can have all the family for a visit". "Who's left babe?' Desmond asked while holding the frame up against the third wall "just mom and dad immediate family that's left". That's great. Let's plan to have mom and dad and your parents as well as your brother and sister for the Christmas holiday. Sidney, Desmond's older brother was in Greece right now covering a news story. We have to call and then make all the arrangements he told her. "That's wonderful I'm glad you agree" no that's not what I'm agreeing to that's okay too. I'm agreeing that this is now the perfect place for the frame thanks hon you can put the ladder away now. Desmond and Mossy had put a lot into designing their beautiful tri-level upstairs home which included a basement game room that cover the entire basement floor. Their master suite was half of the second floor and had a 6-foot long tub with mosaic tile all around it. Overhead they had placed amber colored lights and music from speakers built into the ceiling created a relaxing atmosphere. "I love the heating in the bathroom" Mossy told Desmond. Who with questions agreed to put in the radiant floor heating for early morning or late-night bathers? "I think it's great!" Desmond responded. They did a wonderful job. With all the custom fitting and fine details of the ceiling and closets the Owens had designed a gorgeous home. There was so much open space and both wanted lots of windows to let in all the sunshine of the morning. It was one of Mossy's proud designer moments. She had chosen bright colorful materials to accent the peach wood and smooth lines of the master suite's furniture. Desmond loved his library and of course the game room that by the way was awaiting its furnishings and his spacious yard. He and Mossy had together purchased and collected lots of books over the years that filled one wall of beautiful custom-made bookshelves. And an old secretariat they had restored from down in the basement of the law office was a "prize find!" he said. "I'm going over to "Jon's Home Furnishing's today Mossy would you like to come with me. There's a desk I'd like, that I'm hoping it's large enough for that space in the library." "That's a wonderful idea Mossy said. They loved their new home and often sat in the library talking or going over briefs. They sat in their gorgeous living room with cathedral ceilings and dramatic lines. Desmond in his elegant stoutly wing back chair and Mossy tickling the ivories of her classic piano.

CHAPTER 35

I love you mommy

"How's he doing Jillian?" asked Doris calling to talk with her son. 'He's fine "We're fine. How are you doing? Jillian asked. "Is everything going according to plan?" Jilly questioned. "Yes, as of right now, I'm still in a lot of pain the doctors had to do some extensive surgery. Some parts were badly damaged Doris confided. She sounded muffled. Jillian guessed from the bandages on her face. Jillian's understanding was that only the left side of her face was being reconstructed. Maybe a plastic bone to replace the sunken jawbone on that side and she would be good as new. "Well I hope things continue to stay on schedule for you. Jillian told her. "Thanks Jillian, where's my little boy can I speak with him? Doris said sounding so lonely. "Jillian handed Davie the phone, "it's your mommy" "Hi mommy" I miss you" he said. Then she talked with him for a minute before the next answer. "I'm having fun with aunt Jilly." We play games and we watch movies and we visit Mr. Billy in his big office downtown. Aunt Jilly has a big office too." Doris must have been enjoying hearing his voice. "Are you far mommy?" "Are you coming home today?" "you're coming soon!" okay mommy I'll be a big boy for aunt Jilly" and Mr. Billy too. Aunt Jilly reads me a story before I go to sleep". "My teacher Ms. May says she likes my homework". "I love you mommy! Bye mommy! He handed the phone back to Jillian who was now sitting in her cozy chair wiping tears from her eyes. Davie crawled up beside her and put his head on her lap and she put her arms around him. "I miss my mommy" he said. "I know sweetie, I know. Jillian had asked Doris if it was all right that Davie flies to Washington with her and Billy for Thanksgiving. They were going to visit with Billy's parents. She said yes, and take good care of him and love him for me Jillian and "thanks Goodnight". Jillian was crying after the phone call because it made Davie so sad. She called Billy who was still at his office "Hi honey" "hi" what's wrong Jilly?" hearing the sound of her voice. I'm just feeling sad for Davie he misses his mommy!" "Jillian, I knew this day would come what's left four weeks and two days" just hold him Jilly and love him. He'll be fine and you will too" he said to her. "Tell ya what! I'll stop by with some big ice cream cones for everyone. Are you two going to be up? I know it's a school night so I'll try to get there a bit early o.k. "Thanks sweetheart see you then". "Love you Jillian". That's just like Jillian I thought how is she going to let Doris have her son back in six weeks! And then she has to go to work in New York we haven't even discussed that yet I thought. I sat negotiating a contract over the phone on a conference call. "That's it, we will work that part out after talking with Dunigan and I certainly look forward to our next meeting. Thank you, bye." "Good!" I thought that went well. I signed off on the folder put it in my secretary's in basket, coat over my arm and walked out the door. "Let's see who makes the best cones he thought? I have an idea, I said as I drove out of the garage lot. Thirty minutes later I was pulling into Jillian's driveway it was about 6:30 p.m. He rescheduled an exam for early tomorrow morning so that he could keep his promise to Jillian. Billy walked in carrying a bag from the grocery store. Davie ran over and opened the door. Hi Mr. Billy "Hello!" young man how are you doing? I said putting the grocery bag on the kitchen counter. "Good" he said. "Have you had your dinner yet?" I asked. "Yip, aunt Jillian and I had my favorite pizza!" Billy looked at the large pizza box on the stove top. "Did you save some for me?" he asked teasingly." I think so?" "AUNT JILLY" he yelled to the back of the house. Jillian was finishing up her shower so she and Davie could go through their nightly ritual. Homework read a book, bath and tucked in bed. She came from the back with her long quilted bright colored designer house-dress. "That's pretty aunt Jillian" Thanks Davie" "Hi honey, walking over and kissing Billy lightly on his lips and hugging him gently. "I have a surprise if you've saved me some pizza!" Billy said again now teasing Jillian as Davie looked on wide-eyed. "There's plenty left". She replied "Yeah! "YEAH" Davie said loudly I like surprises. "At school we have surprises when we are good" he said. "Does this mean we're good?" he asked tugging on the tail of Billy's jacket "It sure does!" "Let's see, be careful" Billy said putting David up to the table on a chair. Jillian you get the scoop. "Got it! she said walking over from the drawer. Billy took the large container of Gunther's vanilla ice cream, assorted nuts and candies, chocolate and strawberry sauce, and of course ice cream cones from the brown paper bag. "Oh boy!" said Davie. His eyes were beaming bright. Billy put the container of ice cream in front of him. "You have to be the ice cream man and make a cone for everyone okay" he told him. "O.K!" With Billy guiding his little hands he scooped the ice cream into the cones Jillian was holding in front of him. "One, two, he counted that's a big one". "That's for aunt Jilly he said. We stood there until everyone one of us had a cone filled with ice cream. We had lots of fun choosing toppings and nuts to make each one even more special. Davie had lots of fun Jillian was smiling again and I really enjoyed myself too. Jillian, Davie and I kept each other so busy over the next weeks he hardly had time to miss Doris. Jillian planned outings for him to the big library at the Harvard campus. She stopped in another day to visit his school just to see how things were going and meet some of his friends. "Mr. Billy, aunt Jilly let me push the button on the elevator all by myself." Davie told him on one of his many visits to the Cambridge law office. "HELLO young fellow! Harman Baker saw him coming in to visit another time after school with Jillian. "That's a mighty big backpack you have there!" Harman said. "What's in it?" Davie was looking at Jillian to get permission to speak with a stranger "My books" he told him. "Well and what does a fine young man like you do with all those books, he asked? "I like to read, so I will be smart like Mr. Billy" he said proudly running into Billy's office and sitting behind his big desk. "Bye Mr. Davie said waving as Harman went back to his office smiling. Billy came in from down the hall. "To what do I owe this visit?" I asked coming in giving Jillian a kiss and shaking my future executive's hand as he spun around in my big chair. "Our flight leaves very early in the morning" Jillian reminded me. "Are you picking Davie and I up from the house are do you want me to meet you at yours? she asked. The time to go visit my parents in Washington for Thanksgiving dinner had come and Davie and Jillian were so excited. They had packed their suitcases, watered all the plants, and made sure everything was in place for the week and the big trip. Jillian was so excited she was going to mother Parker's. For years she had waited for this moment but something always came up. Or I would change my mind because of something silly she had done or forgot to do. No matter things were right now and we were on our way. Davie was excited because this was his first plane trip that he's old enough to remember anyway so he's bursting with questions. "Mr. Billy will the airplane take me high in the sky?" "Yes, Davie the airplane goes way up over the clouds I said using my hands to illustrate what I was saying. "Will there be birds up there?" he asked sadly. "Birds do fly in the sky" I told him. "But how does the man in the airplane see the bird so he won't hit him?' he was concerned for the bird's life. "I walked over and put him on my lap. "The airplane flies' way up high above the birds so he never has to hurt or hit them" I said in a way I hoped to ease his concern. "Thank you Mr. Billy I'm ready to fly now he said hugging me around my neck with Jillian standing looking on. We decided because of the early morning wake up to do a sleep over at my house. Jillian and Davie took all their luggage to my place so that everything would be in one location for a bright early start. Jillian went home later again and double-checked to make sure all was well for the week and securing her home. She had given Doris her cell phone number the number to my mom's when she spoke with her on the phone. "Ready DAVIE!" I'm READY AUNT JILLIAN!" they headed to Billy's. Much to their surprise he had sat up a tent in his living room. And the three of them slept in a tent in the middle of his living room. They watched movies, played games and ate sooo! much popcorn they could hardly sleep in anticipation of all the excitement that awaited them on the plane ride to mama Parkers.

'Jillian it is only for a week!" I teased Jilly regarding all the luggage she had brought. There are shopping malls in Washington State you know! After a laugh together we headed to the planes. Jillian was nervous and feeling butterflies in her stomach because of the anticipation of this visit. Davie wasn't saying much. I think he had too much fun the night before and needed some more sleep. I sure hoped he would get it on the plane. After making our way through all of his questions in the airport we boarded the large 747 headed for Spokane Washington. "Buckle your seatbelts!" Billy sat Davie in the middle of him and Jillian on the plane. "Is the sky going to move with us?" came his first question and it was non-stop for what seemed to be an hour. When we got permission to unbuckle the seatbelts Davie sat on my lap looking out of the window at the big fluffy clouds. And he was glad he didn't see any birds. For that matter

I was too. After a while he started to nod. I looked at Jillian who had already gone to sleep. I placed Davie carefully back in his seat and buckled the belt around him. Then I positioned my first-class seat and tucked my pillow under my head. I closed my eyes thinking we have a week before we do it all again.

CHAPTER 36

Toys and Thanks

"David" Tetra said I just came up from our game room have you noticed!" Their game room adjoined the back end of the great room of their spacious home. "You know Billy and Jillian are bringing a little person with them. "We may want to think of getting something around here to entertain him" she suggested. I was just looking at that large empty game room area". "We have the bar and pool table (with its large lion's claw feet at the legs end) but it has seen very little use since Billy left for college" she continued. "There is plenty of seating area's and some quite cozy corners for relaxing and reading very adult friendly" I'm sure Jillian will feel right at home. But there is hardly anything for and active six-year-old boy to play with Tetra insisted. "I'm going shopping David and pick up some games and other toys so he can feel like part of this family" she told him. "Ms. Laine and I have already planned the Thanksgiving menu that as you know always includes a large butterball turkey and all the trimmings" that part is taken care of. David walked around their bedroom after tying his necktie and swallowing down his last sip of coffee. "What little boy wouldn't have fun with a pin ball machine?" he asked excitedly "That was one of my favorite things growing up!" he said. "Wonderful idea dear, "They have changed a lot since then David, but that sounds great, I'll leave that up to you" she told him hugging and kissing him for his suggestion. "We've been so busy at the office since we came back from that conference in San Francisco, I barely have time for lunch" he shared with her. "But we got the contract!" that's what counts David added. I'll make the time today and stop by Farrell's Toy House on my way home. They have a large selection of toys, grabbing his suit coat jacket and kissing Tetra, David walked downstairs to his study. Tetra gathered the breakfast cups they had brought up from the morning coffee and put them on the tray and went downstairs to return them to the kitchen. Ms. Laine was cutting up celery and onions putting them into freezer bags for use later that day. "I'll see you later she told her you have a wonderful day" "You tuu!' Mrs. Parker, Dora said. "Honey I'm leaving I have a very busy day and I have lots to do at the Parson's Center with the holidays coming up", she reminded him standing in the foyer by the front door. "Yes, dear I understand I will be right behind you just getting some papers I need for the office" he said to her coming over kissing her again as she left for the day. David looked around for the telephone number of Detective Masony. The only number he had was from his old precinct. 'This will have to do" he thought. Masony had called while David was at the conference but had not left a number to be reached. "I'M LEAVING NOW"! he yelled out to Ms. Laine as he made his way to the front door. "Ave a nice day sir!" she yelled back from the kitchen. David drove along the highway to his office. "Ring! Ring! "hello" "hello Dad we're landing in four hours. We had a layover in North Dakota and should touch down in Washington around 6pm." Sounds wonderful son I'll let your mom know she's so excited already" dad told me. "It sounds like the bunch of us dad we're looking forward for the holiday time together!" I said to him. "Sounds great son will see you soon!" "Bye dad". Billy hung up his cell phone and Davie asked "is there going to be turkey at your mommy's house Mr. Billy?' Yes Davie! Turkey and all the trimmings and lots of it.

Tetra was scheduling upcoming activities for the children and groups to participate in with their classes and Sunday teachers. This was always a fun time for everyone especially the members. She also noticed there was always a growth in membership during and after the end of the year but mostly due to the holiday season. After she had spoken with her last Sunday school teacher for the day it was 2:30pm. David had called and told her Billy and Jillian was expected at 6:30pm this evening and she still had lots to do. She was excited and happy to have them up for the holiday. It had been to long between visits since Billy was home, she thought. Tetra walked over to her car she stopped and paused looking over at the freshly painted yellow house with white trim and newly constructed access ramp leading to the porch and the front door. "Hello Mrs. Scroggins she said watching her come down the ramp on her Lark that had been provided for her to get around on and then being assisted into the van by a nurse working for the county. "Good afternoon Tetra said walking over and hugging her and gently kissing her cheek. "How are you this fine afternoon" she added. "Oh, I'm fine they's keep me going to the doctor for a checkup and I'm always the one giving him advice!" she told her as only she could. "I'm sure Mrs. Scroggins that's true, you have a wonderful visit with your doctor okay, Tetra replied. "I will baby, I'll be home soon," she said allowing her nurse to close the van door and get in and pull away. Tetra quickly got into her Navigator. She drove the utility vehicle instead of her sporty Benz knowing she would certainly need the space for toys. Heading to F.A.O. Swartz for some toy shopping, off she went. She had solicited a list from some of the young ones at the center on their favorite toys. So, with her list in hand she walked into the large toy store and began looking around.

David was picking Billy up from the airport. He was rushing around his office getting things completed. He shared with Tetra when he called giving her their arrival time. David scheduled a 9:30 meeting for his staff to brief them and update them on the law firm's progress. After answered questions and applauding results they all went back to their prospective offices and areas to continue their work. David had also planned a meeting with one of his dear friends on the golf course and would be gone for the rest of the day. Notifying his secretary of his departure he left heading to Washington Windsor golf course. This beautiful course was very enjoyable for championship golf. David often negotiated many of his contracts with his business clients on the luxurious course. Getting there a little early he had taken out his clubs and sat at the bar having a coke when "howdy Parker" turning to extend his hand to Lon Andersen. "Hello Lon it's been to long" David said holding on with his tight grip. 'Would you like something to drink?" another coke please on my tab?" David requested. After they talked a little regarding their family and business deals Andersen stood up to secure the game taking his card from his wallet. "Well! David said "are you ready?" everything has been taken care of" walking his clubs out to the waiting cart. 'They just announced our tee time". David and Lon put the golf bags into the cart and started to the first hole. "The children loved the game Lon! "Thank you from them and myself' David told him. "Twas, nothing David anytime" Andersen said in his very deep voice. The golf game moved at a good pace they discussed business matters and talked about contract negotiations that made lasting conversations. Coming up to the sixteenth hole with the sun shimmering reflecting the ocean in the background David stood looking at the flagpole he had. David was shooting a three over par and feeling pretty good. Anderson a great golfer who spends a large part of his week on the course usually leads without breaking a sweat. But on this slightly chilly day in November David thought to himself how good could this get! My son was coming for the holidays and all my family would be gathered together. Walking up David lifted his nine iron to the quite sound of the day and celebrated the tough par 4 hole with and eagle. "Won't happen again in a million years!" Andersen said joking coming over to shake his hand and congratulate him. "Great job!" They ended the day laughing and talking and scheduling their next game of golf. They had done this a lot over the years. Getting back into his car after an enjoyed day on the course David headed to Farrell's to purchase a pinball machine. He walked in and found a clerk to assist him with the purchase. "Right this way he told him. "This young man maybe approaching twenty lead him over to a row of every imaginable pinball machine available. There was basketball, baseball, hockey and all the other sports. Every sport was covered in the pinball arena, David thought. Then there were animated character's Simpsons, and Rugrats. After a while he decided on one and asked if he could have it delivered as soon as possible. Paying for it to be delivered in an hour he headed home to wait until it was time to head to the airport. Tetra came in "honey!" please help me bring the things from the car so we can get them set up before he gets here" she said still very excited. "You should see some of the things I have purchased! She was practically out of breath from hurrying around carrying an arm-load of games into the house. David headed outside to see the delivery van bringing the large pinball machine he had purchased. "My goodness David what did you purchase?' Tetra asked seeing the big delivery van too backing up the driveway. "Just wait Tet this will bring lots of fun!" David was excited showing the men where to take and place the large machine. "Thank you he said tipping the men and closing the door. Then David looked in the SUV and saw all Tetra had purchased "it's only for a week!" he exclaimed "What will we do with all this stuff when they leave?" "We'll store it until he comes again or until Billy decides to give us our own grandchild" she said holding David's hand and looking at the now pile of toys lying on the floor. Tetra purchased a monopoly game

Chutes and ladder game, scrabble game as well as chess, bingo a new basketball and something new that had just come out called a video game with cartridges for his age group. They had also talked her into buying a hand held game for hours and hours of fun she was told. Tetra and David had put a basketball court in the back yard for Billy when the house was purchased. He and his friends would play for hours on a Saturday and after school before he left home for college. It wasn't used at all anymore. David would walk out occasionally if he had a recruit over for dinner and maybe throw up a few free throws with him as they talked. That's it. And all of Billy's toys except for a rare few collectables Tetra had given to the churches play Center or charity over the years. Maybe this week the basketball court would come to life again Tetra thought. She prepared a light dinner after getting everything arranged in place. David tried out the pinball machine over and over again. "Want to try it Tet?' I think he's going to like it" David said pulling the lever to push the ball flying forward Ding! Ding! Ding!

They're back! They're back! Tetra said to herself hearing the car come up the driveway. Her heart was pounding she felt it had been so long since her son had come home to visit. She stood at the door and when she saw the turn of the knob Billy walked in. "She instantly put her arms around his neck "oh son I'm so glad to see you come in! do come in! she said shedding tears of joy. "Hi Jillian" hugging her in unison not wanting to let go of Billy. I'm so glad you all came and then holding David her husband's hand was Davie. He walked in "this must be our special guest" Tetra said bending over to his level to hug him. "And what is your name" she asked. Davie looked for Jilly or Billy's go head. "I'm Davie. "Oh my! Tetra exclaimed "isn't he a doll!" holding up his face with her hand. "I'm a boy!" he said not realizing the compliment. Everybody laughed as they walked in to the great room. Tetra now had Davies's hand and Billy's hand leading them into the great room to sit down. She put Davie on her lap and motioned for Billy and Jillian to sit beside her on the comfy Chenille sofa. "You are sure a handsome young man!" Tetra told Davie. He wasn't saying much. Tetra sensing his shyness asked "would you like to play with a toy until dinner is ready?" "Yes' Davie replied. And jumped from her lap and walked into the game area. They all sat and watch him go from toy to toy trying to decide what he wanted to play with. "Are you all hungry?" Tetra asked. To which Billy answered mom you know I'm always hungry." Tetra went to the dining room and got out her china and began setting the table. We'll get the luggage out of the car after we eat son David suggested to Billy. Tetra was still wiping tears and setting her table at the same time. "Mom you cry when I leave and you cry when I come home, Billy teased standing next to her hugging her. "Mrs. Parker you have a lovely home" Jillian said and added I finally got here." "Why thank you Jillian I certainly am glad you could come this trip", Tetra replied walking over to give her a big hug also. Everyone was moving around and Jillian joined right in helping Tetra set the table and little Davie had found the hand held game purposely left where it could be found by anyone looking for it. With instruction from Billy of how to play it, Davie soon became a wiz at the game he was playing. After eating their fill Tetra showed Jillian her bedroom where she and Davie would be sleeping and Billy wasn't far down the hall from them in his old room. Billy and David had brought all the luggage inside and made their way to the study talking shop and all at this moment was right with the world in the Parker home.

Tetra hadn't changed her schedule for the week she just included Billy and Jillian in it. David her husband had showed off the Space invaders pinball machine after dinner the night before and he and Billy had hours of fun playing and showing Davie how to play. David pulled up a stool from the bar and put Davie on it and he played right along with them. Jillian was content in the kitchen with Tetra, looking at her recipe books and talking about cake decorating ideas. The next morning Tetra was up early and preparing to go out for the day." I have to go to the Parson's center" she told Billy. "You know your way around, if you like why don't you bring Davie and Jillian by later" she suggested. David had already left for the office and Billy was up walking around in the kitchen looking for breakfast. "I have asked Ms. Laine to prepare breakfast for you all", Tetra explained "I think Jillian and Davie are still asleep. Not everyone adjusts so quickly to the time zone change". "Thanks mom not a problem" I would like to take Jillian and show her the old neighborhoods and schools around town Billy confided. "You know where the keys are son "I'll see you later. "I don't want to be late" she added hurrying out the door. Tetra was on her own time clock for the most part. But she loved that Center and certain people looked forward to her being there at a certain time. And if at all possible, she was not going to let them down. David arrived at his office walking into his break room down the hall he could hear his private line ringing. His secretary had not come in yet so he rushed over to his office to answer it "David Parker" he answered and waited for a returned answer, "David" Willis Rayford here". It was David's attorney, "Yes Rayford have any news?"' David questioned. "Well it seems this young lady stayed around this area for a while" I talked with a Florence Hening out of Oregon and she was renting a room there for about 8 months". "She thought it was strange that she was living there. Says she didn't look the type". "The place was quite run down and hardly enough room to move around his attorney informed him. "The old beat up car she drove got her around from place to place. "According to Florence she didn't go anywhere much." Except once a month she would leave for about an hour or two. Then come back, change into oversized clothes and sit and talk with the other residence around there". "She kept emphasizing oversized clothes as if that had some meaning Rayford explained. "Seems she always had something to give the others who lived there, "extra food and such". Wasn't like the rest didn't drink or smoke. It seems according to Ms Hening she was careful not to be too showy with what she had." And also, according to Mrs. Hening you could tell she wasn't from those parts. But when she left no one knew it. She didn't say anything to her". There was another girl there she hung with most of the time." 'Never saw her again either she confided to him. "But she paid her rent on time, as she did every month and was gone during the night." "The car? What kind of car?" asked David pointedly? A green 1957 Chevrolet Impala. "Did Ms. Hening happen to get the license plate number?" I asked "No! Her words were, they didn't need information as long as they paid the rent on time" Rayford replied. David thought for a minute trying to put this together. "So, she never came back to the Hening place? "No not according to our detective, but we located the car" Rayford added   still in the area. "How was that?' David asked. Seems Dorca Williams left it at a car lot about a week or two after she left the Henings place. "The salesman remembers a young lady fitting that description coming in with a lot of money. She said her dad had given her the money to go off to school and she needed to have a good car to get there". He said he hadn't heard about any robberies lately and the money checked out good." So, he sold her a brand-new car off the showroom floor 1990 Mazda. She wasn't particular about the color she just seemed to be in a hurry to go. All she said is she had to get to someone and sat anxiously waiting for him to finish the paperwork. Everything checked out so we let her go the salesman told me. He picked her out a black one says it looked fast. Never saw her again. The Chevrolet went down the street to the auto wreckers. "That's all I have David, Rayford explained. I told Masony to call me if he gets anything else" "Thanks Rayford if I have any more questions, I'll give you a call!" David said hanging up and sitting down at his desk thinking. "She's really going through a great deal to hide her whereabouts David thought. "Why?" Then a light came on! "MASONY!" David dialed his Lawyer's telephone number again and then hung up the receiver. "I'll call later he said. Let me try and figure this out first. "Mr. Parker, Herman Fitz is in your waiting room" the receptionist announced over the intercom. David was glad this day would soon be over.

Jilly and Davie were having a good time seeing Billy's old neighborhood and hearing his stories of growing up. He took them by his old house and showed Jillian Glen's old house where they played baseball and swam for hours at a time. The neighborhood looked so small to him now. Nothing looked the same. St Philomene was filled with graffiti and in places the fence was falling down. The school itself had moved to another location in town. They stopped and got out at the park. The trees had grown so tall there was shade all over. Davie ran over to the swings. "Put me in and push me aunt Jilly please!" he asked standing near the swing set trying to get in. He put Davie in the swing and Jillian stood behind pushing higher! Higher! He kept saying. I walked over to the monkey bars. I was taller that the highest bar at its top. I laughed and took my cell phone from the holster case at my side "dialing "ring, ring, ring! "Mr. Reed's office how may I help you?' came a very military sounding voice. "Glen Reed please?' I asked in my business voice. "Mr. Reed asked that you call him on his mobile phone" came my answer or leave a message if you don't have the number". "Glen" I laugh," "Thanks I told the person who answered, "I'll call him there". I hung up and dialed again looking at Jillian and Davie playing and having fun. Jillian had now sat in the swing next to Davie and they were swinging together. "Glen Reed", "man you are tripping! I said laughing after Glen answered. "You're having someone direct your calls!' I added. "Billy my man it's good to hear from you. "I thought for a minute I had lost you" he teased. "So, what are you up too?" Glen asked. "You won't believe where I am right now!' he implied to Glen. "I know you didn't lose your mind and go to L. A." he joked. 'No! Nothing like that but speaking of L.A. have you heard from them?" "Yes, Glen replied. "I finally talked to old girl she said they were offered a spread in playboy." "WHAT!" did they accept it?" I asked surprise. I hadn't heard about it. I hadn't called or return any of Lena's calls of late. "That was last week," she said she'd call "can't take that one home to mama!" Glen joked. "How is Jillian?" 'Jillian's good, as a matter of fact" Glen stopped him in mid-sentence. "I know you haven't called me to tell me I missed the wedding I will disown you forever! "Man stop for a minute with the jokes" "we did it" I told him. Glen now remembering the last conversation he had with him got very serious. "I am glad for you man" Glen said. "GOTCHA," Billy laughed loudly, "O.k. o.k. you got one." Glen conceded. I composed myself saying, "I'm standing smack dab in the middle of the park where we played for hours and I watched you grow up," I laughed. "Are you kidding me?" I had Glen's undivided attention now. "No, I brought Jillian down to visit my parents and I'm showing her around. "You wouldn't recognize your old house it shrunk" I shared which brought a laughed to both of us. I stood and laughed with Glen, describing what ever Glen had asked about and reminiscing our past. Soon we were back in the car and on the highway again. 'That was fun" Davie said riding along the highway to the Parsons Center. There were still lots more stories to tell as I headed to Mt. Nebo. Pulling up we saw people standing in line. "What's going on?" I thought mom didn't say anything about this looking at Jillian as we walked toward the Center's entrance. Then I saw a large banner out front of Mt. Nebo "Pre-Thanksgiving Dinner". "Just like mom" I said walking up shaking my head. Tetra had decided to have Thanksgiving dinner today. She wanted to spend Thanksgiving Day with her family at home. And hated to miss serving dinner for the hungry as she and her husband David had done every year since coming to Mt. Nebo. There was a crew of members already set up tomorrow to serve the traditional day Thanksgiving dinner meals. It had become a church tradition. Mt. Nebo has always served Thanksgiving dinner for everyone who came by on Thanksgiving Day and wanted to eat. The large dining hall seated hundreds and it was filled to capacity. The crowds were flowing in and out all day long. Knowing the layout of Mt. Nebo Billy went around to another entrance to the kitchen area with Jillian and Davie. "Aye! Mr. Billy" Ms. Laine greeted them coming in. Tetra was running up and down the tables serving each plate seconds. Mrs. Guillory, and Ms. Laine as well as some of the other ladies from the women's group were doing their best to assist everyone. But the people just kept coming. 'Hi mom, I was waving letting her know I was there. Ms. Laine and mom had cooked all this food so that "everyone would have a good holiday" as Ms. Laine would say. Jillian grabbed an apron from the shelf and washed her hands in the sink. She motioned to mom who pointed her to the potatoes and green beans. Davie and I washed our hands and went down to the end of the table and let Mrs. Guillory who was falling over sit and serve the dessert 'yum peach cobbler". I took her place craving the turkey and I stood Davie beside me on a large wooden box serving the dinner rolls. "This is fun!" he said holding out his small hand in the large plastic glove. Dad called looking for us because no one answered the home phone. When he got to the church, we had finally shut the entrance door to the dining hall and my little bread server was sleeping in the large nursery on a youth bed. Mom asked dad to take a plate over to Mrs. Scroggins who was out on her porch watering her newly planted rose garden. We cleaned up and finished around six thirty or seven. We got into our car tired but knowing some body wouldn't go to bed hungry tonight. Mrs. Scroggins yelled to us as we left "GOD BLESS YOU ALL!"

CHAPTER 37

Where is Davie?

The only person moving around in the Parker household Wednesday morning was David. Tetra gave Ms. Laine the rest of the week off and she had slept in. Billy and Jillian had not emerged from their rooms and Davie was lying quietly in his bed enjoying playing his electronic game toy. Tetra awoke with David and saw him off to the office and went back into her room to read her bible and just relax after her morning consecration. She walked down the hallway to check on Davie to see that everything was still going well. She knocked slightly and opened the door. Jillian didn't move she was still getting some rest from yesterday's activities. Tetra was so proud of her. Jillian said she had never been involved in anything like that but said she was thankful for the experience and would do it again. Tetra told David her husband "I applaud her; she got right in there and made a difference." "She does seem to be a very nice young lady" David added. "GOOD MORNING!" Davie said to her very loudly, wanting her to be know he was awake. "Shhhh, Tetra said beckoning him to come from the room as not to wake up Jillian. He got up from his bed that was across the room and looked at Jillian asleep as he tip toed out the door. Shhhh, Tetra repeated holding his hand and assisting him from the room. "Let's not wake up Jillian she's still sleeping" She worked very hard yesterday" Tetra told him. "Okay! said Davie "Can I get up?" he starred with his eyes wide awake standing outside the bedroom door. "You sure may". "How about you and I make some breakfast?" Tetra suggested. "Yeahhh," Davie replied. Shhhhh, Let's go down stairs.

David had gone into the office. He had conducted two meetings already and it seems his day had just started. He sat down at his desk and dialed Rayford his attorney to get Masony's number. After acquiring the number, he called. "Masony here" came the stout voice. "Hello detective" David said "this is David Parker" hello Mr. Parker not making the correlation of who he is. "How may I help you?" "I understand you are doing some work for Willis Rayford on a Dorca Williams" David replied. "Yes, but how do you know Rayford?' came his question. "Rayford is my attorney, I asked him to hire someone to look into the Williams case actually we are trying to find her." David added. Masony listened. "I spoke with you several years ago when this case first broke. I came down to your office and you were satisfied that the case was solved" David explained. "So how is it that you are now working on the case again?" David asked pointedly. "David Parker" Masony repeated the name. David could hear pages of a notebook turning. Yes! Yes! I remember, your son was a friend of this young lady." "Yes, that's correct" David now feeling like he was making progress. "Yes, Masony said again, I had satisfied myself with this case until things started falling apart. Some things were just not adding up after I went over the files again. I wanted to reopen the case but after Edith Wright received the death penalty the department wouldn't allow me to reopen it again"!" I'm now retired and have my own private detective agency and that's how I got the case" he concluded. 'I see replied David. "I talked with Rayford and he told me you located the green Chevy and talked with a Mrs. Hening, were you able to find out anything further about it?" David continued questioning. "The car's original owner is a Henry Hemley, Masony said. I'm working on locating him now" he shared with David. "Hemley?" David thought that's the old gentleman who worked for the Demato's. "I have got to get to Kansas he said to himself. "okay Masony keep me posted if you get another lead. Giving Masony his number to be reached and "good job Masony"! David sat for a moment looking and trying to remember the name on the card the young man at the Demato's place had given him. He had tucked it safely in his coat's jacket pocket at home. He hoped Tetra hadn't sent to the cleaners yet.

Jillian woke up and saw that Davie was not in his bed. She lay there for a minute looking at the clock on the wall that read after nine. She hadn't done that in a long time but really with the time difference it was her regular wake up time "but she was in Washington! At mama Parkers AND HAVING A WONDERFUL TIME! She lay there looking around the large guest room with two high poster beds a twin that Davie slept in and a full bed that she was in. Both beds had matching fluffy down comforters in a pale yellow and white. The room had very high ceilings and Mrs. Parker had chosen such beautiful soft colors that made it feel so warm and inviting. The smaller bed where Davie slept was tucked into an alcove giving it a private feel all its own. Then "OH NO! Where is Davie? she thought quickly putting on her robe and heading down to Billy's room. She knocked "come in" he said in his best morning voice "how are you?" "Is Davie here with you?" she asked anxiously looking around another even larger bedroom. Thinking Jillian was teasing him and just wanted to be close, he walked over hugging her and throwing her gently on his bed. "Davie is in your room and he must be sound asleep!" he hinted. "No! he isn't he really isn't!" she told him. Realizing she wasn't kidding he hurriedly got up "o.k. let's have a look around for him he said. Billy and Jillian looked around upstairs. All the doors were closed except the two large double doors at the end of the west hall. David and Tetra had a law library there with a smaller television and two red leather sofas with brad trimmings of gold and a very polished old desk from the turn of the century Jillian thought as she stood looking around in it. 'It was obvious Davie wasn't there and Billy had headed downstairs. She hurried out to follow him, "I don't think anyone else is home?" Billy told her. Davie is probably down in the game room", and laughed as he said it. "You know how he likes that pinball game". They walked down heading straight for the game room. Not a sound could be heard the television wasn't on to cartoons the television wasn't on at all. No one was stirring anywhere. Billy looked outside and in his family's garage. "Well both the car's mom drives are here and dad's car is gone, he told Jilly!" "Do you think he went to the office with your Dad?" Jillian asked concerned. "Let's go ask mom she's probably still sleep after that long day yesterday?" I told her. "Both went back up the spiral staircase to the upstairs stopping to knock on Tetra's door. "Come in" she said in a cheery voice as Billy peeked his head in first and walked in the door with Jillian following him in. "You two finally woke up! Tetra said laughing knowing they were probably looking for Davie who was sitting in his little foot pajama's next to Tetra. Shhh, "we're watching "Bambi" Davie said. And Jillian and Billy sat in one of the two big cozy seating chairs in his mom and dad's bedroom and watched too.

David's first instinct after Masony had given him the news about the car's owner being Henry Hemley was to head back to Oregon and speak with young Henry personally. But he'd hired Masony so he called Masony back and asked that he go out to the farm giving him directions. David told him how he came to have this information and asked that he call him back as soon as he left the Demato place. Masony was right on it! his words. David looked over a few more briefs he wasn't trying to get to involved today. He made busy waiting to hear from Masony. He had gathered his coat and brief case heading out. "Good night" Mr. Parker said his secretary leaving for the day.   Good night Gabriella" he replied to her. "Ring, ring. It was his private line, quickly going back into his office "David Parker" "David" "Masony here" "Yes Masony" Well it seems like Henry Hampster left for Kansas just here on vacation." "That came from a Rebecca says she's his sister" Didn't or wouldn't give me any information or number to get in touch with him" "I'll keep you posted on any progress when I find out more" Masony told David. "Thanks, Masony".

Masony was retirement age and it often showed in his personality. Sometimes David thought he watched to many "Barnaby Jones" episodes. But he was very complete in his investigation. David hung up the phone and dialed to make reservations for a round trip to Kansas City, Kansas for Monday morning. But for now, he was going home to enjoy his wife, son and the special guest who was making this a joyous holiday so far.

The Parkers spent the next day relaxing and having fun in the back yard. David and Billy played a game of basketball with Davie playing their point guard. David would put him on his shoulders allowing him to reach the net high above his head and he'd yell "two points" tossing the basketball into the hoop. Tetra and Jillian spent the day with some of the caterers Tetra used from time to time to make her day and meal more pleasurable. She didn't want to be exhausted and not enjoy her family. She made her specialty dishes and of course her apple crumb dessert a family favorite but left the rest of the meal to her hired staff. Jillian wanted to learn how to make Billy's favorite stuffed dressing "I tried to make something called stove top Jillian told Tetra but Billy didn't like it and wouldn't eat it" "He took me out to eat. "He says you make cornbread dressing? What's cornbread?" Jillian questioned? Is it made with corn on the cob?" Tetra smiled. "No Jillian cornbread his made from cornmeal, and flour Tetra went on with the whole recipe. "Would you like to make some for dinner tomorrow?" she asked holding her hand. Jillian didn't answer but she really wanted to learn to make what Billy liked" "Yes I really would but please be patience with me I have never made cornbread before" Jillian confided lightly squeezing Tetra's hand she was holding. They both laughed. Tetra somehow knew that. Jillian didn't have to tell her! "Get the large bowl from the cabinet over there" Tetra instructed her. Then Tetra wrote all the items Jillian would need for the ingredients on her message board in the kitchen.

Jillian moved around in the kitchen becoming familiar with a seasoning called accent and hot sauce, and greens. "Mama Parker what is greens?' Greens are a leafy vegetable that is very good with cornbread" she told her. It's in the spinach family Tetra added. "Oh, Jillian said "My bread could end up on the table?" Well let's hope so!" Tetra replied handing Jillian the vegetable oil to pour in the pan. "Now I stir it up" Jillian asked as she mixed all of the ingredients in the large bowl. Yes Jillian. Tetra was very patient with Jillian and she was eager to learn. I would bet her cornbread would be on tomorrow's Thanksgiving table. After everything was ready for tomorrow Tetra and Jillian sat in the great room talking getting to know one another better. Jillian was asking question about Billy and Tetra was finding out about Jillian. "Billy never lets me make a mistake," she said in conversation. It's so hard to be like you." so perfect" Jillian added. "I want to have a good marriage like you and David have but I find it so hard to equal what you two have" she said sincerely. "Oh dear, what David and I have took years and years of work" "I'm glad Billy loves me and holds me in high esteem." I spoiled him; he was my everything." So, he sees only my perfection of always being there for him." But David and I both made mistakes and use them to learn from. We forgive each other over and over again" she told Jillian. "But for the same thing Mama Parker?" she asked specifically. "Yes, but not always meaning to. You two must learn to communicate with each other" and voice what's bothering you and treat each other with kindness." Soon Davie came running in from outside "we won"! we won!" "Can we play pinball now?" he asked still excited. Billy flopped on the floor on the large pillow "whew! I'm tired he said. Davie falling right beside him, me too! Everybody laughed including Davie himself. Tetra came out of the kitchen with glasses of lemonade for everyone. "Who wants to play monopoly?" David said holding up the game. "Great idea dad, Billy said. "I need to beat Jillian on my home turf. I walked over and assisted Dad getting the game table pulled to the center of the floor. "Oh yeah!" said "Jillian "bring it on!" and added "Come on Mama Parker we're going to whip the pants off of them!" Jillian walked over and hugged Tetra and whispered thanks for the cornbread recipe but most of all thanks for the talk. Tetra just smiled and said within herself to God be the Glory.!!!

The Parkers had a wonderful week. Thursday Thanksgiving Day was equally fulfilling. The men including Davie made breakfast in the morning for everyone. The women prepared and laid out an elegant Thanksgiving table. They all ate way too much of everything digesting eating and eating again. "Pass the rolls" is there cranberry sauce on the table?" "David, you know what's next" mom said finally sitting down feeling everything was ready. "Let's let Billy slice the turkey this year!" Dad suggested looking at me smiling. I had reached for the large serving spoon in the apple crumble. "Billy it's not time yet for dessert!" I had gone straight to my favorite part. Davie loved the mashed potatoes and gravy. And yes, Jillian's cornbread was the talk of dinner and went very well with mom's mixture of greens.

The whole family including Davie went to Sunday service at Mt. Nebo. I saw many of my old friends and met new ones. Mrs. Ann was still serving with the children. I made a point of going by and speaking with her personally. She was still on the teacher's advisory committee of the church and doing a very fine job. I introduced Jillian to my friend Councilwoman Hathaway who was visiting her parents Dr. and Mrs. Hathaway for the holiday. "Hello William" she said walking toward him after service. "It's good to see, you" she said very distinguished as always. I returned the greeting "You to Mrs. Hathaway." "This is my fiancée Jillian McFinney. "Please to meet you Jillian" Winnie said in her political voice. 'Likewise, Jillian answered extending her hand to Councilwoman Hathaway. Then Winnie turned to me in a playful joust. "I'm just down visiting the folks; you know how that is!" in a humorous voice. She as actually found personality in the political arena I thought. "Nice seeing you Winnie" I remarked. "You too Billy" she said hugging me and going to greet others who I'm sure were waiting to see her.

Their last day was bitter sweet. Mom got up early and made breakfast for the family. Dad was taking us to the Airport on his way in to his office. His flight to Kansas didn't leave until noon so this was a delight for him getting to spend time with us before we left.   He had planned the trip to Kansas for overnight implying to Tetra it was a business trip. He wasn't ready to let her know about the letter and why he was headed to Kansas City. They had just had the most wonderful week with their son and hopefully according to Tetra their future daughter-in-law David did not want to spoil it.   David had invited Tetra to come along with him to Kansas but she decided to stay home. "No David "it's just another business trip, I'll just get bored." Close call he thought "I will just leave it at that. I would surely have to tell her. And I will later! Tetra couldn't bear to see Billy, Jillian or Davie leave she was heartbroken and just wanted the time alone to reflect she told David.

David stood with Tetra by the door holding her around her waist. Jillian wasn't helping she was crying after she hugged everyone and sat on the bench in the entry hall waiting to leave. Billy was consoling her and Davie was tugging on his arm. Davie was sad too. Billy leaned over so that Davie could talk in his ear. Then he ran over to his parents. David picked him up and he hugged them both together saying. "Good-bye Grandpa and Grandma" I love you! Seeing everyone else crying Davie had begun crying too.

CHAPTER 38

A face with a new direction

Billy sat in class at the Harvard Campus. There were only two months left before he would be taking his bar exam and was in his final preparation. Jillian and he had big plans tonight for Davie. It was his last night with them. The weeks after coming back from grandpa and grandma Parkers for Davie had went by so fast. Doris would be home tomorrow according to her last conversation with Jillian. I had gotten used to the constant schedule changes that Davie caused. Jillian had made him part of her life, quite as kept I had too. "Jillian are you picking Davie up from school today?" I would ask scheduling my day if it was my turn to pick him up from school. "No Billy, "I'll get him. Davie and I are picking something up we made for Doris" she informed but I will see *you* for her big unveiling?" Jillian asked candidly. "I'll be there I replied.

Still using her sister's name "Doris", who Jillian knew her as was on her way back to Cambridge for her knew life. That's what Jillian was led to believe. But unknown to Jillian, Doris was coming back to Cambridge with her sister from Los Angeles whose name she had been using since coming to Cambridge. Her sister had found a surgeon in Los Angeles to correct her jawbone, but Doris had chosen to change her appearance all together. "Show me your face?" her sister asked has they rode back on the plane. "Not yet! It's not totally healed, she would say. "You will see it after we get back to Los Angeles". "The doctor says I will be gorgeous" she said proudly to her older sister. So for now still pretending in name to be her sister Doris hid her face even from her. When I get to Davie, I going to leave and not look back she thought to herself". Billy has moved on and I guess I'll do the same. He and Jillian seem to be really in love. They even spent a week at his mother's house. Their relationship seems to be growing. Even after I get my looks back will I still have a chance with him? Doris was starting a new life from behind the sunglasses. She didn't know what her six-year-old was going to think about her new look. That frightened her somewhat. She looked so different. But not even Jillian was going to see it until she went back to her doctor in Los Angeles. As long as her sister was around, she in her disguise still wore her scarf covering her face. She would steal looks in her mirror when she was alone. "If I had not been there during the surgery, I wouldn't believe it either" she said as she blushed before the mirror. She had left Cambridge for what Jillian thought was going to be restructuring surgery on part of her face. But Doris Williams had changed her entire face. No one who knew her would recognize her. And her plans had changed to keep it that way "but how she had Davie! She sat on the airplane thinking about what she was going to do. For years she had hid from the world using her sister's name. No male friends she was too ashamed to share herself with anyone since Davies's father. She was so pretty at one time and had gotten caught up in a bad situation that resulted in her face being disfigured. She blamed her older sister Doris whose name she was using. But it really wasn't Doris's fault she was just trying to help. But now with her new look she had forgiven her sister and is trying to move *on*. There was a time all she wanted to do was hide. But Davie her young son kept her going. Would he accept her looks? One thing for sure she couldn't wait to see him. Now she had the opportunity to live again. She could finish up at Radcliff in the fall and hopefully get a job in her degreed field. She remembers disguised with scarf's she and Jillian often shared homework assignments and studied frequently together. Jillian's major was law. Using the name Doris borrowed from her older sister she had come a year behind Jillian and Billy. When her face got scared, she hid out away from everything allowing her face to heal as best it could Jilly had learned. She also didn't want to risk being caught for what had happened. She had her son to rear. She and her sister patched her up at home, which later in life proved disastrous. She stayed angry for so long. She needed to heal her heart and mind from the damage that was caused. But for Davie she was determined to make things work. She always scheduled her classes around Davie making sure she had time for him. He was her life. Jillian thinks they met by chance walking across the campus. But she knew exactly who Jillian was and that she was keeping time with Billy. She knew Jillian was meeting him at the library on campus. It had somehow become a routine for them. And she was I guess you would say on her way to the library to study. She saw Jillian and bumped into her knowing she was the girl he was spending time with. Aka Doris moved in next door to Jillian and became instant friends. Jillian never knew she was keeping a close watch on their relationship. Jillian wasn't aware she even knew Billy and for that matter neither did he. He had not even thought this girl with a young child to rear was his longtime friend. It was obvious she loved her little boy. She would schedule classes starting after she got him off to school and finishing just before he came home. Unaware to anyone she kept a very close watch on things going on in Jillian's life. Things she had planned were not working out. There were occasional night courses and aunt Jillian as she became known to Davie would keep him. Unaware to Jillian she had grown tired of Jillian always asking her advice of how she looked in a particular outfit or about the dresses she wore out to please Billy! She grew bitter. Maybe Jillian didn't mean anything by it but Doris still didn't like it at all! She says Jillian wasn't taking her feelings into consideration flaunting her beauty in her face. Now she thought I can wear beautiful clothes again too! She had sure planned a shopping spree to add to her new image.

"Please put your seat in the upright position and buckle your seatbelts and prepare for a landing" could be heard across the intercom of the plane. She would soon be home. She then leaned over to her older sister Doris "Here's the plan!

Obermeyer, Finswick and Hannagan" came the voice across the telephone "Good morning may I speak with William Parker please?" David asked calling from the plane. "Mr. Parker, just a moment please I'll ring his extension" the receptionist remarked. "William Parker," "hi son'" "Oh hi dad, is everything o.k. I asked concerned. "Everything is fine. Your mom is fine and she's already planning your next visit" using humor. "Son I wanted to update you on the progress I have made in finding Dorca Williams. It seems she stayed around the Oregon, Washington area about a year before leaving not sure where she went yet" David confided. I've got a lead to follow up on out of Kansas City." "Kansas City?" I exclaimed. "Desmond and Mossy moved to Kansas City" "Well I won't have much time to visit I'm going to talk with an elderly gentleman who worked for the Demato's parents on the farm" David informed him. "What part of Kansas City dad maybe Desmond could help you get around?" I questioned knowing Kansas is a big place. "Hold a minute son, David said rearranging his seat and getting the card that had been safely tucked in his coat pocket. 'Let's see I'm going to call a Mrs. Wheatley when I get settled and make arrangements to talk with Henry Hemley." His grandson was out at the farm and said he had moved back to Kansas City, Kansas." "His grandson dad, how old Is this man?" I asked thinking younger on the grandson. "Oh, I've talked with Mr. Hemley before he is in his late eighties if memory serves me right". David turned the card over for the first time looking at what the young Henry had given him. "Well! David exclaimed! "Seems his grandson is a lawyer" Then David remembered the young man's eloquent speech at the farm. The young Henry worked for "Owens and MacFinney" attorney at law. I was very excited. "That's Desmond and Mossy's firm dad!" "Desmond shared with me he had hired a young attorney!" I replied. "Dad call me please when you get there, our world seems to be getting smaller all the time" "yes, you are right son bye".

Jillian and Davie had stopped by his favorite fast food restaurant and had a hamburger after school. Davie loved hamburgers but he especially liked the toys that accompanied them. He boasted quite a collection from his visits with aunt Jillian. "Where are we going now aunt Jillian, Davie asked has she pulled into the parking lot of the photography studio. "We're going to get our pictures Davie! for your mommy. She will be home soon" Jillian explained. "Mommy will be home soon! Yeah! He said excitedly. Then as they walked into the studio the clerk behind the counter noticed he was sad. "What's wrong, it's fun to have your picture taken?" she told him holding his little face up by his chin in her hand. Jillian explained to her they were here to pick up the mat prints they had ordered. When the clerk went to the back to get the portraits Jillian sat Davie in the big winged chair over by the window. "What's wrong Davie, she asked aren't you glad your mommy's coming back?" "Yes' he said in an almost crying voice. "Well what's wrong sweetie?" she said hugging him gently in her arms. Jillian was trying to be brave for him. She had spent the last two nights crying in anticipation of Doris's arrival back home to get him. She knew she would have to give him back to his mommy but her heart was playing tricks on her and had not accepted it yet. "Will I still see you and uncle Billy when mommy comes back?" Davie asked. Billy had decided after their visit to his parent's house that if Davie wanted to call them grandfather and grandmother then he had to be more than Mr. Billy. So, he asked Davie to call him uncle Billy. He reserved Mr. Billy for Ms. Laine despite his trying to change her. "Uncle Billy and I will always be here" Jillian said now holding David on her lap and dripping tears into the curly locks of his head. "You can come and see us every day, she continued. Do you still remember our telephone numbers?" She had taught Davie her number and Billy's number for emergency purposes and how to use them. "Yes, aunt Jillian "he was starting to feel better. "I'm going to call you and uncle Billy everyday o.k. And every day!" was just fine with Jillian. Jillian paid for her purchase and left the studio to spend her last night with Davie before Doris came home. Doris had called Jillian and said she would be home Friday in Cambridge but she actually got there Thursday. Not going home aka Doris checked into a Cambridge Inn and rented a car. She wanted to try out her new face before seeing Davie. She went to the same stores she and Jillian frequented but now going to the department for herself. She picked out clothes for the beautiful lady she had become on the outside. On her way in the posh boutique some men had complimented her on her beauty. And her taught walk while in LA. was very appealing to her shapely figure. She went to Radcliff and sat around familiar faces but no one recognized her without the scarves and sunglasses. She loved the new her. She sat in the Inn having lunch in her gorgeous new skin. She was on top of the world. The only thing that stood between her new life and future happiness was the drab name "Doris Williams. She was going to leave all the old memories behind and start new. So off she went to the courthouse to change her name.

Billy met Jillian and Davie at "Wally Bear's Pizza house" 'HI Jillian!" I replied speaking loud above the noise of all the young children running around having fun. "Hi uncle Billy Davie said running into his arms to be pick up and hugged tightly. "Come see this" Davie said pulling him to the game he had been playing since he and Jillian got there. Jillian had found a table near it and ordered the pizza and a salad for herself and sat down for a moment to relax from the day. After about twenty or thirty minutes being there, "Pizza's here!" she yelled to Billy and Davie who was less than two feet away from the table. With urging from Billy, Davie came and sat down to at least try and eat some pizza. He was so excited to be here, for that matter every child there seems to have that same level of excitement. The place was in a steady roar. Jillian finally got him to take a few bites from his pizza before he wanted to crawl through the big maze that was filled with children going in all directions. "Please, please aunt Jillian you can see me right there!" Davie said pointing to an opening constructed so they could be seen by on lookers when they reached that place. "Okay. Go ahead" Billy finally said and with Jillian's approval off he went yelling every few minutes 'hi!" to Billy and Jillian sitting down at the table directly below it.

What fun we had. Exhausted Jillian and I finally said. "Okay Davie it's time to go home" Sadden to have to go after two hours but expressed his thanks with a big hug for both of us. Jillian was back home she had tucked Davie in when I arrived. I had come to the Wally Bears straight from the office and stopped by home to change into more relaxing attire. And after Davie's day of excitement he was fast asleep. She and I sat in her living room watching the news and talking about Davie. We made mention of the trip to Washington that she would never forget she told me. "We will have many more" I said in my loving moment sitting next to her holding her in my arms. Jillian loved to hear me talk about our future together. And as far as I knew if there was going to be a future for me Jillian was surely it! She shared later how she often wondered about that fabulous ring she had come across in New York but wouldn't ask. Jillian loved him and no matter what she still had hopes of marrying him. She just was not ready to be disappointed again so soon so she put any conversations regarding the ring on hold. For now, she was content just thinking about it. "Jillian, if I asked you to marry me, would you?" he asked during a commercial from the show they were watching. Jillian sit up and looked at him. "William Parker, I would marry you tomorrow!" That answer brought a kiss that caused them to miss the first few minutes of the segment of the show they were watching. They sat for a moment in each other's arms before the phone rang. "Ring, ring Jillian's heart stopped. She just knew it was Doris saying she was home. She slowly lifted up the receiver of her telephone "Hello, she said in a quiet but audible voice. "Hello Jillian this is Blair Christensen, how are you this evening?' He asked in his usual business voice. Jillian whispered to Billy, "It's Blair" she said moving over to a single big chair in the corner of her living room. "I'm fine just relaxing after a busy day" she said transitioning herself for a business conversation. "Well we need you to start working with us a few days a week to start until after the bar exam" he said "though I don't see us having any problems there" he added with a laugh in his voice" then you can work for us! "Jillian hadn't even thought about what it meant to work in New York. Would Billy move there?" His experience in the Big Apple did not turn out well she thought and then I would surely not see Davie! Everything was happening so quickly. Her voice now shaking because she was realizing all she's giving up for money. Jillian's family had substance. We'll her mom anyway. That's what really caused the divorce Jillian thinks. She sat thinking about everything in that moment with Blair on the other end of the phone. Her mom Frances controlled her real dad with money. And as soon as Bob McFinney earned his own, he was gone. And she guessed they never really learned to relate to one another. Often Jillian wondered if they even loved each other at all. In conclusion she thought was it really worth it? Or merely that she landed this job offer successfully coming out of college that had tempted her. 'Jillian! Jillian! are you there? Blair asked because Jillian was lost in thought. "What days are we talking about Mr. Christiansen Jillian then asked. "Blair please" he reminded Jillian. "Right now, we are full staffed so the choice is yours" he told her. "Call me at the end of the week and let me know which two days you're going to provide us with and I'll send your schedule. "See you soon" he said hanging up. Jillian sat in the corner chair with her head down crying.

I went to work the next day thinking about what Jillian had shared with me the night before. Doris never called or showed up. Jillian was relieved as far as Davie but now she had to decide on the days that she would commute to New York. Sitting at my desk I noticed the note I had left on it the day before when I was speaking with dad. 'Kansas City" was scribbled on a note pad as I talked with him on the phone about the trip he was taking.

David got checked in at the Holiday Inn downtown that sits in part of Kansas City's convention center. It was plenty of daylight hours left when he arrived in Kansas so he settled into his room to unwind. After about an hour he dialed Mrs. Wheatley. "Hello" an elderly sounding woman answered. "Hello Mrs. Wheatley? David questioned. "Yes, this is Mrs. Harriet Wheatley, how may I help you. "Mrs. Wheatley, I'm trying to get in touch with Mr. Hemley is he in?" 'Oh yes, Henry's in, but he won't talk on the phone" she explained. "He's in his room. Are you a friend of Henry's?" She asked questioning the call. "I met Henry a few years ago in Oregon" then she cut in "then you know Clara!" she asked

David "He told me about Clara" David told her still wanting to be able to see Mr. Hemley. "Well I'm sure if you know about Clara, he will be glad to see you!" Mrs. Wheatley said and then added "Well anytime you chose you may come by we're usually here if I'm not at church". She told him very sweetly. "Thank you Mrs. Wheatley" David said hanging up realizing the quickest way to Mr. Hemley was to call his grandson. David called a cab and headed to the law firm of Owens and Macfinney on Jefferson and Pine. The office with its' worn awnings sat on a main street downtown Kansas City. The large brick structure showed the age of the old world building it was housed in. Inside was the smell of fresh paint filtering throughout the air? David looked around the area and, in the entrance, sat a receptionist hidden behind the tall counter plugging in cords on a board. He was amazed she told him it still worked. Looking around there were lots of renovation projects going on in the building. David leaned over the counter "Good afternoon he said. "Yes, may I assist you?" she asked. She almost sounded like a robot. "Owens and Macfinney David replied. "Top of stairs to your right" "thank you" David said moving back to go up the steep staircase. At the top was a door with a beveled windowpane motif. In bold black letters read: Owens, Owens and Macfinney attorney at law. David turned the doorknob and walked in to the twenty first century. There were gorgeous modern furniture pieces in soothing colors. Antique ash colored furniture right out of a 'Todd Oldham' catalog. "Good afternoon" He said loudly entering the office. A person fitting Mossy's description came from the back "how may I help you?" she asked. "He took a chance and said 'Mossy?" 'Yes, she answered reluctantly I'm David Parker" "David Parker" she repeated as if she had forgotten an appointment. "Billy's father "oh Mr. Parker I'm sorry I'm Mostalgia Owens I'm Desmond's wife and the other Owens on the marquee" she added." Please to meet you see you again" she said very nervously realizing she had met him before briefly at their graduation. "Is Desmond expecting you sir?" she asked looking now at the bulletin board on the wall. It had names of potential clients or clients to be seen. "Desmond's with a client right now is there something I can help you with" she asked again. Actually "I'm here to see a Henry Hampster" is he in. "Henry Hampster, I'm sure Mr. Hampster is in I was just speaking with him let me get him for you Mr. Parker. Please have a seat I'll be right back". "May I get you some coffee?" she inquired. "Sure, that would be nice thank you" "sure Mr. Parker just a moment." Mossy walked down a long narrow hall. After a while Henry came from the back "Good afternoon Mr. Parker it's good to see you again so soon" he said in his eloquent sounding voice. "To what do I owe the honor of this visit? "he added extending his hand. David reintroduced himself and reacquainted him with why he had come. 'I see" he replied. "Would you like me to take you to visit granddad?" he asked to which David responded, "I was hoping you would ask". The cabbie who drove me here from my hotel room took so many twists and turns I don't think I could find my way back if I wanted too" he shared with the younger Henry. Mossy came back with the large cup of hot coffee carrying it on a tray, "condiments are over there" she said pointing to a server table sitting off to the side of the wall. The young attorney suggested "finish your coffee Mr. Parker and I'll go and get my coat from my office and we will be on our way. "Sounds good" David said after putting the desired condiments in his coffee. David sat looking around the small but very efficient law office enjoying his cup of hot coffee. After finishing his coffee, he thanked Mossy for it and said he would call Desmond before he leaves town. On their way over to Mrs. Wheatley's Henry shared with David about his grandfather and growing up in Kansas. He said his mother was Mr. Hemley's daughter and then reminded David that he had met Rebecca his sister at the ranch in Oregon. He had always wanted to be someone of importance young Henry shared or somebody of respect. He said he liked reading all kinds of books, he told David his grandmother kept lots of books in her home. David listened intently to the young man who sounded wise for his years. He heard the young man's personality and eloquent style come through his upbringings. Mrs. Clara Hemley was his grandmother and Mr. Hemley's wife. She was a schoolteacher and he had learned so much from her. He promised her that he would make her proud of him. "Her little Henry" he told David "that's what she always called me" They drove a while and the neighborhoods began to turn into slums. "Where are we?" David asked looking at the city's devastation, "This is the southeast area of the freeway he told him." we're almost there" He drove out for about five miles the area had started looking a lot better than the neighborhoods they had just come through. Young Henry looked at him and said, I could have gone another way to get here. But I go through the slums to remind me of the hard work it takes not to be there. And also, I drive through to constantly keep myself striving for a better life". Very wise, David thought, very wise. They soon drove up into a long narrow driveway. At the roads end was a large white wooden house with a long porch and an old wooden swing on the right side. There were six tall steps leading up to the front porch and a beautiful flower garden with every kind of rose imaginable. Mrs. Wheatley coming out met them at the front porch recognizing the car as they drove up. This chubby little lady with beautiful white hair, rimmed glasses, and gingham dress with an apron made from a flour sack came out to greet them. "Hello, Aunt Harriet" young Henry said entering on the porch. "Hello do come in" she said seeing young Henry walking over and giving him a hug then turning to David "Good afternoon son" coming over and hugging him too. Mrs. Wheatley was a very light-skinned woman but David was Caucasian and she called him her son without even thinking about it. "Aunt Harriet this is a friend of granddad's Mr. Parker. Is granddad sleep?" young Henry asked as they stood out on the porch. "No, he just sits in his room, you all come on in," she said opening her screen door and leading them walking across her beautiful wooden floors. Turning the doors' knob, she opened the door to a large bedroom with vaulted beam ceilings. The bedpost on the high oak bed didn't come close to touching it. The shiny wooden floors could be seen underneath the high bed frame. She had charming little rose fabric for the curtain's large windows and an old quilt hanging on the wall to give way to each of the generations. And sitting over in his rocker was Mr. Hemley. David walked in and pulled up a chair. Mrs. Wheatley and young Henry excused themselves from the room to give them privacy. "I'll be right outside if you need me," she said going out and closing the door behind her. "Hello Mr. Hemley" David said. He just sat there. David looked around the room for something that might get his attention. And there it was sitting over on the oak mirrored dresser. A picture of who David thought to be the young Henry Hemley himself and Clara standing in front of their 1957 Chevy Impala. "Color optional the picture was black and white". David took the picture and sat directly in front of him. "This sure is a handsome fellow Mr. Hemley, he doesn't look a day over eighteen" David said to him trying to get a reaction. He still just sat staring out of the window. Then looking again, it came to him. "Who is this beautiful lady standing with him?" David asked Mr. Hemley. His rocker moved. David took the picture and held it closer to his face and pointed. "Mr.

Hemley is this Clara?' he asked again. He looked straight at David. "She's only the most beautiful woman in the world," he said to him. "Did you know my Clara?" he asked now looking at David". No, honestly Mr. Hemley I didn't know Clara. You told me all about her when we met in Oregon" David confided. "Oh, yes Oregon that's where my Clara went home to be with the Lord" And then it seemed like the floodgates opened. Mr. Hemley and he talked about anything and everything. David wasn't trying to stop him from talking or even start a conversation. He just let him lead and he tried his best to follow. "Do you have any children?" Mr. Hemley asked. "Yes, I have a son named William" David replied. "Oh, that's good, that's a good strong name," he told him. "And what does young William do?' he asked now looking at David from head to toe. "He's a lawyer or he will be after he passes the bar," he told him. "Oh, he's like young Henry that boy fooled around and made his grandmother proud me too for that matter" he laughed. They sat and talked and talked. Mrs. Wheatley and young Henry came back in the room and saw Mr. Hemley talking. Young Henry smiled pleased to see his granddad talking again. "I'm sorry Mr. Parker, Henry said. "I have to get back to the office". I have a client coming in and can't be late getting back. He hugged his grandfather and shook David's hand and left. David walked over asked Mrs. Wheatley if she would mind if he stayed a little longer with Mr. Hemley and visit. "Oh yes that's fine with me. 'YOU set a fire under Henry! God knows I tried" she laughed. Would you two boys like some supper to eat?" Mrs. Wheatley asked. David had turned down lunch with him years ago. But he was not about to do it again. When Mrs. Wheatley came back, she knocked on the door. "COME IN" Henry said. She recognized his voice and "MY GOD HAS ANSWERED PRAYER she laughed and clap her hands. WELL SIR JESUS!! Aren't you something Henry!" she said coming in with two big trays of food? She had prepared Greens and ham hocks and cornbread southern style with rice and pinto beans. "You know how to eat this kind of food young fellow?" Mr. Hemley asked smiling." I sure do!" David replied to him and both continued quietly and cleaned their plates. Then Mrs. Wheatley came back with two bowls of something she called blackberry dumplings. Ummm were they good. David would have to confess to Tetra that Mrs. Wheatley's dessert called "blackberry dumplings" was right up there with her apple crumble dessert which was his favorite. Mrs. Wheatley came in to get the finished dinnerware trays. "Did you boys have enough?' she asked earnestly. "Yes ma'am, thank you" David found himself saying" "Plenty Harriet, thank you". "Did you meet Mr. Parker?" he asked Mrs. Wheatley. "Yes, Henry I did" he's a nice man" she told him. "His son is a lawyer you know?" he added. "Just like young Henry" she replied. Then Mr. Hemley laughed as if remembering something. Mrs. Wheatley careful stacked the dishes on a larger tray table and rolled it out of the room. "You two have a nice visit, she stated leaving out. Mr. Hemley tried to get up from his rocker, "My legs just won't do like they used to" he said sitting back down. David walked over and got beside him next to his big rocker and caught him under his arm. "Come Mr. Hemley I'll help you" standing him up and walking him to the door. "Where are we going Mr. Hemley?" David asked, thinking they were just going to walk around the bedroom. I would if you don't mind, like to go out and sit on the porch if you don't mind?" Mr. Hemley repeated again. "My pleasure" David said leading him through the living room. Mrs. Wheatley's little house was immaculate with rustic furniture throughout her lovely country home. To us it would be small but it was a perfect size for her enormous personality she had flowing throughout it. David had learned from Mr. Hemley that he and her husband were furniture makers "made most of the furniture right here in Clara's and Harriet's home" he told him. She had many unique beautifully hand craved tables and the glass front china cabinet that held her precious China dishes could not be duplicated. Mrs. Wheatley was sitting in the living room knitting she saw them coming, "MY, MY, MY!" wonders never cease" getting up to open the door for them to go out and then positioning a chair for Henry to sit in on the front porch. "I'd like to sit on the swing, Mr. Hemley said if you don't mind". David sat him on the swing securely and pulled up the chair. And without him saying another word Mr. Hemley started talking about the picture. "I thought I was something then, he said with a laugh. And as if David wasn't getting it, he said "the picture! I'm talking about the picture". "I had just bought my first car a1957 Chevy and went over to ask for Clara's hand in marriage" and with his distinctive laugh he said" her daddy was so happy he took us outside in front of the car and said "she will!" Mr. Hemley laughed so hard that it became contagious David joined him. After containing himself from the laughter he then said. "When the little girl Dorca came by Mr. Demato's farm wanting to give me Richard Demato's car for my Chevrolet one day I surely didn't want to part with it. It was my Clara!" he told him sadly. "Poor thing was having upset stomach. She threw up a couple of times" Mr. Hemley said. "I went and got her some seltzer water I had in the frigerator. Clara always said it was good for upset stomach you know." She always had it around when she was carrying the children before they were born" he shared. That girl persuaded me to give her my car". I only did it cause I knew Richard". "Said she would only need it a little while and would bring it back" I waited at least a year I know. I finally had young Henry fly down and drive me back here to Kansas in the car she left after I became ill he confided. "I don't like flying" he told him. It's over there" pointing to a very dust covered car sitting on the side of the house not getting any use. David found out later it belonged to the Demato's. 'Don't know if she ever brought back the Chevy?" Mr. Hemley and he sat on the porch enjoying the sunshine the rose garden but most of all each other's company. David asked if he could pray with him, as he was getting close to leaving. "Without an answer, Mr. Hemley caught his hand and nodded his head. "God I truly thank you for this visit today. I have felt your presence around us all day and we rejoice knowing that you are with us. I thank you for Mr. Hemley and Mrs. Wheatley's hospitality opening their doors and allowing me to spend time enjoying the finer things of life. Give them strength in body mind and spirit. Bless their home and their household. I asked all in Jesus name Amen." David concluded the prayer and turned to see Mrs. Wheatley had joined them. Mr. Hemley got up from the swing with very little assistance. And when David left later that evening Mr. Hemley was sitting in the living room talking and laughing with Mrs. Wheatley. David called Desmond from his hotel room and shared with him that he was sorry that he had come all this way and didn't get a chance to see him, but he would make it a point to visit again soon. His flight left out of Kansas City on time. He was flying at an altitude of 30 thousand feet in the air and David was headed home. His cell phone rang in his briefcase. "Hello thinking who could be calling him at this hour of the morning." May I help you? David answered "David, Masony here!" David chuckled. "Yes Masony" following his protocol as to get to the point. "Got a lead out of Kansas City, I'm headed that way now to talk to a Mrs. Wheatley" seems she's housing Hemley there!" he said in his P.I. tone. He almost stopped him But Mr. Hemley and Mrs. Wheatley loves to have visitors. "That's great

Masony David said to him. "There's a car at the Wheatley place go through it see if you come up with something we can use?" He would hate for him to make a blank trip David thought. "I'm on it!" Masony replied.

Doris Williams left the courthouse with a new name. "We will send you the final papers in the mail" the clerk told her "Is the address on the license correct?' she asked. "Please send it to this P.O. box in Los Angeles" Doris requested and with thanks walked out. She hurried to meet the movers. She knew Jillian had planned an evening out. With enough movers they could be out in two hours tops! she thought. She called her sister back at the hotel "You remember what you're supposed to do. I'll meet you at the airport Doris informed her. She was afraid Jillian would talk her into staying in Cambridge and she did not want to see her. She liked Jillian as a person. But her plan to get Billy back wasn't working. She was losing so I'm out! she exclaimed! She knew Billy had fallen in love with Jillian. She figured she had paid her debt to society. Her sister Doris whose name she had been using had built herself a good future in LA. And she was free and no longer needed her protection. Changed name she had another surprise for her sister Doris also when they got back to Los Angeles but they would have to pull this one off first.

CHAPTER 39

Why does love hurt?

FIVE, FOUR, THREE, TWO, ONE BLAST OFF!!!! the count down what a sweet sound. Glen and his crew had been working so hard getting to this day. They now sat tracking the satellite they had been working on for years. Glen's job as an engineer was to rate the efficiency of the propellants in terms of pound thrust. He works in the mission control John F. Kennedy Space Center and had put in tireless hours as they planned the space shuttle's launch. "Glen Reed" he answered, "this is Cheryl, congratulations, "I was just watching the launch on television you must be relieved it's over" she remarked. "Over for now, but thanks we're pretty happy with it" Glen told her. He was starting to think the "pest" was right. He and Cheryl had been dating each other for close to six months and he didn't mind she was the only one. Cheryl Laler had come down to meet him from Austin with his sister Brianna and her husband Meldon. They were taking their daughter Sura to visit Disney World and invited Glen along to accompany Cheryl. Brianna and Cheryl were in a women's group at Shining Star Community church in Austin where Pastor Reed had been sent to over shepherd and they had become good friends. Brianna liked her and decided Glen needed a strong black woman to help him get his life on the right path. That is what Brianna said and so far, so good. Not only did they have a wonderful time at Disney world but they have shared other outings as well, some even including his family. "I haven't seen you in two days what's on your agenda for tonight?' Cheryl asked. "Well babe you know there's a good reason for that" Glen explained and added "you just saw it" speaking of the space launch. "I would love to see you later, but nothing fancy, just need a relaxing evening me and you!" Glen suggested, think you can arrange that?' speaking in his deep manly voice. "Just me and you!" that's sounds inviting" she told him "that's just how I find you" he replied. Glen had all the lines. I called him "the Man" whenever they went out to the club. But Cheryl was different. She had her act together, her own place, and her own job besides her sexy good looks, she had her own money. Glen really didn't mind that he had been seeing her all this time and he didn't feel the need to move on. 'If it ain't broke don't fix it" his motto. "tonight, at your place around 7:00 ish." Glen said waiting for confirmation. "I'll see you then bye for now" Cheryl said using a sultry voice. Glen spun around in his chair. Everyone had disbursed back to their stations and started their regular day's work. Glen along with the other engineers he worked with was working to develop the tracking and communications network for the space program. "I should call wild Bill", Glen thought see what he's up to these days?"

Billy was sitting in Jillian's apartment trying to help her decide what days would best suit her need and commute to the Big Apple. She didn't have to worry about where she would live because her parents lived there. And she and Billy thought living with someone in New York was much better than living alone. "Besides she'd only be there two days a week" he said to himself while he waited for her to come from the back room of the apartment. "If I go on Thursday and Friday then I could relax over the weekend at home she said walking back to the living room sitting on the sofa next to Billy. He had spread his schedule and Jillian's schedule out on the table. They were arranging classes and rearranging work schedules. The law firm where Jillian worked was understanding and said they would do what they could to accommodate her needs during the transition. Still mulling over all the decisions Jillian looked at her watch "I'm leaving soon to pick up Davie, "are you going to be here when I get back?" she asked. "Davie and I usually stop by and get a burger can I bring you anything?" "a jolly toy meal or something!" she teased. Jilly had reasoned "can't cry over spilled milk" so she made peace with her decision regarding New York and hoped Billy would accompany her there. She put her shoes on and reached for her purse sitting over by the chair. Billy beckoned to her "come here pretty lady" extending his hand to her and pulling her across his lap. She put her arms around his neck and they kissed. "I love you' Jilly! he told her. 'I love you too William Parker". Then he tapped her bottom and she walked out the door heading to the school to pick up Davie. She laughed to herself as she drove thinking about her man.

She could hear his voice telling her to slow down. He was always saying she drove to fast in her Infiniti sport coupe, with all its horsepower. She slowed as she came into the school zone "Good she said a parking space near the entrance of the school is open" Davie will be out soon. Looking down at her watch she sat in her car a few more minutes watching parents picking up their little ones. "Where is he she thought?" looking again at her watch he's usually standing right there next to the office. 'Maybe he is still in his classroom Jillian reasoned. She locked her car doors and went across the street to the school. Davie's classroom sits right in front after you pass the school's main office. She walked up to the door and turned the knob. It was locked. Now her heart was starting to pound. She ran back to the place where he usually stands. NO DAVIE! Jillian nervously pulled her cell phone from her purse and dialed Billy. She was so nervous that she dialed her home phone "RANG. Ring! Rang!! She and Billy rarely answered each other's phone at home unless they were there together. He just ignored the ring. That was his idea more than hers. Again, he ignored the ring. Jilly finally realizing that she was ringing her home phone and started to cry because he hadn't answered running around the almost empty school looking for Davie. "Where is he!" she said out loud to herself. "Okay Jillian don't panic it's not that bad. Breath Jillian breath" she said as she dialed Billy's cell number but when Billy answered. "Billy I can't find Davie!" she was crying so hard he could barely hear her. "Jillian! Jillian! Calm down, I can't talk to you until you calm down, he told her. "Now slowly repeat what you said. "Billy, Davie is not at school, I looked everywhere. His classroom door is locked and this school is emptying well practically empty" she told him. Jillian had now flopped down on a bench near the playground. "Jillian? Jillian? Is there anyone in the office?" I asked calmly. "I don't know Billy?" she said. "Jillian go to the office and see if anyone might know where he is! "We left him there this morning, right?" I was now questioning myself. I knew Jillian and I had taken Davie to school this morning, and I walked him to his class and hugged him before leaving. Jillian now afraid of still another locked door went slowly to the office. She turned the knob and it opened "it's opened!" she screamed into his ear over the phone. "Okay Jillian is anyone there?" Yes, Billy I'll call you when I find out something okay.

"O.k. I didn't want to hang up but she seemed to have self-control now so I sat and waited for her call. "Looking behind the counter seated at her desk was the school administrator. Nervously Jillian asked. "Hi, I'm looking for David Wright a little first grader she said. "The first graders have gone home for the day" she told Jillian "I know" Jillian said she was very close to crying again. "I usually meet him right in front of the school and I'm always on time"! she said starting to panic. The lady in the office stood up from behind her desk and walked over to the counter. "Whose class is your youngster in?" she asked pulling out the enrollment list. David is in Mrs. May's class" are you his mother?" she questioned looking at Jillian's frighten state. "No! Jillian said almost crying "I'm his aunt Jillian and I pick him up every day! "Umm let's see David Wright?" she said looking at Jillian running her hand down the list. Jillian stood waiting for whatever it was she was looking at or looking for. "Right here"! she pointed "a Doris Wright signed him out this morning Dr's appointment" reading then looking up for Jillian's response. "Thank you, Miss" she said slowly moving to the door. "Does that satisfied you?" she asked Jillian "That's his mother, that's alright she said going out of the door leaving the smiling administrator to continue her duties. Jillian was satisfied that Doris had signed him out. But she was so heartbroken now that Doris was back. She didn't call Billy back soon enough. Soon his call came in to her. "Well Jillian, did you find him?" Billy asked concerned for the both of them Davie and Jillian. "I didn't see him, Jillian told Billy but I know where he is". "What?' Jillian what are you saying Billy questioned. "I'll be there in a minute" and hung up on her end of the cell phone connection and drove slowly all the way back home. Jillian walked in looking very sad. Her eyes were red from crying and her heart was broken into a hundred pieces. Billy stood up as she walked in. She walked directly into his arms. "I wonder if she stopped and got his hamburger." Jillian mumbled under her voice Jillian! What are you talking about Jilly? I asked holding her and wiping her tears. "Doris checked him out of school earlier today" I found out from the office she said. Then I lead her over to the sofa to sit down holding her trembling body "Jillian we knew this day was coming" I know you are hurting I am too" but that is her son" I kept telling her. "I know Billy, I know but it hurts!" Jillian was crying uncontrollably and I was trying to console her but I was hurting too. Jillian! I finally found a break. "Remember Davie is right down the street he's not that far away." I salvaged something to make her feel a little better it seemed to anyway. I got up and walked to the door looking for Doris's car down the street.

There were only two driveways that separated Jillian's house from Doris's. That was a standard look for anyone staying in residential housing which was near campus. "Her car is not home yet' I said coming back sitting next to Jillian who just could not stop the flow of tears.

David landed and drove down the freeway home. He was back at home in Spokane Washington. He drove along thinking about his visit to Kansas and how enjoyable it was. After landing he immediately called his wife on his car phone "Tetra" "hi honey" David said reaching her at the Parson's Center where she worked.

"David does this mean you're home?" she questioned knowing he had been out of town. "Yes, dear I'm headed home, I'm sure I'll beat you there!" he replied. "That's good, I look forward to seeing you dear. "How was your trip?" Tetra asked. "It went well". He would save the blackberry dumpling story for later. "All right honey I'll see you at home" David said to Tetra hanging up and driving into his driveway. David walked into his house and stopped by the kitchen before going upstairs. He put his briefcase in his study and headed upstairs for a long hot shower. After about forty-five minutes he emerged again. "Whew!" I needed that, David said coming out with a large towel wrapped at his waist. He had stopped and got his Perrier on his way up so he reached for it off the side table and sat in the arm-chair in their bedroom with his feet up on an ottoman. The mid sun was shining through the beaded fringed crepe panels Tetra draped her bedrooms windows with. David sat quietly enjoying the serenity of the moment when. "Ring, ring" hello he answered thinking it was Tetra. "David Parker please?" he knew instantly who it was because no one else addressed him that way calling him at home. "Yes Masony" he replied. "Masony here "I spoke to Mrs. Wheatley where Mr. Hemley lives, they are nice people" he chuckled. Mr. Hemley was on his way to church with Mrs. Wheatley but he gave me permission to go through the car" Masony told him. "Not much in it, needs cleaning pretty dusted" he said. David sat thinking "why am I paying Masony to tell me what I already know? But he listened. "Did you find anything that could possible lead us to Dorca Williams?" David now asked because he felt Masony had disturbed his peaceful moment. "Not sure, found a piece of paper lying under the front seat. Name and address of a Beulah Mae Reeves on Hutchison Grove in Oregon" Masony reported. "Well Masony sounds like you have a lead" he applauded him. "I'll be leaving out tomorrow morning I'll keep you posted Masony added. "Give my regards to Mr. Hemley and Mrs. Wheatley" David told him. "Masony out." David hung up shaking his head not about Masony but Mr. Hemley he was up and going on with his life.

Billy didn't go back to the office he stayed with Jillian who was having a very hard day coping with the fact Doris had come and gotten Davie without telling them. "Why didn't she call?' Jillian kept asking. "Why did she just take him like that?" She kept running the questions over and over in her mind. They both kept getting up going to the door looking for Doris's car. "Jillian please lie down you're going to make yourself sick!" I told her. She would cry for long periods and then ask questions trying to find answers. I was trying to console her in between screening and talking to a clerk down at the courthouse on a few minor cases I was working on. All of a sudden Jillian came out of the back and headed straight out the door across the street. "It wasn't likely but maybe Doris was home and left her car at the airport. She didn't know. All Jillian knew was it had been 4 or 5 hours since Davies school day ended and she wanted to know he was all right. I stood in her door watching Jillian go across the street. She had passed by me so fast leaving her house all I saw was a blur go by me. She walked up to Doris's door and knocked. She looked and Davies's little bear he had taken to school for show and tell was on the ground. She picked it up and hugged it. Then she tried turning the knob? Nothing. She careful walked up to the window not wanting to step on the flowers she Davie and Doris had planted. "Looking into the window Jillian saw an empty house she stood stunned and then she let out a scream that could be heard all over Cambridge. Doris had moved and taken Davie with her!!!!

Glen drove up to the entrance gate of the Kennedy Space Center. He waited for a short time in the line of cars now leaving the facility. The crowds that had flanked the facility ground earlier were down to a minimal. There were reporters and military brass and dignitaries from all over the world to watch the launch of the space shuttle. They celebrated the fact that it had been twenty years since John Glenn the first American to orbit the earth was there this day watching history being made again. Glen stood around for a while and toasted up a few with his coworkers and then excused himself to go home and relax with Cheryl. He had to badge himself out of the gate at Kennedy and head to his condo to prepare himself for a great evening. Glen drove into his gated community as he had done every day. But for months now he had been working long hours, and it was usually dark when he arrived. He had been working developing the tracking system for the launch. Now that it was over, he could start seeing daylight again. "Hi Mr. Reed" the familiar children speaking has he drove in. Most neighbors would say living here in this beautiful community is great. The condominiums had shingle siding, and a lattice gable with a wraparound deck. It presented a very warm welcoming look to the front of each home. Each had their owner's personality and style. There were not many children living there so the ones that were became very recognizable. Horace would see Glen coming through the gate and run alongside of the car with his skate board under his arm all the way to his house. "Mr. Reed can I have your car?" "No! Horace get back from the car before you get hurt" he'd said Horace was usually hanging on the window then. "O.k. well can I drive it?" his next question. "No Horace. "Where's your girlfriend?" "Horace how old are you?" Glen asked. "Why do you think I'm going take your girlfriend"! He'd asked and skate off on his board. His dad was in the military and had been deployed overseas so everybody in their small little community looked out for him. He was only nine or ten at the most and had already learned how to shoot the dozen. His mother worked at the space Center in the administration building so he thought Glen was free for the picking. Glen walked in and looked around his condo.   It seems he was just in and out these last few months. He picked up the pizza box he had the night before and headed to the shower. On his way to his bedroom he picked up the newspaper he had left on the sleeper sectional earlier that morning. Glen's condo was bachelor fabulous. It's very stylish and has a masculine style design. Unless he tells you about the sleeper that's concealed in the sofa it goes undetected. He says it's only used when friends or family stay the night. He had several messages on his answering machine. Checking them "cool" he would answer each one tomorrow but right now he was going to see Cheryl. She was becoming the best thing that has happen to him lately and he did not want to be late. Glen went over to the kitchen turned on his dishwasher. After a long hot shower, he dressed for success! He had stopped by the florist and picked up some fresh roses and a nice bottle of Red wine to compliment any dinner. 'Splash, splash! of his 'Opium' cologne and he was on his way driving down life's highway in a silver roadster convertible knocking on

Cheryl's door at 7:00 sharp. "I'm impressed Cheryl said coming to the door in white jeans that she had poured herself in just for him he said and a white sequined cashmere sweater top. His girl was hot!" She reached and drew herself close to him holding the sides of his face with both hands and brought her face to his and kissed him. "Good evening" Cheryl said in a sultry voice. "It's going to be" Glen said walking into Cheryl's home and sitting the wine on the table. "Let me put these in water for you?" Cheryl remarked taking the box of flowers from Glen's arm and walking over to the table taking them out of the box and arranging them in a vase. Cheryl was expecting her man and the mood she had set showed it. She and Glen had been dating for six months they were mature adults. Cheryl had decided after about three months that she and Glen had something special. She wanted him and spared nothing in pursuing him. She found out what he liked about her and shared the things she cared about with him. He was to her a strong black intelligent man who she could be proud of and live with the rest of her life. She could invite him around her friends and coworkers and be proud of the way he complimented her personality. Not to mention the way he looked with those bowed legs like "Denzel" umm! Cheryl had some classical jazz playing softly, and candles throughout her elegant upscale apartment with the lights turned down low. Cheryl's place was fabulous from the silver sage pinch-pleated London patchwork draperies in her living room, to the French canopy queen size bed with textured vanilla laced headboard in her master bedroom. "She had very good taste in everything" Glen boasted she got me! He would tease. Her place was decorated contemporary but oh so famine! The large bay windows had soft shades that looked out to a row of trees that ran down the walkway outside of her apartment. The parking area where she parked her cute little Toyota could also be seen. When she pulled down the shades it blocked out what was left of the day's sunshine. All the days' light coming in vanished and left only candlelight gleaming throughout. The dining area opened up into a spacious living room filled with white suede furnishings. The snow-white carpeting throughout gave a striking elegance to the entire place. "And right there is where I want you tonight" she told Glen pointing to the fireplace has he stood over replacing the classical jazz to the soothing sounds of Cheryl's "Barry White" collection and other great balladeers he had come across as he looked through her many record albums alphabetized on the shelf. Glen started to sing along to the music and Cheryl was busy in the kitchen setting and elegant table for the night's dinner. Cheryl Laler had only been going to Shining Star for about a year when Brianna invited her to Florida. The two had met at college during a study section. Cheryl already a schoolteacher was doing some follow up study on her teacher's degree and both were busy studying. After a conversation they realized each attended the same church and a friendship flourished from there. Glen and Cheryl were having fun together even though she had not given in to him physically yet. It had come close okay very close many times over the six months. I think that is what intrigued Glen about her he wanted her bad but respected her choice to wait. "I can't give myself to you she said until I know you really want me!" Cheryl told him one night about two weeks into dating. Glen went home puzzled and frustrated but returned out of respect. And was still waiting coming to realize she was worth the wait.

"Glen sat waiting for Cheryl to complete what she was doing. He sat in one of the big chairs in the living room relaxing and listening to the great balladeers of all times album. To keep the mood in check he would ask an occasional question every now and then. Letting Cheryl know to him she had so far planned a special evening. "How was your day?" he'd asked her. "Filled with lots of excuses why they didn't do or forgot their homework she said. Cheryl taught junior high school and she had stories to share regarding her students but not tonight. "Glen please start the fire". I'm just about finished with my masterpiece she told him. Glen kneeled down on the large white bear rug that anchored the fireplace to the room. He moved his vicious teeth away from him. "Are you sure he's going to let me lay here with you?" Glen asked making reference to the bear's big claws and opened mouth. "He won't mind if you are being nice," she said softly. Glen prepared the fire and sat back in the big chair. The fire crackled as it began to burn. "Its ready now Glen said getting up and coming over to the table putting his arms around her waist. "O.k. dinner is ready too"! turning to kiss him lightly on his lips. "Take your sit she said turning down the lights leaving only the fireplace light and the candles that was strategically placed so the light would shine on her face. 'Let me pinch myself Glen said, I have died and gone to heaven and sitting here with an angel," I told you Glen had the lines! "No seriously, this is lovely" he told her "thank you this is very nice." This was the real Glen. He had a facade for the clubs but he was really a down to earth kind of guy. And if he was letting Cheryl see him, he liked her a lot. Cheryl had prepared a crusted snapper with lemon. Using her mother's recipe for oregano vinaigrette, she was going in for the kill. That's woman talked for I've landed this one. The meal she prepared for Glen was to show him. "I want you and I know what it takes to keep and have you". Along with the snapper Cheryl shaved fennel potatoes and made an arugula salad with mustard dill dressing and fruit kebabs to tease him with by the fire. 'Babe you have really out done yourself Glen told her enjoying every bite. Cheryl had prepared the snapper "imacnific!" "Family recipe Glen asked "Does it come along with you?' he asked again flirting during the meal. "Everywhere I go!" Cheryl flirted back putting a bite of snapper from her plate into his mouth with her fingers. They sat talking and having a great conversation enjoying one another. They had been dating each other regularly over the past six months and neither was shy of their wants for each other. They were still finding out about each other's likes and dislikes but for the most part they agreed they wanted to be together. Cheryl was learning more about the Reed family. And Glen liked everything about Cheryl. After dinner they moved over to the fireplace. Cheryl had every intension of pleasing her man tonight and he wasn't backing down from her advances. She excused herself and was gone for a few minutes. He lay there in front of the fire talking to the bear rug he was laying on. Glen had poured another glass of wine into the crystal stemware from the dinner table that he sat carefully on the floor near him. She walked back in. "I needed to relax after eating all that food she said honestly. "She didn't need a reason for him. She came back wearing a two-piece soft red satin sleep shirt with matching bottoms "easy on the two piece "thongs!!!! "Prefect for relaxing by the fire" Glen told her. "Tell me something Glen are you this nice to all the girls you date?" she asked placing her head on his arm. She had two large throw pillows that sat next to the fireplace for extra seating that Glen was using to rest his head on. He was gazing into the fire with anticipation holding Cheryl in his arms. Cheryl liked Glen so she asked the pointed questions. She felt it had been long enough and beating around the bush was over. "I treat women the way they treat me" he said. "o.k. good answer that's being safe" she replied. Glen laid enjoying the sounds of Vandross, Lavert, Mcknight, and of course Barry White playing with a feather Cheryl had lying on the cocktail table near the sofa. He was lightly touching her skin from her neck down to her feet with it and Mcknight was crooning. "She flirted with him kissing his hands. And he liked the cute way she touched his nose. "if you knew my answer would be yes what question would you ask me?" Glen pretended to sit in the position of "The Thinker statue" He turned Cheryl over and kissed her. "Let's see?" he said. And the next line could not have been scripted any better. TURN OUT THE LIGHTS! Could be heard from one of the balladeers and so they did.

CHAPTER 40

Let it snow!

David was home in his study reading his Wall Street Journal. He had the television on listening but not giving total attention to each news stories being broadcast. He often used the noise of his television to break the silence of the house instead of the music. "Hi honey, Tetra said coming through the door carrying a case of bottled water into the kitchen.

David got up hurriedly from his chair "Tetra let me help you with that he said. "What are you doing with all this bottled water we have plenty of Perrier in the refrigerator. "There is also another case in the car. "I bought this for one of the young mother's at the church." Tetra replied to him. She is pregnant and having morning sickness". This will help with the uneasy upset stomach." Tetra added, "I drank it all the time with Billy." David didn't say anything but he was thinking about a lot of things. He put the case of water down in the kitchen and headed to the car. "No, David leave that one in I'll take it to her tomorrow along with some big clothes she can wear to make herself comfortable during this time". "O.k. Tet is that all you have out there I can help you with?" he asked quickly going back to study to get his note pad. The words "uneasy and oversized clothes" kept going through his head. Dorca Williams must have been pregnant that would surely speak to her leaving regularly once a month probably for her checkups. David sat in his study lost in thought reading his notes and did not hear Tetra speaking to him. Tetra had a brochure and had been trying to get his attention. But he was preoccupied with his thoughts of the moment. "David did you hear me? What's on your mind David?" she questioned coming over giving him the ski brochure. "Remember vacation starting the end of the week" pointing to the picture on it. We leave Friday and it's Thursday. Is there anything special you will need? I checked all of our ski gear and ski clothes they are fine and we just purchased new ski's last year" everything is in order there!" she told him, standing across the hall looking into the study. Realistically she was still really talking to herself. "OH! I'm sorry Tetra, David finally said. "It's just this contract I'm working on" finally looking down at the brochure. "Precisely why we're going you have been going and going honey you need to relax get away for a while". "You were always asking me to relax now I'm telling you" "I love you dear, and lately if I don't watch for your well-being you won't." She shared lovingly. "I know honey" and I'm looking for a wonderful relaxing time together with you at Government Camp Ski resort". David affirmed reading from the brochure. "Where exactly is that David?" "Near Mount Hood dear he said. "It sounds fun" Tetra replied heading up stairs. "What would you like for dinner?" she asked walking up the stairs for a long hot bubble bath. I'll get something on the table when I come down" she added. "Sounds good dear. As soon as Tetra was safely in her tub relaxing in a soothing bath David called Masony. He needed to talk through his notes he had gathered. "Ring, ring, ring,' This is Masony leave a message" his recording came on. David left a message and sit anxiously waiting for Masony to call back.

David had everything packed on the car when Tetra came back at noon on Friday from the Parson's Center. Masony still had not called back and he was trying to keep busy and keep his mind on the wonderful time he would have with his wife. He called his office to remind his secretary of his planned vacation. He was not going in that morning and to let her know he was leaving for a week of skiing in the mountains of Oregon and would see them the following week. He called and left a message on Billy's answering machine at home because he wasn't in the Law office and said he'd be off for a while. David figured he was at the university or with Jillian He didn't bother calling on Billy's cell phone but left detailed information on his answering machine of where they would be if he needed them. "Ready Tet let's get on the road we have got a two hour drive up" he said locking his skis to the SUV. It was a beautiful picturesque scenic drive up the hill. It was a very quiet but exciting drive. They watched a family of deer frolicking in the snow and stopped by the side of the rode for a closer look. They passed several snow-plows along the way shoveling snow to the side of the road to keep the traffic moving smoothly. David drove all the way up the highway toward the Cascade

Mountains to the Resort. "Do you plan to attend the class Dr. Edinberg is facilitating next month? "Tetra asked as they drove up the mountain "I do as a matter of fact I planned to invite Billy and Jillian if they are available" David replied. "That sounds wonderful dear". After they had been riding for an hour an a half they saw the turn off sign to the lodge. The snow covered the road and light flakes were falling to the ground. The sun was shining making the weather plausible for skiing. They drove along a long narrow rode for about 10 miles leading up to the front of their cabin. After stopping by the Ski lodge to pick up their keys and cabin assignment, get information regarding their stay at the resort they parked unloaded their things and rested a bit in their cabin. "Honey let's get settled in and we can still get a run in today if we hurry" Tetra said anxiously putting the clothes into the drawers and hanging some clothes in the closet. The lift goes up every half hour, she told him. Tetra was an excellent skier. She as a young Black girl was determined to have a good life for herself. Made her way through college and despite being criticized by her Black friends hung out with Caucasians all through high school and college which eventually lead to her meeting David. She started David skiing and he loved it. The lodge there was so cozy and warm. It had lots of throw pillows on the thick piled carpeting that covered the floor. There were plenty of cozy intimate seating areas throughout for snuggling up to the fire. There were also lots of skiers coming in from other parts of Oregon that David met while parking his vehicle. The main fireplace where everybody gathered at night to mingle was flanked by a familiar stuff moose head hanging over it. The large sunken chenille fabric chairs could hold two people comfortable while sitting and holding conversations together. And most of all you could share stories and enjoy one another's company. So off they went up the lift. 'Let me kiss you now! You won't kiss me after I beat you down this hill!" David said knowing that Tetra was a better skier but he had made much improvement since their last run out. Tetra reached over and kissed him "Good luck" she said "though I'll BEAT YOU Down! David bragged pulling up aside Tetra on the slopes. "here I come I've improved! "OH no! she said you won't and off they went skiing down the mountain. "Watch that tree'! Tetra yelled about two ski lengths in front of David. She was in a ski club in college and was a very good skier. Tetra had won many competitive races on the ski's in her all women events. But David was set on beating her. Several feet ahead of David she threw up her ski poles down at the end of the run, "I won! I won! she said jumping up and down David pulled up and threw snow all over her. "Don't be a poor sport there is always tomorrow she said laughing at David's antics. The next days proved to be equally as competitive Tetra tried to let him win a race by pretending to hit a bump but he saw what she was doing "Don't let me win! I'll do it fair and square" David told her playing with her down the slopes. On the last day of their stay at the cabin he finally put a run together and although it was only by and inch David had something to talk about back at the lodge. Their week together was fun and relaxing. They had something planned every day. Their next day in was an early morning wake up. After two days at the resort David wanted to ride snowmobiles. They were walking over to the designated area after reading the brochure that specified the area for snowmobiles only. On their way over they met Marge and Arnold heading to the main lodge. After meeting and talking about it the couple decided to join David and Tetra on the snowmobile ride. The ladies were very nervous as they got into the back of the snowmobiles with their husbands driving. "How fast does these things go?" Marge asked still trying to position herself in the seat. "Hold on tight David said looking back a Tetra. "These babies go 50mph and some!' he said excitedly and Tetra's heart was pounding. Marge was holding Arnold so tight he couldn't breathe he was laughing so hard. "Marge you have to let me drive or were going to hit a tree! "he teased. What fun they had laughing and laughing as they made their way across the slopes. Everyone made it out of the snowmobile successfully. The guys rode around by themselves after they stopped and let Tetra and Marge out. The ladies decided once was enough and opted not to go again. David and Arnold took off over the slopes. The ladies went back to the lodge and shopped for souvenirs. By the evening after a full day of fun they all sit around the fire that night and had a good laugh. David and Tetra met a lot of good friends even built some relationships along the way. The cabins that were the living quarters had large comfy beds and its own cute little fireplace. Two warm toned comfortable chairs for reading or relaxing in their own private space. David and Tetra decided to have and intimate dinner in their room on their last night there together. "A very fun, decision free, restful week she told David! Thank God he allowed us to enjoy one another. I thank your dear for leaving those cell phones off and the busy life behind for a while. I wanted this more for you than me Tetra confided. I really enjoyed not being disturbed by day to day life. And we met some wonderful friends" Tetra remarked. After dinner David and Tetra loaded up their SUV for and early morning start. "Let's go in the lodge later tonight dear and sit and mingle with our fellow skiers before we leave" David said. Sounds wonderful, Tetra replied, I would love to speak with Marge again. On their way walking over to the lodge from their cabin David was hit by a flying snowball smack in his chest. He looked around to see Arnold ready to toss another. Tetra picked up a snowball from the place she had run to hide and tossed it at Arnold. Marge tossed a snowball back at Tetra then David joined in. Other skiers saw all the fun activity going on and soon everyone was tossing snowballs at anybody in the immediate area. With the fire blazing in the open fireplace of the lodge David and Tetra sat around with other couples holding hands in a large circle. Marge and Arnold and Floyd and Evelyn and Martha, and Ted and Arnie and on and on singing SHE'LL BE COMING AROUND THE MOUNTAIN WHEN SHE COMES...

Billy had satisfied himself that what Doris did was cruel and uncalled for but since Davie was her son there was little, he could do about it. He knew they really had no right to him. Jillian was so torn and broken hearted she lay in her bed for days crying and wondering what had she done. Billy went to Davies school to confirm that it was Doris who had taken Davie. But not to arouse suspension he was trying to help Jillian feel better confirming the signature with the office attendant and other necessary papers needed when signing a child out of school. Doris had left a number but asked that the school not give it out. The school administrator called and Doris Wright spoke with her. Doris also asked to speak with Billy but only saying that she would have Davie call them when she got settled in. She was moving to Los Angeles with her sister. She would not discuss why she took Davie without telling them just hung up the phone. When Billy shared that with Jillian it sent her into a deep depression. Jillian felt she would never see little David again. I was so worried and didn't know what to do. I called mom and dad but they were on vacation. Then I called Mrs. Reed, Glen's mom and asked her to pray for her hoping it would make Jillian feel better. She understood I felt uncomfortable calling her. It had been a long time since I was a little boy running through her home. Mrs. Reed asked me to put Jillian on the phone. I tried handing her the receiver but she wouldn't take It just shook her head no! "I'm sorry BILLY SHE SAID "I DON'T WANT TO HURT LIKE THIS!" Jillian yelled to him over and over again loudly. Mrs. Reed asked me to just hold the phone up to her ear and believe for Jillian. So, I did as Mrs. Reed prayed. It had been a long time since I was taught intersession but I understood that. Mrs. Reed prayed for healing of her heart, restoration of the mind and body for strength to endure the pain and complete wholeness of the inner soul. As I stood listening, I felt so much better when I got off the phone. I thanked Mrs. Reed and she said she would continue to pray for us. She gave me a scripture to read and to share with Jillian. Matthew 9:22. Mrs. Reed also encouraged me. She shared she knew the faith it took for me to call was enough faith to heal my friend. And she was right! I called Mrs. Reed the next night to tell her Jillian was eating. She hadn't eaten in two full days. As I talked to her tears ran down my face. She's resting now I told her but she is being restored Thank God. Thank you, Mrs. Reed for being there I love you".

David and Tetra arrived home to a very wanting home. They had been gone for a week and they enjoyed their vacation but they missed their home, and was glad to be back. "back to the reality" Tetra said looking at David as they lay in the bed. Masony had left a message that he had talked with Beulah Reeves who he found to be a mid-wife of sorts. And she had delivered a healthy baby to Dorca Williams March 1985. So now we are looking for a young Black woman with a child. David had lots to digest and he laid on his pillow holding Tetra and did just that.

CHAPTER 41

The past

Justin was helping the new medical student he thought bring boxes in from her car. That's what she looked like to him walking in with her arms full and a big smile on her face. He had met her in the parking lot on his way into work. She was carrying a big box of medical books and he offered to take them in for her. "May I help you with that?" he asked walking up beside her at the entrance to the hospital reaching for the box. "Hi my name is Justin Parker, I'm an x-ray technician here in the hospital" he added. She smiled looking at his hospital greens he was wearing and teased him. "Oh, I thought you were a fireman, handing him the heavy box "but thank you I can use the help, I have several more to bring up" she replied. Are you new here?" Justin asked. I really don't recall every seeing you before". "You're right, she replied this is my first official day". She had been to the hospital earlier with interviews and getting her paperwork in order. Justin was asking lots of questions as he carried the remainder of the boxes in for her. "Right here she said put them over there, and thank you for all your help". Justin put the remaining boxes down and she extended her hand "Thank you, I'm Dana Williams" she said smiling at Justin. "You're most welcome." "Glad I could be of assistance" he told her looking at his watch "got to go! See you around". He hurried and checked in down on the main floor for his scheduled day of work. Justin was very close to ending his stay at Bowdin and was excited about graduation that for now was still two years away. Kat had forgiven him for not telling her sooner about David and was glad he and David had at least spoken. And for now, she was satisfied. Justin's day was busy scheduling patient after patient in for x-rays. He liked those days. They went by faster and cut his work days in half he'd said. Ariel was meeting him for lunch so he hurried and charted on another of his patients before going down to meet her at the opened air bistro of the hospital. Walking up he saw Ariel already there waiting. "Hi there he said giving her a gentle kiss to her lips. "Hi she said I ordered you pastrami, hope that's alright?" she told him handing him his napkin. "Billy, my brother is having a big celebration next month" he told her. "He has successfully passed the law bar exam!" Justin said proudly. I should get the invite in the mail he bragged but he called already and shared it with me yesterday." "What should I wear? "I mean what's the attire going to be?" Ariel asked. She had of course met Billy and had been to his fabulous bachelor pad! So, she was definitely thinking formal!" "It's going to be held at the Harvard's Widener Library so very formal is the attire!" he told her. Ariel was very excited she was going to a ball with her favorite guy! Ariel worked in the file room of the hospital. She met Justin one day when she brought up some requested files for patient's he needed to x-ray. She had worked hard to get her job paying her way through Business College and then landing a career job there at the hospital. Ariel wasn't use to all the glamour of the life style Justin envisioned for them but she certainly had her dreams. They were learning together from Katherine, Justin's mom. Ariel liked Justin had been raised in a single-family home so they shared a lot of similar stories. "Wow! I'd better start looking for my dress now!" she said moving her drink to the side of the table so the waiter could place their entree's down. "Mine is easy all I have to do is be fitted" Justin replied looking at her. "Yes, Ariel a tux!" he boasted taking a large bite from his sandwich. They sat talking and finishing up lunch and both headed back to finish the day. Justin had to go by Bowdin College for an exam after work. He had shared with Ariel it should last about an hour depending on the difficulty of it. He kissed her and headed back to the x-ray department. Ariel hurried back to the file room with an arm-load of files she had from the surgery department where she had stopped on her way after having an enjoyable lunch with her man.

"Hi mama, Ariel said. She always tried calling her family at least once a month. Her mom accused her of forgetting where she came from simply because Ariel had chosen and made a better life for herself. Her mom had her the eldest and four other children but Rhea couldn't and wouldn't stop enjoying herself to care for them properly. Ariel knew that if things were going to change it was up to her. "Malcolm said you bought him these expensive shoes he's wearing!" Rhea sternly said to Ariel after she called.

"Yes, mama he needed them for school" she explained. "You could have just given that money to me and I could have bought them something to eat as well!" Rhea admonished again. Ariel didn't answer she had tried it all. And nothing worked short of taking the children once a month and as best she could saw their needs were met. She knew they had food she went by every week and took them groceries. Most of the time her mama wasn't there or lying drunk on the very worn out couch. "I just called to say hi" she said "and I'll talk to you soon" hanging up before her mother could say anything else. She usually spoke with one of her siblings. Things were less difficult that way. She loved her family but her mother made it so hard for her to communicate with her. "ARIEL!" her coworker called. "We have to take some files up to OB GYN. "They are waiting for them".

Jillian had somehow through much prayer pulled out of her depressed stay and was doing better. She just wanted to be rid of Cambridge and threw herself into her work. "Billy, I know you've gotten your testing over with last week" she told him calling him at the Obermeyer law office, and I'm going this morning" Jillian was calling me at the office and talking with me about the bar exam she was about to take. "I know Jilly, you're nervous but you will do fine." I said. She hadn't got totally over the Davie incident but was coping with it with his help. "Billy, I think I'm going to move home for a while and just work from there" she told him. Jillian shared she couldn't bear riding by that house where Doris and Davie lived one more day. "Let's talk about that later sweetheart" I replied not wanting her to think about anything but the exam. "But Billy", she said again "Jillian we will talk about it later" "Just keep your mind on what you're doing right now and you'll be fine" Jillian knew this stuff better than I did. So, I knew she wouldn't have a problem passing the exam if she gave it her total undivided attention. "I love you Jillian" he told her hanging up. Jillian left from her law office driving to the state building where the board exam was being administered. Someone gave her a package that had been delivered to her that morning. 'I love you too, Billy she thought to herself as she drove down the road hearing Billy's words going through her head. She had put the package in her briefcase and was trying to focus on the task ahead.

Billy walked in and his phone was ringing "hey bro" Glen's voice was smiling across the phone. "I got the invite" CONGRATULATIONS!" he said. "How is Jillian?" "Jillian is much better" I told him. "Much better is she ill man" he asked concerned. "No, I replied. "Did your mom tell you I called?" I asked him. "No, were you trying to get in touch with me," I've being so busy at the facility but you know how to reach me if you need to!" Glen felt bad he didn't want him to think he was ignoring his calls. "No, Glen I called for your mom, "I needed her to pray for Jillian". Then he explained the situation to his friend. "I'm sorry to hear that he told him but I'm glad things are better" Glen said. I then realized that Mrs. Reed's conversation was between her and I and if I wanted to share it with anyone else it was my call. No one else knew what had happened regarding Jillian except Mrs. Reed. I hadn't even shared it with mom since Jillian had gotten better. "I now was feeling better that my call to Mrs. Reed was personal and private between us. Trust is a beautiful thing I reasoned. "So, what's been happening with you?" I asked cheerfully. "I called to give you the address of where to send flowers" Glen joked. "Flower's? I wasn't getting it yet. Glen sat silent for a minute. "Flower's you got one man!' longer than six months! So that's where you've been hiding!" I said laughing and teasing with Glen. "What's her name? anybody I know?" No! not yet but you will. "I'm bringing her to the party" she's all that and more!" Glen explained. "I can't wait to see the woman who took the Man out of Mac-daddy" I joked. "No, all kidding aside, I am very happy for you, I finally said and Jillian and I look forward to meeting her". "I'm sure Jillian will be happy" I remarked to Glen. "See you soon bye" I said hanging up. I had stopped by and bought Chinese food on my way home so that Jillian or myself wouldn't have to cook. I looked at my watch several times knowing she should be finished by now. Several hours had passed. She knew this law exam inside out. What's taking so long? I thought pacing up and down in my living room. If she failed it wasn't the end of the world. Very few people pass on their first time out. I walked from room to room impatiently waiting for Jillian to come before I sit down to eat dinner. Looking out of my window with every sound of a car that passed and pacing the floor anticipating her arrival had worn thin. I called on her cell phone but was only getting her voicemail and I had left several messages. After about an hour or two of waiting past what I thought definitely was enough time for her to be back I went to Jillian's house. Her car was parked in the driveway and she was home packing her things. "Jillian! I said walking in with flowers and boxes of Chinese food. "I thought you were coming by so that we could celebrate your victory together." How did it go?" I asked. Jillian walked around still tossing things angrily into her suitcase. "Where are you going? I thought we were going to talk about the move later" I said reaching for her hand to hold.

Jillian pulled her hand from mine and continued to throw things into the almost full luggage. "Jillian?" I conceded after seeing she didn't and was not going to cooperate with me, I asked. 'Jillian did everything go well down at the board? I kept asking her any questions I could think of that would put her in this mood. Then I walked over to the table to look at the papered document that she had seemly tossed on it as she walked in. "Congratulations! Jillian" I knew you could do it! I said holding the piece of paper in my hand. Our results I knew would be mailed. I tried again to come over and kiss her she shoved me back and threw a brown envelope at me. "THIS WAS DELIVERED TO MY OFFICE TODAY! She said loudly. "What is this Jillian?' I asked laying it down on the coffee table and walking into the bedroom where she stood taking her clothes from the closet putting them into the luggage bag hanging on the door. "Jillian, Glen called today he's bringing his girlfriend down to the celebration we're having next month". "That's great! Hope you have fun!" she scolded. "Jillian it's for both of us and mom has invited all of our friends". "Desmond and Mossy are coming too and they have a surprise for us" Desmond told me when we talked yesterday.

Jillian stopped for a moment and looked at him. "I'm tired of hurting! I don't want to hurt anymore!" "I cannot do this again! PLEASE LEAVE ME ALONE!" She went back into the kitchen still gathering her things. Then very calmly she said, "I'll come to the celebration because Mrs. Parker has worked hard in preparing it for us. But please don't ask or expect me to be your date Billy Parker! "Why did you do this to me?" And I'm finding out now when you know I am already hurting!" Jillian was just walking and talking and I didn't have a clue of what she was talking about. Things had been going well since the New York trip fiasco. Month's had passed since Doris's betrayal! All I knew is right now we should be celebrating and we weren't. Then she walked over to the table in her fury and tossed the manila envelope to me again "Did you do this Billy?" I caught the envelope before it hit the floor. It was the weight of a magazine. "What's this I said?' sitting down in Jillian's corner chair. I pulled out the playboy magazine and more photos' fell to the floor. I looked at the cover and on the front was Lena and Lexia. The twin bomb shells of New York were the featured centerfold. I didn't dare drop the center page but looked at the photos that had fallen to the floor. IT WAS PHOTO'S OF ME AND LENA. Someone had taken photographs of the gondola ride, the night we went to Omega's. And had even captured my early morning wake up at the Sheraton after my night out with Lena. "You lied Billy Parker and I hate you! Jillian told him going into her room locking the door behind her.

CHAPTER 42

Timing

David kissed Tetra and headed to his office. "Thanks for breakfast" he said heading out of the door. David knew this was going to be a busy week. He looked over his schedule several times before riding in on his way to work. He had his electronic organizer out and was going through each appointment calendared. He was trying to schedule some time to ride back to Oregon and talk with Mrs. Reeves himself. Masony was headed to Los Angeles to check some leads he thought were important. "Mr. Parker" "Mr. Beckner is on line one" Gabriella said over his speakerphone. Picking up his phone's receiver Daivd said "Hello Mr. Beckner, greeting him. Mr. Beckner explained he has been under the weather with a terrible cold and called to reschedule. He apologized for the late call but he was making every effort to keep the appointment. He could have sent one of his associates but wanted to speak to David personally on this matter. "Not a problem" David told him listening to him cough through the entire conversation. After hanging up from his call David gave out a big "sigh" Good! he thought that was my three hours for today. He asked Gabriella to leave his calendar as is do not add he would use this time to catch up on some needed work issues. David saw a couple of his regular clients with one meeting lasting about an hour and a half. "The negotiations went well Mr. Falkner, I think he will be a great asset to your team" I'll be in touch soon bye." David sat back in his leather-bound executive chair with his hands behind his head. Things were going well he thought. Should I stir up this Dorca Williams case again? Billy is fine things are going well with him now it seems. Nobody has heard from her? I should just leave it alone. But he couldn't. David said goodnight walking out of the office early and headed to Oregon to speak with a Mrs. Beulah Reeves.

This drive is getting shorter and shorter he said to himself driving down the highway to Oregon. It was only about three hours round trip depending on your foot. It was about 4:30 when David stopped at a nearby store to look at the directions Masony had given him. "This place is turned around" David thought looking at the street's directions. As he drove along, he looked over and saw the Hening place down the street from the address Masony have given him for Beulah Mae Reeves house. David pulled up and observed someone hurriedly running into the house. Soon an older woman came out to the edge of the fence. David looked around and got out of his car. It was not where he wanted to be when it got dark. So, he was thinking quickly to himself. I'll state my business really quick and leave. "Hi there" he expressed walking up "I'm David Parker. "I'm looking for Mrs. Reeves", he said a "Beulah Reeves?". "You seez her, what can I do Mr.?" And elderly woman questioned looking him up and down. "I'd like to ask you some questions about a Dorca Williams?" David said feeling she was all right with that. "Oh, I thoughts you was somebody else! Come in child come on in" she said. She could barely walk back into the house. It took a while but eventually they made it in. David walked into a house that was so clean you could eat off the floor, he remembered. "Cuse me" she said, "have a sit". And she walked to the back room. David sat looking at the very kept house and wondered about what was taking the old lady so long to come back. After a while a younger woman appeared. "Good evening, I apologize for keeping you waiting, but my little ones have a way of showing up sometimes unannounced" a lady in her mid-fifties said extending her hand "Please to meet you I'm Beulah Reeves". Mrs. Reeves was very well spoken and David was surprised and she knew it. "I have to protect my girls she said they trust me to do so" "How may I help you Mr. Parker?" Mrs. Reeves asked him after she thoroughly checked David out. "How did you come to know Dorca Williams?" He asked her after they had gotten pass why he was here and showing his identification proving who he wasn't she told him. "I'm a registered nurse I like my great grandmother before me am a midwife. "You'd be surprised how many women choose to have their babies away from the hospital" she told him. My requirements are she must have had her regular checkups and keep all of her scheduled appointments with a licensed physician" she went on to say. "They come here and I take them to the hospital every month until their little bundles or ready and they are delivered here. God has blessed me to defer the cost for many of the young ladies that I encounter". "One of the little ones was coming just as you drove up" she laughed "timing they don't have!" "Many of the women I see can't afford to go to the hospitals." "That's what caught my eye about Dorca she really didn't need to be here she chose to." "And that's all right too. I'm here to help not to judge" Mrs. Reeves said lovingly. There was another gentleman here last week. Impressionable fellow!" she laughed. "That would have been Masony, he works for me". "Oh, I see she said nodding her head. "Can I get you something to drink? coffee, tea, she asked before taking her sit. "No thank you, I'm fine. They continued to talk. She said Dorca Williams had stayed at the Hening place like most of the girls do. But she knew Dorca was different. "She took very good care of herself and never missed an appointment. When she delivered her big healthy baby, she was ready to leave this place and that didn't surprise her either. I was concerned about her leaving with the baby in that old car since Dorca said she was moving quite a distance from here". "But when I released her to leave, she asked if she could leave her baby with me for a while until she went and picked up her things from the Hening place. I said sure I didn't have another one scheduled for delivery anytime soon. I sat and held him while he chewed on his fist, beautiful big eyes. "He looked mixed if you know what I mean?" Dorca was almost white, Beulah said. "Dorca wasn't gone long about two or maybe three hours at most she came back with a brand-new car". She paid me and was on her way. "What did she name her baby?" David figured that would give him some extra clues as to finding her. "Let's see Beulah got up and went over to her desk. She pulled from the shelf a folder that was alphabetized from A to Z. W's here it is. Running her fingers down the page "Wright, Wren, Williams okay here it is Dorca Wiliams named her baby David. I remember because I made reference to the bible and told her she had picked a good one" Mrs. Reeves replied. David's heart seemed to stop! he saw image after image going through his mind could this be! NO! common name he conceded. "This baby would be about six or seven years old" Mrs. Reeves said standing there holding her journal open, exactly seven she said looking again at the birth date. "Is there something else I can help you with?" David wanted to ask so many questions but he needed time to sort. "I, I heard you mention the name Wright, tell me her story? David finally got the question out after stammering over his words. It had gotten dark but David was caught up now. "Let's see I have to jar my memory Wright? Yes, Doris Wright she was here about the same time. Though unlike Dorca she didn't have her act together. I'm sure I'll see her again" Beulah told him. 'She had a girl a sweet little girl. I had a family ready for her as soon as she delivered. All Doris wanted was the money to leave this dreadful place behind" she told me. "Things were starting to add up and David wasn't sure about the final sum. "Thank you! he told her; you have been a big help." David was getting up from the chair walking to the door. "Let me walk you out, gets pretty dangerous around here at night I've heard," Beulah added coming to the door to escort David out.

"Mr. Parker, if you have any more questions here's my card. She handed him her business card with name and title RN.

"This is my ministry she told him. I see so many of these young girls, I pray for them and try to help them by being here she told David. "My home address is on the card". David put the business card in his jacket pocket and "thanked Mrs. Reeves again. "He said he would be in touch if he needed further questions answered. She walked David to his car. And he drove away with Beulah Reeves and her grandmother "he's thinking" waving goodbye.

Billy had hurt Jillian and he was not having any success speaking with her. He stayed all night trying to explain away the photographs but the story kept getting worse somehow. The next day had come with Jillian still locked in her room just wanting to go and never see him again. He gave in and decided to give her space and maybe time away from each other is what they needed. She said she would come to the celebration so there was still hope of reconciliation he thought as he left early that morning and went home.

Jillian was so angry she didn't have any tears left to shed. She walked out slowly and saw Billy was gone. She quickly put her luggage into her car and drove away. Her things at Billy's would have to stay she couldn't risk running into him there. She went by her office and gave them the news of her exam. Asked for scheduled time off and headed home to New York. He got the message when he arrived home from his answering machine. "How could this have happened?" I thought. That was so long ago we had mended all of that. Who could have taken those photographs?

But according to Jillian it was never broken. And I hurt her and now she was gone. This should have been a time of celebration but it was the saddest day of his life.

Day after day I walked around the office in a funk. I wasn't returning any personal phone calls. I didn't answer any either, checking the caller I D. and having my clerk screen all calls. My dad was trying to get in touch with me. He had left messages at home and at my office. "Tell him I'm in a meeting!" I expressed to my clerk. "He wanted to know if you were here physically?" she replied. I knew then I had to call him. "Hi dad I said finally calling, "hello son, how are you?" I'm o.k. dad" I told him. But he sensed my tone and began to question. "I have been trying to find the words to say to you for about two weeks now." I said to dad. "How's Jillian and little Davie?" he asked. "They're fine I guess?" I replied. "Son, son what is wrong?" Dad never pulled the "I'm your dad routine on me!" to get me to talk. I needed to talked to someone I had exhausted myself. Jillian had moved in with Kelly and I would have to go through her to even see or talk with Jillian. I wasn't ready for that. "Dad" Jillian has left me and moved to New York. I wanted to tell you all after the celebration but she said she would be there so I decided to wait maybe things will work themselves out." "What happened you all seemed so happy when you left?" David asked. "Well Dad we were happy, very happy I was going to ask her to marry me." I love Jillian" Billy confessed. "I know son I know" David affirmed. "So what happened?" "When Doris took Davie Jilly's world came tumbling down" I began. And" David stopped Billy. "Who took Davie?" he asked. "Oh, Doris his mother came back from Los Angeles and took him back with her." That was a few months ago.

"She didn't even tell us she just took him while he was at school". And Jillian was so heartbroken." So, it didn't take much to push her off the ledge" he conferred. "Stop for a minute Billy, tell me about Doris, David asked now looking at his notes as he sat in his study. "What do you want to know?" Billy questioned. "Anything just whatever you know about her." David replied. "Not much really, let's see, she is a fair skinned woman like me a bit lighter, who lived next door to Jillian." They met one day crossing the campus and became friends, I guess. "What did she look like Billy?" Doris always wore a scarf on her face, beautiful long wavy hair. Jillian said her face was disfigured from and accident or something." She was very careful whenever I was around or even in public Jillian said.

She always had her face covered and sun glasses on". "Did Jillian ever see her face?' "Yes, she and Jillian lived by each other for about 4 years dad! She had gotten use to Jillian seeing her face". "So, Jillian would know her if she saw her?" David continued to question. "I guess dad why all the questions?" I finally asked. "I have still been looking for clues regarding Dorca Williams son and I have linked her with a Doris Wright. "When I heard that name I began to question?" I'm sorry son but I was just pulling at straws" David concluded. Dad, her name is Doris Wright" if that helps". "Doris Wright, that's too much of a coincidence I'll have to check it out" David told him. "Do you have a number where I can reach Jillian, I need to get a description of Doris?" "Hold on Dad I'll get it for you". Billy came back on the line and gave his dad the number to Jillian's cell phone and office. "Let me know if you find out something dad, I added. "I sure will David replied and 'I'm sure what ever happened between you and Jillian will mend over in a few days he told him. "I don't know I hope so. I hurt her pretty badly. I'll have to wait and see" Billy replied. "In the meantime, son, be careful and keep the doors locked. This Dorca Williams story has led me to some interesting people" Most of them have been a blessing, I'm learning God works in mysterious ways." "She's going through a lot not to be found. I'm hoping Jillian can get some answers for me". Take care son!" David got off the phone he didn't want to concern Billy but he was very concerned and seriously thinking something about those names rang true. Dorca Williams or Doris Wright was just too close for comfort. Who were they dealing with?" Ring, ring, David Parker" David Parker Masony here." "All I found out of Los Angeles was a purchase of a cell phone Masony reported. But payments for it is mailed out of Cambridge Massachusetts. I'm on my way there he told David. To which David replied, "I am too!

CHAPTER 43

Hello Kelly

Wanted a live-in single woman child okay. Will live with a sweet self-sufficient grandmother who takes total care of herself, needed only for companionship. This is the email Dana answered after she came to Maine from one of her co-workers. She had gotten settled and her living conditions were a plus. The email came from one of her co-workers whose mother had recently lost her husband of forty years. She says her mom felt the emptiness of her large home and wanted to share it with someone. She had shared with her children she wanted to stay in her home she and her husband had built together. Concerned about her mother being alone she searched for the right person to live with her. She knew her mother was not going to move. Her co-worker was glad Dana had answered the email. That way she could find out daily how her mother was really doing without keeping constant tabs on her. She and her husband traveled extensively and she just didn't have time to devote to her.

David met Masony at his office to discuss and go over the report he had given him from his trip to Los Angeles. Masony walked in letting the receptionist at the desk know he was there. David's secretary escorted him to David's office and Masony sat looking around. "Oh, I see you play golf "he said to David looking at the photo David had of the celebrity golf tournament he participates in every year. "Yes, as a matter of fact I do" However that is a tournament I play in each year for charity, he shared with Masony. "For charity? Masony asked. "Yes, it's a wonderful event and the celebrities are all great that come every year to help out". "There are many organizations who are helped with those type of functions" David concluded. "Now remarked David, turning Masony's head back to why he had come. 'You said something about a cell phone purchase David questioned. Masony pulled his notes from his briefcase he was carrying. I found out at the Henning place that Dorca Williams befriended another young lady by the name of Doris Wright. Now it seems from Ms. Henning, Doris was very controlling of the relationship. Could be to the fact she seemed older Masony informed. Dorca Williams was bidding her time until she had her child. I found that out after I called back to ask Ms. Henning what she meant about the oversized clothes she kept making reference too. I thought maybe it was a weight issue Masony implied." I felt so silly after she told me, Masony said chuckling. Anyway, from an anonymous source "I do have a few contacts up mine sleeve" he said smiling. "A Doris Wright fitting our description traveled to Los Angeles and she and a friend purchased a cell phone. This contract was taken out about four years ago. The payments come from an account out of Cambridge in Massachusetts." So, I need to find out whose account these monies are coming from there" he told David. I will go to Massachusetts and see whose name is actually on this account, Masony voiced. They would not give me any information over the phone or in person I found out later. "That's great news" but let me make a few phone calls before you go. Take a few days off and I'll call you and let you know what information I think we will need or might find" David said. "Are you sure we seem to be getting closer "Masony said with his detective sense. I don't want this trail to go cold!" he added. "No, you're right and I know I don't have to tell you to keep your ears open. However, I don't want us to make a lot of unnecessary trips that go nowhere" David shared with Masony. O.k. so I'll wait for your call". Masony stood and extended his hand and walked out of David's office. David had an idea but first he needed to talk with Jillian and get a description of her friend Doris Wright.

Jillian was still very angry with Billy and moved in with Kelly in New York. She knew her mother would not understand and it would be all her fault things went wrong and let Billy come back before she was ready. She loved him but he had slept with someone else while they were together and then admitted it to her trying to fix the problem. Kelly was so unlike Jillian. Kelly was what you call a fun-loving girl. She wanted to meet the cute blonde guy who worked in Jillian's law firm and badgered Jillian about it every day. "He's my boss Kelly and I don't think he's your type!" Jillian expressed to Kelly. "Do you think you and Billy will get back together?" It's been three weeks!" He calls all the time and you won't take his calls" Kelly asked her. "What Billy and I do is none of your business!" Jillian scolded. "We'll I don't know why you're mad at him" but somebody else is sure to get him if you let him go to long" Kelly remarked. Jillian turned and went back in her room to finish getting ready for work. She didn't care at this moment to discuss Billy with anyone, especially Kelly. Morgan was picking her up for her first full day and she did not want to be late. Kelly wasn't due into Neiman's until nine thirty and she was walking around in her sexy night shirt making herself breakfast. That wasn't unusual they were two girls living alone and Jillian did the same when she had nowhere to be. But today she needed to get ready. "Kelly did you see my mascara?" poking her head out from down the long hallway. "In the drawer under the sink" Kelly yelled back. Kelly had a large apartment so there was plenty of room for the both of them. Jillian just had to get use to Kelly's fun free lifestyle. And she knew that. She moved in to make Billy mad. And to keep him away and so far, it was working. Kelly was sitting in the living room eating her breakfast of wheat toast with butter and drinking her flavored coffee when the doorbell rang. "Jillian! Kelly yelled to her just knowing it was her ride Morgan. 'It's Morgan please let her in I'll be right out" Jillian yelled back. "A few more curls with this iron and I'll be ready" Jillian added. Kelly got up from watching the television news story that was on and walked over and opened the door. Without looking she said "come in." opening the door to their guest who just happened to be Blair Christensen. "Jillian will" Kelly stopped and looked at Blair. She started to head to the back but she could see he liked what he was looking at so she stood in a very inviting stance. "You don't look like a Morgan to me?' Kelly flirted moving her body around. "Morgan had a client waiting at the office I told her I would give Jillian a ride. Is she in?" Blair asked. Kelly was blessed we called her the Dolly Pardon of Riverdale High. "Blair didn't take his eyes off Kelly. According to Kelly no man in his right mind would!" 'What's your name?' Blair finally got around to asking in his British business voice. He didn't always use it but it was his native tongue. "Kelly"" Kelly Lipsney she smiled coming toward Blair giving him her hand. "Please to meet you Kelly, I'm Blair" he remarked. "Likewise, she said sticking out her chest as if she needed to. "I'm ready Jillian said cheerfully coming out of the back and STOPPED seeing Blair standing with Kelly in her night-shirt. "KELLY!" Jillian said turning beet red. "You said it was Morgan so I opened the door" Kelly now using a naive tone. Jillian tossed a throw from the sofa over Kelly grabbing Blair by his arm and leading him out of the door. When Jillian got in the car she apologized for Kelly's behavior, but honestly, she's like that all the time. She wanted to cover for future mistakes that her friend Kelly made. Blair didn't mind he explained to Jillian that Morgan was meeting a client and had asked if he would pick her up. "And on both notes I didn't mind" he said smiling.

Jillian loved her new office and her responsibilities but she was really starting to miss Billy. "I should let him explain?' she thought. But he was supposed to be out with Glen what else has he done?" She sat thinking to herself. "No Jillian move on". She had gotten two written messages from a Mr. Parker today and had no intention of returning Billy's calls. And unaware to Billy, Jillian had changed her cell number. She was angry!

David had traveled a lot from home lately and Tetra was starting to ask questions. He had not told her about Jillian's move to New York though she knew Jillian was offered a job there. Tetra was quite busy herself she had work tirelessly on the celebration for Billy and Jillian, putting many phone hours in with decorators and caters for this celebration event to be held in Cambridge Massachusetts' library. David decided he shouldn't leave again so soon. It may cause needless worry. He would wait they were going down a day early anyway in a week he would use that time to poke around without Tetra even suspecting anything. So, he called and let Detective Masony know the plan and invited him and a date to the celebration. He hoped Jillian would call him back but she still hadn't. He knew what was going on with she and Billy and didn't want to push. He hoped to see and talk with her soon at the Celebration they were giving for her and Billy at Harvard's Widener Library.

Dana sat in her office talking with the head of her department. She had got all of her things arranged in her office and he stopped by to introduce himself and welcome her aboard. "Welcome to our staff" he told her coming over shaking her hand. "I'm Dr. Baisden, Dr. Major Baisden he said looking around Dana's office." I'm impressed!" he said noticing her M.D. on her wall and other accredited degrees in her trained field she had hung over her desk. "Thank you" "Dana replied I really love what I do". "You know where everything is? He asked. Our lounge?" and our board room?" We will have a meeting tomorrow morning to acquaint you and reacquaint others to the changes that have taken place to our hospital this past year," Dr. Baisden went on to say. I apologize for taking so long getting down here to see you but I do hope things are going well" "Yes Dr. Baisden, Dana replied, no complaints." "Well I have been hearing good things about you from this department, keep the up good work" Dr. Basiden said. "Thank you again so much for this appointment sir I looked forward to being a continued asset to this department and hospital" Dana shared with him. 'That's good" he said smiling "see you tomorrow, shaking her hand and leaving. Dana continued to sit at her desk imputing her colleague's names into the email portion of her computer. Her stylish maple furnishing and black leather chair had just been delivered and she was setting up her office for the start of her day. Out with the old and in with the new" Dana said speaking of the new office furniture that was ordered for her. Dana was a psychiatric social worker. She loved working with people, most especially helping them to solve their problems. "Hi!" Justin said looking into her office. I came by earlier to see the movers bringing in your furniture, thought it best to come back later, he told her. "Come in" she said. I'm just getting things set up again". "So where are you headed?" she asked "in such a hurry?" seeing he was still standing. "Have a seat". Dana suggested. "Thanks" on my way out!" Justin said to her taking a seat in one of the mission style chairs in her sitting area. "Your day's over that's great got any plans?" she asked. Justin wasn't trying to date Dana and I don't think that was on her mind. They were becoming friends, and shared a laugh when he thought she was a medical student. They also talked a lot about life. He found her very down to earth Is how he described her to others. Justin had helped her bring the boxes into her office and as far as he was concerned that's all. She was very good looking, Dana looked exceptionally good for her age but she was older than Justin and he knew it. Justin enjoyed talking with her and wasn't trying to go out with her he had Ariel.

"As a matter of fact, I do!" Justin remarked. I'm heading for the airport in roughly four hours for a big celebration!" He sounded very excited. "Wow!" what's the big celebration all about?" she asked getting up putting some pens in her pen container at the corner of her desk. "My brother and his best girl are celebrating passing the laws bar exam!" "It is official now!" Justin said and I'm going to be right there celebrating too!" "Law! Dana's ears perked up. "I have some good friends who are lawyers" she said or should be." Justin was so excitedly happy he could hardly sit down. He didn't hear a thing Dana said. "I gotta pick up Ariel, and go *by* Kat's and head out he said mumbling under his breath "I'll will see you when I come back and tell you all about it "he told her getting up. "Good luck with your new assignment!" Justin said before leaving out of the door. Dana hadn't met anyone yet to go out with so it would be another weekend at home.

"Laney, McCormick and Fry" came the voice on the other end of the phone. "Yes, may I speak with Jillian Mcfinney Tetra asked calling in at her old office. "Ms. Mcfinney isn't in came the voice again. "Will she be in the office later today?" Tetra questioned. She didn't know Jillian had taken her new job assignment and had arranged for them to spend a day having themselves pampered. Ms Mcfinney is no longer in this office, the voice replied. "Then may I have her number in New York please?" Tetra asked knowing how things work in the corporate world. 'Just a moment. She came back on the line and gave Tetra the number to Crawford, Higgins and Applegate in New York. "Thank you, Tetra acknowledged and hung up and dialed New York. Morgan and Jillian were standing talking by the receptionist desk. The receptionist had stepped away to get a cup of coffee from the lounge "Good morning Crawford, Higgins, and Applegate, Morgan said answering the phone for the absent receptionist. "May I speak with Jillian Mcfinney, Tetra asked. Everyone was aware she didn't want to talk with Billy right now. "Just a moment I'll see if she's in" she said putting her on hold. "Jillian it's for you, it's a woman so I didn't bother asking who she was since it is obviously not Billy", she teased. "Thanks Jillian replied "I'll take it in my office" she walked in her office and closed the door behind her. She was thinking if it was her mother, she didn't want things to get out of hand. She sat at her desk and took a deep breath. "Good morning, this is Jillan Mcfinney. "Hi Jillian this is Tetra, how are you?" Jillian's stomach flipped. "Oh hi Mrs. Parker" Jillian said thinking "OH NO! "I was thinking we could pamper ourselves before your big celebration" Tetra said with a smile in her voice. Jillian still wasn't sure of the call and hesitated. "That sounds wonderful Mrs. Parker what did you have in mine?" she questioned. "I made appointments for the both of us at "Che' Moire Pampered Palace and Spa downtown Cambridge." "And all-day treatment for the both of us!" Tetra said very excitedly. "I don't know about you but I sure could use it" she added. "Mrs. Parker that's fine but I'm in New York when is this appointment?" Jillian reluctantly asked. "I' know Jillian, I made it for Friday at 11am, Tetra shared. "You have gotten your gown, already haven't you?" Tetra question. "Oh sure Mrs. Parker!" Jillian had not purchased her gown and now she would hope to find something off the rack that no one else will be wearing. "Oh yes! Tetra said. Jillian sat up in her chair, here it comes! she thought. "How's that cute little Davie?" Then Jillian knew Mrs. Parker had not spoken with Billy and she doesn't know we're not together anymore. Talking about Davie was still very painful. "He's fine, he's fine, Jillian said thinking to herself I sure pray he is. "Give him my love from his grandmother Tetra" she said sounding as if she was wrapping her arms around him. "It was getting to be too much right now for Jillian. With all the speech she could muster without crying "O.K Mrs. Parker I'll see you then" hanging up and reaching for a Kleenex to wipe her eyes. Jillian's case load right now was in her control. She had already scheduled her time off to go to Cambridge for the celebration but she was leaving early Friday. But now with this appointment she would have to take Friday off. That now looking at her schedule wasn't a problem. She sat at her desk going over some briefs and Morgan stuck her head into Jillian's office. "What are you doing for lunch Jill?" she asked passing by Jillian's to go into Blair's office. "Don't know yet!' Jillian replied still looking down at her documents. "How did that phone call go hope you didn't have any problems?" Morgan implied. "No, no problems at all she said. OH! I'm going shopping she said. "What are you talking about Morgan asked. "You asked what I was doing for lunch?" to which I'm replying shopping and Jillian got up from her desk and walked down the hall to the elevator.

Justin stopped by the "Men's Emporium" and picked up his tuxedo. He had been fitted a week before and he was ready for the big night. Walking in doing his Frank Sinatra movement flirting with the young lady behind the counter who was maybe in her last year of high school. "la, la, la, la, la" he said "how are you?" shuffling his feet around by the counter. "How may I help you?' she asked with this blank look on her face. No matter what he said next, that was coming out first. She was concentrating on getting her greeting correctly. Her body language seemed to say follow the manual as she stood thinking. "Justin Parker I'm here to pick up my tux!" She didn't say anything. She immediately turned and walked in the back to get his tuxedo. It wasn't that she was being unfriendly she was following the manual on her job description. Justin stood there humming a tune from old blue eyes himself waiting for the clerk to come back with his tuxedo. He had been fitted and refitted so when she came back and handed him the garment bag and had him to wait while she read all of the instructions to the letter then he was on his way. "He walked to the car standing there with the garment bag over his shoulder searching for his keys. "Oh no he thought. They are on the counter!" He ran back into the store up the escalator to the department on the second floor and the same very nervous clerk came running toward him "I'M SO GLAD YOU CAME BACK!" she said standing nervously holding a tuxedo garment bag over her shoulder. "Yes, I forgot my keys!" Justin told her. She took a deep breath and had now calmed a bit. She walked over and got the keys that had slipped off the counter and handed them to Justin. He turned to leave. "No! Wait! she said, "here's your tuxedo". Justin took the garment bag from his shoulder and rechecked the name thinking maybe she's found her sense of humor while he was gone. The name on it was Justin Barker and his height was only 5'7". To add to her frustration this gentleman, was standing in the garment shop madder than a wet hen. He had gone all the way home with Justin Parker's tuxedo measuring height 6'6". Which could have been disastrous Justin thought pulling up to Kat's house to get Ariel before leaving. Kat was taking then to the airport. She had loaned Ariel some of her jewelry to wear with her beautiful Liz Claiborne gown she had also purchased for her. Kat wanted to be well represented through her son Justin though she never said it to Ariel. Justin was still walking and dancing on clouds when he got to Katherine's "Are you ready to go?" Justin asked reaching for the luggage to put in the car. Katherine had taken Ariel to her salon and Justin did a double take and spun around! UM! He said. "You look fabulous "Let's go.

David and Tetra was sitting in service listening to Dr. Hathaway's message. They knew they were flying out tonight but wanted to get in on the final series of the messages Dr. Hathaway had started a few Sunday's ago. They booked a later flight. They were headed to Cambridge Massachusetts and would not attend Sunday service at Mt. Nebo. They just hated to miss any service. Still they made an effort to attend his weekly meeting on "Healing" before leaving out on their trip. He used a scripture out of Luke 9:6. He shared about the healing that takes place all over the world. He talked about how God sends us out into the world to be a blessing for someone else. David sat and thought about Mr. Hemley, and Mrs. Reeves and their ministry's. Their good friends the Reeds and surely Tetra thought there is a crown for Mrs. Scroggins. David said to Tetra during a song from the choir that filled the air with God's presence "we see his handy work all over if we would only stop long enough to recognize it". The choir sang another melody that filled the eyes of its listeners with tears of joy. "I absolutely love this choir" a woman visiting service reached over to tell Tetra as they sat together listening. "It truly is a ministry in music!" she expressed. "Thank you, please continue to pray for their strength and our strength as a whole. God Bless you", Tetra told her. David and Tetra were renewed in their spirit and soul. Both left rejoicing and blessed.

They stopped by the Crawling Lobster Restaurant before going to the airport to board their flight out to Cambridge. Their flight was leaving at 10pm. And they let Billy know it would be very late when they arrive.

I had been looking through Jillian's photograph collection she had left at my house for photos of Doris Wright but so far nothing. Most of the photographs I had taken of Doris were facing away from the camera. "I had spoken to my dad regarding the time they were due to arrive. I continued sitting in my big chair with piles of photographs and picture albums around me. After talking to dad on the phone I prepared me something to eat and settled in to watch a movie. I had planned to take the day off in anticipation that Jillian might come tonight or call anyway. I sat there longer watching what turned out to be a love story. Jillian still hadn't called so I decided to call her. Ring! ring! "Hello" Kelly said answering the phone. As much as I hated to ask "Kelly is Jillian in?" Whose asking?' Kelly questioned. "Kelly you know who I am, is Jillian home? "'It depends!" "she told him. I reasoned either she wasn't there and wasn't going to talk to me anyway no matter what. And I was quickly tiring of Kelly. "She's in the shower but wanted me to give you our address" Kelly said so that you can come up for a visit. As much as I wanted to see Jillian now, I would have to hear that directly from her. "You know you can always stop by. One of us are always here" Kelly informed me. Jillian, I don't think was there but Kelly wanted to keep me talking to her on the phone for some reason. I did need her address if I ever plan to see Jillian again. "Okay. I said what is it." I wrote down the number and hung up. I hated the fact Jillian lived with Kelly but right now there was not a lot

I could do about it. I really didn't know if Kelly had told her about the night she slipped into my house. That would surely end things with us I thought as I sat flipping the remote looking for something to watch on television. I could only think of Jillian. If Kelly had shared about that night that would truly be the end for us forever. So, I couldn't push. I'd just bide my time. My parents landed in Cambridge Massachusetts Thursday night after a long flight straight through.

Jillian called Billy's house early Friday morning, "Good morning Mrs. Parker, Jillian said knowing her voice over the phone and breathing a sigh of relief. "Yes, Jillian I'm getting coffee and I'll meet you a Che's" Tetra told her. "Sounds great I'll see you there, bye" Tetra and David made it in to Cambridge at 2 a.m. it was 2:30 am by the time they got to Billy's house. Tetra had slept all the way on the plane. She knew her day today would be very relaxing so she was up bright and early. She would surely turn in early tonight she reasoned. David was asleep and asked not to be disturbed by anyone. And Billy who was glad to see them was up still talking after they closed their eyes. He still hadn't emerged from his room. Tetra quickly hurried and drank her coffee down and left out the door for a day of fun.

David finally started moving about 9:30 a.m. Billy had taken the day off and was going to spend it with his dad or Jillian. Tetra had left David a note on the refrigerator spelling out her plans to meet Jillian at the spa. So, plans for Billy wouldn't change he'd hang out with his dad. David got up and showered and had coffee. He had some people to speak with whom he hoped could shed some light in finding Dorca Williams. "Billy are you ready?" David called upstairs to his son who had volunteered to escort him around today. "Coming dad, I'm getting a light jacket this weather here is deceiving" he replied running down with the jacket in his hand. They got in the car headed for the Radcliff's Administration building to see if anyone knew of Doris's Wright's whereabouts. "Good morning, David said walking into the main office. A lady maybe early forties came up to the lowered counter. The main office was at the front entrance. Finding the correct place to go was relatively easy. "May I help you?" she asked looking at dad then me. "I was hoping to get some information on a Doris Wright?" David quickly replied. "Doris Wright, she repeated does she work here?" "Not sure?' I think she was a student here recently?' David added. "Well let me see I can tell you that! But that's pretty much it" she said looking back and forth from me to dad. She put up her computer screen "you're spelling that W-R-I-G-H-T is that correct?' "Yes, that's correct. "Very common name we have lots of Wrights" and some wrongs she chuckled under her breath" looking up at me sitting on the dated wall heater unit of the building. But I'm satisfied we have no Doris's" she said with a tone she was not going to change. "Okay, thank you David said leaving. "This is going to be harder than I thought" he said getting back into the car, "I have got to get a picture of Doris! or whomever she is?' he kept saying. "These are some of the best one's dad maybe we can have them blown up" I suggested handing him the photograph's I had gotten from Jillian photo album. "I need to talk to Jillian, Billy!" "Let's go, David insisted. They drove to the Che's spa and David got out and went in. Stopping short of going through two big frosted glass doors David paused to read the big sign at the entrance embossed with gold lettering it read "women only!" David sat down for a moment on one of the Louis XVI style benches with its' distressed' oak legs and French toile fabric seat taking a moment to think. There has got to be another way he said and turned around to leave. "Maybe later" and off he went back to the car. "I know where we can go" I exclaimed! "I know who will have a picture of Doris Wright" her doctor. "She had surgery on her face. He will have a picture!" "Dad you will have to drive while I look for this number! "Jillian called me from his office one time" he explained. Dad and I exchanged seats and he drove and I went through my contacts on my cell phone. David called Masony and asked him to meet them at a small sidewalk cafe on Lexington and Vine downtown. They sat and waited and Billy continued to look for the number. "HERE IT IS! HERE IT IS!! he said jumping up and down with on lookers. Masony drove up to him jumping up! "I don't want what he's having" Masony joked in his subtle way. "With Masony pulling a few strings down at the precinct we were on our way. We pulled up to Dr. Meloo's office and walked in. "Good morning" David said, "I'd like to speak with a Dr. Meloo". It shouldn't have been that hard of a questioned it was a small private doctor's office that sat in a strip mall in midtown. David was surprised the receptionist spoke very good English. "Just a moment please an Asian lady at the front desk said. "I'll see if he's in". Everybody in the small waiting room were Asian and they were trying to guess what we were having done pointing at our extremities. A man came out from down a short hallway through an office door and introduced himself as Dr. Meloo. Walking out in a hospital jacket with hand extended. I think Masony intimidated him. "Ow may I yelp?' he said in his Asian native sounding tongue. David stood up. "I' need to ask you about a patient of yours, Doris Wright?" "Doris Wright" Dr. Meloo repeated. "Yes" David said. 'What? the doctor wasn't giving up too much information. "Is she a patient of yours?" David then asked. "Do you have any photos of Doris Wright?" David stood looking at Doctor Meloo, who was now looking around at all of us. Masony didn't say anything he just flashed his badge. Closer inspection would have showed it was retired but it was enough for the doctor. "Come" he said pulling us from his front waiting room into his office. Dr. Meloo said something in his native language to his staff. Soon his receptionist brought in a manila packet containing photographs into his office where we were now sitting. She said something to the doctor and smiled at us and walked out. Dr. Meloo pulled out the photos and placed them out on the top of his desk. David knew he had never seen Doris Wright so all the photo's the doctor had laid out were foreign to him. David had to rely on Billy's best recollection of the lady he knew as Doris and Billy had only saw part of her face. He decided after covering the photo to imitate where she wore the scarf, he was sure it looked like her. The hairstyle was the same. So, we went with that.

Dr. Meloo didn't say much just nodded. "May I have a copy of this?" David asked the good doctor. Again, he consulted with his receptionist in their native tongue. I couldn't understand what they were saying but I was hoping it meant yes. She and the other clerk could be seen laughing with each other. She came over and gave another manila envelope to Dr. Meloo. After taking out its contents he just pointed "pick!" he said very serious faced. David chose the one looking at us straight forward. The doctor nodded and put it in the envelope and handed it to us. "Address?" "Do you have her address?" David inquired. He knew he had got away with enough already but he was to close to finding this young lady.

Again, after he consulted with his office staff, he gave David and address for her in Los Angeles. That's where she left going, according to Billy. We left out of the doctor's office satisfied for now. He told Masony we would check it out after the celebration tomorrow night. We thanked him and left from the building. His receptionist and clerk were laughing so hard and pointing about something they were apparently reading from a magazine. We hoped.

Tetra and Jillian must surely be enjoying the relaxing day at that posh day spa. They were sitting in the hot tub with a few other women enjoying conversations ranging from occupations to children and spouses and or mates. "My daughter is marrying this Australian chemist!' one woman bragged through the whole hot tub experience. We heard about the wedding and of course the honeymoon. "Her wedding gown was designed by the same designer who created Queen Diana's royal gown", she boasted with her nose in the air. Tetra leaned over to Jillian "we're in with royalty!" they both laughed. After a while they went in to the sauna "Jillian would you like to tell me about you and Billy?" Tetra asked as they sat in the steaming sauna wrapped in huge fluffy towels. The real reason for this togetherness Jillian thought. "Tell you what Mrs. Parker?" "Well she said with humor mocking the lady in the hot tub. "You have been dating my son now for four years and he has not asked for your hand in marriage" using her best British impression of Julia Child. Jillian smiled but she was thinking, Mrs. Parker doesn't know that Billy and I are not together anymore. "Mrs. Parker" Jillian said moving over to get privacy from the others sitting with them in the large steam room. "Billy and I are not seeing each other right now" she said in a meek voice. "What! Tetra's exclamation came out louder than expected and now others were looking. "That's great Jillian!" they turned back and started minding their own business. Then with only the puzzled expression of Jillian listening, "I'm so sorry to hear that Jillian" "I seem to be the last one to know anything!" "When did this happen?' Tetra questioned, smiling as to not give attention to their conversation. "Just recently she said I found out Billy had an affair on me" Jillian informed her. And he admitted to it trying to make it better" she confided. Some of the ladies were leaving on to continue the next phase of their spa treatment. Tetra and Jillian had fewer ears to worry about. "Oh my, Tetra said memories flashed through her mind. Then she heard the voice. "We go through things that we might help others" If anybody knew how it felt to be betrayed by another woman she surely did! "Jillian, I really didn't know, please don't think that's why I asked you here today. I needed this after a very busy month and I wanted you to enjoy it too" Tetra shared "I didn't tell you how much joy you brought to my life when you came and visited me over the holiday. You, Billy and that sweet little child overwhelmed our hearts and I was just saying thank you", she told Jillian who was now crying. "The steam is getting to me" she said wiping her eyes of tears. "I think our time is up now anyway" Tetra said getting up going out while others were coming in. They went on to the massage room, and facial, and nails complete with a pedicure. They kept conversations very light and void of the situation they were both now aware of. A few more hours in the hair salon and out the door. "That was wonderful Mrs. Parker, thank you" Jillian said embracing her tightly around her neck. "You're welcome, Jillian, you're welcome, Tetra whispered.

"I have an idea!" Jillian said as the two walked out of the spa's concealed glass doors. "If you have time, may I please buy you lunch?" Jillian requested of Tetra. "Perfect! Tetra thought she was not going to over step her bounds with a hurting woman but she wanted to share something with Jillian and lunch was her idea so "Yes I would love to Jillian." Tetra had taken a cab downtown so she got into the car with Jillian. "Have you heard from little Davie?" Tetra asked feeling it was all right to do so now. "I haven't I pray for him every night Mrs. Parker Jillian confessed. "I got so attached to him and I do miss him so much." "When I found out about what Billy had done and losing him at the same time, I just couldn't handle it" Jillian admitted. "Oh, I see, Tetra say rubbing the top of Jillian's hand as she drove. Jillian drove them to a cute little restaurant call "Tea & Empathy". "Very interesting name" Tetra said as they walked in. It was a small establishment with seating for twenty or thirty at the most at one time comfortably. The round tables were arranged for private intimate conversations and the parade of old and new teapots that lined the shelved walls were unique. With tea and scones on the menu it was perfect! They chose a table over by the window that looked out into a garden. As both sat down Jillian mocked, "tea me' lady?" in her best British accent. Tetra and Jillian both shared a laugh. A cheery waitress dressed like a New Englander came over with a menu with every kind of tea imaginable. "Would you two like a spot of tea?" she asked handing them the menu. She could have stood there all day and they still wouldn't have gone through them all. After a while they settled on a black tea called "Mu Dan" a rare Chinese black tea she told them. It was the most famous and had a very distinct flavor so they chose it. They shared with her that they had just been rubbing noses with royalty! So, it is just what they needed. After both had sat for a minute sipping their hand tied with rosette tea, she brought out a silver tray cart filled with sandwiches. Quaint little sandwiches arranged on elegant three tier silver plates. "Choices so many choices" Tetra said looking at all the waitress had brought them. There were sandwiches made with ham, and pepper-cheese and apple she told them. "And this one" Jillian asked "what might this be?" taking one to put on her plate. "That me' lady is curried egg and Swiss cheese, its delightful with your tea" she explained. The antique Baroque flatware and teapot that flanked their table added so much class to their table setting. She didn't stop there. Their gorgeous Swiss rose linen tablecloth was almost covered. They had pear honey cakes and sconces, croissants, grapes draped over a lovely stemmed serving dish, a beautifully decorated cake big enough for two, jams, and butter and peanut butter shortbread perches on a saucer. "My Jillian there's no way we could possible eat all of this!" Tetra said tasting some of the delicious sandwich she had chosen for lunch. They really enjoyed themselves trying to guess what the next bite of an item would taste like. "Tetra then looked at Jillian. "Thank you dear this is truly wonderful. "I love Billy too, he's my son Tetra said. "I don't know what his story is regarding this incident and I really don't want to know that's between you two" I will say what you do is totally up to you. "But for you! Not for him though he needs it also. "Forgive him for hurting you" "I know, I know he was wrong. "I'm not saying go back to him, I'm saying don't lose sleep over hurting, and pain, and hating." He moves on and you're the one who loses." Tetra poured another cup of tea and continued. "I can say this now to you because I went through this with Billy's father. I was very bitter with him for too many years" Tetra told Jillian. I made myself sick." I cried and I cried and I cried some more. I could not and would not forgive him for what he had done." I knew I loved him and through much prayer I came to forgive him for the hurt he had caused, to me and Billy in not being there and when I released it to God He changed David and gave me back a man after God's own heart" It did not erase his past but it allowed me to live in his future" Tetra said teary eyed to Jillian. "But I don't know if I can do that?' Mrs. Parker, I care so much for Billy and when I think of what he did! I just don't even want to be near him!" Jillian confessed. "I moved to the state of Washington!" Tetra said smiling affirming to Jillian that she understood. "Jillian, I know it's not easy. "I'm talking from years of experience. I'm hoping you and Billy will work through your differences and come to and understanding of one another and what each of your needs are" Tetra added. I know Billy loves you" she said sharing Jillian's concerns, and, know this Jillian I'm here if you need me" patting the top of her hand. "Now what's this?' Tetra asked holding up a sweet from the tray with her hand.

CHAPTER 44

An Elegant Affair

The wide-eyed Ariel entered Harvard's Widener Library on the arm of her date Justin Parker. She was wearing her gorgeous Claiborne gown and Justin was looking dapper in his Valentino tuxedo.

They walked into this fabulously decorated room that had been transformed into a glamorous ballroom. It usually lends itself to being the audio section of the library. It had been redecorated into a beautiful oasis of shimmering lights. The room with its already ornate design had come to life with lights, sparkle and color. The lovely prints and verdant colors were bursting out all over. There was lush fabric linens Tetra had chosen carefully for the table settings and very large exotic flower arrangements placed all around to compliment the evening's festivities. Lusciously tinted Venetian glass crystal goblets were gleaming in the candles flickering lights. And Italian dinnerware was set at each table with the Bird of paradise as the centerpiece in a crystal vase. "Hello, David said greeting everyone coming through the doors. "Justin stood still. He felt awkward. He didn't know just how to introduce David to his girlfriend Ariel. "Should I say David? or Mr. Parker? Billy's dad?' he thought to himself. Justin didn't know and Mr. Parker feeling his indecisiveness extended his hand "Hello Justin," David said, It's good to see you made it tonight!" Drawing him in and embracing him with his arm on his chest. Justin just started talking nervously. "Thank you sir" Justin replied this is my date Ariel Hodges. I'm pleased to meet you" she said extending her hand remembering all the instructions Katherine had given her. "I'm equally as pleased to meet you, Ariel is it? David questioned. "Yes Ariel, she repeated. "Justin was still looking for Billy or a way out from his present situation. He really hadn't been around David enough to feel comfortable speaking with him. He stood hoping to see Jillian or Billy. He kept anxiously looking for Desmond anyone just anyone? He stood thinking. He just wanted to see anyone whom he knew on sight. He had met Desmond and some of Billy's other friends at the graduation so he kept looking around for anyone he knew. David noticing his uncertainty explained, "Please call me David, we're all one big happy family here" he told them. "Go right in and enjoy yourselves". "Thank you, sir I mean David," Justin said holding Ariel's hand and walking away. "Oh my, Justin can you believe this place, it looks like a palace!" Ariel exclaimed touching the flowers that set in one of the large arrangements. As they moved in closer the room expanded into this even grander space. The huge crystal chandelier sparkled brightly illuminating the entire room. And standing over at the buffet table they spotted Billy.

He was standing alone in his Gucci tuxedo admiring everyone. But he was the handsome man of the hour. "Billy my man!" Justin said walking up to him. "Justin, so very glad to see you again, and wait don't tell me this is the lovely Ariel?' he playful said to make them feel comfortable. "Hello Billy, this is very nice, thanks for inviting us, she said very humbling. "No celebration would be a celebration without my little brother!" he said embracing the both of them. He was welcoming and being friendly to all of his guests. And yet he was still looking for Jillian. The Jenkins and Reeds had arrived all except Glen but then he always has to make an entrance he surmised. Surprisingly enough the next person he laid eyes on coming through the doors was Winnie. Tetra had invited her when she was down for the holiday visiting her parents. "William Parker" she said coming to him with her hand held out. "Ms. Hathaway what a surprise!" I responded So mother got you to come and visit a friend?" he teased. "I am so glad to see you!" Billy said hugging her tightly. Then composing herself like the lady she is. "I am delighted as well; I would not have missed this moment to officially congratulate you on reaching your goal!" Winnie replied crossing her legs and bowing at the waist in front of him. Winnie looked amazing. She wore a Ruby red iridescent taffeta ball gown with a bustle that cascaded down the back. Her hair she wore pulled up off her face showing off the brilliant sparkle from her handset diamond earrings. "I know you have saved a dance for me?" he implied now standing next to her with his arm around her waist "as many as you like Sir William!' Winnie remarked smiling back at him. They stood and talked about old times, new things that were happening and even Jillian who still had not come through the door. Then up walked a gentleman somewhat balding is how I would describe him over to where Winifred and Billy were standing. The waiter had just made his rounds with the champagne and caviar to all the guests who were now gathering in the large ballroom. "Hello he said in a very deep voice walking up to Winnie. "Sorry Mrs. Hathaway to keep you waiting had a bit of a problem parking, not use to that you know" the valet was taking so long" he said pulling a handkerchief from his jacket pocket and wiping his hands with it. "Oh! Winnie said looking at him then Billy. "William Parker this is Mortimer Van Hellsink" he is my date for tonight she said. "Pleased to make you acquaintance sir" he said shaking Billy's hand. "My pleasure" I returned the greeting. Winnie caught Mortimer around his arm, "we're going to join the others on the dance floor she told me. I nodded and looked at Winnie and whispered, "What's really going on?" "Later Billy, later!" she said walking to the dance floor with her date. The orchestra was playing some contemporary classical music and Ariel and Justin were enjoying themselves. A regular Astaire and Rodgers I'd say. David had longed moved from the door and now was enjoying and occasional dance with Tetra who was stunning in one of her favorite designer's Purcell. Her gown for the evening was a floral taffeta halter-neck ball gown with splashes of pink shimmering through the fabric. Tetra had chosen to accent her gown with precious pink sapphire diamond earrings and a charming diamond bracelet. "Honey you have done a marvelous job here tonight" David said as they waltzed to an upbeat Chopin' classic. "Thank you dear, I am glad we're together to share in our son's success" Tetra affirmed. "Have you seen Jillian yet?" Tetra asked thinking of the wonderful time they had on yesterday but had not spoken with her since." I haven't David said hesitantly to Tetra. "Oh, so you knew about her and Billy?" she asked him. Before answering David spun her around and dipped her in his arms. "Billy told me" David replied. "Ummm, Tetra said looking into David's eyes. "Well I hope things turn out for them I won't interfere" she said spinning around to the music. Billy looked at his watch again. He had just come from the floor dancing with Frances, Jillian's mom who wondered about Jillian's late arrival too. "Thank you, Mrs. Fleming, it was magical" he told her as she stood with her head down blushing. Everyone was mingling and enjoying themselves. Justin had now formed a line and they were taking turns going through it. "BILLY, BILLY come on you have to go through too, they yelled as he sat over with Mr. Fleming. The two of them had moved from the ballroom into one of the sitting areas decorated to coordinate with the other parts of the room for more seating. He got up and ran over and with a couple of twist and a few turns around and around, Billy was through the line. They were laughing at Mortimer who was just right at home with his urban hip- hop version that was truly not his style at all. The band played softly as a few of the members took a break from the first set that had played. The staff was waiting for everyone to get there before they served dinner. "Dinner will be served in an hour" the waiter announced to the entire room. No one seemed to mind they were having so much fun. Justin was meeting everyone and using his intelligence to woo the older ladies into dancing with him. "Thanks Mr. D' Ariel said for this dance, I just didn't feel right calling you David I hope you don't mind?" she told him as they moved around to the beat now playing through the speakers on the sound system. The gowns were magnificent there were McClintocks, and Purcell's, Jones of New York and many others. Mrs. Reed had on an elegant champagne colored pants suit with a delicate sequin top designed by Klein while Frances Fleming felt very comfortable in a black lace sleeve dress by Versace.' The men were all handsomely deck out in tuxedos ranging in various styles. "I'M HERE! I am here! Glen said coming through the door fashionably late. Everyone looked. Mr. Reed just put his head down knowing he came in the airport with them. So why was he so late? He just smiled young men! "Billy walked over to where they were standing. "Glen I thought for a minute you had forgotten about me?' he said embracing him as he joked with him. "Me forget you. NEVER!' he said. I apologize but I was ready and "This is my girl! Glen said proudly sticking out his chest. "Cheryl Laler" I would like you to meet William Parker" my main man no jokes!" he said sincerely. "Cheryl!' I repeated holding her hand. "It is a pleasure to meet you!" I mean a real pleasure" I said smiling at her. She was all that Glen had said. Wearing a satin white fluid gown with the neckline cut in a v to her belly button. But very tastefully done and she had the figure to pull the look off. As a matter of fact, she looked a lot like Lena and Lexia. Only Cheryl had flawless black skin and shoulder length hair with pearl white teeth. I looked at Glen and commented, "she's definitely a keeper" giving a high five to him. "It's nice to meet you also,

Cheryl said smiling at us. "Glen has shared stories about you two." She is charming, I thought. We all stood for a moment talking in front of the entrance door when mom came over. "Please join the others in the ballroom, she said coming over to welcome them. Tetra hugged Glen and met his date and then stood quietly by Billy waiting for Glen and Cheryl to join the others. "We well definitely talk later man!" I added watching them move toward the dance floor. 'Son I'm concerned have you heard from Jillian? she asked. 'No mom, she said she'd be here". I replied and walk back to join the others now dancing again. The orchestra headed back for a second set and everyone went to the dance floor including Mr. Fleming who has dance styles learned from his younger years. The waiter walked as everyone danced happily and sipped on champagne, eating hors d'oeu'vres of caviar with conversations and enjoying one another. I was truly missing Jillian now. I walked over simply by chance and was first to sit in one of the French toile wingback chairs that had been strategically place to face the dance floor for a performance I later found out. "Please clear the floor!" came the announcement from the orchestra's microphone. Mom had invited the dance team of Kent and Villella from the New York City Ballet. And they were going to perform. They were one of Jillian favorites. While the caterers were setting up dinner to be served everyone was moving around to find a seat so that they might enjoy the night's performance. And still no Jillian. Frances had called several times on her cell phone but was only getting a voice mail. Jillian was noticeably missing from the celebration that was supposed to be shared with her. Tetra sat concerned wondering, "Did I say something wrong yesterday to hurt her?" As the performance started Desmond and Mostalgia came in. They had call earlier to ask if they could bring her brother and sister who were visiting them through the Christmas holiday. They walked in quietly and took sits. They watched as the two dancers motioned gracefully to the Mozart X symphony classic. They were making movements that were unnatural for the body look effortless. They floated through the air with long slow leaps. Justin watched intrigued by the perfect balance they kept *has* they spun around like a top without getting dizzy. "Look! David whispered to Tetra at the speed their feet moves". Kent lifted Villella into the air as if she was light as a feather. The entire performance was breathtaking. Tetra was tearing as she sat next to Mossy who was now pregnant and glowing. As the dance team concluded their recital Jillian walked in with Morgan and Blair her new co-workers from New York. Billy looked and sat still until the two dancers took their bows to the applause from all the guests looking on. Then Justin being the first walked over to Jillian. "I wondered if you had stood my brother up?" he teased "Not on your life!" Jillian said. She had been partying somewhere before they arrived there and it was very noticeable to Billy who had now joined the conversation. The orchestra started up. Billy took Jillian and gently pulled her on the dance floor. "Jillian where have you been?' and what have you been drinking?' he asked as she swayed in his arm. He walked her out for some air to a private area and they sat and talked while the others were now enjoying dinner prepared by a master chef Woods. Jillian stated "I'm just fine, I'm forgiving you and I'm moving on" The alcohol on her breath seemed to be doing the talking for her. "Jillian what are you talking about? he asked. "Kelly told me about what you did to her!" "May I explain Jillian?" I didn't want to get into this and there was really nothing I could say to comfort her in this state she was in. Our happy celebration was now totally ruined I felt. I looked at her face. Her mascara was smudged from crying and said Jillian "I love you" and went back in to join my family and friends and pretend to have fun. Frances had come to where Jillian and I had been sitting, seeing me come back through the doors. "Where have you been? Frances scolded. "You have embarrassed me and yourself and you should be ashamed!" she huffed and walked away. Jillian after a while returned back inside. She had gone to the powder room and freshened her makeup and was now playing the same role all's well. But tension was very imminent between the two of them. Both said very little to each other. Dinner was an elegant affair from the loving spoonsful of smoked salmon caviar to the Madeleine's and Clementine's to complete the meal. And then everyone lifted the beautiful crystal stem goblets, in saying congratulations to lawyer William Parker and lawyer Jillian Mcfinney. There was an instant applause all over the room. After a thank you from the honorees extended to all of their guest hugs and kisses were shared by all.

CHAPTER 45

Billy I miss you

I was busy at work still trying to decided what I would do next after passing the bar exam. I didn't know If to stayed in Cambridge with this firm Obermeyer, Finswick and Hannagan they would promote me to accommodate my worth now with a promotion adjustment or just move to another area. Jillian and I shared a few conversations but they all ended up in a big disagreement and more often an argument. Then either would hang up the phone upset with the other with Jillian hating me the more. It had been weeks and going into months and we still couldn't talk civil to one another. Jillian moved all of her clothes back home to her parent's house until she could find a suitable apartment in Manhattan she liked and could afford. She told me she never wanted to see me or Kelly again and disown her as a friend. She hated me for causing that too. She became a workaholic to keep from thinking of me she said. She still loved me is what she told mom. And it seems like I kept adding to her hurt. She had not heard from Doris Wright AND ASKED THAT DAD STOP CALLING AND ASKING QUESTIONS REGARDING HER and it soon became apparent that she would never get over all the hurt that had been caused. She blamed me for all of her hurting and avoided my phone calls even to the office. "Jillian do you want to go out with Blair and I after work?" Morgan asked. Without thinking Jillian just answered "No! no thanks she'd say. "Jillian whatever you're doing it will be there tomorrow!" Morgan told her "I know maybe another time?" Jillian replied. "Suit yourself then," Morgan walked out and entered the door to Blair's office. Blair was a handsome bachelor and he knew it. He made time with all the women in the building. Morgan was just convenient always there. She dated other guys and Blair dated lots of women. Neither he said were about love. I'm sure he never told any of them that. He says he is a fun-loving guy. Maybe that's where she went wrong with Billy she thought. Jillian sat at her desk remembering. Everyone had gone home except the janitors. "That can't be I love Billy! she thought out loud. And he loves me! Everyone makes mistakes! she thought. "Ms. Mcfinney I'm leaving please lock up when you leave" the janitor said sticking his head into her office. She didn't realize how late it was. Jillian had been going over some documents for the cases she had been assigned and loss track of time. She sat back in her chair and closed her eyes. "I'd better get home" she thought. She put all of her documents in the file, logged off of her computer one last look around and swiveled around in her chair to see Blair. "Oh, you startled me!' where is Morgan? She questioned. "Sorry about that" he said I saw the lights on and wondered if you were still here" Blair told her walking behind her placing his hands on her shoulders using a massaging motion. "Whew! Jillian paused that feels great, I can't wait to get home in a nice relaxing tub and forget about this day" as Blair continued to massage her neck.

"Where is the tension? Blair asked moving further down her back gently rubbing her neck. She was very relaxed it felt so good. "That feels great! Jillian said can I pay you to do this all the time?" she teased. Then as she relaxed into the moment Blair reached around under her blouse trying to touch her breast. "Oh, she jumped!" Blair what are you doing?" "Sorry I just got caught up in the moment you're a very attractive lady won't happen again" he said smiling and going to his office. "Jillian sat up in her chair and straighten her clothes. "It's been to long without Billy she thought. Blair's strong hands touching me felt so good. She had avoided Billy's calls for three months now. And she had not felt his touch for a least six she sat remembering. Without saying goodbye or good night she gathered her things turned out the light and left. A few minutes later the janitor came out of Blair's office whistling. "Thanks Mr. Christiansen, putting dollar bills into his pocket.

"Desmond are you and Slovenia going out to get the tree today?" Mossy asked as she wobbled around the house. She was spending less time at the office and her sister Dalmatia "Dal" for short was helping her around the house. Her parents had come for a week and enjoyed "the America" but was missing home and went back to Yugoslavia the following week. Mossy's younger brother and sister wanted to stay opting to go back hopefully after the baby comes in time allowed. Desmond was going out to cut down his own Christmas tree for the upcoming holiday. It had been a week since he said he would go and get it AND Mostalgia was getting impatient. "Desmond if you don't get the tree this weekend, I going out and buy one" Mossy told him while sitting at the breakfast table. "Dal and I bought lots of decorations that are still wrapped in their container packages or boxes, Christmas will be over waiting for you" she stated jokingly. It was only a week after thanksgiving but this was Mossy favorite holiday and she loved to decorate the house and the tree. She and Dal had purchased a lot of decorations for the trimmings. "Henry and I are going out Saturday morning Slov can come too" Desmond shared as they finished up breakfast in their beautiful new home. After a year Slov and Desmond had recently painted the game room and he anxiously awaited his new pool table he had purchased for it to be delivered. Desmond kept busy doing honey do's around the house for the perfectionist Mossy his wife with Slov his brother-in-law helping him. And getting a tree was top priority on his list this week. "Henry knows what he's doing he's from Kansas and he and I are going to cut down the most perfect tree ever" he explained and added "he's teaching me a lot about the Midwest." Slovenia loved the United States too and was learning English well with the help of Mossy and his brother-in-law. He was more daring with the language than Dal his sister. Sometimes his interpretation of the English language came out wrong, bringing lots of laughs. Dal talked only her native language and refused out of bashfulness to try when Desmond was around. She would talk with Mossy having to interpret everything. Slovenia said he wanted to be able to talk to a pretty American girl. "To tell her I love her" he said smiling and raising his brows.

Desmond drove into the office very early. The snowy ice was still being shoveled to the side of the road. The speed on the highway was slow and cautious. Henry was always there first and had brewed the coffee and turned on the buildings heater to warm up the place. Desmond walked in bundled in scarf and down jacket" Good morning Henry" Desmond said looking into Henry's office "Good morning to you how was the ride in from Langley Estates" Sir Desmond?' Henry teased. Henry was so proud to be working for a local law firm and had hopes of becoming a partner in it one day. "Desmond liked Henry a lot a self-made attorney he would say. Henry had shared how persistence he was to furthering his education.

And with lots of help from his grandparents he was able to fulfill his dream and make them proud. His style in the courtroom was smooth and effective. "No holds bar kind of lawyer" Desmond affirmed. Their client's list was expanding and growing. Desmond and Henry worked very well together. Henry was very eager to learn new insights and didn't mind when he had to share the caseload for Mossy when she cut back on her hours until after the second baby comes. Mossy now chose cases that did not require a lot of man- hour's or tie her up in court all day. That allowed Henry to become more experienced in a lot of cases that would have taken him longer to get involved in. 'Henry so you're on for the week end right?" "If I don't get Mossy a Christmas tree soon, she's going to divorce me!" Desmond joked pouring another cup of morning coffee in the office. Desmond was always pouring a cup of coffee. He kept a cup in his hand at all times. Henry teased him about it calling him 'Juan Valdez" of the firm. "Sounds fun Henry replied. "Have you ever cut down your own tree Desmond?" Henry questioned. "No! Desmond replied. "It will be a first! He said laughing. 'I'll be there "Are you cooking breakfast?" Henry asked now walking him back to his office. "If that's what it's going to take to get you there!" Des told him. "Not really Henry said but it would be nice." "Cutting down a tree to accommodate your house is not going to be easy! "You have a big house!" Henry explained laughing loudly. "But I'm up to the challenge." Desmond sat down at his desk "speaking of divorce. I'd better prepare this paper work for Mrs. Toni. She's due in this morning. She wants everything her husband has and everything he ever hoped of having!" Desmond mocked carrying the file into his office to look it over carefully before she gets there. Henry questioned, still standing in Desmond's office, "What did he do?" "Couldn't handle midlife crisis" Desmond confirmed. She even alleges here that Mr. John's was now wearing a toupee on his once bald head" But says he can keep that, Desmond explained now laughing looking inside at her filed papers. "Another old fool trying to be young! Henry concluded walking back to his office. 'I'm headed to court this morning." I'll see you tomorrow" There isn't a problem with helping you get a tree I would love to help" Henry stated leaving the office.

David had several meetings planned for the week. His staff meeting had lasted a little longer due to some additional questions that needed to be addressed. Over all, the meeting went well. He moved back to his office stopping by his secretary's desk leaving some documents for her to type and send out express mail. "Mr. Parker you have a call on line one" Gabriella shared with him as he stopped by her desk leaving the paperwork going to his office. "Thank you I'll get it in my office "David Parker" he answered now sitting at his desk, "Hi dad" Billy responded. "Son, how are you?" Dad I'm better, and I'm finding something to do with myself" he replied. Have you and Jillian resolved your differences?" David asked. "Not really, we're getting better at communicating to each other and I see her maybe once or twice a month" he shared with him. It's been almost a year son do you think you two will ever find what you had? "I don't know dad "I know what I did was wrong, but I love her and I'm trying to give her space to hopefully heal". "But the reason I called is I have decided to stay around this area". "In Cambridge son, at the firm? David inquired. "Not Cambridge dad, I'm moving back to Maine." Everything went silent David smiled to himself. Did you talk to your mom yet?" David asked wanting to make sure Tetra was informed of the things he decided. Especially after the break up between Jillian and Billy she never knew about. And then told David she probably could have prevented it if she would have known. "Yes, I spoke with mom last night" she said it's up to me just make sure it's what I want" she told him. "Dad, I love Jillian, and I'm hoping time apart will help us to realize what we want!" I explained. "Not too much time I hope" Dad posed. "When will you be moving son?" "I'm going down next week and talk with the firm in Maine who has offered me the position." "And Dad I've decided to live in the cottage we have there!" he said excitedly. "Oh, how did that work with Witherspoon?" David inquired, knowing Witherspoon had kept the property in hopes to sell it and make a big commission. "He got a great deal dad!' I had him sell my condo that sold very quickly. And with the commission he received from the sell he's taking a two-week vacation in the Caribbean he told me" I had to laugh. Dad and I shared several laughs regarding the realtor Witherspoon.

David also told him he and Masony were headed out to Los Angeles again over the weekend to check out the Doris Wright story hopefully find her or Dorca Williams and would update him when he came back. "Dad please let me know!" I insisted what you find there. "Her eyes is how I know, that's Doris Wright in those photographs. They reminded me of Dorca Williams I almost told her that once I thought. Honestly that's all

I saw all of the time, her eyes!" I told dad. "I'll let you know when I get moved in. "Give my love to mom". "Oh dad, I almost forgot, I've been attending this Orthodox Church down the street from my house". "It's quite different from what I'm use to but it allows me quiet time to think" I said. "Billy that's wonderful that you are taking time out to serve God anywhere and anytime" David shared. "Just remember he is there even in the Orthodox Church" I love you son bye" David hung up the phone and called Masony to confirm their airline reservations. Masony was picking David up from his home and they would ride out to the airport together.

David had ridden down to Oregon again with the photographs he had gotten from Dr. Meloo years ago. He took the card from his jacket pocket and looked again at the address confirming it and continued driving. He felt very comfortable has he moved along in a neighborhood where there were homes, he was accustomed to seeing big beautiful homes. Pulling up to the address on the business card he saw a beautiful 1700 or 1800's period-built style home. It was a Georgian rectangular shaped with red-bricks and a large front yard. There were thin columns alongside the doors and windows with small panes on each side and above the doorway. David looked again to make sure he was at the right address. He walked up and rang the doorbell. Soon a man opened the door. "Good afternoon, may I help you?' a very articulate tall gentleman answered the door. "Yes, I'm David Parker extending his hand out to him, I would like to see Mrs. Beulah Reeves, David asked?" "Beulah, she's in the garden in the back, do come in I know she's expecting you" "I'm the other half!" Jonathan Reeves, he said shaking David's hand with a smile and a tight grip. "Thank you, David said entering I called earlier." "Come on in he told him "she's right through these doors. Jonathan led David out through two window pane style doors onto a long porch. Well-designed wicker furniture was used to decorate the long porch with its view of a garden setting. There were also two large white wooden rockers and Beulah was sitting out enjoying a good book. "Hi" she said seeing David walking up. "I see you have met my husband Dr. Reeves" closing her book and giving him the attention now. "Please sit-down Mr. Parker can I get you something to drink?" I have a pitcher of homemade lemonade but if you would like something else?' she stated. "No!" "Lemonade is fine David said. She picked up the pitcher she had on the table next to her and poured him a glass of lemonade from the pitcher into the other glass she had sitting on the tray table. "I won't keep you long! David told her pulling the picture from the folder he was carrying it in. Then he refreshed himself drinking from the large size glass of iced cold lemonade Beulah had poured. "Whoa! It is amazing how much those girls look alike Beulah said looking at the photo and remembering. 'It's very hard to see at first their personalities are so different. "I made mention of it when I first met them. I thought them to be related but it's one of those coincidences I guessed. She is definitely her world double" making reference to Dorca Williams and Doris Wright. "You know there's always somebody somewhere who looks like you" Beulah said. "So, who is this one?" David inquired puzzled somewhat pointing to the photograph in Beulah's hand. "This is a photograph of Dorca!" she said to David's amazement. "Doris's lifestyle showed on her if you know what I'm saying," skin, nails, hair those things. "She lived fast and didn't take good care of herself and it showed dark circles under her eyes". Dorca was in very good health and she took good care of herself. With help from Dorca I had trouble telling she and Doris apart when Doris stayed at the home near the Henning's place. Because she ate properly and took care of her body, she too was a very attractive girl. Dorca has a tattoo symbol around her wrist. I remember when she asked if it would affect her baby. "She wasn't going to do anything to harm her precious bundle she was carrying!" Beulah said looking up and smiling. "She covers it sometimes when she wears a watch or bracelet" she went on to tell David" "It's very tastefully done. 'Now may I ask you what happen to her face how did she get this huge scar" Beulah inquisitively asked. "Don't know, David responded, I hadn't seen Dorca since she was a young lady in high school. She and my son were friends and when her parents were killed, she left and we never saw her again." The scaring disfigures her face so it's hard to tell if you have never seen her as an adult" The body changes quite a bit over the years David said conferring with Beulah. "It's her eyes, Beulah reasoned sadly. She always had a look that she just wanted to be loved and free of disappointments." Her hair was wavy compared to Doris's also. "Has something happened to her?' Why are you looking for her?" David reached down and pulled a copy of the letter from is folder of papers and handed it to Mrs. Reeves. He sat silently as she read the entire letter. "I see" she sighed. Well I hope you find her and get some answers" she added. I hope so to David said. Her plastic surgeon gave me this picture of a Doris Wright?' so I really don't know what I'm going to find out in Los Angeles but I going to try". I'm headed out to Los Angeles this weekend it's her last known address after leaving Cambridge Massachusetts" David told Mrs. Reeves.

"Mr. Parker what happened to her child?" Beulah asked appearing to fear the worst. "I don't know, David said shaking his head, it saddens me to say but I really don't know!" There was a lady calling herself Doris Wright who had a young child named David. But she moved on and we don't know where she's gone or even if she has anything to do with this." David was still trying to make sense of anything. "Thank you, Mrs. Reeves you have been a tremendous help" standing and extending his hand. "Let me walk you out Beulah remarked standing up and going to the door. David and Beulah went back into the large brick home. They walked through the living room with its classic empress style window coverings in rich tones, a swag valance with fringe and lots of accent throw pillows on the French provincial furnishings. "You have a lovely home!" David commented heading to the door. He stopped and gazed at a large hand painted portrait that hung over the fireplace. It was a painting of a very young sexy Beulah striking a pose. "Yes, she said before David asked, I know what the challenges are for being young and beautiful" I keep it here as a constant reminder" Beulah told him making her way to open the door. Dr. Reeves came out from his office. They both stood at the door and after they shook hands Dr. Reeves replied, "Again a pleasure meeting you Mr. Parker. "And please let me know, if you find Dorca" Beulah said with a dishearten look on her face. "I will, David said and left. He got in his car and drove away headed back home to Washington.

Masony was there early at the Parkers home. He met Tetra David's wife who would later call him an impressionable fellow. That word seems to follow him. She wasn't the first to see him that way. "Honey I'm leaving I'll see you Monday afternoon. Lunch o.k. David shared with Tetra as he and Masony left for the airport to board a flight to Los Angeles. "Tetra walked David to the door and kissed him waving goodbye to him as he and Masony left. "Do you think I pulled the lawyer bit off?' Masony asked of the story he had thought up to tell Tetra. "I'm sure she thought it was very impressive!' David smiled within to himself.

David and Masony didn't have a lot of time so when they landed, they went right to work looking for the woman on the photograph. They went to the address that was given to them from Dr. Meloo's office. The man at the apartment where she supposedly lived looked a lot shady. But he directed them to the place where Doris worked. They quickly left and walked down the street where they met a woman who was at Doris's apartment also. She left while they were there but was heading back to the apartment and directed them where to go. It was not a place David would have been caught in before he was saved, he thought out loud walking into it. It was a strip joint. "Prizzy Pink Poodle" it was a dive. It was daylight and David and Masony walked in and sat at the bar. The show was about to start and there were maybe ten people watching in the whole place. A blonde came out and did her thing to her screaming fan "oooohey!!!! She kicked high and swirled on her pole wearing hardly anything. Then out came Doris or Dorca, David wasn't sure. She looked a lot like the photograph he was holding in his hand. He would have to wait until she came down from the stage to get a closer look. Nothing was certain as he and Masony sat looking around and all David knew was he just wanted out of this place. As the blonde finished up came another one.

"OH, BABY GO BABY!!" came the shouts as she fell to the floor kicking her legs high in the air. She seemed to be the headliner and David and Masony watched. MASONY got in the act with the dollar bills near the stage encouraging the performance on. Masony was a divorced retired older gentleman who didn't know what to do with himself most of the time David thought "sense of humor, um "dry." David moved over to a smaller table and was being harassed into a lap dance "No thank you!" No! he insisted. "Suit yourself the blonde said walking away huffed. After the other one had completed her swirls and came down to mingle in the few patrons that were scattered at this happy hour club. Masony enticed her to come over and sit and talk with he and David promising her money. "Yes, I'll sit if you're talking right" she said. David had come prepared he pulled out a wad of money from his pocket. "All I want are some questions answered!" David stated. Masony was busy looking in the other direction at some lap dancers in action. Sitting down at the small table David could see she was very attractive and the thick makeup she wore hid a lot of flaws she might have had. Her costume she was wearing though skimpy in material was wrapped around both arms. So, he had to rely on her to tell the truth. "May I ask your name?" David asked "Sunshine" she said. No what is your name?" pushing a hundred-dollar bill over to her. "Who wants to know?' She asked looking David in his eyes. "I'm looking for

Dorca Williams is that you?" David asked wanting to hurry and leave that place. Masony had left the table a few minutes after she sat down to get a drink of water he said. He was feeling a little warm. "She looked down at the one-hundred-dollar bill David pushed over in front of her then he pushed two more. She looked without saying anything. David pretended to put the money back in his pocket and she began looking at the almost empty place. "o.k. she said o.k. put it back!" "I'm Doris. I haven't seen Dorca since she came from Massachusetts with her son, she told David "What do you mean?' he questioned she had piqued his curiosity. "I had been promised a lot of money if I would just stay out of the way. Dorca was using my name and my identity. She is a tough cookie!" Most people don't know that. David showed her the picture. Yes, that's what she looked like. Dorca and I got in a fight with her old nosy neighbor years ago and he hit her in the face with a fireplace poker and broke her jaw. That happened right after we had our babies. I was helping her settle a score. "Why are you coming now looking for her?" she asked David. Whoever this is David thought has rehearsed the story, but this lady didn't know him from Adam. "When I called last month when the cell phone got cut off. I was told Dorca was no longer going to pay for it!" She took everything from me. No one would believe the switch and so I ended up here" she said with a sadden look on her face.

"And I have not heard from her since" David sat and listened things were not adding up. Even if she was telling the truth the acting was horrible.

Dorca has money and lots of it why would she leave a friend in this joint. She could have shared with Doris and a whole lot of other folks and not end up here The Demato's had loads of money. "Where's her son now?" David asked still trying to confirm what he was hearing. He's with her at home I guess or with a sitter" she responded not sure where she went when she left here though she did have her son with her. David needed to see her wrist that would surely tell him who he was talking with. "Dorca? what happened Billy never could get in touch with you when you left Washington after your parents died. David was saying things Dorca should have known about to try and trip this person up. Doris, I told you my name is Doris. This woman was plainly confused and didn't know what David was talking about. "Excuse me she said I have to get something to drink I'll be right back" reaching for the money.

David held his hand on it so it wouldn't move. She walked over to the bar and whispered in a gentlemen's ear and came back carrying a drink and sat down. David talked with her some more. She was giving enough of the right answers that it was hard to tell who she was. O.k. Thanks David said, I'll see you around getting up from the table to look for Masony who had now walked over to the area near the stage and become part of the show. David caught him by his arm and pulled forcefully and led him outside looking back at the stage as they went out of the door. "What are you doing did you get the info you needed?' Masony asked David. No! not really" let's go back in!" Masony insisted. "We need to get the car and come back David informed Masony. Masony who usually never walks that fast hurried to where the car had been parked quickly jumping into it. With Masony leading the way they had walked seven city blocks in just a few minutes. They drove back up to the Prizzy Pink Palace near the employee's entrance parked and waited. They went inside to see another show starting. Again, David pulled Masony back to the car. They were going to wait until the lady calling herself Doris left to go home. They sat and sat for hours in the car outside. Masony left several times for food and water never getting enough he'd said. David had to go and get him out of the Pink Palace a few times during their stakeout. Masony was staying inside to long probably watching the show. At about 2a.m. in the morning she finally walked out to the waiting David and Masony. "Not you two again, I would have noticed that hounds tooth jacket anywhere!" she said pointing to Masony then turned going in the other direction to get into her car. "Please let me buy you a night cap?" David asked or something to eat. There were lights on at the restaurant across the lot from the establishment where she worked so David looked in that direction. "If I have a drink with you will you go? You're making me loose business!" She had now put on her street clothes and coat going home they supposed. "Okay!" she said. They all walked across the lot to Joe's all-night eatery. Masony had snuggled over next to her. She had taken some of the makeup off her face and the lights at the restaurant was less kind to her appearance than the lights in the Pink Palace. They sat and ordered coffee and something to eat. "What are you having David asked trying to get her to relax and take off her coat. The waitress brought over menus for each of them. Masony wasn't interested in food. What he wanted was probably not on the menu. "Order something Masony" David suggested just to keep conversation flowing. Dorca or Doris? David still wasn't sure which had taken the menu ordered something to eat and sipped her coffee. Masony made small talk David had run out of questions to ask her. He doesn't think she was aware what he was looking for anyway. When the waitress came back with their food, she removed her coat. David sat there and took a long look at both of her bare wrist. There were no tattoos on them. "Let's go Masony! David said pulling him up from his food he was now starting to enjoy and the woman still drinking coffee. David got up leaving money on the table to pay for the food and a little extra for her time and walked out. She sat there, very puzzled face and continued to now eat her meal. "What happened? What just happened? Masony questioned going back to the car with David. David still didn't know where Dorca Williams was, but was satisfied that this was not her.

CHAPTER 46

Take me out to the ballgame

Justin walked around in the kitchen whistling a tune. "I'm leaving Ariel and remember I go to the boys club after work so I will be late," he told her gathering up his athletics bag with towel and tennis shoes. He was doing volunteer work for the Boy's club on spring break. Justin enjoyed what he was doing and received college credit for it also. He drove into the hospital garage and parked on the third tier. On his way to the elevator he saw Dana. "Good morning!" he said seeing her walk up to the elevator with her arms filled with documents. "Let me help you with that!" Putting his backpack over his shoulder to free his hands he reached for the large stack of documents. "Thanks, Justin I'm all moved in my new office space again" Dana shared "It seems you're always helping me and thanks I do appreciate it" she told him. "Not a problem we're going the same direction" Justin acknowledged. Justin walked into Dana's office and put the heavy stack of papers on her desk. "I'll see you later!" he said looking at his watch and heading back to the main floor. Dana had progressively pursued were doctorate degree and had settled into her new career. The papers she was bringing up were questionnaires for a meeting she was having with co-workers at other hospitals. Dana liked her new position and enjoyed the people she was working with. Most of all she enjoyed helping people. Dr. Baisden who was over the department was having a social get together for all his new staff that had been hired this year to welcome them aboard. He shared it with them at the last meeting. Dana had not yet acquired a social life to speak of since coming here to Maine. This would be a first evening out for her. The only man she knew was Justin and he was to young and not her type. There was this cute Dr. Dean on staff she saw every morning in the break room.

Jillian had been looking for about two years off and on for an apartment and had found the perfect place for her in Manhattan. It was a Brownstone townhouse with a view. She and Billy were still trying to make it work. Keeping things together, casually dating other people and things were looking up but still day-to-day. She had hoped he'd move to New York with her. But that didn't happen either. Things didn't seem to be going in that direction. She wanted to be able to control her feelings to where he wouldn't hurt her again, she confessed. And she didn't want to lose him. Even though he had explained to her what happened regarding Kelly and apologized over and over about Lena. Jillian's feelings for him were not the same anymore. He had broken the trust. The distance each had to travel to see one another kept things at bay. Billy would come up for a day or weekend and Jillian would exchange the visit the following month. "Jillian hi how are you today?' I had called to give her the news of my new position. "I'm great! are you coming down this weekend to help me move in my new place?' she asked him. "I can if you need me to" I replied. "Do you have the address?" Jillian asked and directions to it, she added. "I have it and I'll see you then," sensing this was not the time to tell her my news. "Was that why you called?" Jillian asked. Things were trying to work between them and keeping this until later just didn't seem right. "No!" I called to share with you that I'm moving from Cambridge. "Jillian's heart thumped! She didn't want to think about being even further from Billy. She wanted him to come to New York and was certain he would because they had for the most part gotten back together. They had even decided the casual lunch dates weren't working for either of them their heart was just not in it. She wanted to be together. There was only silence on the line for what seemed minutes. "Jillian? Jillian? he asked. "Where are you going Billy?" she asked anticipating the worst. "I've accepted a job offer in Maine and I already have a place there!" I was excited Jillian had taken so long to find a place she liked and I didn't have to go through all that. "So next week you can come and help me arrange my place!" I said thinking this will surely please her. What do you think Jillian?" "That sounds wonderful, she replied but truly the wind had just been let out of her sails. Nothing was heard but silence. "Billy's getting further away and I really don't know what to do, she thought. "Sweetheart I'll see you soon okay" she said hanging up before she started to cry. She sat in her office crying. Blair came in with some cases he needed her to work on. "Jillian how's my favorite attorney?" Blair replied, coming in with his always happy mood. She lifted her head surprised to see him standing there. She wiped her eyes. "I'm great Blair what can I do you for? she said turning her words being factious pretending everything was alright. "I have some cases here I thought you might look over and figure out what needs to be done?" Blair replied then looking at Jillian's eyes. "Is there something wrong?' he asked. "No, Billy's moving further away" she said. Blair and Morgan knew Billy and some of what she and Billy were going through from Jillian's stories, so Jillian felt free to share with Blair about it. "Further than a plane can fly?" Blair teased to make her smile and hopefully feel better he had seen it all. It did bring a smile to her face. "Thanks Blair" Jillian said. "No problem he responded just get me some responses on theses by weeks end" putting the files on her desk giving her a wink and walking out. Blair had his way but he was coming around to understanding Jillian. And Jillian was letting her guard down with him.

Billy had things packed and waiting for the movers to load up the truck. Justin couldn't believe he was coming to Maine to live. They often talked about getting together and doing things. Now they were going to be in the same town. Justin was so excited he had called Billy several times that week asking what he needed him to do. Justin was bursting at the seams!! "Billy, I drove by your new place yesterday it's not that easy to find you know calling Billy for the third time this week. "Hey that's good very private, he explained. "Look I'm kind of in a hurry right now going to a meeting" Billy explained again "but we'll do something fun when I get settled okay bro?" "GREAT! Justin replied "bye" Hanging up the phone and happily dancing as he walked down the hall. Justin finished his day at the hospital and jumped in his car heading for the boys club parking his car and seeing Todd coming up "hey Todd, you're doing this for Tess too? Justin asked as they walked into her office at the boys' club. "Yeah man, I did it last year these kids are a blast!" he replied shaking Justin's hand. "Good! You're here", Tess said seeing them walk in. "I thought we were going to have to turn these two young men away?" Tess was now looking at her list of college students and the two young men sitting on the bench near her office who had come late. "What we have done is assigned a boy for each of you" she told them "So we have Billy and Cory here. Please choose one of them and you will be his big brother for the next six weeks" she said giving Justin and Todd the index cards on both.

"I'll take Billy" Justin said. My brother's name is Billy and it will be fun being the older brother for a change" he told Tess. "That's fine then Todd you'll take Cory." What I need for you to do today is acquaint yourselves with each other's likes, dislikes etcetera ". The others have gone out in the recreation area but you can go anywhere on the grounds you like today. Please meet me back here in and hour" Tess told Justin and Todd as they walked out the doors. 'And thanks guys we need all the help we can get!" Justin was happy he had chosen Billy. He couldn't wait to share with his real brother about his new little friend. Billy and Justin walked out and sat on a bench near the large baseball diamond of the Boy's club. "So, tell me Billy, right?' Justin asked sitting next to him. "What's your favorite sport?" "I don't know!" he said holding his head down. "We'll do you like baseball?" That's a great sport!" Justin remarked. "I think so" Billy said very quietly. Then added "I'd probably like baseball if I knew how to hit the ball". "I use to play with my mom sometimes "he told Justin. Justin knew that some of the boys that they were assigned to Big Brother were most likely from single parent homes. He volunteered because he knew how lonely he was without a father growing up so he wanted to make a difference. "Sit right there I'll be right back!" he told Billy running back to the club to retrieve a bat and ball.' All right Justin told him after coming back with equipment to play with. "You take this" handing Billy the ball. "And I'll take the bat" moving back a way from Billy in the open field. "Now throw me a pitch!" Justin told him getting in position to hit. Billy winded up and threw it whewww! right by Justin it went. "Pretty good, pretty good for a young boy" he teased. Justin didn't expect he could throw straight and fast. "O.K he told Billy "let's try it again I'll hit it out of the park!" he teased to make him smile. Billy was smiling he had someone to play with. He wound up again. Whewww! "STRIKE TWO" he yelled. Oh! Justin said, so you're trying to strike me out!' o.k. Make this a good one or I'll hit it out of the park!" Justin mocked. Billy put his head down and tossed the ball into Justin's bat. Whack!! Justin hit it a long way. "Yeah Billy said, we can play baseball again! I let you hit it." Justin clearly saw the ball come slower; he wasn't a Hank Aaron but surely, he could hit a ball of an eight-year-old. 'What do you mean you let me hit it?" Justin teased. Billy sat down on the bench and held his head down. "Hey guy, Justin said putting his hand under Billy's chin and lifting his head up smiling at him. What do you mean?' Justin asked again. "I want you to keep playing with me" he said. "If I strike you out you will not want to play baseball with me again," he confessed to Justin. "Oh, so you think you can strike me out! and that was a lucky hit! Justin said to Billy to build his self-esteem and to help build a relationship like the one he now has with his older brother Billy. All right I'll tell you what? Justin proposed. Billy stood up with his hand under his chin listening attentively to Justin's proposal. Justin wanted to see what he was really capable of his pitches looked pretty good. "If you strike me out, I'll come back every day until I hit a home run!" "O.K. but you asked for it, Billy replied and you gotta come back!" he told him going to his preferred spot to pitch the ball. Justin got in his stance ready to bat the ball. "One, swish! Strike one, two, swish! Strike two swish!!!! strike three, he said laughing at the way Justin was swinging at the ball. 'That's three Justin you want to try again?" Billy was laughing so hard. He and Justin pitched to each other for the entire hour. That for Billy went by so fast. Justin wasn't trying to miss all the balls. Billy was truly a pretty good little pitcher for his age. Walking back in with all the others now going into the Boy's club Justin asked "How did you learn to pitch that way?" "Lots of hours by myself, Billy said. And mom bought me one of those pitching machines". It also teaches you to pitch the ball through a targeted area. I got good so I started throwing against myself increasing my speed!" "It's fun for a while but I enjoyed playing with you!" he told Justin who was now holding his hand on his head as they walked. "Oh, and Justin" Billy said looking up "I'm nine", and smiled. "See you tomorrow sport". Justin said going into Tess's office with the other college students. Billy walked home smiling for the first time in a long time he now had a Big brother.

David had reasoned after his last escapade in Los Angeles he was hanging up his detective shoes. He wanted to find out where Dorca was but truly months had turned into years and the trail had gone cold. Doris Wright the lady from the Prizzy Palace he guesses had given him some clues has to who he might be looking for since it seems Dorca Williams was traveling with her child and she wasn't going anywhere without her son David. He knew he was looking for a woman with a child. He decided to sat down one evening with Tetra and share his concerns. Billy had moved on and maybe Dorca Williams had too. David thought since so much time had passed and they had not heard from Dorca there was no longer the need to fear Billy or his family was in danger. It seemed everything about this case was closed. David sat in his great room waiting for Tetra to finish setting the dinner table. "Honey dinner is served!" Tetra said calling out from the dining room. It was only the two of them but Tetra loved setting her table and enjoyed sitting with David having a relaxing dinner together now and then. David sat down at the head of the table usual spot.

"Tetra this looks wonderful! What's the occasion?' he asked looking at the beautiful candle arrangement she had set. "I had a great day I mean a wonderful week at the Parson Center. "A young mother reported her son got the transplant donation that they had been waiting for and we just rejoiced all over again" "Is that the one Dr. Edinberg announced Sunday during service?" Yes, the very same one!" Tetra said now sitting down to another one of her dinners. She had prepared garlicky grilled chicken. "I was thinking about Billy she said I've been waiting to hear from him since he settled into his place in Maine, have you talked to him?" Tetra asked putting the chicken and the rice pilaf on her plate from the serving tray. "I haven't but I'm hoping we can go soon for a visit and check out the law firm where he's working" David responded "umm delicious honey!" taking a bite of the garlic chicken from his plate. Then David pointed to the table's center "Cherry bruschetta? he asked, "fantastic! as he continued to eat his dinner. "I talked with Jillian the other day" Tetra explained. "Seems she and Billy have moved further apart. As a matter of fact, some guy answered her phone at the apartment!" she said. "That doesn't mean anything you know how this young crowd is they all hang out at each other's place" David said. "I know but I was so hoping Jillian would be the one for Billy, she was such a nice girl". "Did he ever tell you what happened?" Tetra inquired. "No, not really and I didn't ask! That's between them" David said drinking from a crystal goblet filled with wine Tetra had put on the table. "Great for the dinner pallet" he said sipping down another gulp. "Tetra, David paused "speaking of Billy I have been doing some searching on my own for that girl Billy befriended a long time ago." "What girl and why?' Tetra questioned looking directly at David. "Dorca Williams" David told her. "I thought everything with her was closed and settled" Tetra surmised. "I did too! David said until we got that letter years ago, and I've been trying to find her ever since. "Why are you telling me now is there something I should know?" Is Billy in trouble or danger?" Tetra exclaimed. "No at least I don't think so" I have followed this girl to the ends of the earth. I have met some wonderful people along the way" but I still haven't found her. I did find out she had a child though" David replied. Tetra didn't say anything but waited for David to continue. "YES, YES! That's it I don't know anything else. Billy helped me find the girl who was with her at the time but she wasn't of any help in finding her." "David what did she say?" Tetra's mind had begun to work and she was curious as to Dorca Williams whereabouts. "David start from the beginning" Tetra said putting the cherry bruschetta on the plates in front of them. David shared all he knew about Dorca. All the people who had played a role in her life since his search began but the finally result was nothing. Jillian was the only one who knew Doris or the lady who claimed to be Doris that lived next door to her in Cambridge but David said he had not talked to Jillian or showed her the pictures. "So, you're telling me that the lady whose little boy came to visit us has something to do with Dorca Williams?" "I don't know?" David said "She had the same name, but she wasn't the one living next door to Jillian and her story wasn't adding up" David replied. "She said the photograph I had was Dorca it got a bit confusing". "Anyway!" David added finishing up his bruschetta "Dorca Williams according to stories got her faced disfigured, right her in Washington but that's all I know". And the lady who lived next to Jillian kept her face covered with a scarf most of the time because of a disfigurement". She never said why at least not to Billy" David explained. "And Billy doesn't know what became of that sweet little boy Davie" Tetra said wiping a tear from her cheek. "No! David said, but there are people out there who are wondering and praying that he is all right" David told her remembering Beulah and her husband.

David had gotten up from the table and was helping Tetra clear the dishes. He walked over slowly and was carrying the large dinner tray into the kitchen. Putting them down on the sinks counter he put his arms around her. "Just hold me" Tetra said and they stood by the sink and held on to each other. "I don't know the story and I don't know if we ever will, David said embracing her tightly but I hope and pray wherever that child is he's safe and Dorca too". Tetra stood holding on to David and the tears were flowing down her face. Silently to herself she thought, "I have got to speak with Jillian, I've got to!"

CHAPTER 47

And abundance of everything including luck

Dana ended up attending the social Dr. Baisden gave alone this time. The cute Dr. Dean already had a date for that night. She'll surely be ready for the next event she thought sitting in her office waiting for her next client to come in for his appointment. Dana saw and talked to a lot of troubled people. This client she was waiting to see was very unusual. He Dana thought could use his money for something more important like a class on "disarming vanity". Her client was having a problem dealing with his looks. He thought himself to be so gorgeous that everyone envied him and he couldn't understand why no one wanted to be around him. So, he spends his money once a week to come in and talk to Dana about it.

Tetra had an appointed staff from Mt. Nebo who had got things set and going for the Christmas toy give away at the Center. This year had proved to be the biggest give away ever. They were trying to give a bicycle to all the children who were regular members of the children's church. Not only bikes there were other video games and computer equipment and of course lots and lots of other toys. They had interviewed and hired the jolliest Santa they could fine out of all the applicants to make the children happy and to give out the toys to the little ones. The theatrical arts members built a beautiful winter backdrop that served as the focal point for the day. Tetra and her staff had chosen to have the program the day before Christmas that just happened to be on a Saturday that made it perfect. All the children receiving bikes could ride them home during the day to assure they get home safely. Many of the children lived around the neighborhood where Mt. Nebo was located and they came in numbers to children's church on Sunday. The donations were still pouring in and it was a few days before Christmas. Tetra sat at her desk going over the inventory and was just amazed at the outpouring of generosity the community had during the holiday. They had received hundreds of letters from families in need of toys for their children and they had completed filling most of them. Tetra had also spoken with Sarah Clemings who is over the food department. And she advised Tetra that Mt. Nebo has more than enough to fill the number of requests they received for the food baskets. Sarah and Tetra prayed together at a morning break. Thanking God for his abundance in everything.

Tetra Parker was looking forward to a happy holiday for her family, the church family, as well as others. She had been thinking about little Davie since David had shared with her about the unfortunate way his mom Doris chose to take him away. He had brought so much joy to their lives during that Thanksgiving holiday season she felt the hurt for him in her heart. She just wanted him to be happy. She often wondered where he was and she remembered him always in her prays. She had made plans to go visit Jillian after the Christmas Holiday was over and hopes to get some answers as to where he might be. She didn't know why but she felt maybe she could be of help. She had of course prayed and still continues to pray for God's guidance in this situation but for right now there was not much she could do. Billy had invited Jillian to come with him to Washington for the holiday but she was busy with some new cases and couldn't get away so he came alone. "Mom!" Billy said coming to meet her at the Center before she left for the day. "Billy! Oh, I'm so glad to see you! How was the flight?" she asked getting up from her desk to embrace him and kiss him on his cheek. "Oh, mom it was fine" usual, lots of holiday travelers coming and going home to see family" he explained. Tetra was so happy to see Billy he had surprised her and came in a day earlier than expected. "Dear just let me make this one phone call to make sure Mrs. Spade has a way to get her children here tomorrow for the program and we're on our way" she said sitting down at her desk dialing the telephone. "O.k. mom I'm going to walk over and say hello to James, is he in his office?" he asked. "I think so we've been so busy these days making sure all the children go home with toys"." We've been putting in some long hours" Tetra told him. "Excuse me son, the phone is ringing! "Mrs. Spade" Billy walked down the hallway and around the corner to James Captain's office. He had his head down writing when Billy approached the door. "Hello sir", he said smiling and extending a warm holiday hello. "How are you?' he asked walking into the office. James stood up from the desk and came around and gave him a big manly hug. "My, My. It's good to see you you're looking great!" "And I understand that you are now a lawyer of some sort!" he teased looking gleefully at Billy. "That's right criminal law, news travels quickly" he replied. "Good news does" James responded. "Mom tells me you all have out done yourselves with this Christmas giveaway program" 'Oh yes God has surely answer our prayers here at Mt. Nebo" James informed him. "Not only with this but the entire church!" he had gone on to say. "That's wonderful Billy added. "How's your family, and your new little one?" he questioned smiling looking at James. He and his wife had recently within months gave birth to a baby and James had shared with him over the phone how things in the home had changed. "How could something so cute and tiny run the whole house!" James teased laughing and shaking his head proudly. "That's great man I'll be around for a bit I'm sure we will get a chance to talk before I leave" Billy added. "Give my love to the Mrs. and the boss!" he told James standing in the hallway in front of his office door." I'm going to take mom home if I can get her out of here". "This is her second home she loves the Center and the people." "Good seeing you Billy" James said. "You also" I concluded heading back to mom's office meeting Mrs. Guillory on the way. "Little Billy, she said very loudly, coming over hugging him with Tetra looking on. "Yes, he surprised me I wasn't expecting him until tomorrow" Tetra told Christine Guillory who was standing next to Billy sizing him up. "You certainly have grown into a handsome young man" she said holding Billy around his waist looking up to his face. "And you are as pretty as I remember Mrs. Christine" Billy told her and she stood aside of him and blushed. "It is certainly good seeing you and congratulations" she told him. "Tet I'll be talking with you later" she said patting Billy's hand and leaving. Tetra gathered her things and she and Billy walked out to the car. As they drove along the highway going home Tetra questioned her son regarding Jillian. "Billy what happened between you and Jillian?" I don't want details I just want to know something. She seemed like a very nice young lady." "Mom you're right she is, Jillian is wonderful. When she wanted to marry I didn't I just wasn't ready". "Then mom I made some stupid! stupid, mistakes and I think, she tried hard to forgive me but she was so hurt by what happened and I lost her love "Billy admitted sadly. "I invited her to come with me, but she turned me down using her work as the reason"." Now I have to deal with loneliness and getting over her." 'And mom I can tell you it's not fun!" I love her and I didn't realize just how much until she wasn't always there". "Tetra drove up into the garage of her home. Billy had taken a cab from the airport and rode to the Center to meet her. "Billy, I'll tell you I'm sorry this has happened. I liked Jillian too. And I know she loved you, Tetra smiled. "But you never know why things happen everything is for a reason son." I'll continue to pray I know this time isn't easy for you". But as much as I would love too, I can't go through it for you, but I'm always here with you if you need to talk" she said hugging him as they walked into their home after gathering everything out of the car. David had not yet arrived from the office and Billy was spending time in his family's great room on the pinball ball machine while Tetra was in the kitchen making one of Billy's favorite dinners that included fried chicken.

The happiest little boy on earth is what Billy's mom Dana said to him this morning as he left for school. He was enjoying the time he spent at the boy's club and he liked is big brother Justin that had been assigned to him. His attitude a school showed a positive reflection. His studies showed much improvement and he was very happy. After school he hurried home and gulped down a sandwich and maybe a soda. He'd remembered asking his mom to please buy some Gatorade sports drink. Billy walked over and looked in the cabinet "cool! Mom remembered he said getting down a bottle for him and his big brother Justin. "Grandma Bea, I'm headed to the boy's club" he said on his way out the door. Billy was always on time to the boy's club he did not want to miss a minute with Justin. Justin enjoyed him too. He planned all kinds of activities for them to do together. They played baseball almost every day. Justin was helping him with his batting and he was getting pretty good at it. Justin promised Billy he would come out and watch him play with his school team on Saturday when he could get off from the hospital. He looked forward to it. "Justin, are you coming to watch me play Saturday?" Billy asked walking into the boy's club. They had been together three weeks and Justin had not had a day off on Saturday from the hospital. He was the low man on the totem pole in the x-ray department so he got stuck with a lot of Saturdays. He had to work a month of Saturdays to have one off for his brother Billy's celebration dinner. He shared that information with his little buddy to help him understand. He didn't want to promise Billy and then disappoint him. "I'm trying I hope to make one of your games before our six weeks are over" he said putting his hand on Billy's head walking out to the baseball diamond at the boy's club. "Justin will I see you when this is over. I mean where will you go?" Billy questioned as they threw catches to each other. "I'll be here in Maine but the school semester starts and I won't have the time to give with classes and work" Justin replied throwing the ball into Billy's mitt. "Justin, if I come up here to the club will you come by sometime and see me?" Billy wasn't going to let Justin go without trying to keep in touch. "Sure, I'd love to keep in touch I want to know everybody who got home runs off of you!" Justin teased pushing him lightly on his shoulder. "Take your position Billy!" said Justin. Billy grabbed the bat and went to the batter's box. "No one's going to get a homerun off of me!"

"I'm going to hit all the homeruns" Billy said imitating an announcer "HOMERUN!!!' Justin pitched swishhhhh zoom! Strike one. I'll hit it! it's not like you have an arm, Billy teased. Swishhhh zoom Strike two, then he pointed at left field. Justin was hoping he got a hit but he couldn't just give it to him he'd know. Justin wound up and SWISHHHHH ZOOM! WHACK! The ball hit the bat and out in left field he went. Justin was jumping up higher than Billy. Hey, hey, hey! Billy said "told ya!" 'Way to go sport!" Justin said holding his head leading into the boy's club at another day's end.

Jillian sat in her apartment looking out on Manhattan. Billy had asked her several times to come with him to Washington to visit his parents for the Christmas holiday. But she couldn't bring herself to go. Every channel she turned to was singing Christmas carols and they were making her sad. "Why didn't I go?" she questioned. "I'm so lonely. I had not seen Billy in a few weeks and this would have been a perfect get away for me she thought to herself. She had gone out with Morgan and some of her co-workers last night and enjoyed it as best she could, leaving early from the dance club to go home. "Hi sweetheart, I'm glad you had a safe flight" she said sitting in her living room on the phone with Billy. "Are you finding something to do with yourself during the holidays?" he asked. "I sure am!" she didn't want Billy to know what was really going on. "Morgan and I went out last night dancing so who knows what's in store for tonight," she said to get a reaction from Billy. "You sound like you are handling yourself well Jillian" he told her. "But I miss you and I wish you were here!" Jillian sat with her feet up on the sofa. Why didn't he try harder to get me to go? Why wasn't he saying that before he left" she thought. "You're just saying that because I'm not there!" Jillian responded. "That's not true I do miss you, I asked you to come with me" Billy replied. "Jilly I'm going out to the Christmas program today at the church you know how that goes, if mom's, involved everyone is" I love you and I'll talk with you soon". "Mom's sends her love too, Bye Jilly.

Tetra and her staff had put together a wonderful program. The church was filled with people full of holiday cheer. They gave out candy canes with all the programs as people came through the doors. "Where is Santa? A little child asked coming in the door. "He'll be here soon" was his parent's response as they took their sits down front. The church had reserved seating for all the younger member's right up front by the stage. They really felt special. Ages twelve and under were given V.I.P. seating when they came in so no one else could take their seats "See you later mom and dad!" children were saying as they happily went down front to their sits and most parents ended up in the balcony. Only parents with lap babies were permitted on the main floor. The Parsons Center wanted this for the children and they came in excited. As a hush came over the auditorium Dr. Hathaway opened with prayer. We were certainly blessed to have him home for the Christmas holiday. Everyone was glad to see him. "I am so glad to be back with my church family. There is no place I'd rather be during the season". He told them as he addressed the congregation. "Look just look at the church of the future" he said to the applause of everyone in the room. He continued his lighthearted greeting to the congregation ending with "God Bless you all!" he said going back to take his seat that had been reserved for him. The children's choir took the stage, they song some gleeful songs about Christmas. Most had learned them in children's church or at school. Then they conclude with the ever popular "Silent Night." They all quietly took their sits and the young adults presented a play entitled "the Birth" They song beautiful music as each scene unfolded. The mother's board made the costumes and they sat proudly on the second tier looking at their costumed work and remembering all the precious hours that went into them. The play was performed well and brought tears to many eyes when they turned

Joseph and Mary away from the inn. The young adult choir sang "Away in a Manager in the background. When the performance was over people were standing on their feet APPLAUDING!!!!! APLAUDING !!!!!!APLAUDING. A standing ovation was well deserved for this group of young people. The adults sang hymns of joy and Christmas carols uplifting and spirit filled with praise. Everyone applauded again but the biggest applause came for Santa Claus the jolly old elf. He came out to the screaming and shouting of hundreds of children. He sat on stage in this big chair with huge arms facing all of them with his bag of toys visible from the audience. "HO, HO, HO! He said. Tetra thought again of little Davie, she prayed he was enjoying his Christmas. He sure enjoyed all the toys David and she had put in the house for him over Thanksgiving time that year. "HO, HO, HO Santa said again before sitting down in his big seat. "Let's see the first name on my list is Abby Addlersen. The staff had alphabetized all the children's name. So, by the time he got to Zoe Zachary she was fast asleep. "Zoe" Zoie" Tetra said standing over her. Santa's calling your name" She jumped up and ran to the stage "THANK YOU SANTA, THANK YOU, I KNEW IF I GO TO SLEEP YOU WOULD COME!!! She said and everyone laughed. She took her big beautiful doll that was twice her size. GEE! THANKS SANTA and then she looked up THANK YOU TOO GOD!

With toys in every child's hands Mr. Foster recited the poem "Twas the Night before Christmas." The children watched wide-eyed has he gestured each line. Closing with MERRY CHRISTMAS TO ALL AND TO ALL A GOOD NIGHT!!!!

CHAPTER 48

The perfect Christmas Tree

Desmond had taken back the large crane truck he had borrowed to deliver and remove the twenty-foot Christmas tree he and Henry had cut down for his home. They were not prepared for such a large tree. And had to acquire some additional equipment to bring and place it in their home. Mossy's instructions to Desmond were to find a larger tree to fill up the space in the great room magnificently. She also wanted to be able to see it from the window that looked out from the second floor. The very large window could be easily seen from the highway coming into their property. If they sat it directly in the foyer it would be perfect. Mossy and Dalmata her sister had went downtown to Macy's shopping for the perfect decorations for the tree. Mossy wanted it to emulate the tree she had saw decorated in the Macy's Department store's main lobby with all the trimmings of ribbon flowers and silver elegant bells all over its needles. They couldn't wait for Henry and Desmond to come back with the beautiful Christmas tree. What they saw was a huge crane truck and Desmond and Henry with other men who Mossy soon found out were their neighbors coming up to the house with this tree the size of Texas. It looked just like the one they flew in to the White house every year is how she described it. After a few hours and seven men later including Desmond and Henry the big beautiful tree was standing in it's proper place They decorated every inch of it after returning to the store for more decorations of ribbons and bows. They invited their neighbors and friends of course including Henry to a stylish evening hosted by the now very pregnant again Mossy and her husband Desmond. "They wanted to thank everyone for their much-needed help with the tree and to show it off. The sparkle and the glimmering of its lights and silver trim warmed the evening's hours. They enjoyed meeting all their neighbors who they had not met since moving into their new home. One of his neighbors George Phillips who lived near the place where they found the perfect tree heard Desmond screaming has, he hung from the top with a rope around his foot and came to help. But having experienced his own failure in getting a perfect tree, he called Jeb, and Elliot, Kevin and Earl who joined and assisted. They had lots of fun with their new neighbors and their lovely tree. Mossy sat down to play the piano the men including their wives sang Christmas 'carols along with Desmond, Henry, Dal, and Slovenia around the warm fireplace of their home. Hot apple cider or their favorite drinks were served in crystal stemware. Slovenia did a Yugoslavian jig to "We wish you a Merry Christmas" to close out the evening.

Billy hurried home from work. He wanted to see a program on television that featured a debate for an election. Winnie was speaking on behave of one of the candidates who was running for office. She had given Billy her television appearances when she called to tell him about Mortimer Van Hellsink her new assistant. Billy made it a point to watch everyone he knew on television. Dr. Hathaway's appearances and messages, he recorded most of the time to watch at a later date there were so many. He was one every day on the gospel network. "Ring, ring, 'Hello son, Tetra said. "Mom I just got in what's going on?" he asked. "I need to confirm the telephone number to Jillian's office" she replied "I'm going to talk with her about Doris Wright" "Well mom if anyone knows anything about Doris, I guess it would be Jillian" he said. After giving his mom the information, she needed Billy settled back in to watch his program. Tetra had shared with her son about going to visit Jillian and her concern for Davie. She thought long and hard after what David had shared about trying to find Dorca Williams. Then Tetra decided although she didn't know what she was looking for. She felt she needed to try and find Doris. "Something in her wanted to know Davie was alright. She walked into the firm's receptionist area in New York. "I'm Tetra Parker I'm here to see a Jillian Mcfinney" she said to the receptionist seating behind the desk. Ms. Mcfinney is expecting you right this way, leading her down the hall. She took Tetra down the hallway to Jillian's office. Lots of looks were coming from the staff in the offices. They were wondering about who was coming to see Jillian. "Who is this Black woman coming to see Jillian is she a new client?" could be heard as she walked into Jillian's office. Tetra was sure that's what they were thinking anyway. "Hi Jillian" coming up to her hugging her as she entered the office. "Hello Mrs. Parker, it's good to see you, how was your holiday?" Jillian asked making conversation as Tetra entered her office. "It was wonderful dear, and yours?' Tetra asked putting her Gucci bag on the side table. 'It was all right. I missed Billy but I do understand that he spent the Christmas holiday with you? Jillian questioned. "Yes, he did! He said he had invited you also. You know you are always welcome Jillian" Tetra replied, sitting down taking the photograph from her folder she had brought with her. "I don't want to take up a lot of your time dear" look at this photo and tell me who this is?" she asked. Jillian took the photograph in her hand. "I'm not sure she looks like a younger Doris possibly, remember Doris?" Tetra listened. "Remember the little boy David that I kept for a while she looks like his mother but only younger why who is she?" Tetra didn't say anything, she handed Jillian the picture David had gotten from Dr. Meloo's office. Jillian looked at the photograph "now this is Doris!" She said looking at Tetra "why are you showing me these photographs?" Jillian questioned. "It's just a hunch but I think they're the same person." "I can't prove it yet Tetra said. This one pointing to the younger picture is of a young lady name Dorca Williams, it's a feeling I have" Tetra continued to say. "This is the girl who sent Billy that book a long time ago isn't it? Jillian remembered. Then asked. "Is she still around?" "I don't know how did you meet her Jillian? Tetra questioned. "Meet who Doris?" "Umm it's been years let's see. Oh yes, I was walking across campus to meet Billy and she bumped into me" funny because we were going across the grounds. She said she was looking down and we started a conversation" Jillian remembered. "Did you know Billy then?' Tetra asked. "Yes, Billy and I had just started dating' I have known her as long as I've known Billy!" she said much to her surprise, "I hadn't even thought about that. Soon after that" Jillian said "she came over and introduced herself to me. She became my neighbor and then my friend". "This is kinda weird" Jillian added. "What are you thinking Mrs. Parker" Jillian asked looking at Tetra. "Did Doris go to Radcliff?" Tetra asked still trying to indemnify the lady. "Yes, she was a year behind me and I know she did have classes we studied together many times" Jillian informed Tetra. Although her field of degree was not law as I remember, Jilly said. "Doris never told me what happened to her face do you know? Jillian questioned "I mean she said a bad affair or something" Jillian stumbled out her words thinking about things she now found strange. "Well according to David someone hit her. I don't know why or who". That's what I'm hoping to find out maybe that will answer a lot of other questions" Tetra reasoned. "Does Billy know you suspect this to be his friend Dorca Williams?" Jillian asked. "No, I made this discovery on my way up here this morning after I had prayed. I looked again at this girl's eyes." That's one of the things you can't change" Tetra informed Jillian. "You're right Mrs. Parker, I never saw her after her surgery so I'm not really sure what she looks like, Jillian said, sounding helpless in this situation. "I'm going by to see his new place when I leave here and I'm sure Billy and I will talk in great detail, Tetra added. "Mrs. Parker, Jillian paused as she sat there thinking. Seems there were a lot of signs now that I think about it" but I don't think Billy has to worry she liked him" said Jillian. Tetra just smiled. "I'm going to make a few phone calls to Radcliff. We had some mutual class mates even though I was probably the only friend" Jillian said. I'm going to devote time in finding her and Mrs. Parker if I hear any thing, you'll be the first to know" Jillian told Tetra as she left. "Please give my love to Billy tell him I will call soon".

Jillian hugged Tetra and walked her to the elevator and went back to her office and stared into space thinking over the years.

The years went by so fast. Everywhere David, Tetra or Jillian looked they came up empty. Some of Jillian's old friends were glad to hear from her but none knew where Doris had gone and even fewer remembered someone named Doris Wright. Wherever Doris had gone seemed hopeless to find. There was no trace it appeared as if she had fell off the map. Billy went to Dr Meloo's office to find out if Doris had maybe checked back with him after the surgery. The office was now a nail salon. There was no Dr. Meloo insight. He walked in and looked around the office. Then he walked back out and looked again at the building's address, puzzled? The address is correct and things around the area hadn't changed much, he thought standing outside of the door on Vine Street. He turned and went back in and was greeted by an Asian gentleman "Pedicure?" he asked to which Billy turned around and walked out. No one had seen her anywhere. We showed the picture to everyone around the town and no one even knew her. Jillian was sure she could get a transcript or something to help locate her whereabouts. But all of her records were sealed. The folder only had a document stating that all records were transferred to another university. The courts had ordered the records sealed and as far as they knew Doris Wright was the only one who could release it. Without just cause or a real reason they came up empty again. And right now, they had nothing to go on. Doris Wright had really done nothing wrong. She had just move on without telling them. Was that a crime? Jillian found people who remembered the lady with the scarf around the campus but it had been years. The records had been sealed anything to do with Doris Wright from the Radcliff files had been protected and again the trail went cold.

"Jillian and Billy became close again during this time. Spending more time together they renewed their relationship together. Jillian figured if Doris were Dorca she would definitely be competition for her coming back into Billy's life. She really was ready to give Billy up and go on with her life in New York. On the other hand, if it was Doris, she could see Davie again. So, Jillian's thoughts were whoever she is will show up wherever Billy was. She commuted from New York to Maine at least once a month. And Billy would do the same traveling to New York. Jillian and Billy were renewing the love they had lost. She didn't know why? Or what sparked the flame again. It could have been the facts regarding Dorca Williams that Tetra had shared. But what caused the breakup had nothing to do with Doris! or Dorca for that matter. Jillian knew she still loved Billy and had forgiven him for everything, strange how things happen. You just don't know how close you come to throwing your life's dreams away she thought as she packed her suit case once again to go to visit Billy in Maine "William Parker please?' "Just a moment I'll ring his extension came the response. "William Parker" I replied, "Billy my man, how are you?" "Glen hello it's been to long" "You're right are things ok for you, how's Jillian?' Glen inquired "Jillian's good" Billy responded. "You sound like there's something you want to tell me!" Billy said to Glen "Why did you call I just spoke with you last week and you're calling me again so soon what's up?" I asked. Glen was much quieter than usual a mature quiet if you know what I mean. "My, my how you have mellowed since meeting Cheryl" I told him. "I'm trying to figure out a way to ask you something man? Glen responded. "Let's see just put her tongue in motion and ask?" I suggested. "Are your parents alright? "Mom and dad are fine" Glen responded, And Meldon, Bri and Sura I asked "they're fine too. Glen replied. "Then call me back when you think of what you were going to ask o.k. I'm hanging up" I joked. "No Billy don't hang up I'm just teasing with you!" "I WOULD LIKE TO KNOW IF YOU WOULD BE MY BEST MAN!!! Glen yelled loudly laughing, "she got me man, I love that girl, I'm through!" Glen explained. "Billy laughed and laughed after Glen asked the question. He got up from his desk and closed his door. He felt he was laughing to loud and did not want to be a distraction to his office. That's great congratulations! Glen you know I will! You know I will, he said.

Kat and Ariel were meeting Justin for lunch. They had been downtown shopping and thought they would just stop and say hi. "He's usually out already", Ariel told Kat I'll ask at the desk. They walked into the receptionist desk of the hospital's x-ray department "excuse me, Ariel asked speaking with her coworker. Shaquanda Howard was on shift and turned to ask questions. "Ariel girl, how are you?" you off today? Must be nice! What are you doing here on your day off?" After she let her answer, Ariel responded "I'm looking for Justin have you seen him?" "Justin! Have I seen Justin? I've been flirting with that cutie pie all day!" she said putting her hands on her hip. Then she smiled "Justin should be right back his lunch is at 11:30 p.m. he always comes to check out" she said. "Girl I'll see you later I've got to take Brewster's vitals, Shaquanda said to her walking away. Ariel and Katherine sat on the bench for a few minutes waiting for Justin. Then she heard him talking as he came up the hallway of the hospital. She stood up to see Justin walking up with Dana. "Hi sweetie he said coming over to hug Ariel and kiss Kat on the cheek. "This is Dana Williams she works with Dr. Baisden he told Ariel who would know what he was talking about. "Changing her attitude Ariel extended her hand "please to meet you "I'm Ariel Justin's girlfriend" she told her showing off the ring Justin had given her" 'Yes Ariel, Justin has spoken a lot about you, please to meet you". Justin hadn't mentioned her but it really didn't matter her interest in Justin wasn't a love relationship kind. Besides it made Ariel smile and relax. "And this is my mother Kat Heller" Justin remarked. "Please to meet you as well" Dana said. 'Where are you two coming from? Justin asked. "Dana and I were heading to lunch!" He didn't even think about what he was saying. "Ariel found a smile o.k. "a smirk". "Kat and I stopped by to take you to lunch" she said looking at Dana. Who had now started putting her psychiatric skills to work? "Oh, that's not a problem you all are welcome to join us" Dana replied. "Sure, we're going to the cafeteria come on!" Justin said hugging Ariel's cold lifeless body around her waist leading the way. Dana walked behind them. "Kat is it?" she asked walking beside Katherine and her "nobody ask for your company" attitude right through the entire lunch. "My name is Katherine she stated, Katherine Heller. Dana knew this wasn't going to be a pleasant lunch experience. But she's seen all kinds. Most of Ariel's talking was directed to Justin's ears only leaning over to speak into them. Dana who sat across the table looking fabulous in her designer suit had ordered a lush green salad for her lunch. She didn't wear the hospital smock out of her office she wore her regular designer clothes, very stylish and very expensive. Kat noticed that right away. "Where are you two coming from?" Justin posed. "If I know Ariel, she's been spending money downtown" he said eating a large hamburger with all the trimmings. Justin responded to make conversation across the very quiet lunch table "We were shopping if that's what you're asking?" Katherine replied very sophisticatedly looking at Justin to correct what he had said. "Shopping is totally different than just spending money" she added. "Shopping implies you're making decisions about what you're purchasing. Spending money simply means spending money!" Katherine stated. Dana looked at her and smiled and continued eating her crispy green salad with vinaigrette dressing on it. "Dana have you been working for Dr. Basiden a long time?" Ariel asked. "About a year and a half, right Justin. Remember when you helped me bring in the boxes. I think it was about that length of time" Dana said looking at Katherine for a reaction. "Oh, I see" Ariel replied softly. But Justin was enjoying his burger and was clueless to the feelings that were around the table. Katherine kept looking at her watch. She had just about taken all that she was going to. "Justin how long is lunch?' Katherine asked getting very restless and totally fed up with the lunch guest of Justin's that by the way invited herself she thought. "And hour! Justin said finishing up his burger to kick back and relax. Katherine finished the ham on rye sandwich she had ordered and excused herself to go and wait somewhere else. "Ariel, I'll meet you down by the car, I have something I need to do" Son you take care we'll talk soon. And it's nice meeting you" she said walking off. Katherine was not about to sit and hour with that and Justin would hear about it later. Dana was aware of what she had done she wasn't interested in Justin physically. He was a few years younger than her but he was nice a little childish at times but cute she thought. "She finished her salad and excused herself from the table. "Ariel it was nice meeting you, you're sweet you and Justin are a cute couple. She said stroking her ego. And Justin I'll talk to you later take care bye" walking off running into Katherine smoking a cigarette in a smoking area. Dana walked by her and smiled.

CHAPTER 49

Get into the act

Masony called David early one morning he had gone back to Los Angeles to see what he could find out about the lady in the Prizzy Palace. "David Parker please, Masony called David's office. David was not aware of what Masony was investigating after the last time they were together. David had shared with him that he could continue to search for Dorca Williams and he would pay him for it though they had not spoken in a while. "David Parker speaking," "David Parker, Masony here" "Good morning Masony. "How are you this fine morning?" David asked after following protocol. "You'll be glad to know I have a steady girl now" Masony confided to David. "After our talk the last time we were here, I mean when we were together in Los Angeles." "You cautioned me about some things that made pretty good sense, Masony confessed, I'm not a religious man but I did hear what you said". "We may get married but for now she keeps me out of those places" Masony confided. "That's wonderful Masony, David replied smiling quietly to himself but he was glad for Masony. He wouldn't last too long in those places, David thought. He came to learn and realize know no one does. "Any way" Masony said, clearing his throat the reason I'm here in Los Angeles again is because I have been following that lady who we called Doris Wright". She never came back to the Prizzy Palace since that night I'm told. "'What do you mean?" David asked his curiosity peeked now. "I followed this lady who ever she is to a very nice home in Beverly Hills" "There is no way that dive would afford her the life style she's living" Masony reported. "She goes to this high-end fashion house during the day and to a quiet home in the evening. I've been surveying her place for a week. "She uses the name Dorothy Wright. Not married. Has a younger sister. And get this her mother died in child birth with her younger sister and she claims according to my source was tossed around from place to place." "There is no other relative's she's aware of. And is very protective of this sister but no one here has ever seen her." She came here from Washington to pursue an acting career but it never amounting to anything much a few small roles" I was told. Masony continued reading his notes. She started a fashion house and it took off. She now owns a store on Rodeo Drive called "Unique Chic". Comes through every now and then for special clients. So maybe what we got was and acting job!" Masony told David. "I can get in and try to talk with her if you like or what do you suggest?" Masony asked. "Masony you're probably right no one changes from that lifestyle that quickly" "Very good work Masony, David affirmed "but keep a low key, I will try to get there soon". "What kind of time have you given yourself to being there?' David questioned not wanting Masony to be swayed in anyway. "I'll be here until Friday" he told David. "Good I'll get my calendar squared away and I'll see you before then" David shared. "Where are you staying?" he asked Masony. Embassy Suites on San Semen, Masony replied room 567." "Thanks, David said again Masony, good work".

Jillian was sitting on the soft leather sofa at Billy's when his phone rang. He was sitting across the room at his computer finishing up some legal papers he had brought home from the office. He needed to have them completed for Monday morning. "Jillian please answer the phone sweetie, looking as she watched television ignoring the ringing. "Hello" Parker residence Jillian said answering. "Hello this is Justin came the response. "Oh, hi Justin this is Jillian, how are you?" "I'm fine Justin replied, Is Billy in?' he asked quickly. Justin really didn't know what to talk with Jillian about. He had not spoken with her since the celebration a few years ago so he quickly asked again for Billy. "He is, just a moment!" she said getting up to take Billy the receiver of the telephone. "Hi Justin what's up?' "Thanks, for the lunch last week it was good seeing your legal mind at work. Very nice office bro!" "Not a problem we will do it again soon" he replied. "Well I thought you were alone this weekend got some tickets to the Red Sox's game thought you might want to come along". "I'm taking my little buddy Billy to a game for his birthday and he's still looking forward to meeting you" Justin told him. "Wow man that does sound great, but Jillian's down and we have planned this weekend". "You guys have fun and tell him to hang in there we will get together soon".

Billy replied to Justin. "I understand man". "You take- care bye" hanging up the phone. Billy really had no time to do extracurricular activities this weekend he was at Jillian's in New York or Jillian was with him and they usual planned things together. It always felt like they were each other's company. It wouldn't be right for him to leave her alone when she came to visit. So, Billy's time alone was usually Monday through Friday.

Tetra came along with David to Los Angeles. He felt she could share a perspective on things that he or Masony might otherwise miss. David and Tetra arrived on Wednesday and checked into their room at the Embassy Suites. David called Masony to let him know they had arrived and planned to meet him in the restaurant of the hotel for dinner. Tetra had got all the reports together and was looking over them. They were the reports David and Masony had gathered over the years. While she sat in the room waiting for dinner, SHE WENT OVER EACH DETAIL. She sat in the room getting the facts in order and trying to put together the final puzzle piece in place. Tetra listened to the radio softly playing while David was in the shower singing off key to one of the choir's songs. She remembered Billy had shared with her about Dorca Williams real mother and wanted to make sure that fact was brought out when they talked to the lady. But how would they go about seeing this mysterious lady?" David and Tetra walked down to the hotel restaurant and saw Masony sitting having his evening coffee. They walked up to the table. David extended his hand "Good evening Masony, David replied, how are you?" Masony looked up "Wonderful, just wonderful getting up from his seat. "You remember my wife Tetra?" David asked "I do, it's good to see you again Mrs. Parker, Masony said extending his hand to Tetra. "You as well, Tetra said shaking Masony's hand in return. They all sat down at the elegant table to coffee and dinner. The Restaurant served dishes from all over the world. They were internationally known. Tetra ordered Dream Cream lobster cappuccino a soup dish made famous out of New York and David ordered Valley Pearls Salmon tar tare cones from the French laundry. Their main entree Buffalo fillet with Porcini mushrooms were mouthwatering good" said Masony who had eaten all his meals there since coming in Monday. Masony, David and Tetra had chosen dishes that varied in taste but were truly wonderful together as a meal. "Have we decided if we're going to the lady's house are the boutique?' Masony asked. "Well we're not going to her home because we're not supposed to know where that is? David said. "Unless something changes," Tetra added as they sat eating apple pie ala- mode that the waiter served hot right from the oven. The chef had covered it with creamy rich vanilla ice cream. Delicious Masony voiced finishing the dessert. "I have an idea" Tetra said let me sleep on it and we will see you down here in the morning" "Sounds great!" Masony replied. They all got up after signing for their meals and headed from the restaurant. David and Tetra went back to their rooms to plan their strategy and Masony had gotten tickets to the Dodgers game. "See you all in the morning Masony said leaving the hotel to enjoy the baseball game.

Tetra and David went back to her hotel room. After a good night rest, she sat making phone calls around town until she got the one for the "Unique Chic the posh establishment ran by Dorothy Wright. Tetra knew if she called early in the morning, she would probably get a manager who could tell her the place Mrs. Wright would be today.

Pretending to be Mrs. Weatherly of New Orleans who was expecting to see Mrs. Wright personally whenever she was in town Tetra persuaded the nervous boutique manager who was not going to be the one Mrs. Wright fired for disappointing her new client into making an appointment to meet her. Since Mrs. Wright was not coming in today, she gave Tetra the address and made the appointment for Tetra to meet Mrs. Wright for lunch at her Beverly Hills home. "Mrs. Weatherly her body guard David and her limo driver Masony got prepared to go for a nice lunch at Doris Wright's home. David and Masony rented a stretch limousine while Tetra got dressed to meet Mrs. Wright and practice on her classy southern charm. After a while they drove around the corner to the Beverly Hills home where Dorothy Wright lived. Masony pulled the limo right in front of the large glass windows that reached from floor to ceiling. The very wide driveway out front was beautifully decorated with shrubs and colorful foliage flanked by and oversized waterfall attached to a wall that could be seen from the street when pulling up to the wide driveway. Masony got out in his black tuxedo and walked to the passenger side of the limousine and opened the door. David got out and he in turn assisted Mrs. Weatherly a very elegant rich southern lady who only wore high-end fashionable clothing. Mrs. Weatherly and David her body guard walked up and rang the doorbell. A butler came to the door. "Lady Weatherly here to see Mrs. Wright" Tetra said standing in her fashionable big hat and lace gloves. Her matching Lambertson Truex handbag was perfect for a well-dressed lady. David stood quietly by her side. "Do come in Mrs. Wright is expecting you!" he said with a stiff upper lip opening the door wider and standing to the side so that they could enter. "David went in before Tetra looking around as if to check to see everything was safe. As they walked in Doris came from the back extending her hand graciously. "Mrs. Weatherly, it's good to make your acquaintance. David stood looking at this woman who just years ago he had met in a dive at the Prizzy Palace. Now he was standing in this grand three thousand square foot home in Beverly Hills. Each room they passed through was a showpiece elegantly decorated. It had tall vaulted ceilings and designer window treatments. "You have a gorgeous home! Mrs. Weatherly told Doris as they walked into this beautiful family room filled with family photographs all around and a large craved oak desk. "Please sit down. May I get you something to drink?" Doris asked graciously to her guests. "A Perrier would be nice" Mrs. Weatherly replied. The butler standing in the door went to get their request. David walked around looking at the photo's in the room. "Sit down, please sit down" Doris admonished David "You make me nervous with that pacing. You're only here to discuss fashions am I correct?" Doris asked looking at Mrs. Weatherly who had turned to see a photograph that looked like Dorca and Davie on the fireplace mantle. "Lovely family you have, Mrs. Wright." Mrs. Weatherly said taking her Perrier from the butler's tray. "I went by your boutique the other day and I noticed you carry a lot of McClintock's fashion's she's one of us southern girls you know" Mrs. Weatherly said making small talk. "Yes, Jessica is one of my favorite designers too" Doris said taking out her fashion book from the desk. "Here are some of the other designers I carry" Doris told Mrs. Weatherly. And we can order just about anyone's fashions but these are the preferred ones, Doris said pointing to a list. Mcclintock, Purcell, Jones NY, Klein, and Donna Karen and on and on Mrs. Weatherly took her time looking at the list while David was getting a closer look at the photographs. "Is there something that interests you Mrs. Weatherly?' Is there a fabric I might show you?" Doris said getting impatient with the southern lady's decision making. Mrs. Weatherly paused and took a sip of her Perrier water. "Umm" she said looking at some of the fashions in Doris portfolio of styles. "Who did you say recommended you?" Doris questioned getting up to walk over by David who had gotten involved in picking up photos from her displayed table. Just as Mrs. Weatherly was about to answer the doorbell rang. Doris looked to see who was coming since she was not expecting any more company and Mrs. Weatherly was starting to get on her nerve. She is going to speak to her manager at the boutique about this referral she thought. Then as if things couldn't get worse. In walked Masony with bible in hand. David and Tetra had been taking too long and he wanted to know that things were all right. He had changed out of the tuxedo and was parading as a Jehovah's Witness. He came prepared. He had taken the bible from his hotel room before coming to read in the limo while he waited and tucked it under his arm. When Finley the butler refused his offer to let him talk to Mrs. Wright things took a different turn. Masony grabbed Finley and covered his mouth. The smaller butler was carried around in the house until Masony found one of the large bathrooms on the first floor. With Masony's belt and some beautiful fluffy monogrammed towels Masony tied Finley to the towel bar attached to the luxurious Egyptian tub in Doris home. Finley looked shocked and did not have a clue about what was going on. He asked only of the whereabouts of Mrs. Wright his LADY? Finley the unsuspecting butler now sat in the tub after he opened the door for the limousine driver turned Witness. When Doris saw Masony walk into her family room she yelled "Finley! Finley! She yelled again "who let you in here?" she stammered. "Finleyeee!!! Looking for her butler who could not hear her from where he was sitting. Doris walked over closer to Masony who was near the entrance of the room. She was backing along the wall with her eyes steadfast on all three of them now. "It's you!" she said very loudly. Tetra had now gotten up from her chair. She knew things had gone too far in the wrong direction. "That coat! that hounds tooth coat!" Doris yelled how did you find my home? How did you find me? Then she flopped down in one of her queen Elizabeth chairs. "I was never a very good actress!" Doris said looking at Tetra. "Where is Finley? You haven't hurt him, have you?" she asked Masony who was standing a bit frightened at this point. No! Masony stated "he's fine he's sitting in a tub". "Tetra had come out of her hat and gloves and sat in the chair next to Doris "we're sorry. We didn't mean to frighten you. All we wanted was to talk to you about Dorca Williams. We have been trying to find her for years so when we got this close, we got a little desperate" Tetra confessed holding Doris's hand. "You think a little, you lied and you got into my home and

God only knows what you've done to my butler!" Doris stated with a stern voice. "We really didn't mean for it to turn out like this we're sorry! So sorry! Tetra started to cry. She realized the severity of what had just happened and she was ashamed of herself and everything that had transpired. David came over and stood by her and expressed what she had said. "Who are you people anyway?" Doris asked. "What are you to Dorca?" "Dorca was a friend of our son, Tetra said. When her adopted parents got killed, she lived with us for a while before going to her grandparents and we never heard from her again. When we got this letter from Edith, we wanted to find her to ask about the letter that's all!" "Is this a photograph of Dorca and Davie?' David asked going back to the displayed table in the corner to retrieve the photo. "You all went through great lengths to find Dorca you must really be a friend" Doris conceded. "Sit down please, sit down she insisted. "Dorca and I have an interesting story. She is my younger sister. Our mother died in childbirth in having her. "I was only three years older. There was a time when people couldn't tell us apart" Doris said holding her head down. "When I heard from Dr. Meloo in Massachusetts that some gentlemen were looking for a Doris Wright thinking it might be Dorca. I put together that acting job to throw you all off. I thought my little sister might be in trouble". "My mother left me with a friend as best I can remember when she went into the hospital to have Dorca. I didn't know if it was other relatives who raised me or just people." "I know it's not a life to brag about!" Doris said grabbing a hold to Tetra with both hands as they sat in the chair. "When I was older, I found out about Edith. I don't know where she was all those years, we needed her. She said she didn't know about us". "Well I'm still debating on that one?" Doris said smiling. David, Masony nor Tetra said anything they just listened. Dorca and I came together again by chance at the Henning place. Until then I didn't know she was the girl Edith would bring over to this lady's house where I lived when she can for a visit to Oregon almost once a month." "And Dorca would share stories and talk about everything. Then they would leave until the next time" "I envied her. She had a big house and lots of toys she told me. But certain things she said weren't going according to her stories. It sounded just like mine" Doris confided. "When we got back together at Ms. Henning's we both had taken a wrong path we were pregnant". "I was so grateful for Beulah". "She helped lots of young girls including Dorca and myself". Dorca wanted to keep her child. I just wanted money to get as far away from that Hell hole as possible'. I didn't know my sister had money she was living in that place where I was". "But I noticed she never had trouble paying her rent so I hung with her." Masony got up and walked toward the entrance of the room. "Where are you going?" Doris asked. "I'm going to get Finley out of the tub if it's all right Madam", he said. "Thanks", Doris said and added "thanks for not hurting him." Tetra patted Doris's hand for her to continue her story. "Through Dorca I found out that Edith was our grandmother. Dorca came upon some papers Edith had in and old trunk at the foot of her bed. I was very anger and bitter that she didn't take better care of us". "Maybe she didn't know at first about us, she claims our mother left a long time ago but when the Demato's contacted her she had a chance to make things better" Doris said staring coldly aside of the wall at an arrangement of photographs on her desk. "She left me there in that horrible situation with that lady and when Dorca shared her story with me, it had Edith written all over it!" "Money hides a lot of faults you know!" Doris implied. "When Edith claimed the Demato's sent her back to Oregon I had enough!" She stood up and paced the floor. Masony was bringing the scared Finley with his clothes in disarray into the room. "Mrs. Wright are you all right!" this man, Finley started to explain. "Oh, it's alright Finley giving him a hug "go and clean yourself up" I'm fine" Doris told him gently pushing him out of the room. "After Dorca had little David she came and got me from the Henning's place. My child was born a month before hers. "I had spent most of the money I had gotten from the adoption. She had purchased a car and she and I and little David came to Los Angeles". Doris moved around the room as she spoke. "Dorca checked me into a clinic and that's why I'm here today." I still had hopes of being an actress on the big screen" Doris told them. But acting classes did not improve my skills. Dorca and I both knew after a year, my attempts to be an actress failed miserably. We started a boutique and here I am." Where is Dorca and David now" Tetra asked getting to the reason they were here." Dorca used my name and move to Massachusetts to go to Harvard". "Very smart girl" Doris replied smiling proudly. "I found her a surgeon here who could correct her face" Doris confided. "Yes, her face what happened to it?" David asked it looks fine right here" picking up a photograph of her holding David and Davie looks quite young. "That's true, she and I stopped by to visit and old friend before coming here.

"Then Doris's whole demeanor changed and so did the conversation. "Is there something else you want to know?" Doris asked very stoical at this point. "Where is Dorca now?" David asked again. "I haven't seen her since her facial surgery. She and I brought Davie back to Los Angeles. And I got up one morning to a note and she was gone." She wrote me saying she was starting a new life. And that if I loved her, I would leave her alone. She said she loved me very much." "I cry every time I read that note even today, Doris stated. Her next letter to me said too much time had passed and the love of her life had found someone else. Dorca blamed me for her face getting disfigured I was only trying to help" Doris told them tearfully. But I do understand."

"The last letter I received was from Massachusetts she's moved now and I don't know if she will get in touch with me again. She signed it PAID IN FULL. She handed Tetra the letter from a decorative box on the fireplace mantle. It did have the Cambridge address on it. Doris sat crying it seemed like something she needed to do for a very long time. Finley all prim and proper again came to see of his Lady's needs. She stood up and looked at them with tearing eyes. "Lunch was prepared would you all please have lunch with me?" she asked directing them with her hand into the elegant dining room.

CHAPTER 50

Love and disappointment

Dana had made some friends at the office. She had been there almost two years and it was the beginning of June. She had been pretty quiet for the most part staying close to home. And the lady Mrs. Beatrice whom she stayed with was very nice. Ms. Bea as she was affectionately called attended the Lutheran Church. And other than a few of Bea's lady friends visiting now and then the place was still perfect for Dana and her moderate lifestyle. She sat in her office day after day. Ariel as well as Justin was still constant visitors despite what Kat had thought about her. "Halle Berry want a be pretending to be a medical student flirting with a young boy!" is what Katherine shared with Ariel and Justin. Dana was very pretty and didn't look her age but then she did take good care of herself and frequented the athletic club in her neighborhood. She had started going regularly since the weather was nice in mid-April. The leaves on the trees had started to grow out again. So, one Monday she walked into the locker room. She changed into her tights and tennis shoes to prepare for her workout. I'll do about an hour on the treadmill and bars before going home Dana thought. The jazzercise instructor was there Wednesday's and Friday's so she would get a light workout today. Dana put her clothes in the locker and noticed she had forgotten her towel bag in the car. She quickly went back out to her car before she started her exercise workout. Once outside she saw someone familiar. "What are you doing here?" she asked surprised to see him. "I always come by here sometimes to meet my friend" he responded "You need permission to be here and I don't recall giving it to you" she admonished. "I have a pass from the boys club Dana!" he told her pulling it from his pocket. "I'm coming to meet my friend you know the one who takes me to the baseball games". Grandma

Bea met him!" he hurriedly said not wanting Dana to make him leave. "She says he's nice!" Billy told her. "O.k. you be careful and mind what you say" she shared with him. "I will Dana I will" he said and ran off to play with his friend.

"Hi buddy I thought for a minute you wouldn't show" you afraid I'm going to get that homerun today?' Justin teased as he saw Billy running up. "Not on your life!" he joked back with Justin. Billy loved being with Justin. Justin liked Billy too. He took him to the ice cream parlor, baseball games movies whenever Grandma Bea would let him go which was most of the time. Ms. Bea thought Justin was a good influence in his life. They had so much fun in that hour or two sometimes with Ms. Bea's permission. Billy always had something to write about in his super hero booklet he was making at school he told Justin. "I'll see you Thursday" Justin would say to him as Billy left running home from the boy's club.

Billy walked in "Hi Grandma Bea, he said hugging her and kissing her on the forehead before heading to take his bath. "I've made macaroni and cheese!" Mrs. Bea told him as he came running through moving quickly "Gee thanks grandma!" Mrs. Bea loved him and he loved her. He wasn't really her grandson and she knew that but he asked if he could call her that. One of his friends at school called his grandmother that and she had gray hair too he had shared with her. "I'll spank you if you don't" she told Billy, "now run along and wash good behind your ears!" she'd say smiling and going into the kitchen. She made dinner for herself and Billy most of the time and loved doing it. Dana worked late shifts sometime and was glad she had Mrs. Bea to help. "Mrs. Bea" Dana came to her one day after she had run into Billy at the athletics' club. "Billy says he has a pass for the boys club do you know about that?" She asked. "Yes, I'm sorry to say I do" she told Dana. He wanted to play with the other little boys he likes baseball". "I can't throw the ball anymore. I use to" she laughed. "So, he and I walked down to the club, and I talked to that nice lady Tess. "She said there are young men from the college that will be big brothers and women for big sister to these children". "I took Billy one day and signed him up he enjoys it!" And they assigned a real nice young man as his big brother" she said walking slowly back into the kitchen. Mrs. Bea drove herself to where she needed to go. She does walk sometimes, "doctor's orders" she'd said. Dana had a lot she had planned to say about not asking her permission to sign Billy at the boy's club. She looked at Mrs. Bea who barely moves quickly enough around the house to take care of her own needs most of the time. She loved Billy enough to walk three blocks to the boy's club to make him happy. Dana walked over to where she was standing in the kitchen and hugged her tight. "What's that for baby? she asked responding back to the hug "for loving us! For just loving us" Dana replied. "Dana, I may be out of line and please tell me and I want be mad?" 'When are you going to get Billy a father?" She asked as they now sat watching Jeopardy on television. "Oh, I don't' mind you asking. "Let's see when he drops from the sky" she said sharing a good laugh with Mrs. Bea. "Well Mrs. Bea replied, I haven't seen that happen yet but I guess I'll just keep praying!" as they continued laughing. Dana had not figured how to tackle the questions with Mrs. Bea regarding Billy's father. She had only told one person who Billy's father was and was trying to convince herself to tell anyone who asked. But that would just bring more questions. She loved Billy's father and hoped they would get together again. Right now, it didn't look like it was going to happen. "Billy, your dinner is ready!" Grandma Bea yelled after putting his macaroni and cheese on a plate.

It took Tetra and David three months to get the information they needed. And it seemed like they were getting closer to finding Dorca Williams.

It was now June and they still had not found her. All the information they had received from Doris Wright her sister brought them closer but still lead to dead ends. Doris who by the way was now helping them in the search for her. "Hello may I speak with Mrs. Parker? Jillian asked calling to the Parson Center in Spokane Washington "Jillian this is Tetra how are you dear?" I'm great! I found something!' Jillian was excited" "You found something dear what did you find?" Tetra asked. Jillian really had not said anything she was so excited and was talking very fast running everything together. "A friend of mine at the court house came across the name Doris Wright next of kin on some documents she was filing. She remembered me asking about a Doris Wright going to Radcliff. "Yes, dear yes I'm listening. After going thoroughly through some of the names Doris's and Dorca we found "Dorca Williams is aka "Dana Williams" she said. And Dorca who was to me pretending to be Doris Wright transferred her credits to the University of Maine." "So, Mrs. Parker you were right she is in Maine, somewhere" Jillian said. "She's following Billy!" Jillian added. "No if she's there she was there before Billy even knew he was going there"

I think?" Tetra said. "But that's great news I'll tell David". "Thanks for keeping your eyes open Jillian." "So how are things going with you and Billy?" Tetra asked. "I'm still waiting to be a grandmother you know! she said sharing a smile with Jillian. She was thinking about fate and people. How quickly things happen. "They are great we're going to Glen's wedding at the end of the month I guess we'll see you there" Jillian stated. "Yes, David and I are spending a few days with our old friends while we're there. "I love you Jillian thanks for calling" Tetra responded. Tetra didn't know why but she felt sadness with Jillian. She didn't know if finding Dorca had anything to do with it but the closer they got to finding Dorca Williams the sadder the feeling inside her grew for Jillian.

Tetra shared with David the information Jillian had given her. But told her husband she wasn't going to travel right now to Maine. She would like to stop by on their way from Glen and Cheryl's wedding in two weeks. She shared with him that she wasn't feeling well and had made an appointment with her doctor. 'I know already what Dr. Hansen is going to say, I'm over worked and need to rest". "But I enjoy my work at the Center" she said to David. She knew her doctor was right. Tetra had started out helping in the Center and it had turned into a full-time job. But she loved it

So, to keep things going David sent Masony to see what he could find out in Maine regarding Dorca Williams. He gave him a starting point of the University of Maine. Check all names used not sure what you will find. David told Masony. "I'm on it!" he said.

Tetra got a clean bill of health from her doctor with advice to rest. "You cannot solve all the world's problems in a lifetime!" her doctor advised her. Off to Austin they went. David and Tetra arrived in Austin a week before the wedding. They had called to let the Reeds know they were in town and would see them tomorrow but got no answer. They had left several messages on their answering machine. David or Tetra had been trying to call since they arrived that morning but got no answer from anyone. Not getting anyone on the phone the Parkers decide to go and get something to eat. They had just ordered when Tetra's cell phone rang. "Ring, ring" hello" Tetra answered. "Mom, "yes Billy. "Hello son are you here in San Antonio yet? She asked. "No mom I'm not, I called, he replied. "We have been here all morning and we have not been able to get in touch with the Reeds" she Interrupted him sharing. "That's why I'm calling you. "The Reeds called me! "Well are you here yet, why are they calling you?" Tetra was full of questions. "No! but I'm coming. The Reeds just called apparently there was an accident at the Space Center. Glen has been badly hurt." he told her. "No, oh no! Tetra said. She sat in the hotel's restaurant crying for her friend Phyllis's son. David took the phone from her. "Son, WHAT'S GOING ON?" David asked trying to calm Tetra's wailing. "Let's go honey we've got to get out of here and go to the airport." Tetra was speaking through the tears. Billy stayed on the phone explaining it to his dad. Glen and his crew were working an experiment with one of the shuttles. He slipped and fell from the pod and somehow was pinned under it. "That was earlier this morning" Billy shared and they had rushed him to the hospital in critical condition. He informed his parents that he was getting the first flight out to Florida and would see them there. After about two hours David and Tetra were back on a plane leaving San Antonio to Florida. They were hopefully going to be a comfort for their dear friends Wallace and Phyllis Reed. Once they landed David rented a car and went directly to Bayside Medical Center in Florida. Tetra walked into the waiting room. All the family had assembled. Mrs. Reed was in with her son behind the large closed doors in intensive care. Cheryl was crying so hard and Bri was crying holding her arms around her to comfort her. "Cheryl, you have to be strong for Glen, Tetra shared with her as she came over to relieve Brianna. Tetra had gotten all of her crying out on her plane ride there "They have stabilized him honey don't make yourself sick!" Brianna kept saying to her. Mr. Reed sat silently. He clearly looked tired and worn from the day. We understood they had been there since early morning and it was now very close to midnight. Tetra now quietly over with Cheryl sat holding her and began to pray. Somehow Tetra found strength in the tears of Cheryl. "Could this situation be the feeling I'd been feeling for so long" she thought sitting there in a hospital waiting room. Everything was going through her mind Sura so full of life running around asking questions trying to make everyone smile and Glen fighting for his life in the other room seemly all by himself. "Sura has grown so much since you all last saw her. She's five and just moves around a lot asking a lot of questions no one could really answer" Meldon shared with the Parkers. "Dad, Brianna replied to Pastor Reed we're going to take Sura and put her to bed. "It appears they have done all they can do tonight" she said "that was the last report we got" "I'll be here early in the morning. I have to make some calls to our jobs in the morning and let them know we're out of state and the reason" she told them gathering up her things to leave. Brianna walked over and hugged her dad and kissed Tetra and David before leaving. "Where's grandma, mommy?" Sura asked after jumping from Pastor Reed's lap. "I always kiss grandpa and then grandma" she insisted. Bri got down in front of Sura." Sweetie grandma is in with Uncle Glen right now we will see her tomorrow" she told her. "O.k. mommy" she said starting to cry. Meldon picked her up and put her head on his shoulder then said good night shaking each one's hand as they left.

Tetra asked Cheryl who was plainly sickened with grief if she wanted to go home and rest. She hadn't moved all day, Tetra was told. "She got there soon after Glen's office called her. When she got to the hospital, she contacted us. Cheryl went in to see Glen and the nurse brought her out and got Phyllis. Cheryl still did not want to move out of this waiting room. "I love you" she kept saying they all felt her pain" Pastor Reed shared this with them as they sat waiting to hear from Billy. Tetra, David and Pastor Reed prayed a fervent prayer as they waited in the waiting room to get some additional information about Glen. When Brianna got to Glen's home, she called Cheryl's sister to go and get her from the hospital. She was down from Austin helping Cheryl finalize her wedding plans and then they would fly back with her to Austin. She and Glen had stay away from each other during the week in anticipation of the wedding night. Now to see him this way! "She needs to rest as best she can Bri shared with her sister." Please bring her here to join us at Glen's house in case we're needed back at the hospital fast". "Heaven forbids!" she said. When Cheryl and her sister arrived, Brianna gave Cheryl something to help her sleep hopefully long enough to wait for news tomorrow.

Billy arrived alone Jillian was still in New York. He planned to call her early the next morning when he found out something about Glen's condition. After saying hello, he went directly into Glen's room in intensive care. Mrs. Reed and Tetra had secured pillows and blankets and was resting their heads on the arms of the cold steel chairs with mock leather seats in aqua blue. David and Pastor Reed were coming up from the cafeteria with coffee. "Good morning David said handing the sleepy-eyed Tetra her paper cup of hot coffee. 'This is the best I can do with a vending machine" David added offering her some type of cinnamon roll wrapped in a clear package." 'This is fine she said sitting up to take the hot coffee and roll. "I'm really not that hungry right now anyway, thanks dear" reaching up and kissing David on his cheek. Wallace was sharing the same breakfast treats with Phyllis.

Billy went into the room. He reached up with his hands and wiped the endless flow of tears from his eyes. He looked at Glen lying in the bed with tubes all around him. You could hardly see him for all the apparatuses they had him attached to. "He hasn't said anything since he's been here but the doctors have stabilized him" the nurse told Billy. She had just taken another set of vitals and things for now were holding. He pulled up a chair closer to the bed and careful put his hand on Glen's hand. He could see all the needles and tubes they had running through his body. He tried hard not to cry but the tears would not stop flowing. Billy finally conceded and with tears wetting the side of Glens bed covers where he laid sleep in an unconscious state, he prayed. "Dear God, who am I that you spare me time and time again. I am so undeserving of your love and your grace yet you keep giving it to me. Right now, all that I have belongs to you. I can't face this situation without you. You know both of us. We go back a long way and I have come to what was supposed to be a happy occasion. It has quickly turned into gloom for me. Dear God I do recognize that you are still in control and I ask that you help each of us accept your plan. Billy sat there and talked to God about he and Glen's life with non-stop tears streaming down his face. If Glen heard it, he didn't react, but God had heard! Billy knew it for God dried up his tears and renewed his spirit as he petitioned him to heal and make whole again his friend.

Billy, Tetra, and David left the Reeds going back home after a week and much, much prayer and tears shed. After about two weeks Glen was moved from intensive care into a private room. He was still lying In bed not speaking. And though Mrs. Reed and Cheryl would stay constantly by his bedside they couldn't see much improvement though the doctor's said he was improving. Even at times when asked with his big strong hand holding hers, he could give it a positive squeeze that he understood. Jillian had called Billy every day to get the updates on Glen's progress. And has the weeks went by he was improving the more. By August he was sitting up in bed and though still not able to use his legs his outlook was positive. "Honey I don't know how I'm going to make this up to you"

Glen told Cheryl at one of the visits" I love you and right now I can't walk you down the aisle of a church" he told her holding her hand." Cheryl looked through her tearing eyes at his tears and said "Glen just last week you couldn't even tell me you loved me with your voice" You barely knew who I was! And you just said to me "I love you" "You like I know nothing is impossible with God!" And Cheryl stood by his bedside hugging him gently and remembering.

Masony had called Doris Wright in Los Angeles and asked if she could possibly come to Portland Maine. He had run into a snag with legal paper work that required a relative and would gratefully accept her assistance. Billy had heard about the progress being made in finding Dorca Williams from Jillian. And though he asked to help over and over again his dad had asked him to stay out of it for now. "Keep your distance son we will let you know what is going on" he told him. Again, Billy couldn't believe Dorca had been by him all these years and he never really knew. "Dad" Billy said calling him one day. "How are you son?' David asked. Billy had called him at the office "I heading up to Jilly's in New York so if you need me that's where I will be" he confided. "How's Glen?" talk with him lately David questioned. "Every day dad with morning coffee" He's in good spirits still giving those guys in the hospital a tough time and he says physical therapy is coming along, disappointing sometimes he told me" "Good I talked with Wallace and he seems to be positive things will work out alright". "Phyllis is still praying it's harder on her Wallace implied to David. Well David said "Wallace says it didn't get rid of Cheryl and I thank God for that" Billy laughed thinking about the loved Glen and Cheryl shared. "That is a blessing" David added. "Yes son, life is so uncertain we're on top of the mountain one day and in deep, deep valleys the next. That's why the bible admonishes us to be content in all things, David replied." I know dad, I've been thinking about that. I have been with Jillian all this time and truly I don't think I'm going anywhere without her. I mean I love her and we will probably be together forever." Billy confessed. "We'll son only you can answer that question but I do think it's time you made a decision regarding Jillian. David shared with a fatherly heart. "I know dad, I know we will talk soon" Billy said. 'Have a safe flight son.

Again, Billy had boarded his plane to New York but this time he had made a stop by his safety deposit box and got out a small black box to give to Jillian in hopes the answer was still yes. He thought about Glen and Cheryl's misfortune how quickly life changes. It was September and another year was coming to an end "Jillian hello darling!" Picking her up and swinging her around at the airport. She had come to pick him up during her lunch hour and to take him to get settled in until she came back home from the office. "You're in a good mood" Jillian said as they were walking over to get his suitcase from the circling luggage belt in the airport. "I'm here to see my best girl, maybe take in a show and relax!" he told Jillian "you have a problem with that?" No! not at all sweetie let's go!' Jillian took Billy to her apartment and she headed back to her office. Billy had made plans for Jillian but first he was going to watch his high school friend Seymore play basketball with his overseas team. He loved the foreign travel and was playing basketball overseas after coming out of college. He had played a few years and looked good out there shooting that rock. He relaxed and watched as Seymore hit two free throws to put his team into overtime. He sat alone in Jillian's apartment enjoying the game as he went over plans for his big evening with her.

Masony now with Doris Wright, Dorca's sister from Los Angeles walked into the University's office. The bright-eyed clerk at the counter came over to them "Have you been helped or may I assist you in any way the clerk asked. Doris shared she was looking for her sister who graduated from here as best she knew. They had already been to the courthouse and found out about the change of names but for some reason with all the documents Doris had produced they would not release any information to her. Doris said only enough to get cooperation from the skeptical clerk. "Her name was changed through the courts look and see what you have on a Doris Wright, and a Dorca or Dana Williams. "Thank you we will wait." She was gone about twenty minutes and came back with nothing for them. "There are several Doris Wrights is there a middle initial are something else birth date something!" she sneered. There are only a few Dorca's she said. The last name Williams run the gamete she told us. 'What did you find under Dana?" Masony asked has he stood listening to the conversation. The agitated clerk now looked at Masony without answering. Doris figured she doesn't seem to stray far from the names Wright or Williams. "I do understand sorry to bother you." Doris said getting on the clerk's best side she hoped "Is it possible we could have a list just within the last two years of everyone with the name of Williams or

Wright she asked smiling at the clerk. Who now was willing to give them what that asked for. She quickly pulled up the names and handed them to Doris. "It's only names no other data of any kind" she told her. "Thank you very much you have been kind!" she told her thinking she may need her services again. Masony and Doris found a quaint little coffee shop near the university and sat down. Masony took the list for Williams and Doris looked at the one for Wright. After a light lunch and reasoning what Dorca might do they headed back to their hotel rooms and a telephone. They were going to try and find telephone numbers for these 347 people total on both list and start from there.

Jillian walked into a trail of rose petals starting at her front door. She could smell the fragrance of flowers in the incense that filled the air. The music was playing on her stereo and candles covered her dining table as well as the fireplace mantle and… She walked into her bedroom smiling knowing her man was treating her to a romantic evening. She slowly approached her bed and heard the water running in her large tub. Looking in the bathroom she saw him sitting in a tub filled with bubbles and sipping champagne that had been taken from the beautiful sterling silver ice bucket on the tray table by the tub. Seeing Jillian, he asked "caviar madam?" holding it up above the bubbles of the water. The caviar was also sitting on the elegantly decorated tray table that boasted a single red rose. "Oh, my Billy this is so charming!" she said. "Won't you join me he suggested taking a bite of the caviar on its wafer "Ummm good!" Jillian had already put her briefcase down by her desk in her bedroom. She slowly started to remove her clothes. With every piece she removed he would again sample the caviar. "Ummm good! he'd say. Jillian put her toe in the water and then her whole self was in the water. "Ummm very good" he said handing her a glass of champagne to sip. "Jillian looked into his eyes "sweet heart it's been too long and I have really missed you!" He leaned into her and they passionately kissed. "I'll drink to that" he said. "He then lifted the crystal goblet in the air and Jillian did the same. They gently let the goblets meet then brought them to their lips. Jillian was swept away by everything going on. When she put her glass up to drink something touched her lips. "What's this? Through her tears she could see the sparkle of a gorgeous! Fabulous! Fantastic! Handset Diamond Ring! "OH MY! SHE SAID OH MY! THIS IS BEAUTIFUL! She was reaching over hugging Billy and soap bubbles were flying around the room. Oh my! She kept looking at it holding it in her hand. After she calmed somewhat, Billy looked her in the eyes and asked "Jillian Mcfinney will you marry me?" oh yes Billy oh yes! She exclaimed. Billy took the large stoned diamond ring and placed it on Jillian's finger. I'll leave the end of this story to your imagination. "Jillian's a very happy girl!

CHAPTER 51

Mr. Masony I presume?

Doris had helped all she could and had to get back to her boutique and her home in Los Angeles. Masony had gone back home too but returned the following week to finish going through the list of names they had the clerk pull from the computer at the University. They had narrowed it down to one hundred and fifty-six names. Masony had crossed all but seventy-five from his list. He never realized Williams came in every nationality possible.

Knocking on door after door with no results he stopped and sat on a bench in the park. Masony took out his list and began to mark off the names he had already contacted and eliminated. Then out of the sky came a baseball "WHACK!" right beside him on the bench. Masony jumped! Then he saw the baseball. Up ran a young boy "sorry mister my friend Billy and I were playing ball over there" he said pointing to the empty field except for one young boy. Masony looked intimidating but he really wasn't. He sat tossing the ball up in his hand. Then up ran the other young man. "Did you get the ball Tommy?" Billy asked. "He still has it, pointing to Masony. "Hi mister, Billy said "may I have our ball?" "Sure, young man just be careful though" Masony said tossing it to him. "I'm Masony", "are you two pretty good ball players?" "We sure are you want a play with us?" Tommy asked. "Let's see you're Tommy and you're, Masony now was looking at Billy. "I'm the pitcher if you want to play mister!". Billy replied. "Sure, I'll toss you a few. "Why are you here mister?' Tommy asked. Just resting worked hard today!" Masony told the inquisitive Tommy. Masony played a little baseball in college and had a pretty good arm.

They ran over to the vacant diamond in back of the boy's club. "Can we play?" Can we play?" several other boys who were standing around waiting for a team game ran over. They formed teams and Masony pitched a no hitter in the last inning to win the game. "Not bad mister, do you live around here?' Billy asked. "Not far Masony said speaking of his hotel room. He didn't want the young men to be afraid of dealing with a stranger. "I'm Billy Wrig I mean Billy Williams he said. I pitch for my team. I come up here often to play with my big brother Justin, Billy told Masony "Oh, so you live near this nice boys club?" Masony asked, to get Billy's mind off what he really wanted to find out. 'Well that's nice your parent's let you come here! he said. "My mom, I mean my grandma Bea lets me come we only live a few blocks from here" Billy added. "O.k. well I've got to go you boys run along it was fun maybe I'll see you all again" Masony told them pretending to walk away. Billy and Tommy said goodbye to their friends and slowly walked home. "That old guy is pretty good! Billy said. "Maybe he'll come back again" Undetected at all Masony had followed Billy home and wrote down his address and would come back later. Very smart kid Masony thought knows how to tell a story.

Jillian was so happy the next day she went looking at wedding gowns. They hadn't planned the wedding she was just getting a head start. She was hoping it was Monday so that she could show everyone in her office her gorgeous white gold diamond ring. As a matter of fact! Jillian thought. She got on her home computer and emailed everyone in her directory at the office. She walked around all weekend looking at her hand. If this was a dream, she didn't want it to go away. Jillian called her mom and invited her out to lunch while Billy practiced hitting some golf balls at a course near her apartment. He had shared with Jillian that he was finding himself having to hone his skills for the clients "Okay, I'll take mom out to lunch and share the news with her while you're out sweetheart." She said as Billy departed for a day on the golf course. Jillian had made reservations for she and Frances at "Cornucopia's a restaurant they had frequented many times. "Hi mom, Jillian replied walking up to Frances waiting at the door. "Hello Jillian, you're looking happy, where's Billy I thought you two would be together what happened?" she asked concerned things had again turned. "Oh, mom he's on the golf course somewhere not sure right now Jillian said just to throw Frances off she looked so worried. "Now Jillian you can't expect Billy to come here to see you and you just send him off! Frances admonished. "Mom I'm not worried and you shouldn't be" she told her. "Jillian Mcfinney "I'm not going to go through what we went through a few years ago!" Frances said sitting down to the table. Jillian continued to ignore her and picked up the menu the waitress had left on the table. "Mom I'm going to have the lobster and corn bisque and the virgin ear corn" Jillian said. "What are you having?" she asked. O.k. Jillian but mind what I say!" Frances added. The waitress stood by the table waiting. "Give me the crab cakes Frances said with cilantro sauce and the western cornbread bruschetta. And please bring me the corn salad. "I will never understand you modern women!" Frances went on to say. "You simply take things for granted" Billy's a good man he's not going to be around all the time Jilly mark my word!" Jillian turned her head around. She was doing all she could to hold a straight face with her mom. She wanted her to notice the ring on her own but she couldn't stop fussing long enough to do so. Jillian sat making small talk about the office or anything else Frances found no value in at this time that Jillian couldn't be with Billy. After their meal was served Jillian sat looking at the table "Mama Parker taught me how to make cornbread it's one of Billy's favorite foods" Jillian explained. "It's good something came out of the time you spent there!" Frances was not going to let up on Jillian no matter what she said. "They continued eating and finished their meals. The waitress came back to check regarding desert. "We will both have a large slice of lemon meringue pie to celebrate" Jillian told her. "Celebrate! What are we celebrating now?" What kind of promotion did you get this time Jillian?" Frances stated. "Mom, calm down" Jillian told her handing her napkins in disguise of showing off her ring which by the way a blind man could see that rock! She held her hand up even after Frances had taken the napkin and wiped her mouth with it. When the waitress brought the two large slices of pie Jillian handed her mother another napkin. Frances took it, then Jillian handed her another napkin, "Jillian don't be cute I'm not that messy!" she said. "One can never be too careful" Jillian said again and held her hand out. Frances stopped and looked at Jillian "this is ridiculous!" she said. Jillian didn't take her hand down. Then the lights hit it just right and "OH MY GOD JILLY! "Why didn't you tell me?" "You just let me go on and on!" "Like you are doing now mom" "Jillian said smiling. Frances held Jillian's hand "Jillian I'm so glad for you!" getting up from the table and hugging her. "Thanks for telling me" Frances smiled.

Masony kept surveillance on the house he had followed the young man to. He told David he heard without question how the young man changed his name several times. It could just be a coincidence but worth checking out Masony thought. "Be careful Masony, Tetra and I will be down this weekend. Billy and Jillian are planning a big engagement party David told him. "You're welcome to bring Irene" he added. Masony always walked around singing about sweet Irene McCockney the love of his life. 'Good thanks I'll do that!" he said "Masony out". Masony saw the comings and goings around the young man's household for a few days. He noticed the young lady came in late sometimes and leaves early other times. And she fit the age description David had given him about Dorca Williams.

The young man was pretty constant and liked the boys club a lot. Masony even saw him playing with his big brother who strangely had blonde wavy hair. Then there was and older lady who drove a Buick that was in immaculate condition he reasoned. She was probably the original owner Masony thought. One morning he saw the younger women pulling from the driveway and followed her around the corner and to the freeway. He almost lost her in the freeway traffic but spotted her again after someone got pulled over for speeding. She took the exit off the freeway and two blocks down turning into the hospital's parking garage. So far so good Masony thought, we're looking for someone in this field. Parking as to be unnoticed he followed her into the hospital down the hall. She stood for a moment maybe checking her mail or something Masony wasn't sure. "Good morning Dana" came the young hospital worker "You're here early he said. "Oh, good morning Justin, yes I am, I have a client coming in who likes early appointments" she told him. Masony stood with his back toward them a quick look told him the young man was Billy's older brother. He quickly jotted down her name and waited for her to go in an office or somewhere. "I'll talk with you later Dana told Justin. "Oh yes Dana, Justin remembered. "My brother Billy is having an engagement party this weekend thought you might get a date and come. He said. "Sounds fun I'll let you know?' she said gotta go!" She rushed down the hall and into an office. "Psychiatric Department". "Not hearing all of the conversation Masony had many conclusions to draw from what he had just seen and heard. "How can a ten-year-old have an engagement party he thought at first? Then this lady dressed in street clothes just went in to see a psychiatrist ummm! "I'd better call Mr. Parker he reasoned.

Jillian's week at the office was futile. She couldn't concentrate on anything but the engagement party, and of course the fabulous wedding. Frances came by everyday making sure things were planned out to the letter. "And Jillian "I have already reserved the room at Trump towers for the wedding" she told her. Blair and Morgan both congratulated her along with many others who had received her earlier email. Morgan had planned for Jillian an office shower after the formal announcement in Maine. She was inviting her co-workers and Billy when she returns to New York. Blair and Morgan were now openly dating which came as a surprise to no one! "Jillian, I know this is going to be a fabulous evening Blair and I are looking so forward to it" Morgan said standing in the boardroom after their meeting. Blair was out of the office with a new client and was expected in later. By days end Jillian ran into Morgan again leaving the office. "Morgan here's the invite for you and Blair I never saw him today" Jillian confessed to her. "Blair called he got tied up with a client but I will see that he gets it". She said to Jillian. "That's fine I'll be here late tonight I'm taking off Friday to get an early start on the party" she told Morgan "so I'll see you all Saturday alright." They gave each other the business hug and Jillian went back into her office and closed the door. 'Hi honey! Jillian said calling Billy at home. "I was just saying goodnight" I have some work to finish up if I'm going to take off tomorrow" she told him. "I LOVE YOU JILLIAN!" he said lying in his bed remembering her touch. I love you too Billy "and my ring is much grander than I remembered" she said. "then you remembered?" Billy questioned. "You know when you gave it to me" Jillian recanted the line. "Oh, Jilly that's alright, I knew you had moved it from the suitcase that night, I wanted to give it to you so bad but you just wouldn't tell the truth about meeting Blair and I didn't know what to think". "Will you ever forgive me he asked "Forgive you Billy it was my fault, I should have told the truth and saved a lot of headaches Jillian said. "Jilly I'm glad we got it right this time!" I really miss not being with you and starting a family and he went on naming the future teasing her about a dog and a picket fence. "William Parker, she said I wouldn't trade you for the world". Jillian Mcfinney will you marry me! "YES, Billy without questions. "Yes, I will marry you!"

Jillian got off the phone with Billy realizing what a good man she has. She had almost lost him for good and let her self-get swept away by Blair's charm. She sat and remembered how Kelly intervened. Jillian was angry with Billy's continually putting her off and flirted with Blair leading him on. Kelly being a true friend told Jillian it was her fault Billy had mistaken her for Jillian that night. And the hot and bothered Blair went into Kelly's room that night instead of Jillian's which was fine with Kelly. Soon Jillian heard someone talking outside her door. It was Blair! Jillian quickly gathered her things and hid under the desk. "Blair walked into her office he wasn't alone. "The janitor must have left the lights on!" Blair said clicking it off and leaving Jillian in the dark under her desk. He and this female voice walked into his office and with the sounds coming from the room Jillian hurried to the elevator and out of the building with work to finish at home.

David walked over to his fax machine in his office. He had received an unexpected fax from Doris Wright. She was giving him the details of what she knew about the night she and Dorca visited Mr. Grover and the happenings in the Richvale home. David sat and read it. He couldn't believe things for this young lady had gone undetected so long. He didn't want to upset Tetra and so he waited to share it with her later. David folded the faxed paper and put it in the pocket of his jacket for safekeeping. He wanted to hear Dorca Williams story and awaited Masony's call. Soon Masony called David Parker and he instructed him to find out about Dana. "What's the last name?" Why was she there" inconspicuously Masony! David added. We caused enough flare ups remembering Doris and Finley. Masony went back up to the office after he had coffee of course. He walked in "May I help you?" Dana asked sitting behind the desk now wearing a smock. "Do you have an appointment?" Thinking he could be one of her clients. 'I'm looking for a Herbert Finderstien?" Masony said pretending to read it from a card. He was in this office?" "No! I'm sorry I'm Dana Williams, Dana Williams", she said getting up to shake his hand. May I help you?' she asked the confident Masony "Thank you for your time but I got it now" walking out leaving Dana raising her brows to "it takes all kind.

Masony quickly called David back giving him all the details. He had stood in her office long enough to see her degrees were from University of Maine. "I'm sure of it Masony told David. David quickly got on the phone to Tetra at the Center. "I think Masony has found Davie. Well the kid is the right age. He says is name is Billy. But Masony says usual if a person is hiding out, they will use a name that's easiest to remember. "Did

Masony get a look at Dana or Doris you know what I'm asking Tetra said nervously now things had come this far. "He did but says it's hard to tell". O.k. let's calm down we don't want a scene like we caused in Los Angeles. I hear there's an elderly lady there also. Tetra added. "David, we have time. Have Masony take a photograph of Dana and fax it to Doris in Los Angeles. She can positively identify her and that will save us a lot of embarrassments. "I want this over as much as you but let's do it correctly I don't want to interrupt anyone else's lives.

CHAPTER 52

Explanations are in order

Jillian called her mom when she got home. "Mom you're still up? I was hoping you would call Jillian. I wanted to talk with you about the dress you let me pick out for this occasion. "That was so sweet of you, but now I'm worried you won't like it or it won't fit right? Frances said "mom I'm sure it will be fine" you have been buying my dresses since I was born!" she told her which Jillian felt still did not ease her concern" "Mom, would you like me to come there tonight?" Jillian asked. She had finished the papers and would fax them into the office tomorrow. "Are you sure Jillian?" "I'll be there soon mom" Jillian replied. The trip to her mother's didn't take that long. When Jillian walked in her mother had two dresses lying out for her to choose from. "Mom I told you it was your decision?" I trust your judgment you were right about Billy, weren't you?" she teased Frances to get a smile. "This one is fine mom" Jillian said picking it up from the bed. "Are you going to try it on?" Frances asked. She wanted everything perfect for her daughter's party. "It's late mom!" Jillian explained. After a pause and sigh she went into her old bedroom and put on the dress. She had to admit "its gorgeous mom" she said as she walked out to the teary-eyed Frances. "My baby is all grown up!" you look stunting Jilly, absolutely stunting. "Oh yes before I forget call your dad and give him the address and directions to the hall in Maine. He still has not gotten his invitation he's been traveling he says, Frances huffed. "I will mom first thing tomorrow morning on my way out" Jillian explained. "Roger and I have a later flight but we will be there in plenty of time." "I love you Jillian giving her daughter a big hug. "See you tomorrow mom" Jillian said leaving to go home.

When Doris got the fax, she wasn't sure who the photograph was that Masony had taken and sent. "That's not Dorca! she thought. Masony has messed up again. She got ready to call David and tell him when the photograph fell to the floor. Picking it up she stared right into the face and captured the eyes. Doris fell back on the chair. "Oh, my she said, that surgeon changed her face!" "Oh my God it is Dorca!" She's totally changed I wouldn't have known her if she had walked into the boutique. "Oh my, she thought. Doris got her purse and went out of the door. She drove along the highway headed to her boutique. She turned into the parking garage and got out. Quickly moving into the crowded elevator up and up it went. When it stopped on the tenth floor she got out. The sign on the door read: Dr. Alan Mosby surgeon to the stars. Doris walked in, "she had no time for the receptionist. She was carrying the photograph in her hand. 'Excuse me! Excuse me! the receptionist said as Doris pushed her way into the surgeon's office. Seeing it was Doris, the doctor held up his hand for the receptionist to stop. "She's fine" he said. "I was wondering when I'd see you in here" Dr. Mosby told her. "But you changed her whole face! Doris screamed in his face. "That's what she wanted. I tried to talk her out of it especially since she had a child it's harder on them" he told Doris. "So, you found her anyway, Dr. Mosby said standing now holding the photograph of his work in her hand. He had shared with her she was spending a lot of money. But someday someone who's really looking will find you he had shared with her. "I'm sorry Dorothy you had to find out this way. But I'm glad you found her for the child's sake anyway." How long as it been?" years?' the doctor questioned. He did so many without looking at his records he couldn't say precisely how long it had been. "Thanks for talking" Doris said. She couldn't really be upset with Dr. Mosby. Dorca was strong willed and she would have it her way. Doris left withered. She got home and called David and Tetra. "She's Dorca but don't expect to see the same girl you knew years ago she said and went on to explain to Tetra.

Masony was standing outside on the step of the hospital when Tetra and David walked up. Good afternoon sir" Masony said to David and nodded "madam" "Good afternoon" they said together to Masony. "She's in her office the last time I checked unless there's another way out. Masony informed them. "I had a very long talk with Doris in Los Angeles, Tetra explained "I would like to talk with Dorca by myself David if you don't mind!" she added" Are you sure dear?' David asked concern something could go wrong. "Yes, David I will be fine, though I'm sure you and Masony won't be far behind if I need you, Tetra said standing outside of Dana's office waiting to go in. "Honey I'll be right here!" David replied securing a spot on the wall directly in the path of the door. "Tetra walked in "Excuse me, how may I help?" Dana said seeing a lady walk in. Tetra looked at the walls where Dana had displayed her degrees. "Very impressive" Tetra acknowledged. "Excuse me ma'am this is a doctor's office is there something I can help you with?" Dana stated she had stood up and was coming around her desk. "You don't remember me?" Tetra asked. Dana looked it had been years and she really hadn't seen Tetra up close in a very long time. Tetra removed her winter hat revealing her face. Dana looked and sat back in her seat. "How did you find me?" She asked. "It really doesn't matter Dorca or do you prefer Doris or Dana!" oh excuse me Dana!" Tetra said a little teed she had to go through this concern for her son. "Have you seen Davie?" Dana asked. I haven't but Masony says he calls himself Billy!" It was easier that way Mrs. Parker, Dana explained. "Easier for whom?" Tetra questioned. "He was so young, and when Doris my sister came and we got him from school he was so hurt and so devastated. I'd call him Billy and it made him feel better." "I was going to come back after I got beautiful again for Billy but by then Jillian had stolen his heart and Davie's too". She had Billy; I could not let her have my son David!" Dana explained as she sat crying behind her desk. Tetra pulled up one of the mission chairs in her sitting area and sat down. "Who sent that horrible letter and the bible to Billy?" 'Now that was not nice!" she said not feeling Dana's tears right now. "The letter? What letter? If a letter came, I don't know about it. I had nothing to do with it. I gave Billy back the bible in hopes he would know I was still around" Dana informed Tetra, "one had nothing to do with the other. Just a coincidence" Dana said. "When I heard Jillian had moved to New York I figured Billy had moved on too". "Davie seems to be adjusting and has found new friends it's not easy Mrs. Parker I'm sorry." Dana sat waiting for Tetra's next question. "Edith said in that letter she didn't kill the Demato's if she didn't who did?" Tetra questioned. David stuck his head in the office. "I'm fine David!" Tetra stated LOUDLY to him. David quickly removed his head back outside of the office. "I really don't know. Doris Wright came down from Oregon and picked me up from school. "When she got to Washington I don't know?" Doris who I found out later through papers Edith had in an old trunk was my older sister. She took me down town to shop for a dress by myself!" After an hour or so she came back to the same boutique. Then she took me to a hair salon and told me Edith had asked her to do it for me." She said Edith was still at the farm. Then Doris dropped me off in time to meet Billy and told me my parents the Demato's had went to Oregon". 'She was very upset they had sent Edith away and left me that's all I know". Dana replied. Tetra was halfway home in her questioning. Now she had come to the one that was really the driving force behind this whole fiasco they have been going through "Well tell me Dana who is Davies's father?" Tetra asked. Dana stood up and walked around her office. There were things she had to say before getting to that. "Why are you asking?" Dana questioned looking at Tetra. "Because Billy told me what happened prom night and putting years in prospective it could be so" there is a strong possibility he is my grandchild so I'm asking?" She said reasoning through her thoughts with Dana. "I really didn't know until after I had him Dana said. He was darker than I thought he should be in the circumstance" she said. "I only involved Billy when they sent Edith away! I felt I had no protection from anyone. I really didn't like her smothering me but I really missed her when she was gone" she kept saying. She was still being vague in her answers. Grover was going to tell me what he really saw that day in Richvale if I did meet his request just one more time. "I thought Edith had come back and murdered them after Doris told me she knew what was going on in that house. Edith confessed to protect me but I didn't do it. Doris and I went back after our children were born just to talk with Grover. He panicked and hit me with a poker from his outside fireplace". I tried to help him after he fell down holding his chest but Doris threw me in the car and drove away!" Dana continued to say, "He was lying there kicking and I never looked back again" she said "Doris pulled a patch of his hair from his head". That's what we used to prove he wasn't the father" she said. "So, what are you saying Dorca! Tetra stood up "David!" she yelled he came running in with Masony right behind him with his weapon drawn. Dana looked. "No! no! Tetra said "put that away!" "I called you in to tell you that Davie is our grandson! He is!" she said holding on to David. Dana looked at Masony, "You're the man who came in here this morning" she said now realizing what was going on. "Dana where is he can we see him?" Tetra asked it's been so many years. "Don't cry dear, don't cry" David told her but he was shedding tears too. "I'm so glad we didn't give up" she said.

David then turned to Dana who he now knows is Dorca and caught her by her arm and looked at the tattoo that encircled her wrist. "You met Beulah Reeves" Dana stated "I did David said. "Do you have a shredder?' he asked. A shredder looking confused but Dana pointed to her corner wastebasket. "Thanks David said walking over and taking the paper from his pocket. "What's that" Tetra asked. "Something that I should have deposed of at my office David told her. "Closed case from long ago, pushing the button turning the shedder on the document. "Davie gets out of school at 3 "o'clock p.m. Here's my address he'll be there" Dana told them. Tetra and David hugged Dana "thank you dear" thank you." Dana sat back in her chair thinking.

Billy ran in 'Hi grandma Bea, I'm getting a sandwich, some Gatorade for me and Justin and I'm headed to the Boys club he said moving around the house like lighting. "Billy your mom called she's on her way home she needs you to be here" Mrs. Beatrice told him. "Oh why?" I'm meeting my friend Justin today. Tommy and I and some other guys are on the same team, I can't be late I promised." he pleaded with Mrs. Bea. Dana had called and explained it to her without going into a lot of details, but Grandma Bea. still couldn't make Billy understand why he couldn't go to the boy's club today. When she was just about to give in Dana pulled up in the driveway and so did another car. David, Tetra and Masony parking in the driveway of the modest home own by Beatrice Flowers. Everyone got out and Dana invited them in. Mrs. Bea, this is David and Tetra Parker Davie's grandparents" she said proudly. Billy was sitting over in the big chair unhappy. All he was thinking about is Justin would come and leave and he would never see him again. And this is Mr. Masony, is it?" she asked hoping she had it right. "They've all come to see Billy she said "I mean Davie. "This is so confusing Mrs. Bea said. "I know Dana told her I'll explain later". "Please to meet you ma'am Tetra replied. "Please sit down" Dana said speaking to everyone. She went over to the chair where Davie sat pouting "and this is Davie" she explained. "Tetra looked at him with loving eyes. Davie looked sad. "Dana, Davie said "Justin's is going to leave and I won't get to play with him today. Then he looked up "Hey you're the guy who played baseball with us the other day! looking at Masony. "Why are you here?" he asked. "Mr. Masony helped your grandparents find you?" Dana told Davie confusing him more but nothing right now was clear. "Davie?" "Remember you're supposed to call me Billy! Davie replied. "No Davie, it's alright now they know who you are", Dana confirmed. Grandma Beatrice had gone into her room so they could talk. "Billy these are your grandparents David and Tetra Parker". She stood holding him facing the Parkers on the sofa. "Hi, he said quietly. "Hello sweetie Tetra said she wanted to squeeze him so tight but held her feelings. "I remember when you came to our home. "My you have grown" Tetra said to him holding his little hand. "You liked that pinball game we played with our son Billy and David my husband she added to help him remember. "Are you?' he stood for a moment "Where is aunt Jillian?" "Aunt Jillian, you remember aunt Jillian?" Tetra exclaimed she was happy he remembered something of his past. He looked at Dana and held his head down. "Davie it's all right telling them what you remember" she told him. He ran into his room. "I'm sorry!" she said "it's going to take some time," Dana reasoned. Then he came back with something in his hand. "He walked over and gave it to David and Tetra see "I still have it I play with it every night!". "Uncle Billy said he would remember me always if I kept this and so I did!". Where is uncle Billy?" Tetra, David and Masony were beaming with joy. "YOU WILL SEE HIM SOON?" Tetra got excited then calmed to say "if it's all right with your mom". Grandma Bea had come back out of her room and stood in the door smiling "Thank you Jesus" she said quietly. "I have an idea!" Davie said. "Let's go to the boys club and meet Justin please! Please!" David looked at Dana and everyone including Grandma Bea went along. Justin and the boys were just finishing up and Davie ran over to Justin. "Hi Justin I'm sorry I didn't get to play with you today will you come back again?" he asked "Sure I will sport but where were you today we didn't have a pitcher" Justin questioned putting away the gear they had used to play with. Then Justin walked from the equipment room into some familiar faces. "What are all of you doing here?" Justin asked very surprised. "Dana and Mrs. Parker and Mr. Parker going down the row. Justin was puzzled. "First my name is not Billy! It's David. Like my grandpa" Davie said smiling along with David Parker. "This is my mom Dorca not Dana! And this is my Grandma Parker" and Grandma Bea you met her, Davie said waiting for Justin's reaction. Tetra hugged Mrs. Beatrice. "What? what? Justin stood rubbing his head. "I'll explain later Justin" Dana said "if you will".

Billy had got to his office early poured his second cup of coffee when his cell phone rang it was Jillian calling from the airport. "Hi honey

I'm on my way I'll see you in about an hour" she told him. "I'll be there, he said. Billy was picking Jillian up from the airport in Maine she was coming from New York for their engagement party. "Oh Jillian, Glen sends his love. He regrets that he and Cheryl won't make this party but they are planning to be there for the wedding day". "That's wonderful to know he's getting better Jillian replied. "I agree Billy said I've asked him to be my best man". "Desmond will be there of course but he may not be readily traveling with another little Des so close on the way" he said sharing a laugh with Jilly. "I talked to my dad Bob. I gave him your cell number if he gets lost trying to find us tonight" she told Billy. "That's wonderful I look forward to meeting Robert Mcfinney he teased using her real father's name. "SWEET HEART I LOVE YOU! Jillian repeated. "O.k. Jillian I love you too! Now get off the phone and get here so I can hold you in my arms, Billy said hanging up.

"William Parker you have a call on line two" the receptionist at his law firm "Ridgeway, Banks and Brown announced over the intercom. Billy walked into his office. William Parker" he answered. "Hi Billy, 'Oh hi mom are you here already? "I am and I have some good news!" "Well I just heard from Jillian so I don't know what news could be better!" he joked. "Well dear, we have found Davie!" Tetra replied. "What! You have? He exclaimed jumping around his office. "Where is Doris?" oh never mind where is he?" mom!" Billy didn't know what questions to ask first. "Jillian's going to be OH MY!!! Billy EXCLAIMED! Where are you mom?" Billy asked. "We're on our way to your office. There is a lot to explain" she told him hanging up the phone.

As Billy sat in his office anxiously waiting for his mom to bring Davie he heard a lot of commotion coming from the break room at the law firm. The television was on and they were making an announcement. Billy stood watching and his cell phone rang again. Everyone was talking so loud as they gathered around the television set "Something was happening in New York! Somebody yelled. "Hello, Billy said trying to hear through all the noise in the room "Jillian! Jillian! Sweetheart! he said louder. "O.k. there you are I thought for a minute I had lost you he told her. Positioning himself in front of the television"

Then his phone went dead as he watched the plane hit the tower.

www.ingramcontent.com/pod-product-compliance
Lightning Source LLC
Chambersburg PA
CBHW051135300726
48978CB00011B/280